PATTAYA 24/7

Also by Christopher G. Moore

Fiction

His Lordship's Arsenal
Tokyo Joe
A Killing Smile
A Bewitching Smile
Spirit House
Asia Hand
A Haunting Smile
Cut Out
Saint Anne
Comfort Zone
The Big Weird
God of Darkness
Cold Hit
Chairs
Minor Wife
Waiting For The Lady
Pattaya 24/7

Non-Fiction

Heart Talk

PATTAYA 24/7

A NOVEL BY

CHRISTOPHER G. MOORE

Heaven Lake Press

Distributed in Thailand by:
Asia Document Bureau Ltd.
P.O. Box 1209
Bangkok 10110, Thailand
Fax: (662) 260-4578
Web site: www.heavenlakepress.com
E-mail: editorial@heavenlakepress.com

Editors: Rhea Tregebov, Merrill Fearon, Busakorn Suriyasarn
Jacket design: Jae Song

Web Site: www.cgmoore.com
E-mail: chris@cgmoore.com

ISBN: 974-92066-6-5

For General Vasit Dejkhunjorn and
Mark Abel

ONE

LUNCHTIME at the Lonestar Bar in Washington Square, the same six or eight middle-aged *farangs* leaning over their plates cutting into pieces of meatloaf. It was mostly the same old faces. One of those Galapagos Islands meeting places where exotic species cut off from the outside world gather, their evolutionary divergence displayed in sexual selection practices and mating rituals, livers, immunity from alcohol damage, and an unhealthy appetite for meatloaf. The owner, George, never ate, and sat watching the rain fall. He was fat enough to raise suspicion that he ate large amounts of food. But when did he eat? Darwin would have netted him and hauled him back to England for further examination.

Most of the regulars figured George as a candidate for the secret eater award. McPhail said that George knew secrets about the kitchen and that was why he didn't eat. He might not have been watching the rain; he could have been waiting to find out which of the six or eight regulars would croak first. He didn't wait in silence.

Sitting at a large booth under the stuffed water buffalo head, George nursed a beer surveying his empire and barking orders at the staff.

"Change that goddamn music. I want country. Fucking country. Do you understand a boy band isn't country?"

"Yeah, change the music," shouted Ed McPhail. "And turn the volume way the fuck down. Can't you see I am trying to have a conversation? Jesus, George, we'll be wearing hearing aids."

McPhail wore his black dyed snakeskin trousers with a white cotton shirt. He slowly pushed a Marlboro into his ivory cigarette holder.

"I am eighty-two and can hear more in one fucking ear than you ever hear in a lifetime," screamed George.

McPhail made his free hand into a talking-head puppet, his fingers moving up and down over his thumb like lips over a stick jaw. McPhail gestured at George. George got the message. The DJ got the message, changed the music and turned it down.

Calvino poured more salt onto his french fries as McPhail found his lighter.

"As I was saying," McPhail said, lighting a cigarette. "I had this uncle named Harry. He lived in a trailer a couple of hours out of San Francisco. He collected stuff. Clippings from newspapers, magazines, junk mail, and brochures. He had stacks and stacks of clippings, all a dirty yellow color—like nicotine-stained fingers yellow. That's age, man, age. Getting old and going nowhere. Understand what I am saying? He had all of this shit everywhere: tables, the floor and the sofa, on chairs. There was enough heat pumping through that mountain of paper that the whole place could have gone up in blazes.

"Uncle Harry kept all those clippings because they had some tiny piece of wisdom, some insight into the workings of the universe, and one day he was going back to read them all like one long narrative. But he never had time to read. All day he spent clipping more pieces and making new piles. Harry thought he would find a window into the human condition.

"You know what he claimed? Swear to God. Harry said he had invented the TV and microwave but some assholes had robbed him of his inventions—stole his ideas. He said, 'Son, I've always been ahead of my time.' He planned one day to get all of his inventions back. He wrote every fucking law firm in the state asking them to take his case. He never got one reply. Not a single fucking letter. But the man believed in his own wisdom. All of those news articles had made him wise. Listen to this: Harry said that he invented the Internet in 1949. He had the proof. A piece of paper where he wrote down 'internet' and it was somewhere in one of the piles. He had other papers that showed he had invented the TV and microwave. Harry was a dreamer. He wanted to make good. He fucking tried. But he couldn't get it together. He once said to me, 'All I needed was a million dollars and I'd have left Bill Gates eating dust.'"

"After everyone becomes a millionaire, then what?" said Calvino.

"Then I'm putting up the goddamn prices. And when that day comes, maybe I can get someone to put on some goddamn country fucking music," screamed George. "If the fucking Arabs don't blow us all up before we can spend our money." One of the demimondes sauntered over to change the music. She put on the country song about how in country music no one ever says the F-word.

"Vinee, how the fuck are you going to make a million doing legwork for insurance companies? Man, there's no money in chasing down live people pretending to be dead."

Looking around the bar, Calvino wondered if there were a number of dead people pretending to be alive. And it crossed his mind that he could well be one of them.

"Bar *yings* understand the answer, McPhail."

"What is the answer to my question?" He had forgotten for a moment what his question had been. What remained in his head was now a blur—how does a private dick working small cases ever hope to make any real money?

"*Yings* know in the service business you need to understand the price issue."

"One thing's for sure, bar *yings* ain't gonna be millionaires any time soon."

"There's more to life than supply-and-demand and making money."

"Try living without any fucking money," George shouted down from his perch.

"Everyone needs some money, George. Not being a millionaire doesn't make you a failure."

"Bullshit, everyone wants to be rich," said George.

"He's right, pappy," said McPhail.

Calvino looked around the bar. He didn't see any dollar millionaires; he didn't see any millionaires, spooning their vegetable soup and reading the sports page of the *Bangkok*

Post. "The word is, terrorists from the south might export their violence to Bangkok," said Calvino. "You get blown up, what good is a million dollars?"

McPhail rolled his eyes. A couple of the regulars looked up from their fried chicken. "You can get run over by a bus or a motorcycle, Calvino."

"Or a water buffalo," shouted George.

"My secretary's fortuneteller said this would be the year of a major disaster."

"Fortunetellers, what the fuck do they know?"

"What did your Uncle Harry know?"

"What I am saying is, Uncle Harry spent his life clawing through some stack of newspapers looking for something and he never found what he was looking for. He wasted his life. What else has a man got but his time?"

"His dreams," said Calvino.

"Calvino, you're too fucking old to have dreams."

"McPhail, you're too young to have stopped dreaming."

TWO

THE GPS digital panel read N 11° 28′ 22.0″ and E 101° 45′ 17.7″. Six small black bar graph spikes appeared on the panel, one after another, each one indicating a connection had been made with a satellite. Each satellite confirmed the co-ordinates. Two hundred dollars of GPS had plugged into a multi-billion dollar grid. Unlike the old days, when the best sailors would get lost, the Sunday sailor now had an instrument that made certain he would never be lost. The fading sun touched the horizon of the sea. Nothing but water—no pattern, no design, and no texture—and the sea was called the Gulf of Thailand. The trawler could be anywhere, anytime, any place—no landmarks to judge time or place. Water stretching as far as the eye could see. The GPS device allowed Captain Suthan to plot his trawler's position with an accuracy of thirty meters. He shook his head. It was unbelievable to hold such an instrument. No smuggler could ever have made a better investment.

From the center of the sun-reflected surface, a fishing boat sped across the open waters. The boat approached from the starboard side. Shielding his eyes against the brilliant sunlight, he raised his binoculars. Captain Suthan slowly pulled the focus sharp and tight, until he gradually made out the outline of three men inside the approaching boat. Two men huddled on a bench at the bow while the third man crouched at the stern, operating the outboard engine. The wind had died and as evening came, the hot air cooled. From the quarterdeck of the trawler, the captain watched the progress of the boat.

The man working the engine also had a GPS, the glass catching the reflection of sunlight. The captain slowly lowered his binoculars and glanced at his watch, making note of the time. The fishing boat had appeared exactly on time. The rendezvous had been precise in place and time.

Considerable care had been taken in selecting the right location for the rendezvous. Sailing too close to sea-lanes disputed by Thailand, Cambodia, China, Vietnam or the Philippines invited the attention of patrol vessels and inspection by naval personnel. The captain had long experience in these waters and knew the risks of being spotted and stopped had grown after 9/11 and exploded after the school burnings, bombings, and killings in the southern provinces. It was a time of turmoil and suspicion and crackdowns and strange, terrifying diseases. Being at sea, one felt safe, isolated from all the threats, Captain Suthan thought. His pulse quickened. His trawler had entered a zone of danger.

Few of the safe harbors from the old days remained. Places where smugglers operated with the kind of liberty that was unlikely to return in this life. Technology had cut both ways. While it was easy never to become lost, it was more difficult to not be found. Through his binoculars, the captain scanned the horizon for any other vessels. He saw nothing but the vast, open sea. He called down to the men to prepare for the fishing boat coming alongside. He had informed his crew only an hour before that they would be taking on board a man who was in need of urgent medical assistance. How did he know this? Captain Suthan had told his crew that he'd received an SOS call about the medical emergency. As the captain, he had a duty as the closest ship in the vicinity to give aid and assistance. This was a rescue procedure and the crew would assist in doing their job.

Questions immediately came into the minds of some members of the crew. No one else on board had heard the emergency call come over the radio. How could such a call come from such a small craft as was approaching? Small fishing boats didn't have such advanced electronic equipment. The captain assured them the fishing boat had taken the ailing man from a larger trawler. Why hadn't this trawler helped the man? Why had they put him on a fishing boat? Those amongst the crew with these questions kept them to themselves. The atmosphere on the trawler, as they waited, grew tense; the men waited, watching the fishing boat as it closed in.

The captain ordered the crew to keep their distance from the sick man. He was infected. But the captain didn't say what disease the man in the fishing boat carried and was bringing onto the trawler. The captain used the Thai word *tid-rok*. This was a nicely vague term. It could have meant anything from diseases such as AIDS or malaria, to the bird flu. Rumors had circulated that SARS had re-emerged out of China and people were dying. More rumors circulated that bird flu had mutated with ordinary flu. And no one was certain if the authorities had covered up the latest outbreak. It didn't take much imagination for the crew to assume the man coming onto the trawler had something deadly, something that might infect them.

Their main reassurance was that the captain loved life as much as they did and he would be just as vulnerable to infection by a strange disease as any member of the crew. If he hadn't shown concern, then what reason was there for them to feel unsettled and anxious? The stranger had filled them with dread from the moment his boat had been spotted. One of the Cambodians, or Khmer as the locals called them, said the captain would avoid the infected passenger, and that his plan was to throw the crew into the line of fire. The sick man's breath would be on them. He would touch them. The disease would be passed on. The crew argued whether they should allow the infected man to board the trawler. Captain Suthan raised his binoculars and watched the crew, picking out the ringleader who had stirred up the others. He made a mental note as he focused on one of the Khmer.

He felt Captain Suthan's eyes on him. The Khmer glanced up and saw the captain training his binoculars at him. They locked eyes for a long second. The Khmer was the first to look away. He blinked. The captain lowered his binoculars and yelled down at the crew to prepare for the arrival of the emergency medical case. The fishing boat left a long wake as the boat glided across the sea. The captain signaled the man operating the engine. The men on the fishing boat waved back. The men on deck scrambled pushing a rope ladder over the starboard side. If this man was infected, no one wanted to be too close to the ladder when the man emerged onto the trawler.

The Khmer and Thai crew discussed plans for what to do in the event the man in medical distress was unable to board without assistance. No one could agree what should be done. No one volunteered. Captain Suthan hadn't given an order. The captain, one of the Thais argued, wanted to see for himself the condition of the passenger, and only then would he give his order. The boat drew close so that the crew and captain could, for the first time, see for themselves the faces of the men in the small boat. It wasn't obvious which was the sick man. None of the three men looked any less able-bodied than the others. This left the mystery open as to who would be joining them on board the trawler. All they knew was that if he needed assistance, then no one had volunteered to go to his aid and the captain had given no order.

The wind had picked up. The boat was fifty meters away as the first whitecaps appeared, rolling it slightly from side to side. Ten meters out the pilot of the fishing boat cut the engine and let the momentum carry it forward. The two men in front were dressed in old trousers and long-sleeved shirts. Under their balaclavas they wore white surgical masks. The sun caught the whiteness of the masks. A sense of alarm rose as a gasp from a couple of members of the crew. Experienced seamen understood the art of smuggling. The appearance of an unexpected visitor with pirated merchandise wasn't something that disturbed the crew; such an incident meant side business with an additional profit potential and could only be welcomed. This felt like something quite different from ordinary smuggling. Too many news reports of fatal diseases had filtered down, and the appearance of the masks played to their fears. Except for their masks, the men in the boat could have been fishermen or rice farmers or laborers. Or they were smugglers delivering goods. The men on the boat might have been of any nationality. They might not have been men. They hung fenders and dropped the boarding ladder over the side.

The first attempt to pull alongside failed. The fishing boat hit the hull, and bounced away, churning water as it spun around. The pilot started the engine and slowly edged forward.

Cautiously he navigated alongside the trawler. On this attempt, one of the men in the bow grabbed the boarding ladder and steadied the boat. The Khmer ringleader reeled away from the railing as one of the two men removed his white mask and cursed at the pilot of the fishing boat. Captain Suthan had told them they were taking on board an ill man but he hadn't warned of possible infection. The crew, taking the lead of the Khmer ringleader, froze with fear. Two of the Khmer who had knives drawn bent over and tried to cut the rope ladder. The captain ran down the starboard side of the deck. He shoved the Khmer with the knife away from the boarding ladder and slapped him. He called them stupid water buffalo. His hands balled into fists, his voice roared with anger. He threatened to throw both of them overboard. At first they recoiled but slowly they stepped forward. They had a job to do. And the captain told them that under no circumstances would the rescue operation be aborted. No one on board had any choice but to participate; it was their duty. Was his intention clear enough for them to understand? They glanced at each other, out at the sea, was there any real other choice? The men begrudgingly returned to their hard work. Unless they were quick, there was a good chance a hole would be punched into the side of the small fishing boat. One of the crew leaned over with a long pole and one of the men in the bow of the boat grabbed hold, steadying the fishing boat. A choppy wave hit the boat, nearly knocking the man overboard.

"*Inshah Allah*," the man yelled, and his mask slipped down around his throat. "God willing."

He quickly pulled the mask over his nose.

The crew thought that they had heard curse words. There was no need to speak a language to understand the hint of warning embedded in such words. The sounds were unlike Thai or Khmer. Whoever the stranger was, his speech wasn't Thai. One of the men, the mask still covering his face, had begun to climb the rope ladder. The fishing boat rocked alongside as the slender bearded man with large brown eyes showing above the white mask wheeled himself over the railing and jumped down onto the deck. Whatever the cause of his illness, it wasn't apparent. His eyes were bright and clear and his movements agile and quick. The captain approached the man. His greeting was neither a *wai* nor an offer to shake hands. The two men simply nodded to each other. The captain ordered the crew to lower the main net. Two members of the crew worked the winch and the others pushed the netting over the side. Slowly the net touched the boat below and the two men remaining in the fishing boat struggled to load a large crate-like object inside the net.

The sun quickly dropped into the black sea and the men below worked under the beam of a flashlight. The captain ordered one of the Khmer down the ladder to help secure the cargo. In darkness, guided by a crewmember's flashlight, the Khmer disappeared down the rope. A quarter of an hour later, the three men managed to lift the cargo into the net, and moving the flashlight from side to side, signaled they had finished. The captain signaled for the net to be raised. The wheels and gears of the winch groaned as the net slowly rose. Under two flashlights, the crew saw for the first time that the cargo was a large footlocker. Inside the net, it banged against the hull. The stranger who had just boarded barked through his mask in broken Khmer at the men to be very careful with the cargo. He hung over the railing watching the progress and directing the man at the winch. The Khmer who returned from the fishing boat came up the ladder just behind the net, guiding it as it slowly rose. It required the full crew to land the net and footlocker on the deck. The Khmer and the other crewmembers stared at footlocker, at the stranger wearing the mask, then at one another. They all had had their fair share of experience in the smuggling game. All of them had seen smugglers loading sealed footlockers. The one pulled out of the main shipping net of this trawler was no different in any tangible way.

With the footlocker safely on board, Captain Suthan turned, looked over the side and waved his flashlight at the fishing boat. The pilot waved his flashlight in reply and started the engine. A moment later the fishing boat slipped away into darkness. A foreigner, who spoke broken Khmer with the men in the boat, appeared on the deck and, after exchanging a few words in highly accented English, he disappeared with the captain. The men had an uneasy feeling about this smuggler.

In his hand was a well-used copy of the Koran. Call it an omen. As he stood on the deck, the surgical mask obscured the stranger's face. He could have been anyone. He could have been infected with any kind of disease. He clutched the book, turned his back and was gone. Like a ghost.

Later that evening one of the crew crept past the captain's quarters. He saw through the window as the foreigner, the surgical mask hanging around his neck, counted out stacks of American hundred-dollar notes. The captain sat passively on the edge of his bunk, not blinking. He showed no fear of being in close proximity of the infected man. The captain coolly smoked a hand-rolled cigarette as the stranger counted out hundreds and hundreds of hundred-dollar notes. When the sailor returned to the crew quarters, he shared the story of the stranger and the money counting. He might not have known who Benjamin Franklin was, but he certainly recognized his face.

"How much money did he pay?"

In Thailand there were three standard questions: *Where do you go? Have you eaten rice? How much does it cost?* The question that mattered the most was the last one. The only person other than the stranger and the captain who had the answer was a simple-minded boy of eighteen. But the young spy hadn't a precise answer. He said that he'd never seen so much money. American dollars, too. Having gone to a village school for four years, he didn't think in large numbers, so he replied with the largest number that he could think of: "Many, many hundreds."

Vagueness in thought and ambiguity in answers had its rightful place on board the trawler and on shore. The crew understood that a great deal of cash had passed from an infected stranger to a captain who had no concern that the stranger had removed his mask. The mystery of the footlocker with its secure locks stored away on the quarterdeck remained unsolved. None of the crew spoke as they went about their work. The captain let them know he expected them to forget about what they had witnessed. The man they'd rescued was in serious distress, despite what any of the men thought. The captain did what any captain would do to render assistance. Then he smiled and broke out beer for them. It was the day before New Year's Eve. A new year was about to arrive and the old year's work was nearly behind them. The trawler would soon return home. The trawler was scheduled to return in time for the crew to celebrate the New Year. The captain had calculated the timing. To have returned to port too early would have invited questions. To have docked without a catch in the cooler would have ensured the wagging of tongues. His men were exhausted from five weeks at sea. The unscheduled pick up at sea had unsettled them and threatened to delay their return home. Sailors loved routine. What had been thrust upon them wasn't an ordinary work detail. Some of the crew—egged on by the Khmer—wondered if they would be paid a bonus. They had only been at sea for thirty-five days. They calculated the captain would pay them for that time. With the money that the infected man had paid, it was only right, they decided among themselves, that some kind of New Year's payment was fair compensation for the added risk.

The next morning, no one saw the stranger, who stayed in the captain's quarters. Food was taken to the door and left. The captain talked about disease and infection in a round-about way. He claimed to know a great deal about both and about how to protect against the spread of infection. He explained that to prevent VD all one had to do was apply a tab of Darlie toothpaste into the penis after intercourse. The active ingredient killed the germs that made a man ill. The captain swore an oath that this was the truth and that he had never been sick after sleeping with any woman, no matter how long she had been on the game. No one among the crew had the nerve to ask whether Darlie toothpaste might cure whatever disease had afflicted the stranger. The next morning the empty dishes were left outside the stranger's door. While the stranger might be suffering from some rare illness, whatever the nature of this infection, it hadn't lessened his appetite.

That evening a launch from the trawler was lowered, and the men worked up a sweat lowering the footlocker to where others waited inside the launch to guide the cargo downward. The captain, a crewmember and the stranger climbed into the launch. The trawler had anchored three miles off shore. The coast was a tiny white ribbon in the distance. The crew waited as the launch took the stranger to shore. Thirty minutes after leaving the trawler, the launch reached the beach. Not more than an hour later, the launch returned with the captain and crewmember. With the captain on board, the trawler set course for home. The captain, all smiles, had pulled a case of beer from the huge, nearly empty freezer hold for the crew. He handed around chilled bottles of Singha beer. The hold was filled with fish. The frozen fish would fetch a good price, the captain told them. The men said nothing, drinking their beer. The Khmer broke the silence as he asked about a bonus. It was a vague question, but the meaning wasn't lost on the captain. The captain grunted and his face darkened. Hadn't he always looked after his men? Hadn't he given them more than any other captain? Why were they so ungrateful, after all that he had done for them?

He didn't finish his beer, throwing the bottle overboard. He walked over until he was a couple of inches away from the Khmer. This man was a troublemaker, the captain said to himself. He looked at the Khmer as he spoke to the entire crew: every man should keep his mouth shut about the stranger. After they reached port, everyone should stay to themselves and wait until he sent for them. This was not a request. It was a direct order. A threat on a ship was different from one made on shore. Surrounded by water, no man needed to be reminded how a captain could make an example of a sailor for everyone else on board to fall in line and, once in line, that line would hold once they reached shore. The Khmer's knees were shaking. He held onto the railing, eyes down. He wished he hadn't asked the question. He apologized to the captain and said he didn't mean anything. The captain thought about the apology. He didn't commit himself one way or another. None of the usual *mai pen rai*. One of the crew handed him a fresh beer and said not to worry so much. Thay had their fish. And in a week or so everyone would return to sea together. The same sailor lit a cigarette and handed it to the captain, who said nothing as he turned and looked out at the moonlight on the sea.

THREE

THE trawler tied up at the wharf in the early morning. The captain had phoned ahead and arranged for transportation. A good catch was on ice and the trucks would deliver the fish straight to the market. He also radioed Veera that the trawler was returning to port with a full catch. This was more than a simple courtesy call; it was expected and necessary, as Veera controlled the port, the loading, and the unloading of trawlers the way he controlled many other activities from hotels, massage parlors, billiard halls, restaurants, and shopping centers. The captain and Veera went back a long way. Captain Suthan's trawler was one of the last that Veera made the effort to meet personally. As a man of stature in the community, he dispatched a *luuk nong*, a second in command, to look after his interest. Protocol required that old friends not hide behind their success. Of all the trawler men, Veera had maintained the closest relationship with Suthan. They had done various business deals over the years. Their fathers had known each other. Their families had intermarried. There was a history of money, blood-kin, and friendship. Money. Captain Suthan owed Veera a large sum of it. The captain had used the money to buy the trawler and had borrowed more money to refit it. His loans to Veera had been overdue for more than eight months.

For the first few hours, everyone was as busy at the port as they had been at sea. There was little time to talk. Unloading the fish from the huge freezer hold in the trawler required brawn and patience. It had been easier loading the fresh catch than it was removing the frozen carcasses.

When the last of the catch had been loaded in the back of pickups, the captain was ready to pay his crew in cash. They stood around the wharf waiting for him to reappear with white envelopes containing their money. Each of the Khmer had an extra five-hundred-baht note in their envelope. Each one *waied* the captain, thumbs touching their forehead, the envelope pressed between their fingers. They smelled of fish and the sea. Once on shore, a swagger returned to their step. They were free of command and work. Food vendors had setup stalls hawking noodles, beer, and fried rice. Another vendor had a tray of flowers weaved together for an offering. Four or five Thai men in their early twenties were at the wharf waiting. They wore green vests with a number stitched on the back. A couple of men squatted along the road; the others sat sidesaddle on their parked motorcycles. They stared at the Khmer walking towards them from the wharf. Word had spread that Captain Suthan had returned with a full load of fish.

The boss, a decade older than the taxi drivers, was stocky; hung on his barrel chest were one-baht gold chains each holding three amulets. He combed his thinning hair back from his forehead. His pencil mustache and scraggly beard suggested the conflict between a career of smash-and-grab and poetry. On his left pinky finger, he sported a long fingernail. Three, four inches and perfectly manicured. He wore a quasi-military shirt and trousers. He watched the Khmer from his white plastic chair as he picked his teeth with the tip of his long fingernail. As the Khmer reached the road, the boss leaned over and spit. All eyes at the taxi stand focused on the men clutching their white envelopes; the whiteness gleamed, as it was set off against their dark skin. The crew seemed smaller, thinner and more fragile on the vastness of land. The Thais had no trouble knowing who belonged and who were foreigners. They had no trouble spotting the two dark-skinned men as Cambodians. The Khmer walked towards them with their pockets full of money. With money came women, liquor and face, and that was just the start of it. Foreigners wanted to grab what wasn't theirs.

One of the Khmer hesitated as they walked past the motorcycle queue. The weight of all those stares made him swallow hard. Slipping under the waves in the middle of sea. On board ship, the crew looked after one another. It didn't matter who was Thai or Khmer; they faced the same dangers. On land, the bonds of the sea dissolved, and there was no one to rescue them. The Khmer had entered deep waters even though it was bone dry land and they felt totally alone, and abandoned.

"Where you go?" one of the taxi boys asked the Khmer in Thai.

One of the Khmer spit out the name of a karaoke bar not more than half a kilometer away. The boy kick-started his motorcycle and patted the back saddle. The Khmer swung a leg over and sat behind the driver. "Fifty baht," said the driver.

The Khmer knew the local price was five baht. Knowledge wasn't always a good thing to have. He shrugged off the extortion and decided not to challenge the driver as the other motorcycle drivers looked on. "*Mai pen rai*," said the Khmer. "No problem." He ate his own words as if they were a bitterroot.

His friend, whom the captain had seen as the ringleader on the trawler, tried to hop onto the back of the same motorbike. The two men were small enough to fit on the saddle. Upcountry, entire families were loaded onto the back of a motorcycle. The boss leaned forward in his chair and waved off the Khmer.

"No, cannot," he said. "You must take bike, too. You break the law, I think. You pay one hundred baht."

The Khmer slowly got off the first motorcycle and, showing no expression, walked over and started to mount the next bike in the queue.

"I say you give me one-hundred-baht fine."

The two Khmer were outnumbered seven to two. Weightwise and in terms of weapons, it was more like twenty to one. Those weren't good odds. Whatever the motorcycle taxi drivers demanded, the Khmer had no choice but to comply.

The first Khmer had disappeared on the back of a motorcycle—he had no choice, no chance to help his friend, as the motorcycle taxi driver gunned the bike, heading to the village. His stranded friend looked helpless as the members of the motorcycle queue surrounded him. The Khmer opened his envelope and offered the queue boss a hundred-baht note. The boss looked at the note, and then with pure hatred in his eyes looked at the Khmer. "Next time, you pay me two hundred baht, okay?"

A new Mercedes Benz pulled alongside the parked motorcycles. The tinted back window silently lowered and a well-groomed Thai greeted the motorcycle queue boss, who returned a full *wai*, and bowed his head.

"Have you eaten yet?" asked the man on the passenger side of the car. "*Krap. Taan tan khaow rue yang*?" Have you eaten, sir?

Veera could easily have been mistaken as an ethnic Chinese. He had light, clear skin and a rounded face, flat nose and large puffy bags under eyes hidden behind a pair of designer sunglasses. The eyelids drooped, revealing an age somewhere between mid-forties to early fifties. Veera carried himself like a much younger man. He lowered his sunglasses, nodded and grinned at the motorcycle queue boss, who showed his submission the way an omega animal prostrates to his alpha superior. The alpha showed his rank with the car, driver, and the twenty-baht gold chain around his neck, catching the sunlight. On three fingers of his left hand, he wore rings festooned with rubies, diamonds and sapphires. On his wrist was a gold Rolex thick with diamonds studded around the twelve points of time. One by one, Veera hooked his fingers over the edge of the glass. The Rolex appeared and the sun caught the diamonds in a cold glittering white swirl of light. His little fingernail was half as long again as the motorcycle queue boss's prided pinky nail. No animal in the wild kingdom mustered a better display of power and influence than a local gangster. Every attention to detail was a conscious choice, a sign that he'd established himself at the top of the food chain. Big fish ate little fish and Veera was the biggest fish in the area. Trawler captains occupied a status far below his. Veera controlled the waterfront. He was the man who decided who came on his turf and the price for that privilege, who lived and who died.

"I am late. Or Khun Suthan was early. What do you think?"

"I think that Khun Suthan was early."

The second Khmer had escaped on the back of a motorcycle. The captain arrived a moment later carrying a bag. He *waied* Veera, who climbed out of the back of his chauffeur-driven car. Veera returned the captain's *wai*. "I think you bring in a very big catch," said Veera.

"Okay catch. As far as fish go."

Veera lifted his head back and laughed. "You always joke me. But you are my very good friend. I understand you. And you know that I love my friends."

The captain sighed. "I could have a small problem."

He passed the briefcase to Veera. A broad smile crossed his face.

"Khun Suthan, you never worry about small things. Please, come to my house and have lunch with me and my wife and son. Don't say no. I won't hear no."

In the back of the Mercedes, Captain Suthan hinted that the two Khmer who had been on his trawler might cause a problem. He wasn't sure. They'd overheard him speaking Khmer and English. Maybe they would make trouble, maybe they would shut up. Who knows what a man will do when he's away from the boat with a few drinks inside him? The captain had done his part; he had delivered the money to Veera. Some lingering doubt told him not to trust the Khmer. With the attack on the southern armory and the stealing of M16s, gun smuggling had reached a higher level of danger. The captain assumed weapons were in the footlocker. The crew made the same assumption. Not all of the crew were Thai. Like the Burmese, the Khmer were devious, unreliable, and had to be carefully watched. That's what schoolbooks taught. Who would doubt the wisdom of one's teachers?

Veera opened the briefcase and glanced at the cash inside.

The trawler was at last mortgage free. Captain Suthan was at last his own man. As far as one could be one's own man in a world of Veeras.

That evening as the Khmer stumbled out of a roadside bar, three men and the boss from the motorcycle queue waited.

The sound of men singing and talking spilled out into the street behind them. That wasn't the only sound. The sound of a drum echoed and merged into the lower frequency sound of a steel beam as it caught the first Khmer on the forehead, and bone and brains splattered in a shower onto the road. The blow made a loud, sickeningly hollow sound, a half-cry, and then the singing from inside the bar once again filled the night. The second Khmer, the ringleader from the trawler who was one step behind broke into a run. Two of the men kick-started their motorcycles and within twenty meters the runner lay in the road, blood pouring out of his head. The boss pulled up in a pickup and the second body was loaded next to the first one. One of the men carefully slipped a slightly soiled white envelope from the back pocket of one body, and then patted down the other body and rolled it over as the pickup headed along the road. He found the other envelope and held them both against the back window, rapping his knuckles against the glass. Slowly the boss turned and smiled.

FOUR

FROM the third-story office window, Calvino looked down at the street choked with double-parked cars and vans. It was eleven in the morning. A skyward flash of brilliant light caught his eye. Rain clouds from southern China streaked with jagged white cracks cut across the sky. A pause followed the flash; the silence was punctured by a loud boom that rippled like a series of explosions. In that split second the window shook and the sky turned brilliant white. The semi-feral dogs in the *soi* howled. Maids sucked in their breath, afraid of ghosts, afraid of flooding, afraid of the looming premature darkness. Vincent Calvino turned away from the window as the first drops pelted against the glass. Motorcycle taxis scattered for cover. On small *sois* off Sukhumvit Road, the traffic had slowed and soon like sticky rice would become glutinous and messy.

Ratana had phoned half an hour before, talking about her Chinese lessons and her confinement to her mother's house. She checked in five or six times a day. Whenever she was bored, she picked up the phone and rang his number. He answered knowing it was his secretary. Her voice was deep, thick with mucous that came with flu-like symptoms. She had been ill. That was one reason she was home. And her tone carried a sense of the worry planted in her mind by her mother, turned nurse, turned Chinese-language instructor. The unrest in the south and rumors of violence spreading to Bangkok was the other reason. She said that she understood now what people who had gone through the Cultural Revolution had experienced. Storms clouds weren't the only thing breezing down from China. One of those animal-to-man diseases had hitched rides on migratory birds or spread inside planes over all Asia, attaching itself to the lungs, nose, mouth and eyes of passengers—sniffling, coughing, hacking, spitting passengers, sweat pouring out of them. It had gone dormant for many months and then suddenly resurfaced with a vengeance, killing the young and the old, the feeble and the helpless. Nine days before, Ratana had returned from a shopping trip to Hong Kong and immediately her mother had placed her in quarantine. It had happened so quickly that she hadn't had a chance to think, and once she did, the depression set in. Her lifeline was the telephone to her boss. Vincent Calvino listened to the phone ring, knowing who it was and that she was depressed and scared and anxious; he stood watching the rain hit the lane.

The old world of Bangkok was undergoing change. Closing hours had moved to midnight. Disease alerts. Rumors of terrorism were whispered in the ears of Ratana's mother; she whispered them to her daughter. Calvino was undecided what it all meant. Were these rumors and events ordinary volatility within an existing phase of the Thai life cycle? Or were they evidence of something deeper, more fundamental, and far more radical—a phase transition to a different cycle, a new life? Like when ice turns to water. A disease that killed hundred or thousands caused phase volatility; one that killed millions could trigger a pandemic, a phase transition. Like when water turns to steam.

There was no way to know until it happened, Calvino told himself. Meanwhile there was nothing to do but wait. The days since Ratana's return from Hong Kong had been one of life's low points. He had no secretary and no outstanding cases. In between jobs, in between lives, as he watched the rain, he thought his own life might also be in for a phase transition. Heat and energy made all the difference. The difference between work and being jobless. The difference between a prostitute and a nice girl. The difference between a bandit and a terrorist. The difference between life and death. The same thing, but in a different phase. Ice to water to steam.

The wet streets below reminded him that he had forgotten to close the window in his apartment. The thought of damp sheets on the bed was depressing; Ratana's absence had left the office a lonely, silent and grim place. He fought against the urge for a drink.

He looked over at the ringing telephone. He was still blinking from the blinding flash of lightning. It was her call for help, he thought. Her Chinese lesson would be finished by now and she would need the comfort of his voice. A halo of sound surrounded the telephone. He knew this wasn't a divine message. The divine was in light, not in sound. He picked up the phone. It was Searles Valentine, an old friend and client, calling from Pattaya.

"Is it raining in Bangkok?" asked Valentine.

"Pouring," said Calvino.

"It is very good for the garden."

"I don't have a garden."

"Pity."

His new generation of friends in Thailand called him Valentine. A few close friends from school called him Val. Calvino called him Valentine. He seemed to like that. Only his mother and schoolmasters had called him Searles until one day, he took Calvino aside and said, "About this name Searles. I'd rather you didn't call me Searles. Please call me Valentine. I would consider it a favor."

Calvino didn't ask why calling someone by their last name as opposed to their first name could be considered a favor. He assumed that Valentine had his reasons. People had funny quirks about names. As if what one called a person or a thing mattered in a world of nameless pain and suffering.

This time when Valentine called, Calvino had a good idea that he wasn't making a personal call. A couple of days earlier, Valentine had made that clear in an email. The morning he'd received Valentine's email, there had been eighty-three emails—offers to increase his breast size, penis size, stock deals, special deals to Disney World. After he deleted the spam, only one email was left. It was from Valentine. His message had been simple and to the point. *I'd like to engage you in a matter. I'll phone with the details. Valentine.*

Calvino read the email several times, looking for some other hint of what Valentine had wanted. But there was nothing below the surface of those stark, cold words. Valentine had a problem and he wished to discuss it at a time of his choosing. Calvino imagined that it was a delicate problem that required complete confidence. When the call came in that morning of the lightning and thunder, Valentine told him the story. His gardener, a man name Prasit, had apparently committed suicide, but some of the people employed on the estate were convinced that Prasit had been murdered. And what did Searles Valentine believe about the cause of his gardener's death? He didn't speculate about alternative causes, and knowing Valentine—not well but well enough—Calvino guessed the cause of death didn't much matter one way or the other. Suicide was as good a cause as any, so why not just leave the matter as the police had left it? That was Valentine's attitude. What mattered most to Searles Valentine was his demand for peace, order, and tranquility. Calvino's job was to reinstate the old status quo to this small kingdom. How was he to perform this act of magic? By magically lifting all doubt as to the gardener's death and reassuring the insecure employees that the poor man had indeed killed himself.

"A death here and there is really nothing in the grand scheme of things," Valentine said. "Really all I need is your professional confirmation of Prasit's suicide. It's really quite simple. Then all will return to normal."

On the surface, it appeared that Valentine would have made a good fascist, or Stalinist for that matter. This was unfair. His personality and talents were too complex to label. In his honesty and frankness, there was something touching, refreshing, without artifice, screens, rationalizations.

He lived on twenty *rai* of land on a lush estate eight kilometers outside of Pattaya. On the phone, he invited Calvino to spend a few days on the estate—a grand, overused word and one that Valentine avoided himself—in describing the large grounds with gardens of coconut trees and flowers and scrubs, outbuildings, farm land, goat enclosures, forest land, the moat stocked with eels and catfish and the rambling hacienda deep inside, out of sight from the road, a place of refuge.

As Calvino listened to Valentine's plea, he wondered what the point was of staying at the office in Bangkok. The phone pressed to his ear, he looked out the window at the steady rain. There was nothing keeping him in Bangkok. A chill of loneliness spiked through his body and he shuddered. There was no reason to not take the case. He stared at the rain-swept street. How many times had he willed a client to phone so he'd have enough money to cover the monthly expenses? Now he had a client *begging* him to take a case. Was he that proud? That crazy? Sitting on the edge of his desk, he listened to Valentine pleading and offering money. He remembered how well Valentine played the piano. The man was a genuine artist and the death of the gardener had caused *his* world to come unstuck. And that was the only world Valentine cared about. His personal bubble world. His cocoon stuffed with hand-picked butterflies. That's when a private eye knows he's in business: a man who is used to absolute control finds it draining out of his life and he'd do anything, pay any amount to have it back again.

"Vincent, you are tormenting me," said Valentine.

"I don't get many clients from Pattaya."

"My friend, Doctor Iain, says never ask, 'What are the pros and cons of Pattaya?' Ask instead, 'Who are the pros and cons in Pattaya?' and then you stand a chance to understand how the system works."

Calvino smiled to himself. Valentine was quick-witted. Spending time working for a man with some good humor and talent wouldn't be a bad thing. Valentine heard nothing but silence and interpreted the absence of a response to be some hesitation to leave Bangkok.

"It would be dreadful to work for what the average man would pay you," said Valentine. "But, you see, I am not average. I am willing to pay the full rate. Are you accepting my invitation?"

"Is this a social call or work?" asked Calvino.

"Both. As I meant to say in my email, what I have in mind is social *and* business. Whatever your usual fee is won't be a problem."

What he meant and what he said were different orders of communication. One had been in the email; one had been left out.

"Three hundred dollars a day and expenses," said Calvino.

"Perfectly reasonable, my dear fellow. I can give you an advance if you like. I normally don't advance funds to *anyone* in this country. It's an abhorrent practice guaranteed to make a man come to grief. There is a saying that once you put sugar cane in an elephant's mouth, you can never retrieve it."

"*Ooy khao pak chang*," said Calvino, translating the saying into Thai.

"Very good. You've been studying your Thai."

Valentine was rich, distinguished; a famous pianist. He was recognized internationally as one of the great classical pianists. He had a following in London, Paris, New York, Moscow, and Berlin. His CDs had sold half-million; not Madonna or a boy band's worth of CDs, but by classical standards, he was a superstar with a following.

"My gardener hanged himself inside his room and it is quite annoying."

"Thoughtless," said Calvino.

"My feeling exactly. If he was going to kill himself, at least he could've gone into Pattaya and hanged himself off the premises. A thoughtful employee would have done that. But he was of the gardener class and obviously one can't expect too much."

"Obviously not."

"Don't mock me, Vincent. I see no reason to get sentimental. Prasit was a good gardener. I am sorry he's dead. But I am more sorry about how he's gone about inconveniencing me. After all, I had paid him well and treated him fairly."

"Why not let the police deal with it?"

"Some of *my* people believe that it wasn't suicide. The police think the opposite. So there we are. A division of opinion."

Valentine had a feudal lord's notion of the people on his estate. They belonged to him. Some of his chattels obviously had a different point of view from their lord.

"Who's questioning the police report?"

"My Number One. I can't shake her from the silly idea. I am certain that Prasit's widow has put this silly piece of nonsense into her head. I need you to remove that nonsense."

"How do you propose I do that?"

"You drive down to my house and stay here. Look at the scene, draw the logical conclusion that Prasit hanged himself, and explain it to her. It's very simple."

"Why would she listen to me, if she won't listen to the police or to you?"

"My dear fellow, women only listen to and believe the men they don't sleep with. It's a variation on the theme that no man is a hero to his valet. Prasit's widow is an exception to the rule. I don't sleep with her. But she won't listen to me. And she certainly doesn't believe a word the police say."

Outside the window the rain fell. Nothing moved. "Is it raining in Pattaya?"

"Beautiful, clear skies," said Valentine. "Can you come this evening? I will see a splendid dinner is prepared and then you can start putting the puzzle together."

"Dinner. I'll be there."

A death inevitably disrupted the life of those close to the scene. If the death were a murder, that was an entirely different level of disruption, as police investigators, reporters, and others appeared on the doorstep asking questions. Treating everyone as a potential suspect. Not to mention the slow accumulation of neighbors and assorted onlookers drawn to the scene of the drama. Valentine's inconvenience would have happened on several fronts: from supervising the early morning feeding of the goat herd, returning to the main house for breakfast and reading the morning papers, sipping tea, a swim in the pool, checking email, then a nap, followed by hours at the grand piano, and at night one of the *sanoms* visiting his quarters. Each stage of the daily cycle had been disturbed, blurred, making him miserable.

Calvino thought, as he put down the phone, that this appeared less of a murder case than a crossword puzzle for Valentine; one of those difficult five across words that was just on the tip of his tongue. If only that word would come; but it remained out of reach. Prasit's death became an amusement presenting multiple possible solutions. In Valentine's mind the gardener's death had only one obvious cause. The man had awoken one day thoroughly depressed, understood his lot in life—which was one of servile, demeaning work. His wife was away and so she wasn't there to comfort him, and he removed his belt, looped it around his neck, fixed the buckle to the door knob, sat down and bent forward in his chair until his life slowly slipped away. In the case of a suicide, most people who knew the deceased sought an alternative explanation which would exonerate the dead man; to make him non-culpable for his death. To find an exterior cause to explain this terrible effect. Like many people, Valentine understood how easy it was for others to project their sensibilities onto another, or their situation, or indeed their death. Despite his annoyance, he felt the widow's refusal to accept the police report was perfectly understandable and that Vincent Calvino was the man to talk sense to her. A domestic murder case was just what the doctor ordered, thought Calvino. Getting lost in an ordinary murder case would divert him from contemplating the meaning of the changes swirling in the polluted Bangkok air. A break from news flashes about viruses, bombings, terrorists, and the creep of what increasingly felt like a gradual slide into martial law.

FIVE

RATANA'S mother was nearby. Both women wore white masks. Except Ratana had taken hers off to allow for a thermometer to be slipped under her tongue. The mother moved around her daughter like someone who was half picador and half mad scientist.

Answering the phone, Ratana removed the thermometer from her mouth and handed it to her mother. Her mother slipped on her reading glasses and examined the thermometer closely.

"Normal?" asked Ratana.

Her mother said nothing, wiping the thermometer with a piece of cotton dipped in alcohol. Calvino waited as the voice muffled into a sound track of non-words. In the background, he heard Ratana's mother whispering, but he couldn't make out the words.

"My temperature's normal," said Ratana.

"It's not about the flu or SARS," said Calvino. "It's irrational."

"I know that. You know that."

"But your mother doesn't know that. Let me talk to her."

He heard Ratana arguing with her mother.

"She's gone."

Elvis has left the building, thought Calvino.

"My mother's been listening to a talk radio show. People are calling in and saying it is the foreigners who are responsible for SARS and bird flu. Foreign birds. Foreign people. They are the carriers. These people are screaming into the phone that *farangs* must be avoided, and my mother is listening and nodding."

"She believes them?" asked Calvino.

"Who knows what to believe? She spoke with her fortuneteller today. He predicts something terrible is about to happen," said Ratana.

"Such as?"

"A terrorist attack in the BTS."

Ratana came to work on the sky train. The possibility of such an attack would have the desired effect; it would help keep her away from Calvino's office.

"He also said that Muslims would hit those working for Jews."

Calvino didn't like where this was going. "My mother was Jewish," he said. He knew that Ratana's mother also had this knowledge. For years the family had been working to separate Ratana from the employment of the *farang* private investigator. The new viruses and terrorism had given the mother a new arsenal to launch a new attack.

"I can't change who I am, Ratana," he said.

"No one said that you should."

What she meant was everyone, including her mother, knew that was impossible. Since he couldn't change mothers, and his Jewish blood put her at risk in her mother's eyes—or those of her fortuneteller—what hope did he have of persuading her that her mother was wrong? She could become collateral damage. Anti-Semitism was the long nightmare that had no exit. He had had his final reason to leave Bangkok for a week or so.

"I am going to Pattaya. I phoned Valentine. His gardener died and some of the staff believes he was murdered. I told him I'd take the case."

"Pattaya is a dangerous place."

"I am trying to think of a place that isn't."

"You know what I mean."

"His house is outside of Pattaya. I don't anticipate a problem."

"In five more days I'll be back to work," she said. "My mother agrees. If I am not sick in five days, then that makes fourteen days inside and I must be okay."

"What about the prediction of attacks against Jews?"

She cleared her throat. "Khun Vinee, I am not afraid."

He wasn't certain what he wanted to hear. Five more days of fortuneteller predictions of violence imported from the south might cause her to change her mind. He decided to leave it open. To give Ratana an easy way out if she needed one.

"You think about it. After five days, you tell me how you feel about coming back to work."

"How did the gardener die?"

"The police say he hanged himself."

"If he had a disease, he could have lost heart and killed himself."

"Or someone could have killed him."

There was a long pause.

"Take care of yourself, Khun Vinee. And thanks for being so understanding about everything. My mother really means well. I hope you believe that."

"Yeah."

SIX

VALENTINE'S estate was a two-and-a-half hour drive east from Calvino's apartment on Sukhumvit Road. The rain had eased once he hit the outskirts of the city. Half way to Pattaya the sky turned blue, the road surface dried by the heat of the sun, and the high temperature had the highway drivers boiling as they gunned along the shoulder at 140 kilometers an hour to pass slow-moving trucks. He'd seen Valentine in Bangkok over the years every few months. He tried to remember the last time he had driven to Valentine's estate. Six, seven years ago, he guessed. Valentine had personally designed a grand estate some eight kilometers outside of Pattaya and then acted as his own contractor for its construction. Before the expressway and the eastern seaboard opened, the terrain between Pattaya had been fields and a series of sleepy villages. Calvino had been invited to Valentine's house-warming; the surrounding landscape was a rich, upcountry place dotted with green rice and sugar cane fields and water buffalo, pigs, and chickens. Since that time, the city of Pattaya had burst out of its borders and rapidly expanded, swallowing up great parcels of farmland. Converting paddy into an ugly sprawl of shops and houses. Within a few kilometers of Valentine's estate, Calvino saw how much the land had changed. That feeling he had had years ago of an isolated pastoral enclave had been lost. Most of what had been traditionally rural was now dotted with newly constructed suburban styled houses with blue tiled roofs and freshly painted walls.

Turning off the main highway, he pulled in front of a shophouse—the metal gates were rolled up to the ceiling. Inside on the concrete floor were fifty-kilo bags of animal feed stacked to the ceiling. The Chinese owner, his shirt unbuttoned to display a half-dozen amulets on a thick gold chain, squatted on a stool behind a large desk where he kept a watchful eye on the road and his employees. Valentine had phoned Calvino and asked if he could stop and pick up three bags of feed for the goats.

"For goats?"

My dear, fellow, I raise goats. Don t worry; it s not for our dinner tonight. The feed is paid for. All you need do is use my name and one of the men who works for the owner will load the bags for you. There s not much to it. It shouldn t take five minutes. It would help me a great deal.

Calvino understood that whenever someone said there wasn t much to doing something, this meant to expect trouble, delays and anxiety. Otherwise, they would have done the chore themselves. Normally I don t run errands such as picking up goat feed for clients, said Calvino.

"Now I've hurt your feelings. Of course I have. And you have every right to feel aggrieved. In your place, I would likely feel quite the same. All I am saying in defense of my indefensible request is that the shop is on your way. And if you weren't a friend, I wouldn't have asked. If it is too much trouble, then I'll find another way."

Guilt usually worked wonders on Calvino. "Three bags?"

"And no heavy lifting. The men will do the heavy lifting. There is no smell. The bags won't leak. And my staff will take over when you arrive. But if this offends you..."

"Valentine, I'll pick up the bags."

"Good man, Vincent Calvino. You are a very good man."

Tell that to Ratana's mother who assumes her boss will spread rare and lethal viruses to her daughter, and that Muslim terrorist who had targeted him in Bangkok.

SEVEN

AS the road curved to the left, it narrowed to a dirt track. Calvino turned onto the path and drove another thirty meters. He passed an empty lot; a water buffalo tethered to a stake grazed on tall grass. At the end of the road was a gate and on either side a high wall with rows of medieval-looking spikes on the top. The wall snaked around the perimeter and finally disappeared, like the Great Wall of China, out of sight. The blue steel gate marked the entry point to Valentine's estate. There was no name; the number 88/9 was etched into the side of the wall. Calvino shifted his car into park and honked his horn. He waited for one of Valentine's servants to appear and open the gate. He left his car engine running. Looking through the windshield, he saw that the huge gate was locked. The sound of several barking dogs rose from the edge of the gate. After a couple of minutes he honked again, waited, and finally opened the car door, climbed out, and walked to the gate to peer through a peephole halfway up the right hand side. He saw no one. A large dog and two much smaller mutts snapped and growled from behind the gate. Calvino returned to the car and dialed Valentine's number. He had just been talking to him. Obviously he'd been expected. So why hadn't Valentine sent someone down to open the gate?

Meanwhile, Valentine had switched off his cellphone. There were clients who had the habit of using their cellphones only to make calls and then immediately switched them off. Calvino sat in his car and waited, drumming his fingers on the steering wheel. He saw a couple of chickens pecking the dirt not far from the water buffalo. He thought about the air-borne diseases and the scare they had caused across Asia, and how this had provided an excuse for Ratana to be held hostage by her mother, and he thought of the hard, driving rain he'd left behind in Bangkok; in other words, he cheered himself up by thinking about all the factors that had driven him out of the city.

Five minutes later the dogs stopped yapping; he heard a human voice.

"Coming."

A moment later she pushed open one half of the gate, and then the otherside.

"I am Vincent Calvino," he said.

She nodded, her eyes darting from side to side, looking him over. "Yes, I know. We are so busy. It is my fault. *Nai* will be angry. He told me to wait for you at the gate. He will punish me. It will be terrible. Please, please, understand that I am sorry to keep you waiting."

Her English was good. Her tone was anxious and despairing. She used the Thai word for boss—*nai*. In most places of domestic employment that was all the Thai an illegal immigrant needed to know to keep her job.

"Maybe I am early? But I thought Valentine was expecting me. Then I thought I was wrong. He changed his mind," said Calvino.

"No, no. He not change his mind. That's impossible. Everyone who lives here has been waiting for you. We wait for many days. Ever since. . ."

"Everyone?"

Calvino's question startled her, reminding her that she had said more than was intended. Her job was to greet him. And before she could stop herself, she was gushing about him like he was a visiting star on tour.

"*Nai* said to ask if you picked up the goat feed. He worries too much about his goats. Like a father worries about his children."

"Where are the others to help?"

She looked at him, then away, patting one of the dogs. "They are on strike."

"Strike?"
"They stop work."
"I know what a strike is," he said.
She looked down and said nothing.
"The bags are in the trunk," said Calvino. "All 150 kilos. One more bag and the front wheel of the Honda wouldn't have touched the road. I am joking; I'll help. I am not on strike. Not yet."
She laughed. "You joke very good. My name is Som. I will help you. Follow me."
"What's your job here?"
"I am a maid."
"And you do farm work as well?"
She nodded. "Everyone helps with the goats. It's a rule. Follow me."
"I am glad I didn't break the rule," said Calvino.
She ran ahead with three dogs sniffing at her heels and pointing as she ran, leading him to a parking shelter. Parked inside were an old Toyota station wagon and a pickup truck. Calvino pulled alongside the battered, rusty pickup, stopped and got out of the car. He walked around the pickup as Som returned from the front gate. Dented and weather-beaten, the pickup looked like it had been hit on one side, rolled over a cliff, pulled back onto the road, and driven back and parked in this spot.
So much for no heavy lifting, Calvino thought. He leaned into the trunk, picked up a bag and slung it over his shoulder.
He tried to place the maid's accent. "You don't sound like a Thai."
"Shan," she said, smiling. "My Thai name is Som. I was born in the Shan state. The Burmese army killed my brother and two uncles. Please give the bag to me. *Nai* will punish me if he sees you carrying the bag. That is my job. Shan people can carry a heavy load. We don't complain."
A sense of pure pride came from her lips. It had to be cut with a large element of hurt and sorrow. Some women were damaged beyond repair when their fathers and uncles were killed. Others found an inner strength. Som was a survivor. She'd found a way around the killings. Father killed. Pass

the rice. Uncles slaughtered. Time to go into the fields to plant, weed, or harvest more rice. He wanted to ask about her mother and aunts but thought better of it. Sometimes it was better not to ask too many personal questions too soon. He would have the chance to interview her later.

Som couldn't have weighed more than forty-three kilos. The name "Som" translated as orange. The color orange or the fruit, depending on the context. Or a name used by a Burmese woman on the run from a violent past.

"The bag has seven kilos on you. Let me give you some help. We won't tell *nai*, will we?"

She stared at him for a moment, wondering if he was playing a mind-game, and when it appeared he was genuine, she smiled. "You a very good man," she said, her head inside the trunk of the Honda. She rose up with a bag of feed on her back. "We put them here for now."

They stacked the bags on the concrete floor behind the pickup truck. The dogs sniffed around the bags. As the Great Dane hiked its leg, Som shouted in Thai for him to stop. Its head turned, the brown eyes sad and defeated, and dropping its leg, the Great Dane, head lowered, approached her. She patted its head.

"Tomorrow, the strike is over, and I can get someone help me move the bags."

She walked ahead. Calvino stood beside the bags, the Great Dane sniffing his pant legs. "Dober doesn't bite," said Som.

He looked back at the dog, wondering what kind of name "Dober" was.

"I am not worried."

"*Nai* is expecting you. We must go."

Som led the way, crossing the arched bridge over a wide moat. She looked down at the water as she waited for Calvino to catch up. He looked down. In the muddy water below, the large head of a catfish broke the surface, its whiskers beaded with water, only to submerge itself, the tail flicking the water as it closed over the large fish. Calvino had drawn alongside and watched the fish. Insects glided over the surface. Fish jumped, snagging dinner off the surface of the water, then disappearing as fins and tails lashed the water. There was something medieval about a moat and something totally in place at the same time.

A splash carried over the bridge. "They feed this time of day," said Som. "It is very terrible and very beautiful." The Great Dane and the other two dogs came to a dead stop at the foot of the bridge. The dogs sensed where the line had been drawn, and beyond that point they couldn't go.

On the opposite side of the stone bridge, through a narrow passageway, the path opened into a small Bali-style courtyard. Wild orchids and banana trees grew along the verge running beside a whitewashed wall. Shoes had been carefully lined up in pairs near the threshold to the main living quarters. Som slipped off her sandals, squared them so that the toes and heels were even, and waited until Calvino finished removing his shoes. She lined them up as well next to her sandals. He followed her inside.

There was a series of single-story buildings with gabled roofs arched together. They had been built so the windows overlooked a central swimming pool. On the night of the house-warming years before, Calvino remembered, the pool had been dotted with white lotus petals. Incense burnt in pots along the edge of the pool and Valentine's guests sat in deck chairs watching as one of Valentine's women languidly swam laps in a tiny bikini. This time the pool looked different, less exotic and more functional—like a health-club pool. No white lotus petals floated on the surface nor were there incense sticks burning in clay pots nor were nubile women swimming to the sound of Mozart piped from Bose speakers hidden among the banana trees around the perimeter. On that evening seven years ago, a Mozart recording was playing; it was a recording from a Royal Albert Hall recital with Valentine on the grand concert piano. That was before he had as the Thais said, gone *lud lok*. Before he had fallen off the world.

As Calvino entered the world Valentine had fallen into, the feeling was that it was the same but changed in subtle ways. Oil lanterns with large upside-down cones lined the perimeter of the large pool. The surface of the pool was placid and smooth, and the grounds empty of people. He wondered about the strike. There were leaves floating in the pool. It hadn't been cleaned for a couple of days from the look of it. He expected Valentine to pop out at any moment, but he wasn't anywhere to be found. Having done her primary duty, Som disappeared. Without a word, she had gone back over the bridge to the outbuildings where the kitchen was located. Left alone, he wandered around the dining area enclosed by a wall on two sides and above by a heavily beamed roof with a rotating fan. In the center of this room was a long teak dining table. Dinner service was set for three people. Calvino wondered who the third guest would be. If he were a betting man, he would have put money that the third chair would be used by one of Valentine's harem. He liked the company of beautiful women. That much Calvino remembered. In the kitchen area, he walked past cupboards and a long wooden counter. He continued to the far end of the kitchen and examined a number of jars lining one shelf. Each jar contained snakes. Some with stripes and others with dull green skin, dull lidless eyes. Calvino picked up one jar and examined it. Valentine silently crept up from behind.

"That one is not lethal. It is an adder. The one next to it is a banded krait, and would kill you within thirty seconds. More people die from a falling coconut than from snakebites. Which merely proves the obvious—most seemingly safe, ordinary things in life may be more lethal than the dramatic strike of a banded krait. We shouldn't fear snakes. We should fear coconuts." Valentine paused, taking the jar with the banded krait snake curled inside. He sighed and put it back on the shelf. "Prasit had absolutely no fear of snakes. You could almost say he loved catching snakes. He had a great deal of knowledge about them. He knew the various kinds of adders and cobras. What snakes were aggressive and which would give a nasty bite but wouldn't kill you. Collecting snakes became a hobby that we both enjoyed. Now I am without my gardener, and my collection risks a halt. I trust your journey was without incident." It was an innocent question. One that Valentine assumed could only be answered in one way. There had been no problem.

"I delivered your goat feed. The bags are behind your pickup."

Valentine sensed something hadn't gone right.

"Som didn't organize that?"

"She organized it perfectly. Just as you promised, no heavy lifting."

"See—what did I tell you?"

"You are a man of your word."

"Welcome to my humble abode."

"For a man with most of your employees on strike, you seem to be relaxed, even comfortable."

"Som told you about the strike," he said with a shudder. "Som can be a naughty girl. Spreading our family secrets to guests. That's disloyal. Beyond that, what she said is inaccurate. It isn't really a strike so much as a misunderstanding. It can and will be cleared up very quickly."

"Misunderstandings, like strikes, can go on for a long time. What makes you think this one is about to end?"

"Because you are here." He smiled, his arms open, and embraced Calvino.

Valentine's face and neck were tanned. Calvino thought the tan came from working outside in the garden, walking his estate, looking after the dogs and the livestock. Also, Valentine's short-cropped hair was grayer. Standing at six three, he towered over the Thais. With a swimmer's slender body, Valentine still had a boyish face, grinning like a twelve-year-old after landing his first fish—or snake. When he sat at the grand piano, he seemed larger than life; a presence that commanded awe. The music flowed out of his fingertips.

"Come over here and sit down," said Valentine. "I am afraid my *yings* won't be happy with me as long as you are on the premises. Competition is such a bore when it comes to women. They thrive on it and I find it not worthy of my attention. I have too many other things to concern myself with."

"I'll keep a distance," said Calvino.

"That will only make you more irresistible."

Valentine wore a white shirt open at the neck, sleeves rolled to the elbows, and unbelted baggy tan-colored pants. The casual look of a man relaxed.

Two Thai women in their twenties carrying plates and bowls followed in orderly procession behind Som. There appeared to be an order in their entrance. They set the dishes down on the counter saying little as Som lifted the lid on the large porcelain bowl heaped high with rice and came to the table. She served Calvino first, scooping out one large spoon of white rice and then another until Calvino raised his hand.

"Enough," he said. Swooping in behind Som, a young Thai woman dressed in black shorts and a black T-shirt—"Hazard Design" written in white—held a plate in front of Calvino. Asparagus tips and sliced mushrooms basted in butter. She waited until Calvino helped himself, lifting the serving spoon and fork from the side of the platter.

"This is Maew. She's my Number One," said Valentine. "Maew, say hello to Khun Vinee. He's a *nak suep*. The private investigator I sent for."

"My first assignment was to deliver three bags of goat feed," said Calvino.

"I am afraid *farang* irony isn't her forte. But she has other more important skills. Maew has been a very bad Ubonratcha Thani *ying* of late. She's the ringleader for the wildcat strike. Isn't that right, Maew? She has insisted on wearing black as a protest. Her behavior has not exactly been what one would call a show of loyalty."

The young woman smiled as Calvino returned the serving spoon and fork to the platter. She moved over and stood beside Valentine, who helped himself. "And the *ying* offering you that rather succulent steamed sea bass is Kem. Who, despite her nickname, isn't salty at all. She is my Number Two and is from Buriram. You can see the Khmer influence in her cheekbones. The high forehead is a dead giveaway. My Number Three, Gop, is in the kitchen slaving over a hot oven. Soon she will bring out a very nice green curry."

Calvino glanced at the empty place across the table. "You're expecting someone else?"

Valentine stared up from his large piece of sea bass. "That is for the gardener. Or should I say, for his spirit that I have been assured lurks nearby. The women organize an offering to his spirit every day. It is in their heads that with you coming to look into his death, a place should be set for him. I'm informed that they believe his spirit hasn't left the premises and that his ghost continues to wander the grounds. And

Prasit's spirit will not leave until his murderer is found. That, I tell them, is difficult, as the poor man hanged himself. A fact confirmed by the police. A fact confirmed by the medical examiner that inspected the body. Obviously facts aren't what these ladies are interested in understanding. Savages believe in the occult, mysticism and black magic, and those dark forces can be expelled only by using supernatural means. Speak not to them of reason or logic or science. Savages live in a world of speculation, rumors and gossip, fearful of unknown forces and unseen worlds."

"I am an investigator, not a shaman," said Calvino.

"There is no such distinction. And I believe that Sherlock Holmes would have agreed with me. How is the fish?"

Calvino looked up. "It tastes like fish."

Valentine grinned. "Better than chicken. No one eats chicken. We all live in a world imprisoned by our own worst fears, wouldn't you agree?"

He pulled out a chilled bottle of Pouilly Fuissé and poured Calvino's glass half full, then filled his own. Valentine raised his glass, swirling the white wine around the inside. He stood up from the end of the table. "I propose a toast."

Calvino rose to a half-standing position, holding his wine glass by the stem until it touched the rim of Valentine's glass.

"To exorcising Prasit's ghost and any other ghost haunting this place," said Valentine, his fingers dancing along the stem of the glass. "May the poor man rest in peace. Did you know that spectrophilia is a condition that means a person is sexually aroused by having intercourse with a spirit or ghost?"

Calvino admitted he hadn't heard the term.

"I am beginning to wonder about Number Three in that department."

Gop, hips swaying as if she were listening to music inside her head, appeared from the kitchen carrying a bowl of green curry. She was the youngest of the three serving women. Her playful eyes darted from Valentine to Som and back to the bowl. She grinned like a hooker who had spotted her all-time big spender just come through the door. Her painted red nails matched her lipstick. Gop liked to dress up and go out for fun. Instead what she had to settle for was carrying in bowls of curry and serving up Valentine, a middle-aged private investigator and a ghost. Valentine wrapped his arm around Gop's waist and reeled her in.

"You, my little frog, are late. You've been painting your nails and leaving us without our curry. What shall your punishment be? You are already my number three *sanom,* so demotion is out of the question. Later we can discuss something suitable."

Calvino then drank, then swatted at a squad of mosquitoes launching a simultaneous attack from overhead and at ankle level. He reached down and smacked his ankle.

"Damn, mosquitoes," said Valentine. "Som, please light mosquito coils."

As the mosquito coils were lit and slipped under the table at the feet of Valentine and his guest, Som served another helping of rice from a large bowl. Splashes of lantern light reflected in the calm surface of the swimming pool. Some bamboo leaves floated in the light.

Calvino nodded at the empty place set for the ghost of the gardener. "Tell me what happened."

"I've already given you the general outline. But of course you need more information. Right. Prasit was very good with the goats –"

Calvino interrupted. "How long had he worked for you?"

"Nearly two years."

"And before that?"

"He had been unemployed. And before that he had worked as a handyman, and before that? I have no idea."

"Was he having any personal problems? With money, booze, or his wife?"

"None. That was the thing about Prasit. The man seemed problem-free. He never complained. He never beat his wife. He rarely left the compound and then only to buy supplies or goat feed. Until a couple of weeks before his death, I never saw him upset. He was a happy man. Well paid. He had his housing and food provided. He was in paradise."

"What happened to him in those two weeks before his death?" asked Calvino.

"He seemed depressed. His work became uneven and sloppy. He slept in late and started drinking."

"Any idea why?"

"I asked him. 'Prasit, what is happening to you? Why are you falling apart?' And he said, 'My brother died. I feel bad.' And I thought, the man's suffered a personal loss. That is understandable. Cut him a little slack and let him bounce back to his old self. But he went the other direction into pure despair. And inside that black cloud he killed himself. It happens frequently. People give up. And when you look at most people's lives, it is a miracle that it doesn't happen more often. I would like you to spend two or three days here. Talk to the *yings*. Talk to Prasit's wife. Talk to anyone you wish. I will see you get a full list of all the people employed by me. Listen to all of their stories. And, at the end, tell them the police and the doctors were telling the truth. No one is hiding anything."

"You've had the monks in?"

"Yes, of course. They came, performed their ritual and went. You'd think that would have appeased the ghost. The monks didn't work. The strike continues."

This was a serious problem, thought Calvino.

Valentine had made up his mind. The job had been offered in order to give the appearance of addressing the concerns of the household but Calvino had grasped what was required of him—to confirm the master's opinion. The last thing Valentine wanted was an investigation. Not because he had anything to hide. His motive was not sinister; it was selfishness. Like most very rich people, Valentine was proudly selfish. He simply wished to end the turmoil Prasit's death had brought to his estate. He wanted his peace of mind restored. He wanted his women to smile again and stop shivering every time one of the dogs howled at night.

"What was the brother's name?"

"Som, what was Prasit's brother's name?"

She looked up from the bowl of rice. "Sombat."

"When did he die?" asked Calvino.

"Early July," said Valentine.

"How did he die?"

"Shot. That was the first week of July. The police say he was silenced by gangsters in the drug business."

"Was he in the drug business?"

"Good God, how could I possibly know?"

He had a point. Valentine couldn't even remember the dead man's name.

"How long between when the brother was killed and Prasit died?"

Valentine sighed. "Prasit died last month. The 27th of August. I very much hope that I won't have to spend days answering so many questions. I said Prasit was depressed because he brother died. Other than that, the rest seems impossibly irrelevant. And I don't see what I can usefully add."

Calvino put away his notebook. Three weeks has passed since Prasit's death. He watched Som clear the table. The *sanoms* one by one vanished from the dining area without a word. Valentine looked alone sitting at the end of the table. It wasn't going to be an easy investigation. No murder investigation ever was. Calvino told himself that work was the antidote his spirit needed. And when that work was establishing why and how a man died, there could be no greater puzzle to solve.

EIGHT

CALVINO stretched out on the bed. The room provided by Valentine was large and clean. Tiled floors and a king-size bed, a nightstand with a pitcher of water and a glass. The toilet, washbasin and shower were in an area behind the room and ran the entire length of the room.

He held the cellphone between his shoulder and ear, writing as he spoke to Ratana. "My father taught me a Chinese word," said Ratana.

He waited.

"Aren't you going to ask what word?"

"What's the word?"

"The Chinese word for marriage. It is woman plus the symbol for blurry vision, confusion, or lack of consciousness."

"A form of mental disease?"

She laughed. "It's true."

"Your mother didn't tell you."

"Father said she only teaches the Chinese she wants to teach."

"He sounds very wise."

"What did Valentine say about the murder?" she asked.

He liked the fact that she had gradually eased herself into the business question. "He doesn't think it was murder. He wants me to back him up and say that the gardener hanged himself."

"Did he?"

"You know that Thai proverb about the strand of hair blocking the sight of the mountain?" asked Calvino.

"*Sen phom bang poo khao*," she said.

"In Valentine's case, there are three strands of hair. His three *sanoms*."

"I am about to lose consciousness. He has three wives?"

"They have gone on strike. Tomorrow, I'll interview them and find out why. I have a feeling something is going on that no one's talking about."

"Are the wives beautiful?"

"A reasonable collection."

That isn't what she had wanted to hear.

"It's because he was famous."

"He was a big celebrity once. Or maybe he still is. Anyone that famous has advantages. That's one of the things that I am sure is in the back of his mind."

Ratana's mother had come into the room. He could tell because Ratana had started talking through her mask. "Mother said two more police were killed in the south yesterday. One shot and another one hacked to death with a machete."

"Any news of violence spreading to Bangkok?"

"Not yet," she said.

That was the end of the conversation. Calvino climbed off the bed, stripped down, and entered the Bali-styled bathing area. A wall that came to his shoulders surrounded the bathing area. He crossed the tiled floor, turned on the water and eased himself under the showerhead, looking into the night beyond. Beyond the trees he saw the moon through curved iron bars spaced three feet apart on top of the wall. Rows of flowers grew in a three-foot space that ran next to the wall. And creepers had begun to snarl their vines around the iron bars, softening the feel of the enclosure, making it a kind of moonlit paradise. That had been the word Valentine had used at dinner. Paradise. Prasit had lived in paradise but even people in Eden killed themselves.

As the jet of hot water massaged his shoulders and back, Calvino breathed in the air. He held it in his lungs. Bangkok air was something taken in small sips and immediately exhaled before any residue of dust, pitch, tar, and fumes could stick. Here the air was sweet and clean. He smiled to himself as he stared at the dark outline of forest and above the trees, the night sky dotted with bright stars. He wondered if it was still raining in Bangkok. He'd forgotten to ask Ratana. Insects bounced off the mirror just below the light and fell into the washbasin. A couple of cats perched on the wall, slinging down low, watching him under the shower.

Coming from a settlement of squat houses beyond the rice fields, above the sound of the running water, he heard the sound of laughter and singing and loud music. The pounding of a drum and playing of flutes. Not the lilting classical music of Valentine's grand piano crowd. But a deep, immediate, earthy music, beaten out frantically with drums, accompanied with the howl of horns and reed instruments. The music of intense passion. Earlier in the car as he had driven along the country road off the highway, Calvino had seen a group of crudely built shacks made of wood and cement blocks and built on stilts. Chickens that had survived the culling pecked in the dirt. Small children played with a battered football, kicking it so that he had had to stop his car on the main road while one of them ran after the ball. The music and laughter came from the direction of where the people lived in those houses. A wedding, a funeral, or someone had won the lottery. Slums were what people called places like Klong Toey where thousands of upcountry poor people lived in makeshift wooden shacks built over black, swampy land. They came to Bangkok to find their fortune and instead mostly found a life that was even more miserable, dangerous and hopeless than the one they'd left.

Like in upcountry New York, clusters of people who lived in rural poverty had some small dignity that came from being part of village life. There were no city folk to look down on them. But with city and villages running together, that time was ending. The sprawl had begun the long process of connecting Bangkok and Pattaya. In ten years, no patch would be left without its accumulated mass of houses, factories and shopping malls. Maybe it was a myth that there was a time when everyone enjoyed a life filled with playing, fun, not thinking too much, and no problem that was larger than the phrase *mai pen rai*. Or maybe there had never been such a pure time. Hearing the racket in the distance was a reminder that life was on an uncertain course of change, and that the time for play and fun was being constricted by new laws and old grievances, and nearly everyone was thinking too much, and the new set of problems promised to swallow and spit out *mai pen rai*.

Calvino toweled himself, feeling the night breeze blowing through the trees and rustling the leaves that curled around the iron bars. The cats silently watched him from their perch on top of the wall. With the moonlight on his face, he felt oddly at ease and happy. He might have stood there half of the night if it hadn't been for the sound of the door from his room to the bathing area. It disturbed the tranquility of the moment. Alert and cautious, he wrapped the towel around his waist and quickly turned, his fists clenched, ready to strike the first blow. Two women stood side by side in the doorway. He recognized Maew, Valentine's Number One, but the second woman, whom he judged to be in her thirties, he hadn't yet met.

"Do we disturb you?" asked Maew.

A Thai-like question. Of course they had disturbed him, and of course they knew they'd done so but expected him to smile and shrug off the intrusion. Having entered the guestroom, and not found him inside, hearing the shower, they had no inhibition against opening the door the moment the shower had been turned off.

"Do I look disturbed? Undressed. Wearing only a towel. But not disturbed."

"That's good," said Maew. "This is Fon. Her husband was Pee Prasit. The gardener. Her English isn't so good."

"How good is your English?" Calvino asked Fon.

"She asked me to help her," answered Maew before Fon could reply.

"She has something to tell me?"

"She was the one who found her husband. And she *knows* he didn't kill himself. I believe her."

He looked at the two women. Standing in the night with the breeze coming in from the forest, he had begun to understand the alliances that had been formed following the gardener's death. "Let me get dressed; then we can talk."

"Okay, we wait you outside," said Maew. She turned at the door. "We thought you might have a gun. But you don't have."

They had searched his room while he'd been in the shower—no, they had waited until he was in the shower and then searched in room. It was a calculated act. He wasn't about to tell them that he had left his .38 police special in his car.

"You think I need a gun?"

Fon's expression never changed. One of those neutral expressions that one could read anything or nothing into. "I can get for you," she said.

Bringing Maew in order to act as translator had been an excuse. She had wanted someone from the household for emotional support. Going into a strange *farang's* room at night alone wasn't something a respectable Thai woman did. The way Calvino figured it, Maew had the status of being Valentine's number one mistress, and also she was younger, meaning she would find it difficult turning down Fon's request. Not that Maew struck Calvino as someone who needed much encouragement. It hadn't taken much observation to see that Maew and Fon were likely the strike organizers.

"We can always send out for handguns. It would be a good idea to talk first. If for no other reason to establish who needs shooting."

After he dressed and combed his hair, he walked down a dark path to a series of buildings. A halo of light shone from the kitchen that was the center for cooking inside the compound. As Calvino stopped at the entrance to the kitchen: he noted the sinks and ovens and burners and large fridge and shelves of canned food. Spotless. Above the rear door was a pyramid of finger marks left by the monks. Ghosts on the prowl refused to cross a threshold so marked. That was the underlining psychology. He continued walking until he reached the staff living quarters. "Staff" in the sense of *sanoms*—a fancy Thai word with multiple meanings. Valentine used *samons* to refer to his three mistresses. Windows in each room faced the path and each of the rooms which were half the size of the guestroom, was designed with the same basic setup: bed, lamp, TV, fan, and small fridge in the corner. In Bangkok most upcountry working *yings*—those who worked in the bars, massage parlors, karaoke places, pool halls—lived this way in the *sois* off Ratchadapisek and the high end numbered *sois* off Sukhumvit Road. No curtains or blinds covered the windows. Anyone walking past could stare in. But other than the gardener, the only other male was Valentine. In one room Kem—*sanom* number two who had served sea bass as her dinner duty and disappeared to her room because she had a stomach ache due to her *mens*—lay with a pillow under her stomach, balancing herself on her elbows, and watching MTV. In the next room, Gop—*sanom* number three—sat on her bed, looking at herself in the mirror, her legs folded beneath her and her hands with the pretty painted nails at her side. She appeared absorbed in her own image, glancing up to check the cartoon station on TV. Each of the rooms had been hooked up to cable; there were upcountry families who lived on less money than the cost of the monthly cable bill. Valentine had shelled out all the funds necessary to keep the *sanoms* occupied in their off-hours. He not only knew about music, the man was an expert on employee relations, and on relations with employees. The next room Calvino walked past was dark. A few feet ahead, Maew and Fon waited in the half-darkness of the path. Fon knelt on one knee and stroked the Great Dane, drool hanging from the edges of its huge, floppy lips. The animal had a head the size of a grown man. As Calvino approached, Fon rose and rubbed her hands.

"We go to my house to talk," said Fon.

She walked ahead with a flashlight and Maew followed her. They hadn't waited for a reply. "Better stay on the path," said Maew, glancing back.

"Snakes," said Calvino.

"You smart man," she said.

"I saw the row of jars with snakes inside. An impressive collection."

It was a couple minutes walk across an open field. The three dogs came sniffing along the edges, following behind on the off chance there might be a meal ticket. Fon stepped out of her sandals and opened the door to a small cottage, walked inside barefoot, and switched on the light. After Calvino and Maew entered, she closed the door. Mosquitoes flew inside. She got a can of spray and soon a gray fog clouded the room. Calvino tried not to breathe in the fumes. He gave up in less than a minute taking as his punishment for not breathing an even larger hit of the poison. Two wooden chairs and a coffee table were the only furniture in the main room. Fon sat on the bamboo mat and Maew joined her. Fon pointed to one of the chairs. Calvino shook his head and slowly eased himself down onto the mat. "It's okay, I can sit on the floor," he said.

Fon, her eyes intent and fearful, continued to point at the chair. "I found him in that chair," she said. She pointed to over Calvino's shoulder. He turned and looked at the chair. He touched the chair the dead man had been found in as if to show he understood the importance of that piece of furniture.

"Your boss believes your husband killed himself."

She shrugged as if it wasn't very important what her boss thought on such matters. "He's wrong."

"And the police are also wrong?"

Fon rose to her knees, and then raised herself up with the agility of a dancer. She slid across the bamboo mat over to an interior door. She glanced back at Calvino and smiled. "There is something I want to show you."

Fon struck Calvino as someone who once had smiled a lot; the smile had been her default face to the world, then her husband died and the default setting changed. Death and divorce reset the default expression. The new setting converted a smile into a serious, saddened flat-line look of desperation; or, depending on the circumstances, death healed a sour face, turning the lips upward into a glowing smile. It was a question of whether the passage of the person from life to death had been seen as a loss or gain, and in Fon's case, it was a certainty that Prasit's passing had been a great loss. Her expression spoke about the true nature of her feeling and spoke volumes about how her husband hadn't failed her. He had only gone away when he should have stayed. She wished none of it had happened and now that it had, she was duty-bound as his wife to see his memory wasn't tarnished by a verdict of suicide. Fon was, in other words, a fighter, and she had found something worth going to battle for.

NINE

FON had found her husband in a chair, leaning forward from a door. Not an ordinary door. She stood beside him as Calvino examined where a monk's index fingerprint had left a smudge of white paste on the door. The smudged paste had hardened, turned flinty, and the edges of the fingerprint swirled out from the center. Starting from the bottom there were four neatly placed fingerprints, in the middle row were three-print, and at the top row were two more fingerprint marks. A triangle of prints expertly centered. At the four points of the compass around the finger-painted three rows of prints was the Thai script for the number nine, looking like an ancient Thai dancer's headdress or, to an American eye, a Dairy Queen ice cream cone. A dead dragonfly had been taped in the southern position of the Thai script. A large dragonfly with its four long translucent wings—two on each side of the dark, shrunken body—a system of tiny ribbed translucent veins against the door. The tail curled into a semicircle like a scorpion's in the strike posture. The markings left by the monk were in a similar pattern to the ones above the door to the kitchen. Such markings were common occurrences above the doors of a room, office or above the rearview mirror of a car. Thais believed that the monks' blessing ceremony, with the impression of a set of his fingerprints, acted like amulets, stopping evil from entering through the door. They promised protection from evil.

Calvino had never heard of a monk killing a dragonfly and taping the creature to the ritualized markings as the *pièce de résistance*. The ritual had nothing to do with Buddhism. It was a leftover from the animistic world. Still, monks, even when performing quasi-Buddhist rituals, remained under a vow not to kill, and that applied to all creatures. Not even a mosquito sucking blood fell outside that vow. The dragonfly stuck to the door bothered Calvino; it was at direct odds with custom and tradition. Something strange had happened and this was the first evidence that somewhere something out of the ordinary, something connected to black magic, had entered the gardener's house. Then it wasn't a custom to hang oneself using a belt on a doorknob and leaning forward on a chair. The door, belt, chair, the death—all of it was weird.

As Valentine's story of the falling coconuts hinted, the dangers of life were in the mundane, the innocuous things that blended into the background. A simple door was the site of a violent death. Valentine's opinion was that his gardener was fearless. Assuming Valentine had been right about his lack of fear about snakes, it didn't necessarily follow that Prasit was not haunted by other fears. The black magic images stuck on the door told a different story; of a superstitious man who sought refuge in omens and magic. It would have been the rare gardener or servant who wouldn't have shared Prasit's beliefs.

"When my husband wasn't working, he spent many hours inside this room," said Fon.

Maew watched as Calvino stared at the door, running his hand around the doorknob. The belt would have been looped around the doorknob. Prasit would have leaned forward on the chair, and slowly, he would have strangled.

"Pee Prasit put the dragonfly on the door," she said.

"After his brother died," said Fon.

"Did you ask him why he did that?" Calvino asked. Valentine had said his gardener wasn't a man who was afraid.

Fon nodded. "Yes, I asked him why he had done that, and he told me, 'For power and protection against the bad thing.'"

"What kind of bad thing?"

"I want to show you his room. He felt safe inside."

"Safe from what?" asked Calvino.

"The most brave man can have weakness. Don't you agree?"

"I agree that you don't need Maew to be your translator."

As Fon opened the door, there was a strong smell of dead flowers and stale incense. The smell hit him like the stale air of a closed tomb. His eyes immediately began to water. He followed Fon inside, thinking, why had a gardener like Prasit living on a wealthy *farang's* estate required the protection of a dragonfly on the door to his prayer room? Animism and Buddhism often walked hand in hand with upcountry people. But there was something more involved. Fon flipped a switch and a string of Christmas lights that stretched over several tables came to life, spraying the walls with reds, blues, and greens. The small room was an elaborate shrine. Looking around, Calvino concluded that it was no ordinary Buddhist shrine. Many Thai houses had such "prayer" rooms. A sacred place inside the house decorated with Buddha statues; a sanctuary where offerings of flowers and food and prayers were made. Prasit had created a holy room using Buddhist objects. There the comparison stopped. He also had taken pagan objects as the central motif, and these objects suggested dark, compelling forces. Why had this gardener gone to all the trouble to build this shrine adorned with animal images and covered with pots of flowers?

Fon slid across the floor on her hands and knees, and, stopping to strike a match, reached over the table and lit each of the nine yellow candles. She worked silently as she performed the candle ritual. Maew sat on a bamboo mat a few inches away, her hands cupped in a *wai*. Shadows from the candles flickered against the walls, illuminating the flowers, Buddha images, and offerings; the candlelight revealed layers of old editions of *Thai Raht* newspapers. The newspapers had been carefully laid in front of the ceremonial tables. Care had been taken to preserve the pages. Calvino thought of McPhail's uncle who collected newspapers. This collection served a different purpose, Calvino thought.

Fon sat back and cupped her hands together, her eyes closed; she bowed from her hips, hands stretched forward, until her forehead touched the floor. She bowed two more times, then sat straight up, shoulders arched back, and ran her hands through her hair. Maew performed the same ritual.

Fon pushed the Start button on an ancient tape recorder, which was within arm's reach of where she knelt. Twin speakers were positioned on opposite ends of the tables. From the speakers came the voice of a middle-aged Thai man, soft and soothing, speaking deliberately, as if giving comfort. He spoke of dispatching a spiritual bodyguard whose job was to protect Prasit and Fon. The bodyguard would become the spirit of the place. The voice dissolved into a chant. Pali chants boomed from the speakers. The expression on Fon's face was serene. The chanting was one of those ways of transforming the mind to a state of elevated awareness. Maew's face was a blank—whether that was elevated awareness was anyone's guess. She might have been bored, stoned, or her mind turned off. Or she might have been drifting. Wherever she was, it was a place beyond where the chanting could reach her. She appeared to have entered another universe.

Calvino sat on the floor, listening to the tape and watching the women, as the yellow flames from the candles gave a strange sense of unity to the series of small ceremonial temple tables. The tables had been pushed together to form a seamless surface and on top were bronze statues of monks and Buddhas and cheap vases with real and artificial flowers. The real flowers were shriveled, dying, drooping and lifeless. One of the bronze statues, a monk, appeared in the dim light to be larger than the others and tiny, thin pressed gold sheets had been stuck onto the bronze. Among the statues were plates of bananas and oranges, unopened boxes of milk and juice. Scattered here and there were small statues of two-headed elephants, snarling monkeys with pointed incisors ready to draw blood, and turkeys with tails fanned as if seeking to mate or escaping the monkeys. Some of the incense sticks stuffed into a vase were half burnt, others untouched. On the floor, bamboo mats and cushions were laid out over newspapers. Fon knelt on one of the mats. From the amulet on a gold chain, the empty one next to her must have been Prasit's prayer mat—not a difficult guess. The gold chain was wrapped in a circle from left to right around the amulet encased in a small coffin-like case. She gently brushed the amulet with her fingertips and, fingers splayed, ran her hands through her hair.

This was the place a frightened man had taken refuge.

These were the things that had given him courage.

What a man clutched onto as he stared into the void left an imprint of his fear.

Somewhere between a man's dreams and his fears, he saw a truer reality. Maybe Prasit saw that reality and couldn't live with the image and decided to end with a dragonfly taped on the door behind his back.

Beads hung from a hook on the whitewashed wall. A toy TV and baby bottle straddled the sides of a plastic doll in a gold uniform holding a sword upwards. This had to be the bodyguard, thought Calvino. Flowers—pinwheels, orange, white and yellow—lined the wall where the tables ended. Beside another doll figure were large fake carnations in gold and white. Pink lotus like polished hard rock candy.

Near where he sat, by candlelight, Calvino noticed that the tiled floor was bare except for many old newspapers. As his eyes adjusted to the dim light, he examined the newspapers more closely. They had been spread out to form a rectangular shape. It wasn't apparent at first. But each of the newspapers had photographs of the dead. Smashed, broken, torn, shredded, drowned, bodies; headless bodies, bloated and ripped as if beasts had taken them in the dark of night, eaten their meat and left the carcasses behind. Calvino removed one of the candles and held it over the newspaper. He examined the photographs by candlelight. The large headlines in Thai script above one of the pictures spoke of murder. Uniformed police officers and a couple of farmers stood beside a well. Two of the cops wore surgical masks. Behind them in the distance a tarmac road wound through a sea of rice fields. Calvino bent closer for a better look at the photo. In the foreground, on a white ground cover, human bones were visible—a skull, sternum and ribcage, femur, and scapula. The muddy bones had bits of cloth attached. From the way the bones had been laid out, it appeared that a paleontologist had reassembled bones from an ancient burial site. Inserted beside the photograph of the officials and the bones was another smaller photograph of a young Thai man wearing a shirt and tie, a narrow mustache on his lip, very much alive and smiling into the camera. You didn't have to read very much Thai to figure out that the bones in the one photograph were the remains of the grinning man in the other photograph. Calvino moved his attention to another Thai newspaper a foot away. A body slumped over the wheel of a Honda that had smashed into a utility pole appeared in another picture. Others had bodies with gunshot wounds in the chest and face, with the eye socket empty from where a bullet had entered. One body lay face up in a field with burnished pills spilled over the arms and shoulders of the dead man. As Calvino looked over the newspapers, the chanting from the tape echoed off the walls in the small room. Fon sat in front of the ritual images on the table, a million miles away, her lips moving and her hands in a *wai*. More photographs of bodies in the street, beside a canal, along a dirt road, in the driver's seat of a van. Many of them had pills sprinkled around them. Bodies spilling pools of dark blood and small reddish pills. There wasn't a newspaper covering the floor—and dozens of newspapers appeared to be laid out according to an order—which didn't have the lifeless form of someone found dead in a public place. He made a mental note to check the dates and names of the Thai daily newspapers.

These newspapers were Prasit's prayer room legacy. The carefully preserved papers were the pages of his photo album of fears.

The chanting stopped. Fon leaned over the table and switched off the tape recorder. Maew sat back, relaxed, and managed a smile as she waited for Fon to switch on the ceiling light. The small room was hot and humid. Sweat ran down Calvino's neck.

"A week before my husband died, a snake was found over there," said Fon. She pointed to a row of milk cartons behind the bodyguard doll. "If it had bitten him, he would have died."

From the jars of snakes, it seemed that being bitten by one was an occupational hazard for any gardener. Valentine had said a falling coconut was, in percentage terms, a greater danger. But coconuts don't fall inside a prayer room. She waited for some reaction from Calvino. "Snakes in a house are common."

"You don't understand. This wasn't an ordinary snake. It was a Siamese cobra. These cobras don't live in the province of Chon Buri. They live in the south."

The Siamese cobra had had some assistance in its migration from the south. The connection with "south" inspired a sense of fear and suspicion. Her tone was the same as his secretary's on the phone.

"She speak English very good," said Maew with obvious admiration. She had already forgotten her cover story that her presence was needed to translate for Fon.

"Because I am a gardener's wife doesn't make me stupid," said Fon.

Fon was not the average gardener's wife. She was articulate, educated, and intelligent. It didn't take much of a leap to conclude that the objects in the room, the recording, and the strange beliefs in invisible bodyguards had originated out of Prasit's personal fight with demons.

"Whose voice is on the tape?" asked Calvino.

"Ajarn Sawai."

A monk was offered referred to as "ajarn." "Who is Ajarn Sawai?"

"He gave my husband strength," she said.

"They were friends? Or he was his guru? How did it work? Did he pay Ajarn Sawai to make the tape?"

She shook her head. "No, Ajarn Sawai never accepted money."

If mysticism was a source of strength, it hadn't been enough for Prasit, thought Calvino. The room had voodoo sensibilities. The practitioner hadn't done it for money. Fon spoke of him with reverence. Had she been wooed by the art and music and chanting?

"Were you in this room when your husband saw the snake?"

"No. I was in the goat pen. And when I returned, my husband had already killed the snake. He told me not to worry. And I said, 'Someone put that snake in our house.'"

"Did he say who that someone was?"

She blinked and looked down at the floor.

"Did you ask him?"

"He had no idea."

"Do you know if Sawai is from the south?"

Her eyes grew wide. She looked offended. "He's from Chon Buri province."

"It's my job to ask questions, Fon. I need to know what happened and who the people are who are involved. That means personal friends, business associates, strangers—anyone who had access to this room."

"I understand," she said.

"What did your husband tell you?"

She explained how he had believed the snake wasn't in the room by accident. A deadly cobra had been let loose in the prayer room, slithering over the sacred images on the table, a couple of feet above the floor lined with newspaper photographs of horror and death. Prasit told his wife that he had been praying but at the last moment he opened his eyes. The bodyguard of the monk had spoken to him, warned him of danger and saved his life. In the middle of his prayer, Prasit looked up and saw the snake, its hood open and ready to strike. The presence of some force—from the revered statue of the monk—came through and gave him courage. He stared at the snake a few inches away, hissing, raised up between the flowers. Slowly he reached under the table, his hand grasped a knife, and without blinking, his hand came up, cutting the snake in half. He brushed the dead snake to the floor. He went out into his shed and found a jar, washed it out, and deposited the two pieces inside. He slipped into the dining area that evening and left it on the shelf with Valentine's collection of jars. The Siamese cobra had been the last snake killed by the gardener.

Fon said that she hadn't told anyone, including Valentine, about what had happened that night. From the grim expression on Maew's face, Calvino felt this was the first time that she had heard the story. This gave Fon's story credibility. To test that credibility, Calvino had some questions. Why hadn't she told Valentine that Prasit had killed the snake inside his room and carefully placed it in a jar that same night?

"He said he found it near the moat," said Fon.

"He lied to his boss?"

"My husband didn't know how to tell him what had happened. It might have caused a problem." If she had told the maid or one of the other women, by the next morning all of the women in the compound would have known. Everyone would have been afraid of finding a deadly snake in their room.

That was plausible, thought Calvino. And there were other reasons. Thai workers rarely passed bad information to their boss. To say that a snake had been in the house might have alarmed Valentine, making him believe that his gardener had attracted bad luck or bad karma. Who would admit such a thing except to their wife? It was the kind of leap of assumption that Prasit could have easily made. It fit a personality profile. Servants don't bring bad news to their boss. They do everything to reinforce the order and stability of their boss's universe.

"Let's say someone put the snake here. They had to know how to get into this compound when you were away, and they had to have some skill in handling such a deadly snake," said Calvino.

"What if I told you that the police say Sombat, my husband's younger brother, was shot because he had a conflict with a drug dealer? But it wasn't true. He never took drugs. He never sold drugs."

"You think the police killed your brother-in-law?"

She slowly exhaled, as if her patience was being tried. Recklessness on the road killed tens of thousands. "When my brother-in-law's body was found, a Siamese cobra was coiled near his body."

"The same species? Are you sure?"

"Sure."

"How did you find out about the snake?"

"My husband talked to the man who found his body. He saw the snake. My husband knew snakes and from the description, he knew it had been a Siamese cobra."

"The police didn't put it into their report." He hadn't seen the report; he was guessing. If it had been in the report, Valentine certainly would have said something about such an odd occurrence.

"It had disappeared into the fields by the time the police came."

"Were there any bite wounds on Sombat's body?"

"I asked my husband but he wouldn't say."

"Would he have told you had he known?"

"He told me what he thought kept me safe. He was a very good man. Good men don't hang themselves."

She had his attention. "Not usually," said Calvino.

"And have you ever seen a cobra inside a coffin?"

Now she had gained his full attention.

Calvino had lived in Thailand long enough to know that most people feared an attack by a king cobra. The Thais called them *ngu jong-ang*. The police were often called to residences in the Sukhumvit area to kill a cobra—*ngu hao*—a different species of cobra—that had crawled into a house. In the rainy season, when it flooded, the snakes hid under the surface of the water. Only the brave ventured through knee-deep water after a storm. There were several other types of cobras and other types of venomous snakes. Added to the list of snakes that could kill in minutes were sea snakes, banded kraits, Russell's viper, Malayan pit viper, green pit viper. The most dangerous and aggressive was the Siamese cobra. Despite what Valentine thought about coconut deaths, a fair number of people died from snakebites in Southeast Asia each year. It was a slow, painful, terrible way to die. Snakes had their territory.

There were two brothers from the north; each had left home to find work in Chon Buri province, where jobs were easy to find as the eastern seaboard expanded. Each brother had, or at least from what appeared on the surface, experienced a nasty confrontation with a Siamese cobra that was native to the south of Thailand. Both men had died. But neither brother had died of a snake bite. The gardener died by hanging himself on the prayer room door underneath a dead dragonfly. In one way the death was bizarre, but in another way it was an ordinary, common death that happened frequently and was hardly newsworthy. If either Prasit or his brother had been killed by a cobra—that would have been news. There would have been graphic photographs splashed in the local newspapers.

A connection might have been drawn between the troubles in the south and the species of snake, leading to a conclusion of terrorism and violence. But it hadn't happened to the two men or anyone else. If it had, Calvino was convinced that the newspapers carrying the photos of the victims would have been preserved for floor coverings in prayer rooms.

The widow seemed to read Calvino's mind.

"My husband and his younger brother were killed."

"But not by snakes."

"By someone who knows snakes very well."

"Tell me about the snake in the coffin."

"It happened at my brother-in-law's funeral."

TEN

THE crematorium was on a knoll surrounded by a heavily wooded area. A few miles from the *wat*, the mourners had a short journey through the town before arriving at the crematorium on the other side. A small *sala* with the coffin inside had been lifted and placed on a flatbed and hitched to a pickup. The truck led a procession through the village. A monk sat in the front of the pickup. Nine monks waited inside a large open-air *sala*. Rows of folding chairs had been placed in the *sala* waiting for the funeral party to arrive. On the opposite side of the road from the *sala* was a crematorium with its sliding metal gate closed. The moment Fon saw that the gate was closed she knew the family, friends and neighbors were in for something unpleasant. Prasit standing next to his wife said that she wasn't allowed to walk down the hill. She was to stay at the *sala*. He had wanted to spare his wife what he sensed would be a gruesome ordeal. Friends of his brother, men from the village, worked stacking wood and tires into a platform. Sweat rolled off their arms and necks as they worked.

Fon had to stay behind with her mother-in-law, uncles, cousins, and friends who had the good sense to not get too close. Prasit had rarely ordered his wife to do anything against her wishes. She didn't question him when he ordered her to stay away from the cremation site. As Prasit walked down the hill he looked back and saw her with her back turned, and saw her turn, and look towards the pyre. It was the last family affair they had attended together. For a moment their eyes met over the distance. She felt that he was very far away and she resisted the urged to break into a run and go to him. Instead she did what he had asked. She stayed back and waited.

One hundred meters down a narrow dirt road, which led from the open-air *sala*, the platform had been piled in layers—planks of wood and underneath the wood, old threadbare car tires were wedged between the planks. The pyre was finished by the time Prasit reached the bottom. A signal was made and a half dozen of the neighbors pulled the trailer with a blue-roofed sala to the edge of the makeshift platform. Prasit, an uncle, and his brother's friends lifted the coffin and nestled it on the wood and tires. The men gathered around the coffin as the lid was removed. Prasit swung the axe to cut a coconut and poured the coconut milk onto the head of his dead brother. Prasit handed the axe to one of Sombat's friends. The other friends and Prasit stepped back from the platform. They watched as a friend handed the axe to one of the attendants who had earlier walked down the hill from a shed opposite the closed permanent crematorium. The attendant, a bald, middle-aged man, held the same axe that Prasit had used to split open the coconut and, hovering over the open coffin, swung the blade into the body lying in the coffin. The attendant leaned over the corpse and hacked open the stomach, the sound of ripping of flesh carrying up the hill. With the stomach split open, the axe moved down the body, chopping long, deep gashes into the flesh of the upper thighs. He sunk the axe into Sombat's flesh with no more expression than a butcher. Prasit watched a couple of feet away, his face pale, wiping the beaded sweat away from his brow. The attendant who had done his job with great efficiency, suddenly looked up, a half-scream in the back of his throat as he stumbled back from the coffin. He dropped the axe and ran. One of Sombat's friends caught up with him and led him back to the coffin. He swore that he had seen a cobra inside the coffin. He howled with fear as the friends dragged him to the coffin. Each cautiously approached the pyre and looked inside the coffin. The attendant gave them no time as he turned, lit a match and threw it into the wood, igniting a raging fire. Prasit ran forward but it was too late to look inside. The flames had engulfed the coffin.

Had there been a snake coiled inside? The attendant swore on his amulets he had seen one. Sombat's friends hadn't seen one. The flames were a solid sheet and whatever was inside the coffin had been consumed. The axe had done its job as the flames burned the body without any explosions erupting from inside it. The last thing family and relatives needed to hear was a loud bang as the stomach filled with gas exploded into a ball of flames, leaping skyward to burn the leaves off the nearby trees.

Prasit told his wife that his brother had looked peaceful. He had been killed outright. He hadn't suffered. Later that day, when they returned for the ashes, Prasit found the incinerated cobra. It had been coiled at the bottom of the coffin.

ELEVEN

FON left the prayer room, returning after a moment carrying a chair. She stopped at the entrance. In one hand she had a man's leather belt wrapped around her fingers. Maew's smile evaporated. Ever since the discussion of snakes, she had sat upright, raising her legs up to touch her chin, her eyes scanning the room. Vigilant, watchful, and uncertain what lurked in the shadows.

"Go to your room and sleep," Fon said to her in Thai.

Maew was grateful for the suggestion. It meant that her obligation to Fon had been satisfied and she could go. She scrambled to her feet and walked out of the prayer room. A moment later, Calvino heard the entrance door close. He was alone with the widow.

Fon wasted no time positioning the chair against the door and looping the leather belt around the doorknob. Calvino watched her re-create the death scene. It was common practice to reenact a crime. In the case of a death that could be murder or suicide, reenactments were also staged; those who favored suicide produced a reenactment to support their theory as those who claimed murder adjusted the scene for their purposes. She sat on the chair and described how the police and doctor believed that Prasit had put a chair next to the door of the prayer room, looped the belt around his neck and leaned forward, not so much hanging himself as strangling himself. The metal buckle had tightened hard against the right carotid artery, cutting off the oxygen. Strangulation hadn't taken long. His neck hadn't been broken. There were no signs of bruises or violence. It had been Prasit and the dragonfly hanging on the door. His brain no longer had the supply of oxygen to function, closing down each and every system of the body.

"I had gone into Pattaya. *Nai* wanted to buy syringes to inject the goats with some medicine. He asked my husband to go. But after Sombat was killed, my husband never left the compound. He always sent me or someone else. I used our motorcycle. I am a careful driver. I couldn't have been away from the house for more than two hours. When I came home, I found him in his chair."

What she described wasn't anything a wife should ever have to witness. Prasit's tongue lolled from the side of his mouth. His face had gone puffy and purple and bloated. His eyes were bloodshot and yellow and wide open, as large as saucers. His favorite amulet hung on a gold chain from his neck. This was another small detail in Fon's mind that convinced her that her husband hadn't killed himself. He would never have hanged himself wearing an amulet around his neck, or do such an act of self-destruction on the entry door to the room he held sacred.

She pointed out the contrary argument by the police. The main one was that there had been no sign of a struggle. It was difficult to believe that a man would voluntarily allow someone to hang him with his own belt without putting up resistance. Besides, no one inside the compound had seen anyone come or go from the house. Behind the house was the edge of a forest. In theory someone could have slipped over the fence with the forest as cover. But none of the neighbors had noticed any stranger or any unusual movements around the compound. Someone would have seen something, the police had said. The widow's opinion had been less persuasive than she had hoped for. Valentine felt the police had examined the evidence and reached a logical, sound conclusion. The widow, in Valentine's view (one shared by the police), was simply being a hysterical woman—emotional, unstable, illogical—falling apart as a result of grief suffered from losing her husband. An understandable (and regrettable) premise made of sorrow, but life had factors other than sorrow to consider and Valentine insisted that what Fon believed was fundamentally unsound in its premises. Another Thai woman might have given in. But not Fon. She had allies in the compound. Maew, Valentine's number one "creature," occupied the official position as the senior employee in charge of feeding the goats. Her unofficial position was number one in ranking of those invited, from time to time, to occupy the bed of the goat owner. Maew had agreed with the widow, and applied the kind of pressure that only someone with number one ranking who sometimes shared a bed with the boss can apply. She organized a strike that had forced Valentine to bring Calvino to Pattaya.

Exhausted by reliving the events, Fon collapsed forward on the chair, hands covering her face. Calvino waited until she composed herself and then left the house. As he was on his way back to the guestroom, Maew stepped out of shadows. She followed a couple of steps behind him. He stopped, looking over his shoulder a few feet beyond where she should have turned to her own door.

"You've passed your room," he said. "In fact you should have been in your room a long time ago."

"I am not sleepy," she said.

Calvino leaned against the wall of the building.

"You have been waiting for someone," said Calvino.

"I wait you."

"Is there something you want to tell me?"

Maew smiled and stepped two paces closer. "*Pee* Fon's very clever. She's not a stupid girl like the rest of us. I go to *mor sam*. Junior high, then I leave school. Fon go to university. And she graduated from university. She worked as doctor."

"A doctor?"

"For animals," said Maew. "But she married a stupid gardener. He was from upcountry. Like me, *pee* Prasit go only to *mor sam*. Then finish. Why she do like that? Marry a stupid man like him? She's *dtok khob*. I go to university, I get the paper, I not work for Mr. Valentine. I marry a very rich man and he buy me a house and a car, and I work in a office and have my own desk."

"Maybe she loved Prasit," said Calvino.

"If she could love Pee Prasit, then she could love someone else, too."

Dreams and fears were manufactured for most people. What they wanted and what they were afraid of were identical to links of sausages on a conveyor belt. The same product filled with the same material. Calvino walked ahead, stopping to open the door to the guestroom; he thought about what eyes were watching from the darkness. It didn't matter, he thought. If Maew had something to say, she could come into the room and say what she had on her mind and leave. Instead, she walked straight into the room, walked over and sat on the edge of the bed.

The gardener and his wife had rarely been apart. In the last couple of months, Fon hadn't been herself. She was less friendly. Prasit seemed nervous, jumping at the slightest noise, distant and remote. They both did their work but kept to themselves. Fon had stopped smiling long before her husband was found dead.

Something had bound them together. "A secret," said Valentine's number one girl.

"What secret?"

"If I tell you, then it won't be a secret."

Calvino rubbed his eyes, walked to the door and opened it.

"Wait, don't go so fast. I can tell you something."

Maew, easy and relaxed, was happy to play the game, and Calvino stopped, rested against the wall and glanced outside. The giant Great Dane came sniffing and slobbering around the verandah. He closed the door and turned back towards her.

"Fon go upcountry."

"Thai people go upcountry all the time," said Calvino.

"Not Fon."

Maew had been surprised that Fon had left the compound and traveled alone to visit her family upcountry. Such a solitary journey was unusual. Fon had told her that her mother's sister had fallen ill and had asked for her. What could she do but comply? The aunt had a long history of illness and there was nothing to suggest that she was any more ill than usual. So after a day, Maew saw that Fon had returned with a handgun and had hidden it in the prayer room. The next day she had gone into Pattaya on an errand. When she returned, Prasit was dead. The gun remained where she had hidden it. She had found him sitting in his chair, slumped forward from the door. If he were going to kill himself, she had told Maew, he would have used a gun.

According Maew's account, Fon was thirty-seven years old and came from a long line of freethinkers. Fon's parents had been communist in the 1970s and she grew up in the jungle with her parents on the run from the army. It was only later that her father, a university-educated engineer, found work in Singapore and saved money for Fon's education. She hated the government for what they had done to her parents. Alienated from students who spent more time on their make-up and clothes than their studies, she decided on a non-traditional lifestyle. She always wore baggy jeans and old shirts. She studied science and earned a degree. After university, she qualified as a vet. The middle-class Thai seeing her at a distance assumed from her dress that she was a peasant. She liked that assumption and did nothing to dissuade others from looking down on her. She said this gave her more freedom than those who drove imported cars on credit. And freedom was the most important thing in the world. She learnt the secret when she was young: giving up face in return for freedom was a small price to pay.

Most Thais lived their lives mainly to acquire a "big" face. Face was their reward. Without a big face—and that took money, power and influence—all else in life was thought to have been lost. And to lose face was the next thing to losing one's life. Such a loss led to rages, threats, irrational outbursts; it also led to murder. Then Prasit ran into someone like Fon who failed to play the face game to type, who had turned the absence of face into an art form.

She had met Prasit five years earlier. At the time, according to Maew, Prasit had worked as a gardener for a resort in Pattaya. Fon was an assistant vet at a south Pattaya pet clinic. He had been a diligent worker. Starting as a member on the ground crew, he ended up as foreman. He had taken a great deal of interest in learning about plants and wildlife. One day he brought a poodle to the pet clinic where Fon worked. A guest at the hotel had asked him to take the dog for a wash and cut. The day they met, Fon had said that it was Prasit's love of animals, his kindness towards people, his knowledge of plants and flowers that had touched her. They saw each other two days later. Again they met the next day and then daily meetings occurred outside the workplace. She had known her fair share of men before. Prasit was the only man whoever allowed her to trust herself to be faithful. Even well into her thirties, Fon possessed a beauty and elegance the farm clothes could not disguise.

In the prayer room, Fon had played with her husband's amulet as she spoke. Play didn't quite capture the caressing game, one finger at a time, massaging, touching, stroking as she spoke. The skin on her hands and face were roughened by the sun. She had milked the goats the same day she found her husband dead. She was at the work the next day. During the entire ordeal she never missed a day's work. She did her husband's chores as well as her own. She worked from early morning until late at night. No one could believe her energy or her determination to lose herself in her work.

Maew said she didn't think that Valentine would keep Fon on at the compound for much longer. She was the gardener's wife; what she did was work as part of a pair, and the pair had been broken. The fact that she continued to occupy the gardener's house was a circumstance forced upon Valentine by the other women living in the compound. Until she left, he couldn't hire another couple. The gardening work of the huge estate was disrupted despite the double-duty shifts that Fon pulled. And Valentine had pointed out that it wasn't that Fon had no other place to go—she had family upcountry, she had marketable skills. She refused to budge until the manner of her husband's death was resolved. Valentine had suggested that she was stalling, being quite comfortable in the gardener's house from which she showed no signs of voluntarily leaving.

"The gun was the secret?"

Maew smiled. "Yes, but there was another secret."

"Better than a gun?"

Maew leaned forward and whispered, "When she found Pee Prasit, there were *yaa bah* pills sprinkled over his clothes.

The same as had happened to his brother. *Pee* Fon threw them away and made me promise not to say anything about them."

"Did she tell you why she did that?"

"She said a bad man had put the pills on her husband."

"Do you have any idea who the bad man is?"

Maew stretched, arching her back. "I go now," she said.

"Stay a minute. I want to ask you something," said Calvino.

"No good for me. People see me leave your room they say the bad thing to my boss. Then I have a problem. You understand me?"

Calvino understood her all right.

She smiled, and bounced off the bed and out the door.

TWELVE

IT was nearly eleven. Calvino opened his cellphone. He wondered if it was too late to phone Ratana. Her mother's enforced quarantine hadn't excluded phone calls. There was an unwritten rule that she wasn't allowed calls after 9.00 p.m. Fon's rebellious state was contagious. Ratana had the same impulses as the daughter of the jungle fighters. Parents made a difference. Ratana's mother taught her the Chinese symbol for a woman and Fon's mother had taught her how to field strip an AK-47. The phone was Ratana's only outside link with the world. He auto-dialed her number. It didn't connect. He lay back and thought about Fon's devotion to her husband, and how she continued to demonstrate this loyalty even after his death when everyone else said she should accept the police report. In his secretary, Calvino had witnessed similar acts of caring and support. He redialed her cellphone number. This time the call went through. She answered on the third ring. She sounded sleepy.

"The gardener's wife has a gun," said Calvino.

"My mother wants to buy a gun."

The first step was buying a gun; the next step using one. Fear had a way of making people feel a weapon was a source of comfort. Like the dead dragonfly and monk's markings on the door had given Prasit comfort. Shooting at shadows out of fear was a good way to kill someone you loved.

"It is a bad idea."

"The neighbors make her paranoid about Muslims who want to kill Buddhists. She has nightmares of terrorists breaking into the house and hacking her to death."

Many people were already armed. The last holdouts were the little old Chinese ladies like Ratana's mother. People felt a sense of helplessness. Security and protection businesses boomed.

"Talk her out of it," said Calvino.

"I'm trying my best. You know how mothers are."

His own mother had been headstrong, self-willed. She had owned a handgun.

"The gardener's wife also has a university degree. She's a trained vet."

"She married a gardener?"

The reaction was forceful and immediate. The social distance between them had to have been large. They would have had little hope of acceptance of their marriage by those around them. Someone like Valentine wouldn't have cared. He'd have shrugged and dismissed Fon's degree and training.

"They seemed to be happy."

Ratana was silent with a gray horror that happiness could ever be found in such a union. She struggled to find words to express her troubled thoughts.

"Could she have murdered her husband?"

"Because he was a gardener?"

Calvino smiled, rubbed his eyes, opened them and looked up. He saw a large house lizard on the ceiling. "She's the one who wants an investigation. Everyone else is content to say it was suicide. Valentine lives in a fantasy world occupied by his big-hearted creatures. He doesn't want that world disturbed. He doesn't want reality to intrude on his fantasy life. He doesn't much like Fon."

"Who?"

"That's the gardener's wife. I was saying Valentine wants Fon off the premises."

"Is that why he hired you?"

Calvino thought for a moment. Ratana had a way of seeing through to the truth of a situation. "Yeah, that's a large part of his motivation. Fon's a modern woman. Valentine wants his women from the Middle Ages."

She paused. "Do you know what it means in Chinese when you put the symbol for woman and modern together?"

"I give up."

"Prostitute."

"There were no rural prostitutes in China?"

"That's what I asked my mother."

"What did she say?"

"Modern city life has destroyed our values."

"I thought Buddhism taught that all life is about accepting impermanence."

"I thought of that, too. My mother said a good Chinese girl listens to what her mother teaches. Everything else can be impermanent."

"What does *dtok khob* mean?" he asked. Maew had used it in reference to Fon marrying a simple, uneducated gardener.

"It means someone who is off the margins. Someone with an alternative lifestyle. Like a hippie. Or a rebel. For example, an educated Thai-Chinese girl who works for a *farang* private investigator. Her mother might say she's *dtok khob*. Off the page and into the unknown. Or you can say *nok krob*. Off or out of the frame."

"Or a university graduate who marries a gardener," said Calvino.

"I almost forgot—Colonel Pratt phoned. He's going to Pattaya."

Before he could reply, the line went dead. He tried phoning again but there was no signal. He sat back and thought about what she had replied to her mother. "I am a modern girl but not a prostitute." Or, "My duty is to myself." Or, "I don't want to live on the page composed by you." It seemed close, but none of it quite fit what Ratana would actually have said. Most people accepted the page or frame manufactured by parents, teachers, and movie stars. There were so many subtle ways that mothers used to keep their daughters on frame, on the page. Ratana was in the process of undergoing an intensive indoctrination. He watched the gecko on the ceiling hunting mosquitoes.

All that he had intended was a good-night call, but the call had ended before he had accomplished his task. It was unsettling. The way cut-off phone calls always were. In the grayness of existence, the figures that broke the surface of consciousness lurked in the shadows, waiting for the right moment to play their tricks and hook their victims, pulling them down below the surface line until they no longer breathed. It was this world that Ratana's mother instinctively feared. The one she wished to keep outside the door of her daughter's life. It was that world of darkness that Calvino had represented: hidden, dangerous, and mysterious. His was an alien world to a traditional Chinese-Thai mother. He repeated the phrase *dtok khob*. To fall. To fall off the margin and into the void. Was that what he was doing with Ratana's life? The most that could be promised was that he would not expose her to the frontline of his work. She worked behind the lines, knowing that she would be safe and that he would keep himself one jump ahead as the long shadow fell.

Calvino found himself listening to the buzz of the air-con. What stuck in his mind was the way his secretary had dropped the information about Pratt. The colonel would have wondered why his friend had gone to Pattaya without calling him. He didn't have a direct answer other than the frustration of Bangkok, the tangles of traffic and heat and thunder storms, along with a sense of doom prevailing among most people as stories of disease and terrorism continued daily in the press. Colonel Pratt was on his way to Pattaya. There hadn't been time to find out why his friend, the colonel, was going to Pattaya. He conjured up the image of his friend. He lived and worked under the protection of Colonel Pratt. "Protection" wasn't quite the right word. He sheltered under the colonel's wing. The colonel had been the slender thread on which to build a life in Thailand; no foreigner could exist for long in the private investigation business without a patron. Friendship with the colonel was better than owning a gun.

In the darkness, he saw in his mind's eye the prayer room in the gardener's house and the ritual markings and dragonfly taped to the door; heard the taped voice chanting and talking about spirits, bodyguards, and princesses. Faith that below the surface lay a world of forces—good and bad—that could be appealed to for protection. For Prasit, it had been more than mere faith; this place represented the forcefulness of Fon's belief in her husband and his inability to take his own life. She *had* made a case for murder, thought Calvino. But it wasn't conclusive. Life proved always to be filled with surprises about the capacity and motivations of others; hidden, dark sides of personalities that suddenly exploded without warning in an act of violence or self-destruction.

It was hard for others—wives, brothers, mothers, fathers, neighbors—to reconcile that the membrane of life rested on a sea of deep forces lying beneath, the seen co-existing with the unseen. Until there was a break and all hell was blown through that cracked membrane of what had been solid and good. He imagined how Fon would have returned from her trip upcountry and carefully wrapped the gun in a sacred cloth, placing the weapon in the prayer room for the eventuality that her husband's prayers went unanswered, for the day when the unseen crept into their lives and other means had to be used. The gun must have been in reach that day; if it was, then why hadn't Prasit gone for it? It was possible that Prasit and his brother had both been on drugs. *Yaa bah*, pure speed, made people crazy. It made them do things they would not otherwise dream of doing. Either Prasit didn't know that he was in mortal danger or, as the police report concluded, his mortal danger came from unknown forces deep in himself.

The Thais had a saying about people who spent a lot of time thinking about such matters: *rok kriad*. In the land of *sanook*—the land of fun-making and play—one stayed on the same page and seriousness was often viewed as a kind of disease. *Rok kriad* translated as "the disease of seriousness." The cure? In Thailand the prescription was simple: Stop thinking and have fun.

THIRTEEN

"I trust that you had a good night's sleep," said Valentine as he eased into his chair at the dining table. Breakfast of cereal, banana, honey, milk, juice and coffee was laid out on a bamboo mat. "Creature number two crept in last night for an unscheduled visitation. Do you know what sexually arouses her?"

Calvino shook his head. He had no idea. He wondered why Valentine had a deep-seated need to share intimate information about his staff.

"Rubbing her cheek against my sweaty old baseball cap. It's a known condition. The literature calls such an arousal complex *mysophilia*. They are aroused by various smells of unclean underwear, hats, or socks. After she left, I dreamt I was in England. I was standing on the stage of the Royal Albert Hall and the audience waited for me to play. Only there was one slight problem. There was no piano. What do you make of that? An audience in anticipation, and my instrument had vanished into thin air."

"I dreamt of a cobra. Not unlike the one in the jar on the shelf," said Calvino. He nodded in the direction of the collection of jars with the preserved remains of snakes at the far end of the table.

"You are a New York City boy," said Valentine. As if that fact had particularly serious consequences in dreamland. "The country often gives people nightmares of the jungle variety. Our ancestors, after all, lived in the bush. They were eaten by large beasts and sometimes killed by snakes. That primitive fear is in our bones."

As Calvino had said to Ratana the evening before, Valentine was not so much a romantic as a hardcore fantasist. One had to be medicated to have more illusions than Valentine about the nature and purpose of relationships. His sexual partners were off the frame. *Nok krob*. The whole setup was of another world.

"I have a few questions."

"I should hope so. That is the reason you have been invited, sir. To ask questions and to seek truthful answers."

Calvino opened a small notebook and uncapped his pen. "When did Prasit die?"

"That's easy. The end of August."

Calvino looked up. "Do you remember the day?"

"It was the 27th. A Wednesday."

"Where were you on that day?"

"I was at my piano. Music will always remain my true passion." Valentine laughed and spooned in another mouthful of bananas and cereal.

"Did Prasit ever use drugs?"

"Antibiotics on the goats."

"Did Prasit take drugs?"

"Good God, no—I would have fired him on the spot."

"You said Prasit gave the goats antibiotics. Not Fon. She is a trained vet."

"She worked in a bloody pet shop shampooing poodles. Prasit knew more about goats than she would ever hope to know. And why are you asking if he took drugs?"

"People who use drugs sometimes deal drugs." He didn't wish to break Maew's confidence that *yaa bah* pills had been sprinkled over her husband's body.

There was an admission of agreement in the expression on Valentine's face. "As I said, Prasit didn't even drink. Can you imagine a gardener who doesn't live for Singha beer or Mekhong whisky?"

"I drink Mekhong and Coke," said Calvino.

"If you are after the gardener's job, I might overlook your peasant drinking choices but I am afraid I couldn't quite set you loose amongst my creatures."

"You don't like competition," said Calvino.

"Don't like it? I loathe competition. That's why rich people use their money to buy monopoly power. They don't wish to compete."

"It's in our DNA," said Calvino.

"Well said. We all carry the gene for monopoly. In most people it is mercifully recessive. So they don't suffer in their powerlessness."

Calvino looked down at his notebook. "Did you see anyone coming into the compound that day?"

"Nothing out of the ordinary. It was just another day."

"One of your employees might have mentioned something."

"The creatures were questioned by the police. I questioned each of them. But by all means feel free to question them yourself. They saw nothing. They saw no one. I am paying for this investigation in order to satisfy the creatures. Fon put Maew up to nonsense."

"What kind of nonsense?"

"She had Maew organize a strike. Despite her ill intentions, my desire is to be fair to the woman. But the harsh reality is, at the end of the day, she must go. I *need* a new gardener, and the new gardener and his wife *need* a place to live. I have two very important, unfulfilled needs. Meanwhile, Fon is stalling. She loves it here. And why wouldn't she? My lovely gardens are returning to their feral natural state. Her point is that I will lose interest in her husband's death if she leaves."

"She has a point," said Calvino.

"Of course she has a point. I tried to pay her off. I offered her quite a large sum of money to leave. But she's very stubborn and refused. I guess there is no harm in having someone investigate. That is why I chose you. To come and ask and prepare a report saying poor Prasit for reasons only known to himself and God decided to hang himself. If you ask me, it was his wife that drove him around the bend. The last month or so, she was always on about something or other. The woman's relentless. I don't think Prasit ever had a moment's peace."

"That was about the time Prasit's brother was killed."

"The brother was on a motorcycle. He was shot. This happens all the time. You drive in Bangkok. Try driving upcountry. How many times have you wanted to shoot one of these motorcyclists? You see one about to slam into you. Blindside you before you can react. If you had a gun, then you might use it. Upcountry it is five, ten times a day. Recklessness doesn't quite describe this behavior. Inebriation along with the mistaken view that they will be born to a better life makes it seem like they expect someone to shoot them."

"The police found *yaa bah* on the brother's body. And bullet holes in his body."

"The police are always finding *yaa bah* and bullet holes in dead bodies. If he was shot, then it was road rage or he was robbed. Or killed by rival drug dealers. There's a crackdown. Don't you read the newspapers? If you get knocked down outside my gate, they might find pills on you. And bullet holes. So be careful." Valentine broke in a wide grin. He had finished his breakfast and signaled the maid to clear the table.

"How many ways are there in and out of the compound?" Calvino asked.

"Now that is your first good question. You are using your brain. And to answer that question, I will take you on the grand tour of the grounds. You can inspect the boundary of my property. Then you tell me how many entrances I have."

"You don't need an entrance to get access to this place. Someone can easily climb over a wall near the goat pens. Am I right, Valentine?"

"Ah, now you have pleased me. You have used the right name. And yes, you are right, this isn't a high-security prison. If someone wants to get in, they surely can find a way."

"Let's have a look around the grounds," said Calvino.

Calvino finished his coffee and closed his notebook. As he rose from his chair, Valentine leaned across the table. "My maid tells me you made a visitation to the widow's house last night."

He had his spy network, noted Calvino. He may have had an intelligence network—and likely did—to report what was really going on inside the compound, and inside the heads of people living in the compound. Or the source of the information might have had a more simple explanation. Maew could have had her own reason to snitch on Fon. How Valentine had obtained the information was, for the moment, less relevant than finding the true motive of the person providing it.

"I asked your staff a few questions, if that's what you mean. That's what I am here to do. Are we working off the same page?"

"Of course we are. Did Fon reveal anything of interest?" He had gone straight to the point. Valentine remained fixed on Fon as a window to understanding her attitude, intentions and plans.

"She has an abiding desire to prove her husband was murdered."

"Murdered? Ridiculous woman."

Valentine was visibly annoyed. He stared at his sandals, stroked his ponytail several times, pondering his Burmese *ngats* in the alcove outside the main entrance. When he looked up, he had regained his composure. This ability must have come from long years of learning how to quickly recover and mask that one has hit the wrong key in a complicated piece of music.

"Before taking the tour, let me show you my studio," said Valentine. "I've made some changes since you were last here." A tour of the grounds was exactly what Calvino had in mind. The diversion to the studio, however, seemed like an indulgence, a great waste of time. Valentine had already shot ahead, talking about why he had walked away from such a career. Valentine explained that on his last night at the Royal Albert Hall, he had felt something touch his soul: He would never—could never—play that well again. It was like being twenty-three years old swimmer and winning the gold medal for the 100 meters. It happens once. After that you swim but you don't swim for gold. No matter what reserves might be called up from his depth of talent, inspiration and intuition, at the very best, his performance might come close to that moment. It would never exceed that moment. He had, in his modest estimation, hit the artistic equivalent of the speed of light and the realization had terrified him. He clung to that one gold medal; it had been enough.

They reached the outside door to the studio. There was a series of doors. The outside door opened first. They entered a chamber that could have been a drug contamination airlock between a hot-zone lab and the world of health and innocence. The dead space created a barrier between the searing tropical heat on the outside and a Steinway grand piano on the inside. Valentine explained, "Without temperature and humidity control, the love of my life would soon bleed into a tuneless hag. Therefore, we must maintain strict temperature control. I open this door. We enter. The first door is secured. That means closed, shut tight. Then we open the next door and enter. It is slightly tricky as there is no light in the passage." Valentine let out an awful laugh as he opened the outer door.

As the outside door closed and the darkness enveloped them, he continued to talk about music and the life of a concert pianist.

"What was the point of continuing? I would have practised for twelve hours a day. I would have made myself drunk on music. You can have no other life. Visitations from creatures were a rare luxury. I figured out that evening the meaning of life. I didn't want to make that large a commitment to my art. I wanted other things."

Valentine opened the inner door and walked ahead into his studio, a vast, open space with Persian carpets over polished hardwood floors. "Of course, you might say, I could still have made a living as a concert pianist. That is true. But knowing what I had achieved and knowing what it took to maintain that peak level made me utterly miserable."

He sat down at the Steinway and played Mozart, his fingers rolling down the keyboard, his eyes half-closed in a state of total feeling for the music. Suddenly, he stopped and looked up at Calvino.

"Have you ever faced personal disappointment? Of course you have. Men like us know the meaning of disappointment. It doesn't help when fools sing our praises because we know that fools can't help us. Their foolishness makes us more desolate and alone. I knew in my heart of hearts that my performance was falling lower, failing, and that I had nothing left but vanity to grab onto. After a certain age you no longer can compete at the same level."

His fingers frantically raced down the keyboard with self-assurance.

"I faced the horror of a free fall into mediocrity."

Valentine's hands danced down the keys.

He spoke as he played, "Who in their right mind wishes to experience such vulnerability, such a constant fear of personal disappointment? Not I, sir. So I retired and disappeared to Thailand. I built this compound with my own hands. Every flower, bush, and tree I chose the way a conductor chooses his orchestra. And it has become this grand daily performance—walking the land, smelling the flowers, seeing what I have planted in the earth bear flower and fruit."

Valentine stopped, rose from the bench, walked across the room and poured himself a glass of ice water. He stood looking across the room at the concert grand.

"Each afternoon, in the hottest part of the day, I retire to my studio and play for myself and sometimes for the amusement of my employees, who were raised to think of music as banging drums. I can't tell most people this story. They can't believe a musician of my stature would have turned his back and walked away from fame and a brilliant career. I knew the truth. I was playing for a dying audience. Taste, vision, and a brilliant ear for a perfect tone were traits being bred out of our species. Weaned on a diet of MTV, pop radio and movie soundtracks, my audience was on the way out. I was unwilling to sacrifice my life practising and playing for a diminishing audience. Because I am selfish, the world is without Searles Valentine, his concert recitals of Mozart, Liszt and Brahms. But Searles Valentine has his interests, hobbies, and diversions. He has a wonderful life. But, and this is where you come in, there is a problem. A man killed himself and my creatures are in revolt. Now we can go on the grand tour."

Valentine talked about himself a great deal. Another symptom of someone who had fallen off the world.

Calvino's Law: People who talked about themselves in the third person had the personality equivalent of a detached retina; they could no longer see themselves except as a blurry vision projected by others. If Valentine had been a New Yorker, the remedy would have been a couple of decades on a therapist's couch. As Valentine lived in Chon Buri, his therapy was working with his goats, secretary, vet, gardener, and his specialized staff of *sanoms* with tailored sexual fetishes. He didn't seem to be getting better. But he did seem, except for the strike and dead gardener problem, a happy man.

FOURTEEN

AROUND eight in the morning they left the main house. A windless, hot, dry morning sun hovered above the horizon. The air clear and pure, Valentine inhaled, eyes half-lidded, and slowly exhaled. That air is a tonic. A drug. An addiction.

"Was Prasit ever involved with drugs?"

"I thought I answered that question earlier. I told you that as far as I knew, Prasit never touched alcohol. Drugs? Did Prasit take drugs? Highly unlikely." He shook his head violently.

"I didn't say *take*. I said *involved*."

"You are a born lawyer. And that's why you are here. But to answer your question for yet another time, Prasit was *involved* with the gardens and the goats. Believe me, this is a full-time job. Other involvements would have been impossible."

Valentine had cranked himself up into the gentleman farmer, tour guide mode, cocking a battered straw hat over one eye, and wearing an expensive pair of sunglasses as he charged over the drawbridge, kneeling down on the other side where three dogs waited, tails wagging, yapping, fawning, the Great Dane sniffing and pawing. Below in the moat, the lotus blooms had opened and the brackish water was dotted with dozens of white lotus blooms. The dogs followed as they walked ahead passing the guesthouse and kitchen. Bees appeared along the verge, diving and darting among the flowers as they walked. The stillness of the air made the bees' presence all the more noticeable. Valentine hurriedly moved down a narrow stone path through a grove of towering coconut trees. He would suddenly stop as if he had heard a voice or had a thought, cocking his head to the side.

"Prasit loved this garden." Valentine shaded his eyes with his hand and stared up at the green coconuts hanging in clusters under the long green leaves. "*Ton ma-phraow* that is "coconut tree" in Thai. We were going to buy a monkey and train it to fetch the coconuts. We had many more. But I had Prasit cut them down. Danger of coconuts landing on one's head is not some remote possibility. Finding monkeys for the trees that remained was another disappointment, I am afraid. But these coconut trees are the percussion section of my naturally grown orchestra. They are tall, strong with the potential to create the canon fire of the 1812 War. Aren't they magnificent? I read somewhere that thirty people are killed every year from a coconut falling onto their head. Death is such a terribly random visitor and with such a sense of humor. Killed by a coconut. Not the kind of thing you want on your death certificate. Hanging by your belt is bad enough."

"Have you ever been married?" Calvino asked.

Valentine laughed. "Good, God, no. I suffer from gamophobia."

"Which is?"

"You, my dear fellow, didn't study Greek or Latin. It means fear of marriage."

After walking another thirty meters, the pathway cut between rows of mango and lychee trees. All evenly spaced and, from the soil around the base, recently watered. The long stems on the mango trees were thick with green fruit the size of bloated green kidneys. "My French horns," said Valentine, pointing at the mango trees. "And my flutes." His hand gestured towards the lychee trees. Behind the mango trees were two rows of jackfruit trees. "Drums and snares," he said nodding at the jackfruit trees. Coming out of the orchard and into a field was a tall evergreen with star clusters of green oblong leaves. "Do you know the name of this tree?"

Calvino had already told him he didn't know the name of any trees.

"It's the devil tree," said Valentine. "It is the conductor of the orchestra. And on the other side of the devil tree are horsetail trees. Look at the fine green leaves. Each leaf is like a slender spike on the body of an exotic sea animal. The Thai name is much nicer. *Son pradiphat.* 'Horsetail' is too common for such a splendid creature."

He wasted no time cutting around a thick curtain of bamboo; the large yellow stocks streaked with green veins were old growth supporting the weight of a thick umbrella of green shooting skyward until the weight bowed the bamboo carrying the green leaves, like weeping willows, back to earth.

"With Prasit's help, all that you see we planted on this land. Before it was barren and without order and structure. We brought design and meaning and music to the landscape. To live well in the world, you must know the names of things. Without knowing the names you can't truly see or appreciate them."

In Valentine's mind, he had created a private world-class orchestra. He was the conductor and Prasit had played first violin and of course any conductor knows that losing your first violin is a huge loss. And a powder room also constructed from flowers, shrubs, vines and trees. Prasit had played a key part in this comic conspiracy between desire, nature and music. Following his boss's instructions to plant a string section, and brass, and oboes, horns and chimes. The flowers and trees and shrubs weaved a harmony from color, order and beauty. The notes were perfect. It was Wagner and Beethoven in flowers and leaves and bark. What those great composers had done with music, Valentine had done with plants. Calvino looked around at the garden in full bloom as Valentine inside his head waved his arms like a conductor, playing a most beautiful melody that only he could hear. What was left for Calvino standing on the path as Valentine conducted? He stopped, looked around, smelled the flowers, and listened. What he heard was near total silence.

Beyond the gardens was a large open pasture with goats. He watched as the young women he had seen from the night before were inside the enclosure housing the goats.

"You see my creatures are working."

As Valentine unlatched the gate to the fenced area where the goats were kept, Calvino answered his cellphone. Colonel Pratt's voice was distinct and clear.

"I heard you took a new case in Pattaya," said Colonel Pratt.

"I am at my client's goat farm."

Colonel Pratt hadn't expected this answer.

"Khun Ratana didn't mention anything about goats."

Colonel Pratt was smiling to himself, Calvino thought. He thinks I've hit a new low. A *farang* private investigator reduced to slumming in a goat pen.

"The client's gardener died. The police say suicide. The widow says murder."

"Any evidence of murder?"

"I am investigating the possibilities," said Calvino.

"Let's talk about it later." The call ended.

Pocketing the cellphone, Calvino walked through another gate. Valentine had already stepped inside one of the holding pens and ruffled the ears of a goat. He talked to the goat in baby talk. The goat's ear shivered, its tongue lolling out of the side of its mouth. "You, my lovely, are an adorable creature. Soft and beautiful. Your eyes are like jewels. Her name is Bach. Don't look surprised."

"A goat named Bach?"

"Why not?"

Calvino shrugged. "A friend once named a fighting cock after me." That had been Edward McPhail and (except for the first fight) the cock had gone on to never win another fight. Calvino decided to keep that bit of information to himself.

Walking down the rows, Valentine bent down and looked inside, "Elgar has a runny nose." He moved over to the next pen, "Sibelius is suffering from an iron deficiency. That's why she's looking not at her best." He turned to Calvino. "To have all the world's greatest composers healthy and giving you milk from which you can make cheese and yogurt is one of the great mysteries of life."

Valentine with Bach beside walked between the rows of wooden pens. Valentine walked with one hand looped around Bach's neck. On the side of the gate of each pen, a plastic sleeve had been attached and inside was a printed card with the name of the goat—Handel, Schubert, Delius, Elgar, Strauss, and Debussy.

"Smell this goat. Bach never smelled so clean, pure."

"Like the perfume tree or was it a shrub. Or maybe a case of mysophilia?"

"Very good, Vincent. Someone sexually aroused by a goat. That as it happens isn't one of my fetishes. What I am trying to show you is a perfectly ordinary day in my life. You do want to know something of Prasit's duties?"

Somewhere between the boundary of duties and household rituals, the mystery of Prasit's death would be unraveled, thought Calvino. The world was divided between those who had a huge desire to *know* and those who wished to *avoid knowing*. Facts, reality, evidence and clues belonged to the first kind of person. Illusion and fantasy belonged to the second. Calvino had made it a point to take assignments from clients who genuinely wanted to know the truth, and had developed the habit of distinguishing between fantasy and reality. On the other hand, Calvino didn't have a lot of clients.

Watching Valentine with the goats after a tour of a garden planted like an orchestra with a powder room attached, the feeling was becoming clear which world Valentine occupied. The more he saw of Valentine's constructed world, the more he thought that suicide was the more likely possibility. Sucked into a world of evergreen instruments, creatures with names and numbers, and natural powder rooms, it wouldn't take much to push someone a little too far until one day he snapped, slipped a belt around his neck and leaned forward in a chair.

In the far corner of the goat pen, Fon looked up as she raised a bucket of feed and poured it into a trough for several of the goats. She quickly looked away before he could establish eye contact, turning her back as if neither her boss nor he were in the goat pen. Another woman helped with the morning chores. From the evening before at the dining table, Calvino recognized her as Kem—*sanom* number two, her eyes watery and red, sniffling, as she squatted before a spigot waiting to fill a bucket with water. This was the *sanom* who became, according to Valentine, sexually aroused by the smell of sweat on his baseball cap. Her lower jaw quivered, the shudder of someone who had been sobbing. Valentine took no notice of either woman. Why was the young girl crying? Had she had a fight with Fon? Where were the other girls? He scanned the goat pens looking for the others. They must have stayed in their rooms.

"Prasit was a gardener. But he also helped with looking after the goats?"

"Of course Prasit helped with the goats. He was an exceptional worker. He was up and running around doing chores hours before I arrived. Watering the flowers and shrubs. Pruning. Planting. Sweeping up leaves. Then he would wait for me here inside the goat pens. He loved these creatures almost as much as I do. In the morning, we inspected the goat herd. We have twenty-five goats. And one of them is always either coming down with or recovering from a health problem. I would make suggestions about treatment. I'd check the feed, the water, the condition of the animals."

Each of the pens was built on a concrete platform and separated by a wire fence. The breed of goats was called Nubian and they had long floppy beautiful ears and markings, along with the nobility and stature of a fallen celestial being making do with their lot, giving their milk, waiting for a new life they once knew far beyond the horizon of this planet. As Valentine stopped talking, Kem had taken the water into one of the pens. She sat down on a stool and milked one of the goats.

"Why is she crying?" Calvino asked.

Valentine looked up from Mozart, continuing to stroke its head.

"Because she's a silly creature. Kem refuses to accept the first principle of the goat business. A goat can produce five liters of milk a day. And from that we make cheese and yogurt. It is a cottage industry but it teaches the employees the value of industry and independence. All of the profits go to those who work. Everyone has their task: building fences, enclosures, cleaning up, feeding, getting the product made and marketing. Maew delivers the produce. She doesn't really like goats. But she can market, so she receives a share. Gop, my Number Three, has no feeling for the goats or the business at all. She neither feeds nor grooms the goats. When she sees the others making profits, she will come around. Money is such an effective spokesman for labor."

"I asked why Kem was crying."

"Quite right, and I gave a lecture on goat economics. Kem is crying because she is sad. And why is she sad? Yesterday I told her to separate the newly born kid from its mother. This had to be done before the mother could lick the membrane from Mahler's eyes and mouth. Mahler's a splendid name for this kid. But I digress. The newly born kid must be separated the moment it leaves the womb to be nursed by a human. Elgar, Bach, Wagner—they've all gone through this procedure. There can be no bond; no visitation between mother and offspring. You may think that is cruel. Kem obviously feels it is heartless, and one must admire her delicate disposition. But one of the first things about raising goats is that the kid must be separated from the mother at birth or the kid drinks the mother's milk and without the milk to make into cheese and yogurt there is no business and without business there is no profit. And without profit there is nothing to show for one's labor."

Valentine had an answer for everything. Sometimes a man with too many answers has no interest in questions, especially ones asked by others investigating a death. Calvino figured him as an eccentric, industrious, slightly mad, gamophobic—to use Valentine's own diagnosis—middle-aged *farang* who had slipped off the edge of the known map of life, opted out of reality and settled into an enclosed way of life invented by himself. Valentine knew what he wanted and he wanted precisely what he had. The only fly floating on the cream was the strike to withhold sexual services (which worked imperfectly as Kem has taken a bribe the previous night to slip into Valentine's room). Organized by Maew who fronted (for reasons of her own) for the gardener's widow, the strike was inconvenient and had created a black market for sexual favors for those who otherwise had been paid to deliver them. Except for this blip of organized resistance on Valentine's radar screen, the cottage industry and the rest of the household appeared to function normally—if such a word could be wedged into a description of Valentine's life.

"She will get over it. She's young and silly the way young people are. She transferred her maternal instinct to that of a goat. The goat feels no great sense of loss. It has no more emotion for its kid than it does for the feed I hand it." He looked out over the pasture and sighed.

"You are doing this business for the women?" asked Calvino. While Valentine had many talents and impressive qualities, altruism didn't seem to be on either his short or long list.

"Absolutely. The *sanoms* need a sense of purpose and discipline. They can't be expected to properly look after me if they can't look after this small herd of goats. Without close supervision, at the moment, I am afraid it would all come to grief."

He scooped up a handful of feed and fed it to Mozart. The feed was gone in an instant. "The expansion of the herd is linked to the expansion of the women tending the goats. Two goats can sustain one woman. And a household of self-sustaining women is a good thing. When the times come for them to leave, they will have accumulated a substantial sum."

Valentine's fingers played the top of the fence like the keyboard of the piano as if he were hearing music, and as the chords became louder and louder his fingers rose to find the right keys to match the sound in his head. The goat enterprise was a separate universe of milk and cheese and yogurt, of labor, of grooming, feeding, and cleaning. Fon, the ex-vet, took a syringe from a plastic box, inserted it in a small vial, and then Calvino watched as she injected one of the goats. The women worked a couple of feet apart but with very little conversation. It wasn't clear whether this was caused by the presence of Valentine or for some other reason.

"When do you decide to dissolve the ménage à trois and add a new member?" asked Calvino.

Valentine sighed. "It's not a ménage à trois. It's *troilism*."

"Trolls?" asked Calvino.

Valentine threw back his head and laughed. "Not mystical creatures. Troilism is three people having sex. You don't necessary sleep with them at the same time. A *ménage à trois* is where say Maew and I are a couple and we seduce another woman to sleep with us. While each of my *sanom* has a different rank, each is a separate lover."

Calvino frowned. "You have three sexual partners. Plus you that makes four people. How's that *troilism*?"

"At least you're not mathematically challenged. Or perhaps you were trying to trap me." Valentine narrowed his eyes, trying to read from Calvino's expression where he was going with this line of questioning.

"It's not a trap. Two, three, or four. The number doesn't matter," said Calvino. "How long will one of your lovers last in this arrangement?" In the back of his mind, Calvino thought if one of the *sanom* was under threat, she might have turned to the gardener for moral support. Love triangles were a leading cause of death.

Valentine shrugged. "There's no set time. Perhaps after two or three years. Who knows? George Orwell said, 'All animals are equal but some animals are more equal than others.' The same applies to all creatures. One might last much, much longer. It all depends."

"Depends on what?"

"Performance."

"You mean fetishes."

"A man should be greater than the sum of his fetishes. Performance is the measure of all human activity and endeavor. Whether you are sitting at a grand piano at the Royal Albert Hall or working in a harem, a bank, a factory, or an office. One must be up to the task or one is let go."

"Or weaned away like the newborn kid," said Calvino.

"Young girls are filled with false emotions. With a kid, the mother's milk is for sale. It isn't for the offspring. The same system applies for my creatures. After I decide one should leave, in theory she must go immediately. That is the optimal system. With Fon the theory has broken down. I could just kick her out. That wouldn't be rational. And at the core of my being, I am a rationalist."

"Other than Kem, were any of the *sanoms* unhappy? Or possibly think they might be cut from the team?"

"Team? I like that," said Valentine. "And I am the coach."

Valentine knelt down in the corner of the pen and let out a long sigh. He called out, "Kem, stop that blubbering and come here immediately." He tugged on the end of his ponytail. His face looked bloodless and older as the sunlight slanted across his jaw. She pretended not to hear him.

He called to her again, "Come here quickly. I know you heard me."

The conductor had issued a direct order to a member of his private orchestra. Calvino leaned over the pen and looked down at the concrete floor. Valentine knelt beside a small pile of tiny wet pellets. Goat shit. To his right was a bucket of the goat feed that Calvino had hauled in from the shophouse near the main highway.

The feed the goats ate looked no different from the turds, except the feed was dry. In the passage from the lips to the anus, the feed had been wetted before being expelled. Valentine explained that it was Kem's job to clean out the pens. Everything was to be swept up and put it in plastic bags that were hauled away. As Kem slowly walked over to the pens, Valentine continued. "The most important thing to remember with goats is hygiene. If there is filth or dirty conditions, everything is ruined. This is why there is bird flu. The chickens are raised in filth. A virus thrives in squalor. We must purify to save ourselves from disease. I teach this to the *yings*." The *yings* washed their hands before touching the animals or the feed. They were required to sweep the pens and clean the stalls. Their obligation as an employee, an oath given to Valentine, was to maintain cleanliness. In the enclosures and in the bedrooms, they understood the importance of a sterile hand as it came into contact with another life form.

Kem sulked; her chin lowered, dried tears on her cheeks, as she walked inside the pen.

"Do you see this? It is obviously not clean."

Valentine pointed down at the small pile of turds in the corner.

She shrugged, turned away, and reached for a broom.

"This will cost you fifty baht," said Valentine.

Kem frowned, sweeping the shit into the bag. "That's not fair."

"It's a question of following the rules, Kem. And if I inspect the pens and find that you haven't cleaned them properly, you are fined fifty baht. Does this look clean to you? No, it's not clean."

Fon wandered over and waited until Valentine had finished. She pulled notes from her pocket and peeled off a fifty baht note and gave it to Kem. "It's my fault; I asked Kem to feed the kid before she cleaned the pens."

"Right," said Valentine with barely concealed anger. "So you decided to change the system. I will let Sandra know that she should deduct that sum from your monthly share."

Sandra was on the list Calvino had made of the people working on the estate. This had been the first time Valentine had mentioned her. "I'd like to talk to her at some stage."

Valentine smiled. "By all means. She's a wealth of information."

"What are Sandra's duties?"

"Nothing sexual if that's what you are implying."

"I wasn't implying anything. You seem defensive."

"No. Not at all."

Valentine explained that all of the cash earned from the milk, cheese, and yogurt passed through Sandra's hands. His constant fear was of being cheated, the victim of fraud and double-dealing. His secretary, an Indian from New Delhi, had been with him since his London concert days. If the cottage industry of goat products was going to succeed, Valentine convinced himself that all rules of work, hygiene and money had to be faithfully obeyed.

"The incentive to increase one's wealth is basic to the human condition," said Valentine as they left the goat pens. "And the gardener's widow, as you saw for yourself, is undercutting my authority at every step. Changing the rules. Turning my creatures against me. Please, Vincent, settle this matter of Prasit's death quickly so that I can be satisfied that this woman's husband killed himself and I can at last see her off the premises with a clear conscience."

Sandra struck him as someone on the outside of the *sanom* system. But she had one leg inside the business part. Anyone close to the money and with a better life than the others had to be an object of envy, thought Calvino. The reference to sex and Sandra had thrown Valentine off balance. He had recovered his composure in a heartbeat. More than money connected the two.

Once they returned to the sanctuary of the main gardens—the goats hidden away—Valentine sang and danced. In his mind, he had left this world for the world of his hallucinated orchestra. His imagination possessed him. Why is it that illusions make some men carefree, and some women murderers? It is a question to which there is no answer. The man who had sat across from him at the breakfast table had gone through personality alterations as he waltzed through his day. The confrontation with Kem was instantly forgotten as if it had never happened. Valentine lacked the capacity to retain anger or harbor a grudge. Such feelings discharged from his mind within minutes of their appearance. It became clear why the problem with Fon was such a serious one; it was constantly challenging him to remember something that he wished to forget.

Calvino had planned to use the time with Valentine to gather pieces of something which one couldn't quite call evidence; it was thinner, more fragile than hard facts. Desires, secrets and disappointments were more like psychological tea leaves, and a private investigator learned from experience how to read the language of betrayal, cruelty and murder from a glance, a tear, the posture of the body, and the tone spinning around the edges of a word like a fully loaded weapon. The relationship to sex. The relationship to power and money. Valentine had been right about one thing: there was a system of living and working and relationship, and there were those who work inside and outside it, and the way they worked side by side was through deception and threat of harm to anyone destroying the illusion of harmony. Because the entire setup, to use the Thai expression was *dtok khob*, thought Calvino, didn't mean that in an off-margin world there wasn't the same desire for peace and tranquility. It was for this world that Calvino had been hired as the chief restorer of what had been lost.

FIFTEEN

THE main bar inside the Tequila Reef was packed with American soldiers. Young men and women—short hair, no overhanging bellies or flappy arms, the toned bodies of efficient killing machines—who drank Singha beer straight from the bottle. They were seriously fit and seriously into the mode of having fun. A couple of Hispanics danced in front of the jukebox. They had *soldier* and *American* written all over them. They had arrived in Pattaya as part of an advance team for the Cobra Gold exercise—the annual military exercise conducted by Americans and Thais in the fine art of coordinating killing machines. A surfboard from Hawaii hung over the door. The waitresses wore Hawaiian skirts and leis and behind the long counter was a row of frozen margarita machines. In the corner a couple of black women engaged in a speed-drinking contest with strawberry margaritas. A roar of laughter erupted as the winner slammed down her glass and grinned. Thirty or so soldiers shouted, cursed, talked, belched, filling the main floor with loud vibrations and gas.

In the back, sitting alone at a booth, Colonel Pratt sat with a glass of orange juice reading about the latest bombings in the south on the front page of a Thai newspaper. Calvino walked his way through the crowd and slid into the booth. Colonel Pratt lowered his newspaper, folded it neatly and put it on the table. Calvino, looking upset, sat across the table.

"The noise is terrible. This isn't music. It's jackhammers against the skull," said Calvino. "Let's go someplace else."

"Noise is good."

"Since when?"

"Who can hear us talk above that sound?"

A waitress came to the booth and Calvino ordered a Singha beer.

"You never order beer," said Colonel Pratt.

"Who would recognize me if I am drinking a beer? They might think I am another soldier in the advance Cobra Gold team."

Colonel Pratt nodded and smiled. He didn't think anyone would mistake his friend for a soldier. They didn't come that old except in the movies. "Like the noise, beer has its bad and good points, depending on the context."

"As I said earlier, I am investigating a death. Suicide? The police report concludes Prasit killed himself. Murder? The widow is convinced he was killed."

Colonel Pratt sipped his orange juice, looked over at the soldiers. "It could be both."

"Either the guy killed himself or someone killed him." He wasn't certain whether Colonel Pratt was trying to provoke or teach him. Knowing Pratt, he would say one is required to produce the other. "Okay," continued Calvino. "How do you murder yourself and then say that isn't suicide?"

"Sometimes a man wishes to die. He can't or won't do it himself. So he incites someone to do the dirty work. So what do you call that? Suicide? Murder? Suicide by murder?"

"Assisted suicide like when someone has a fatal illness?" asked Calvino.

"Or someone is tired of life."

Calvino was suddenly sorry that he had opened up a possible third explanation for Prasit's death.

"Why are you in Pattaya?" Calvino asked. "It's not exactly your beat."

"A murder investigation. A reporter—or what remained of him—was found in a well. He had been shot and his body dumped. The local police have found no clues. The family asked why the police haven't found the killer. They've had a couple of months and come up with nothing."

There were layers of truth—some even claimed that there were *degrees* of truth. The colonel chose for reasons of his own to state the upper surface. He knew Calvino well enough to know that he'd pick up the highly unusual nature of a Bangkok-based colonel assigned to investigate a killing in Chon Buri. Many possibilities could be read into such an assignment: the importance of the victim, some cross-jurisdictional power conflict, or a possible connection to an unrelated case in Bangkok or elsewhere. In the case of Thailand, it could be all three possibilities along with a dozen more. Years ago Calvino had learned never to press Colonel Pratt for more information than he was willing to offer. It was an attitude that was rare; it was an attitude that allowed the colonel to be at ease in the presence of a *farang*.

Colonel Pratt continued. "My superiors have an idea that I might find what has been overlooked."

"Finding the overlooked." Calvino paused. "That's the sort of thing that can get a reporter killed. Find that and you find his killer."

Calvino's Law: The dark forces and influences who contracted for hit often had enough juice to guarantee that a curious policeman would finish his career walking point duty along the Burmese border.

"How long are you in Pattaya?" Colonel Pratt asked.

Calvino thought about the newspapers spread on the floor of Prasit's prayer room. One of the photo spreads had been of a reporter's remains being hoisted out of a well, the bones displayed on a sheet in a field. There were only a few Thai words Calvino could read on sight: *farang*, reporter, murder, and sex. Not always in that order, and not always in the same story. But the words often appeared in bold-printed headlines.

"A few more days," said Calvino. "Maybe longer."

"You heard about the travel advisory from Australia?"

Colonel Pratt glanced at the soldiers dancing in front of the jukebox.

Calvino shrugged. "Every month there's a new terrorist warning." He drank from the Singha beer and made a face.

"Sooner or later everyone gets to be right," said Colonel Pratt.

"And you think someone is going to be right this time?"

I don t know. But no one knows when it s their turn.

"Meaning?"

"I am having a look around."

"What's the primary mission? The murder investigation or checking out if the *jihad* in the south has moved north?" asked Calvino. Silence followed. "Or maybe it is a two for one."

This brought a gentle smile from the colonel. Strike at the golden calf and Cobra Gold. He had read the phrase in an intelligence report.

Colonel Pratt's choice of bars hadn't been a random act. Calvino knew the colonel had a good reason for choosing a particular place and time. Even with limited intelligence sources, it wouldn't be difficult to learn that the Cobra Gold advance team had chosen this bar as their place to hang out and unwind. The bar, with its American theme, music, food and management, made them feel comfortable. A joint in a strange and foreign place that acted as a home away from home. The kind of designated playing field that a terrorist dreamt of targeting. Pattaya bore the stain of *jahiliyya—barbarism.*

"My client wants a quick resolution."

Silence fell between them, the void filled with the hollering from the bar.

"You're under pressure," said Colonel Pratt. "And so am I."

Ever since Calvino could remember, his friend had played a dual role inside the department. He was admired and held in awe because he understood the mystery of how *farangs* thought. Not only the process, but also the rationale underlying the process. At the same time, such knowledge caused a sense of unease, distrust, and created distance as his superiors and others in the department were fearful that his knowledge might suddenly turn and shift and double back in unforeseen ways, in directions that they could not control.

Overhead the air-conditioner groaned, straining at full blast to cool down the hot, throbbing bodies; men and women letting off steam, knowing what lay before them was an exercise and not the real killing experience. Calvino looked over the tables and the bar. If he were a terrorist, he thought, where would he *hide* a bomb? Or would he park a motorcycle out front, walk away, and push a detonator as he walked along Beach Road? Or would he walk in with the explosives concealed inside his clothing, walk up to the jukebox, drop in a coin, push the number for Eminem and listen to the lyrics: *Look, if you had one shot, one opportunity to seize everything you ever wanted... one moment.* Listen real hard because those might be the last words anyone inside would hear, as the bomb went off and he cleansed the planet of infidel soldiers.

Calvino watched the soldiers dancing to Eminem's rap. He tried to erase the apocalyptic image from his mind. On one level, he wanted Pratt to know that he could handle his own investigation. But the images of a bomb exploding stayed inside his mind. He told himself that he didn't need anything from Pratt. But he wasn't so sure. Everyone had been living under the terror of code-orange alerts for months. It didn't stop anyone from going to a bar. Most of the time no one gave the possibility of an attack a second thought.

"Khun Ratana's under pressure from her mother," said Colonel Pratt.

"She's learning Chinese. Did you know that?"

"She told me."

"Her mother wants to buy a gun. That's not dealing well under pressure."

"Most people don't hold up well under stress," said Colonel Pratt.

"Staying in quarantine hasn't helped."

Colonel Pratt sipped his orange juice. "Tomorrow Ratana plans to go to the office."

"She told you that?" It was news to Calvino.

Colonel Pratt nodded. He liked dispensing good news for a change.

"I hadn't heard."

"You know secretaries, they like to surprise their boss."

Calvino felt awkward talking about Ratana as if she were someone who would surprise him. He told himself that she was his secretary. An employee. But even Pratt knew there was something more unstated between the two of them. A personal bond that neither of them had yet found the words to express.

"Any idea who wanted to surprise the reporter with a bullet?"

"A couple of ideas," said Colonel Pratt. "He was working on a story about the disappearance of a crew who worked on a fishing trawler. One of our sources said the bodies of the two Khmer were burned and the remains dumped in the sea."

"And Pramote thought there was a story to investigate," said Calvino.

"How did you know his name?"

"I read it in the papers."

"I didn't think Pramote's murder ran in the English newspaper. And even if it did run, they would have buried it in the back pages. Besides, the report was in the papers months ago."

"Last summer, wasn't it?" said Calvino. "I have a good memory when it comes to murder."

"A long memory and a good memory aren't necessarily the same thing," said Colonel Pratt.

Calvino let the remark pass, raising his Singha beer. "Is there a connection with the men who got burnt and the reporter? Maybe he got whacked because he found something he shouldn't have found," said Calvino.

"And what might that have been?" asked Colonel Pratt.

"That's what you're figuring out. Does anyone kill a reporter without someone important giving the okay?"

The case had the fingerprints of the local mafia on it. There was no need to say the word: *jao poh* or gangster or warlord. Chon Buri had its fair share of gangsters running women, drugs, and guns. They ran their local turf with brutality, and violence, and kindness and handouts. Protection and safety were guaranteed for those who bowed to the godfather's authority, and a spot at the bottom of a well was reserved for those who challenged him, failed to heed a warning to back off. Those had always been the sub-rules of the game—the official rule was to deny the existence of *jao poh*. It was crazy. A world of denials and a world of containing the power and influence of what was denied. Pramote wouldn't have been the first reporter to suffer from the illusion that his press credentials would shield him. He got it wrong. The influence didn't get any darker than the one in the provinces. Gangsters lacked a reputation as original thinkers. As men of action, original thinking was of secondary importance. Finding how to get things done without getting caught, that required a lot of thinking.

Colonel Pratt said that the Cambodians came into port on fishing boats at the end of every month to unload their catch and to get paid. These were poor, uneducated peasants. They worked for two weeks, a month, six weeks fishing offshore. It was hard, backbreaking, dangerous work. They worked long hours, surviving on rice and fish. Surviving wasn't the best description. They were likely fed well enough to be kept strong enough to work the bone-crushing hours. The colonel admired the Khmer's determination to make money for their families in Cambodia. The big boss paid in cash. They walked away with four, five, even ten thousand baht, depending on the weight of the catch. This was a lot of money.

Colonel Pratt fell silent. Calvino knew how to fill in the blanks.

It was too much money for people in the village not to notice. Local officials and gangsters setup roadblocks, stopped them and demanded their money. After the extortion team struck, the worker might be left with five hundred baht. They should have been grateful to walk away with one baht; that was the attitude of the locals. The men at the roadblock could have taken everything. But this was the middle-path, leaving something for the unfortunate victim of fate. Let him go back and fish again and try his luck. Maybe his karma might improve. There was always the chance he could escape the roadblock next time. That was enough of a chance for them to return to the trawlers to try one more time to avoid highway robbery. What was clear, though, was that no Cambodian fisherman should complain to the police or to NGOs, or especially take his cause to a reporter or a foreigner.

"Karma is a hard thing to understand," said Colonel Pratt.

"I understand enough. A man gets himself killed. He dies on the job. Because he found out who did the fishermen. Someone talked to him. He got the story."

If this breach of the rules happened, or was rumored to have happened, the fishermen's bodies would be found—sometimes, or sometimes it would disappear at sea. The fishermen were shot, stabbed, drowned—the method was less important than the certainty that death served as a warning for each man to honor his fate and that of others destined to a better place on the wheel spinning the cycle of chance. In this life, it became the nature of their relationship with those waiting onshore. Next life, who knew? The situation could be reversed. *And indeed it may have been reversed, so why should I have my chance? It was given to me*, thought Calvino.

Colonel Pratt had pieced together most of the story from several sources. It was always surprising how much people talked about things they shouldn't talk about to each other and even to strangers. Each person had a tiny piece of the story. To them that was the whole tale. It was likely that the dead reporter had somehow stumbled over enough gossip to start making a few too many inquiries.

The puzzle Colonel Pratt cobbled together was of the day the men died in the village. Several fishermen had been seen in a fight outside a bar, and not long after that, plumes of smoke rose in the distance from a forested area. Later the charred remains had been scooped up from the gooey mess of smoldering tires and dumped into a bag, carried onto a boat, taken out to sea and thrown overboard. They had returned to the sea where they had worked and they vanished without a trace. No one had been arrested for the murder of the Cambodians. No one had been arrested for the murder of the reporter. It was the way things worked. Or the way people with authority and influence worked the system: without fear that came with the knowledge they were untouchable.

Someone reached over the bar and rang the bell. Peels of laughter and shouting followed as the soldier kept ringing the bell. A couple of moments later, a waitress brought another orange juice and Singha beer and set them down on the table.

"Looks like good luck," said Calvino. The colonel was right: there was no such thing as luck in the abstract. In the abstract luck was just another chance that could go either way. Not unlike love, stud poker or the lottery.

"Depends if you like Singha."

Calvino liked that answer. He raised his Singha beer and toasted Colonel Pratt.

"Here's to New York City on the day you drank your first Coors."

Colonel Pratt raised his orange juice and touched the rim of the Singha bottle. He looked around the room at the young soldiers enjoying themselves, drinking, singing, and joking around. "It's hard finding truth in a crowd."

That had been one of Calvino's mother's sayings. Long before Pratt became Colonel Pratt, he'd been a student in New York City. He'd spent many weekends at Calvino's house. Calvino's mother loved cooking for him. Over chicken soup she'd say things like, "You can no more find truth in a crowd than you can find compassion in a pack of jackals." The colonel had loved Calvino's mother like his own. He'd promised her when her son came to Thailand that he'd look after him. They had a strong bond, a connection going back twenty years, and each man had come to accept that there was a piece of destiny stringing together their personal and work lives in a circle. It had happened before in assignments in Cambodia and Vietnam, and it was happening again in the heart of mobster country. The history made Calvino a half-believer in *karma*. And what about the other half of his beliefs? Like just about everyone else, it was up for grabs.

"And what will you do if some of *your* people are involved?" asked Calvino.

He kept away from the word *uniform*. It wasn't just authority, it was immunity and impunity. The uniform was a full house at the karma poker table.

"My people? I can't answer that until I know the situation."

"You'll figure it out depending on the situation?"

"On keeping a balance."

"The Tao," said Calvino. "Neither day nor night."

The colonel nodded.

Colonel Pratt had the Taoist belief that there was no black without the white, no good without evil, no beauty without ugliness. To eliminate one was to eliminate both, and since that couldn't be accomplished, the best recourse was to establish a careful equilibrium. No matter how long his friend Vincent

Calvino had lived in Thailand, Calvino still couldn't accept a world which was both black and white; a world where the forces found a way to co-exist, and such an existence meant a mutual acknowledgment that one could never totally defeat the other. The metaphor of light and darkness failed to deliver the essence of what the colonel felt. But there was a breathing meditation that did. The physical act of being mindful as the lungs inhaled, held the breath, then exhaled. Mindfulness of that act, an act with two motions, one in and another out—that was being mindful that without each, the body would die.

SIXTEEN

AFTER feeding a bottle of milk to the kid named Delius, Sandra had walked from the goat pens to the guestroom and slipped an invitation under the door. Calvino saw a piece of paper sliding under the door. He picked it up. He opened the door and spotted Sandra walking quickly away from the guestroom. He stepped onto the verandah. Outside the guesthouse two of Valentine's dogs chased each other around in the grass. The Great Dane pushed its nose inside, watching him and sniffing at his hands. He pushed the dog out, closed the door and read the paper. A handwritten invitation announced a recital by Searles Valentine would commence at 7.30 p.m. that evening. Mahler and Sibelius were to be performed and other surprises would be announced at the concert. And, as if the invitation wasn't strange enough, Valentine had scribbled, "I will tell a touching and true story called "Lotus Shoes." A new word for you to learn: *podophilia*."

It didn't seem to matter that Calvino was in the middle of a murder investigation. Valentine had arranged for a recital and a story-telling session. And, no doubt, there would be more lectures on sexual fetishes. Was Valentine so cut off from the outside world that the death of a gardener was one more management problem to deal with? The presence of an investigator into that death certainly hadn't caused Valentine's routine to change. Except for the breakdown of his rotation system among his *sanom,* everything else in his life appeared much as it had always been. The issuance of the recital invitation was a confirmation that Valentine would not let anything or anyone interfere with the way he ran the life of the compound.

Having instructed his secretary to hand-deliver an invitation at dawn appeared as natural as asking Calvino to stop for a fifty-kilo bag of goat feed. Valentine was a man who needed an audience. He needed a witness to his performance. He was at his best in front of an audience. A captive, private audience was the best. Some men liked showing off their women in a social setting. Valentine had loved showing off a harem as he sat behind a piano. This would be no ordinary recital. That was to be expected. There was nothing ordinary about Valentine. Why had he gone to the trouble of mentioning lotus shoes?

As Valentine's secretary was about to slip away, Calvino called after her. "Does he have regular concerts?"

She turned back and stared hard at Calvino; the features of her Indian face twisted into a slow burn of rage. "The master plans a recital whenever he feels like having one. This is his place. His life. We exist in order to feed his damn goats, water his plants and listen to his music."

"You don't like him very much, do you?"

Her mouth moved and no sound came out.

"He has been good to me and my family." The words came out like a stock phrase; something that she repeated to herself every six hours as she sat on a stool and waited until the newborn kid sucked the contents of the bottle dry.

Calvino walked down the path to meet Sandra. He held out the invitation. "Does he normally tell stories about shoes at his recitals?"

"There is no normal in this compound. Or haven't you noticed?"

"Maew said you hand-feed Mahler," said Calvino.

"And Delius. Every six hours. They must be fed. Goats come before people. As do trees, shrubs, flowers and other things I'd rather not talk about."

"My job is to ask people to open up about the things they don't talk about. It is one way to help me understand how Prasit died."

"You can stay here for years and you will never understand."

She turned and walked away. Her disposition had been cranky ever since the kids had been born. She had been assigned the duty of bottle-feeding Mahler and Delius every six hours, and feeling sleep deprived, she had fallen into a dark, foul mood and otherwise had made life miserable for everyone else in the compound. She had justified her moody behavior as the cost everyone had to pay for this unnatural separation of mother and child. After a week the mother would sniff the kid and walk away. The mother would make no claim on her child. There would be no bond. The kid's diet had to be carefully monitored. Any deviation from the strict measure of the feed and the feeding time would subject the kid to all kinds of potential illnesses.

Any deviation and Sandra would have a deduction from her salary.

Being in a bad mood was a one hundred-baht fine.

Missing a feeding was a one hundred-baht fine.

Calvino wondered if the system of deduction might have had something to do with the death of the gardener.

SEVENTEEN

IN the late afternoon, Valentine drove his beat-up old pickup into Pattaya to drop Calvino off away from the main drag. He stopped and put the pickup in reverse, and without looking, backed up. He hit the brakes hard. He had nearly collided with a new Toyota. The driver of the Toyota jumped out of her car and squatted down in the road looking for damage. Valentine squatted beside her.

"You should look where you are going," said Valentine.

"You back into my car," she said.

"Where's the damage?"

Her eyes examined every inch of the car.

"You lucky," she said. "Next time maybe not so lucky."

Valentine climbed back into the pickup. "They should make cars from wood. At the end of the day, you park your car and sand down the bumps and scratches, slap on a little paint, and you're ready for another day of driving in Thailand."

"Thanks for the lift, Valentine."

The blood had drained out of Valentine's face. His hands trembled as he held the steering wheel. Calvino hadn't wanted Valentine dropping him at his exact destination. After the near accident, Valentine was so preoccupied he wouldn't have remembered in any event. Nor did Calvino want locals tracing the registration of his own car. Valentine dropped him about a five-minute walk from the pet clinic where Fon had once worked. There he could blend in as a tourist. Valentine looked around the area and was about to ask why Calvino had wished to be dropped in this dead zone of local shops, which had nothing to offer a *farang*. He thought better of it.

"You can make your own way back to the compound," said Valentine, drumming his fingers on the steering wheel. He pursed his lips together as Calvino opened the door. "Don't forget, there is a concert this evening. I wouldn't want my guest to be late. It would set a bad precedent for the employees."

I am an employee. Calvino said to himself. "I'll be there at 7.30."

"Good, then be off and do what snooping you must do. Whatever you can find in this wretched neighborhood, I say, good luck to you. I have a bit of snooping of my own to do. Seven thirty and please be on time."

"On your way back, you wouldn't mind picking up some goat feed, would you?" asked Calvino as he leaned down, one arm resting on the car door.

"I hope you won't be the one to write my obit. Because I fear you will never let me live that down."

Calvino shut the door and waved. He watched from the pavement as the concert pianist, gentleman farmer and harem keeper drove away in his ancient pickup, a plume of bluish black smoke gushing from the tailpipe. The pickup was a perfect disguise. No one would have looked twice at him, or thought that he had once been famous, that he was a man with a fortune, a payroll, and a dead gardener. Only someone who had no concern with face could possibility have driven such a vehicle. In a land of face, the best disguise for wealth was displaying poverty. He walked along the *soi* until he came to a market selling fresh fruit and vegetables. The hawkers called out to him, offering him fruit to taste. He cut in between a couple of stalls and saw a small shorthaired dog lying on its side under the shade of an overturned crate. He knelt down and looked at the dog. A woman selling mangoes hovered above him with a piece of fresh mango offered out in her hand. He took the slice and slipped it into his mouth. It was sweet. Calvino stood up from the dog.

"How much to rent your dog?"

The smile vanished from her face and she wiped her hands on an apron.

"What are you going to do with her?"

In Pattaya this wasn't an inappropriate question to ask a *farang*.

"Take her to the vet."

"Lucky isn't sick. She's a very clean dog.

"She looks tired. Lucky needs a check-up."

The woman looked down at the dog.

"One hundred baht. One hour. But you can't hurt her."

"I'll be gentle. Promise. And I'll need a leash."

The vendor pulled out a frayed leash and handed it to Calvino.

"Twenty baht for the leash."

"That makes a total of one hundred and twenty baht," said Calvino.

"And you buy from me one kilo of mango. I give you a good price."

"Good idea. I'll take two kilos. When I bring Lucky and the leash back, I'll pick up the mangoes."

The clinic was in a row of shophouses. It was sandwiched between a beauty parlor and a mom-and-pop shop—one of those last holdouts against the horde of 7/11 and other chain convenience stores that, like a contagious virus, had taken over much of Pattaya. Valentine had been right: the neighborhood was wretched. When the Australians or Americans issued their travel advisory about possible terrorist attacks against foreign interests, this was not the kind of place they had in mind. This was the kind of non-descript neighborhood that terrorists blended into. Inside the clinic, middle-aged housewives and teenaged maids sat in plastic chairs. Dogs on leashes lay at their feet or slept in their laps. A couple of dogs yapped, pulling hard on their leashes. Excitable, sick animals with yellowish eyes and dry, rubbery black noses.

Behind the reception desk, a middle-aged Thai woman, her glasses on the end of her surgically altered nose, flipped through a box of small index cards. She was looking for something. Calvino waited with Lucky at the end of the leash as she fingered through the cards twice. It could have been a nervous habit, a way of looking to be doing something, Calvino thought. He stood there and she never looked up. He decided to interrupt and ask a few questions about prices and treatment. She pretended not to hear him. He repeated the last question twice, "My dog has a cold. How much for the vet to see her?" Before she answered, a needle must have been inserted into the hindquarter of a dog and it howled and then cried in pain. The dogs in the reception room looked up, ears erect. The perfect-storm look of terror reflected in their eyes. The woman behind the desk had the sullen look of a casino dealer eyeing a table of New Jersey pensioners. She glanced up from the card shuffling. She looked over the counter at the fruit vendor's dog.

"Lucky," she said.

Of all the dogs he could have rented, this one had to be recognizable by the card-shuffling woman with a bad attitude and nose job at the local pet clinic.

"I want her checked out before I buy her. See if she's got any problems. Before, there was a vet working here named Fon. She looked after my dogs for years. Then I went back to America. I am back and I'd like Fon to run some tests on Lucky."

The receptionist had a blank look on her face. She either had never heard of Fon or she was a first-class actress.

One of the customers waiting with her dog cleared her throat. "Excuse me, did you say Dr. Fon?" Lucky had brought him some luck. He sat down next to the woman and she opened right up. The woman knew the history of the clinic. She had been bringing her dog here for ten years. She remembered Dr. Fon. Most importantly, she was willing to volunteer information.

"Dr. Fon leave a long time ago," said the woman in the faded blue dress.

"And her boss, the guy who owns the clinic, I guess that he probably left, too?" asked Calvino, turning towards the woman with the white poodle.

She shook her head and turned the page in her magazine. "No, Sia Veera, he still lives in Chon Buri. He has a big name. I never see him anymore."

"Is he the big man in the province? That Veera?"

"He is very important. His name is loud," she said. "Big politician." In Thai the name that made a big noise was a famous name.

"Thanks," said Calvino. "What's wrong with your dog?"

"He's too old. Sick. Can't walk good. I come to have him put to sleep."

She flipped another page, smiled, and patted the dog on the head.

"I don't walk so well myself," said Calvino.

He had the name he'd wanted to find. There was always the chance such a common name could have belonged to someone else. Calvino was familiar with Thai names like Lek, Narong, and Toi. Veera could be added to such a list. But there was only one Veera who was known as an influential person in Chon Buri, or what the Thais called a *jao poh*. The woman had been clear this was the Veera with the big, loud name. Veera's picture was often in the newspaper alongside local officials and politicians at some birthday, wedding, funeral, or opening celebration. The fact that Veera might also own a pet clinic was not a surprise. That was assuming that what a busybody in the waiting room believed was the name of the owner was the truth. In Thailand it was often impossible to determine the identity of the true owner of a business or a property. Title was channeled through a system of wives, minor wives, sisters, cousins, gardeners, maids, and *luuk nongs*. The truly rich and powerful had a lifestyle not all that different from the Pope, living in grand palaces decorated with art, collections of jewels, swords, scrolls and paintings, and traveling in specially armored vehicles. But on paper they were paupers. When it came to directly owning property, the gangsters understood that like the Pope, it was better to keep ownership and title separate from the authority they wielded.

"The vet will see Lucky," said the receptionist.

Calvino was at the door. "She's feeling a lot better. That won't be necessary."

"I thought you wanted an examination."

He leaned against the door. "I am thinking to myself. She will just get old. Sick. Won't be able to walk. Then I'll have to get her put down. I've decided not to get a dog. But thanks for all of your help."

He walked the dog back to the market stall and paid for the two kilos of mangoes. Lucky crept back to her spot in the shade of the crate, though the sun had moved and the shade was only a tiny shadow. The vendor gave Calvino back his change. "You can tell your friends about Lucky. They want to rent for one hour. No problem. She's a very friendly dog. I think she like you very much."

"I'll be sure to keep in touch," said Calvino. Like drop her a postcard with just a few choice words: *Hello my big, big bow wow.*

EIGHTEEN

VALENTINE, giggling and smiling, jumped out of the pickup and ran around to the passenger side, opening the door for a slender young Thai woman. She stepped out smiling as she caught her first glimpse of the gardens. She had the pale-skinned Chinese complexion, narrow face, not young—mid-twenties—and an easy, confident smile. Dimples small black holes on both sides of her mouth like they had the gravitational force to suck Valentine's eyes out of their sockets.

Two hours later Valentine appeared dressed in black tails, white shirt, and white tie. He walked into the piano room as if he were walking onto the stage of the Royal Albert Hall. Following two steps back was the *ying* from the pickup. She wore a silver sequined dress and carried a matching bag. Everyone else had been waiting for twenty minutes before they arrived.

Valentine couldn't stop looking at her, smacking his lips and jutting out his jaw and proclaiming to no one in particular, "Her name is Jirapan. She is our special guest of honor tonight. Along, of course, with our own private investigator, Vincent, who you will now have all met."

Sandra leaned over and whispered, "This is another *sanom* audition." She had the passionless tone of a county coroner performing a 2.00 a.m. autopsy while dictating notes into a microphone.

Calvino nodded, wondering what sexual deviation had brought her to Valentine's attention.

Jirapan sat on a chair next to the grand piano, facing the other people in the room. Sitting down Valentine, because of his height, was eye-level with each of his *sanoms* who were standing. He had to look down to catch Jirapan's eye. She wore a dress and nylons and sat with her knees locked together. Slowly Valentine returned to the keyboard; his hands came down onto the keys. A Mozart concerto thundered out. Valentine, his eyes half-lidded, slipped into a private world far removed from Thailand. No one else in the room followed him in his dream-like fugue. Jirapan's reality was too large of an interfering presence for the *sanoms* and other women. She occupied the chair traditionally reserved for Maew, which translated as cat. This was the chair designated for Valentine's number one *sanom*, though he had initiated the idea of rotating the privilege of sitting in the chair among the three. Number One was followed by Number Two, and finally by Gop. The frog, his Number Three, filed past last. That way, Valentine had reasoned, everyone had the chance of being admired and recognized as the chosen one. Jirapan had usurped the rotation. It had been Maew's turn. Everyone in the room except Calvino and Jirapan knew it was Maew's turn. Sitting in the first row, she appeared to be one substantially unhappy cat. Her face lay on the chopping block. And there was Valentine in his own world, fingers gliding over the keyboard, his ponytail swinging from the back of his head as his head moved in tempo with the music.

Ever since Prasit's death, and the de facto strike if not organized then inspired by Prasit's widow, Valentine had retaliated the only way he knew how. He knew bringing back strange girls would cause a disruption to the usual protocol. It was management's way of breaking the strike. If they were going to turn the social arrangement on its head, he would see that their face suffered as a consequence. This tit-for-tat low-level warfare had been going on for weeks. No one in the room was secure in her position. The presence of Jirapan was just the latest aggravation to the tense domestic scene. Management on the piano; employees in the audience lined up by seniority. Next to Maew in the front row was Kem followed by Gop. They automatically sat in accordance with their ranking: Number One followed by Two and Three. None of the women in the front row smiled or listened to the music. They couldn't take their eyes off Jirapan.

Kem whispered that she must have used cream to lighten her skin. No one was *that* white. Gop said she thought her long legs and large breasts also came out of a bottle. No urban myth can hold a candle to a rural-urban myth. Kem whispered, "No, not a bottle, a knife." They had an argument about whether a doctor could make a woman's legs longer. Fon and Som, with Sandra, Valentine's secretary, sat in the back row. There was a lot of whispering back and forth. Valentine was oblivious to the background chatter ten feet away. Jirapan averted her eyes, her hands folded in her lap, knowing the women were staring and whispering about her.

Valentine's workforce formed a solid block—despite the fact that Som was Burmese and Sandra was Indian—one united by a common suspicion of any new female who might be an intruder onto their turf. No one could quite determine her status: had Jirapan been invited to hear Valentine play or was she coming to play with Valentine? No one knew, but that didn't stop the front row from speculating in loud whispers. The *sanoms*, despite their obvious hatred and the prejudice and fear it produced, were right about one thing. Jirapan had translucent white skin, the blue veins showing in her neck and hands. This had been their first calculation. A woman with dark skin was often from Isan or a Khmer or from the south. Women with light- colored skin felt superior to anyone whose skin started toward the copper end of the spectrum and moved down to a hue of teak to cobra black. Dark meant peasant stock. Dark promised evil and suggested dangerous and threatened dirty. Dark-skinned people—particularly women—were *the other, the outcast, the outsider,* and *an undesirable.* There was no such thing as too white. Valentine's invitee to the recital had skin close to the edge of albino. Any damn fool could translate white as meaning high-class, good, and desirable. And more than a few fools did. As Valentine played, he turned once and smiled at Jirapan.

She applauded. "Not yet, sweet Jirapan. You must learn when to applaud. Never too soon, or too late," he said, continuing to play.

The *sanoms* stopped talking the moment Valentine spoke to Jirapan. They didn't wish to miss a word from Valentine's lips that might be a clue as to his intentions. Once he returned to his playing, they immediately resumed chattering among themselves, the conversation growing more emotional and shrill as they talked about Jirapan as if she weren't within listening distance. The Thai word for white—*khaow*—rose up again and again only to be pushed under by the Mozart coming from the grand piano. The thing was, this Thai with too-white skin had created a presence that made them feel as if they had been transported against their will into a world of inferiority. In the world of skin color, Jirapan sat at the top of the highest order. If the *sanoms* and other employees had held up scorecards, Jirapan would have scored a perfect ten from all six judges. Add white along with her proximity in the room to Valentine, and Jirapan was a gale-force storm blowing through their lives, rocking their little boats, threatening to capsize them. The best thing against that feeling of drowning was to hang onto each other, brace against the hard wind, and wait until the storm blew over.

Among Valentine's staff, the ultimate humiliation was having someone else make them into that *other* woman who felt that she was looked down upon. When Valentine had started the concert, Calvino had watched the women, thinking about how little encouragement most people needed to sign on to the whole fascism and racism program. Calvino had an uncle in New York City—his mother's younger brother—who said that the human species had been hardwired for fascism; it was the default operating system for mankind.

Valentine switched to a Liszt concerto he played by heart. As his fingers touched the keyboard, Kem held up a photograph of the goat named Liszt, showing it to Valentine, who nodded. She lowered it to her lap. Expats could be a strange lot, but Valentine was in a category all by himself, thought Calvino.

Halfway through the Liszt, Valentine stopped and looked up at the women, who were now almost shouting. "Creatures, please. You are making it very difficult for me to play. If you are such savages that you can't appreciate Liszt, then please remain silent so others with more refined taste can enjoy the music." The front row averted their eyes and stared at their hands. No one responded. The room was silent except for the hiss of two large humidfiers. Valentine resumed playing and the women resumed talking. After he finished the Liszt, he looked up. Jirapan was clapping her hands politely. A moment later, Valentine's secretary joined in the applause, followed by the maid, Fon and Calvino. Without question he had a true feeling for the music he played, bringing a sense of urgency and drama. But not everyone in the room agreed; those seated in the front row sat on their hands smiling nervously, not certain what was coming next. The degree of refinement and appreciation and loyalty rolled out in the order in which Valentine had expected it.

"As my creatures don't appear amused by the music, it is time perhaps to tell a story. It begins with my mother and her friend. Without doubt the most enduring influence in my childhood was my mother's friend. Her name was Sutida and she was from Thailand. Sutida was an intellectual. She loved Bach, Mozart and Beethoven. She was also left-wing, and that made it dangerous for her in Thailand. She chose to work as a laborer in a factory even though she had gone to university. She sweated in the factory as a show of her solidarity with the working class. Her grandmother had been Chinese. The grandmother's feet had been bound when she was four. Her feet, as a result, never measured longer than five inches. They were eternally the size of a four-year-old's. She had been crippled and hobbled. Why would the Chinese do such a cruel thing to a child? Making her into, in our eyes, a cripple?

"This was done to enhance her sex appeal to men. And for the usual Chinese reasons: power and money, and beauty and grace. The grandmother had a collection of lotus shoes. Beautiful, ornate decorated silk slippers. Blue, red and gold colors. These silk slippers fit easily into the cup of the hand. Then after the Republic came to power, the practice of foot binding was officially banned. Fines were imposed against any family who permitted this feudal practice. What had been the height of sexuality became, in a few years, a disgrace, or burden, and something to be hidden from sight. From sexual arousal to disgust in less than a generation.

"The practice of foot binding started with a consort in the Chinese royal court in the 10th century and lasted nearly a thousand years. First they bound the feet, then the mind, and finally the soul. That is the history of China. Submission started with the feet and worked its way up to the brain. Giving one's self up for family, for a man, for fashion, for a look. The feet were admired and adored. They aroused. At weddings and at funerals the tiny lotus shoe clad feet were displayed. The woman's feet were a status of their class. Much later the peasants got it into their heads that by binding their daughters' feet they could be associated with—or more likely confused with those who didn't know better—the higher classes. Farmers' wives had their feet bound. The most striking thing about the grandmother was the absence of hatred or even regret at the outrage. Think what it would mean to have a deformity imposed upon a woman. She could hardly walk. But she possessed a serene aura, a pride and dignity bestowed by her suffering. She wore her deformity as a badge of courage and honor and beauty. What she had done at the urging of her mother was to repay the debt she felt she owed to the family. And what was her obligation: to bring the best possible suitor to the doorstep. She did this with her tiny feet inside a pair of lotus shoes.

"Khun Jirapan, as I've come to learn, also had a great-grandmother whose feet were bound at a young age. She has shown me a pair of her great-grandmother's lotus shoes, which have been handed down as a treasured family heirloom. She has them with her tonight. Please, Jirapan, show these people in the audience a gift of insight into their lives. Show them to those who think that they have suffered an injustice. Show them the shoes your great-grandmother was made to wear after her feet had been bound. Did she ever complain? No. She never had an unkind word or a wish to have been someplace else or born in another family."

Jirapan pulled the lotus shoes from her handbag and handed them to Valentine. He rose from the piano stool and walked over to the corner where he pulled back a cloth to reveal a glass case on a stand. Inside was another pair of lotus shoes. He plucked a key from his pocket and opened a small lock, pulled open the glass door and reached inside for the shoes. The pair easily fit inside his palm. He walked back to the grand piano with the shoes. Sitting down on the bench, he produced, as if by magic, a small ruler from inside his formal black jacket and proceeded to measure the shoes from the glass case and the shoes Jirapan had given him. He measured them twice. The *sanoms* and others watched as if they had never seen something like this before.

When he looked up, he said in a loud, clear voice, "The shoes worn by Khun Jirapan's great-grandmother are half a inch longer. Lotus shoes to be sure, but still slightly larger than the ones my mother's friend gave me on my sixteenth birthday."

He went back to the case, replaced the lotus shoes and locked the door. He addressed the women in the front row. "You think your life is hard. Please have a look at these shoes. Remember next time you are crying yourself asleep over some nonsense that if you had been born in China a hundred years ago, you wouldn't have a nice man like me looking after you, providing you with a degree of luxury others would love to have, and fresh air, and music and consideration. So I think each of you should begin to put the past behind and let us all start again fresh and new. Remember when you believe that your suffering is the greatest that there is always someone who has suffered a half an inch more."

His speech meant nothing to the *sanoms*. The shoes were thought beautiful and elegant and made them wish for smaller feet. They knew almost nothing of Chinese foot binding. For them, the message they took into the night was that Valentine had found yet one more fetish to amuse himself.

NINETEEN

CALVINO arrived mid-morning at the house of Pramote's widow. She waited inside the door as if she were expecting a visitor. She betrayed no surprise at the arrival of a *farang* in a sports jacket and shirt open at the collar, smiling. One thing she was certain about: this had little chance of turning out to be a good-news smile. Since Pramote had gone missing in February, there had been no good news. When his body was found in June, those who came to her door with the news had been smiling. Her four year old daughter, a curtain of straight black hair hanging above her eyes, hugged her mother's leg. The widow looked him over, making up her mind whether to invite Calvino inside or to close the door and back away. Holding her eighteen month old baby cradled onto her side, she shifted, using her free hand to take a long drag off a cigarette. Her hair, uncombed, the ends twisted from the baby's tiny hands, looked unwashed. She wore no make-up. She'd gnawed her fingernails down to the flesh. They looked red and swollen. At the first knuckle, her fingers had turned nicotine yellow. Her T-shirt was soiled from the baby. Food, snot, or shit—it wasn't immediately clear from color or smell which orifice the stuff had leaked from. Calvino imagined she had once been beautiful, fire in her eyes, a ready smile and laugh. Some pure energy of youth had ignited inside her and burnt brilliantly, hard and fast. Then the fire had gone out, leaving a shell of grief and suffering, and the smile extinguished. What he was witnessing were the ashes of that stellar beauty.

“My name’s Vincent Calvino. I have a few questions about your deceased husband.”

As he looked at her and thought of the mental and physical weight of her two kids, he thought about the newspaper photos of her husband’s bones stacked beside a farm well. What had once been a flesh-and-blood husband and father and reporter following up a story was no more than a pile of discolored bones. That was the memory she had been left with, the one she had to find a way to prepare her children for when they were old enough to be told why their father wasn’t with them.

“What kind of questions?” she asked.

“A few basic things. Like what your name is? That kind of thing.”

“Nueng.”

“And this one?” Calvino nodded to the eighteen-month-old boy.

She put down the toddler, who peered up at Calvino.

“This is Daeng.”

“And her name?”

“Jep.”

The toddler drooled, staring at Calvino. She wiped his mouth with a cloth.

“We don’t get a lot of foreigners coming here,” she said.

“My face normally doesn’t scare children,” he said.

Just as Calvino had finished with his ice-breaker questions, feeling that his friendly reassurance was working to gain the widow’s confidence, Daeng’s mouth went crooked. “*Farang, farang, farang*,” he repeated, before tears spilled out of his eyes.

The widow snapped back into defensive posture.

“You didn’t come here to ask our names.”

Calvino nodded. “That’s right. I am here because of what happened to your husband.”

“I don’t understand. Why does a *farang* ask about my husband?”

“I am a private investigator.” He showed her his ID. She glanced at it and shrugged. “I’m working on a case and need to ask you a couple of questions. It won’t take long.”

Her haunted look turned to suspicion. No one helped anyone without wanting something in return. “I think the police already know everything. Ask them your questions," she said. "There's no secret."

"One day your children will want to know why their father died."

She sighed and looked around for an ashtray to stub out her cigarette.

Calvino continued, "Your kids will want to remember their father as a brave man doing what he believed in."

"Is that what you think?" The disbelief swelled in her throat. She coughed, that low hacking cough of a heavy smoker.

Calvino nodded. "That's exactly what I think."

"I'll tell you the truth. If he thought like this, my husband must have hated us. If he cared about us, he would take the money and forget the story. If he did that, then I would have a husband and they would have a father. Now we have nothing. That's not brave. That's stupid. What he did was foolish."

Bitterness twisted her face. She lit a fresh cigarette and drew in hard.

"I heard that he was a good man," said Calvino.

"A good man stays with his family. He doesn't get himself killed."

They were nearing a standoff.

"A good man sometimes dies for what he believes in."

"If the police won't help, how can a *farang*?"

"By looking in different places and asking different questions," said Calvino. "All you have to lose is twenty minutes of time. And what you have to gain is a chance to understand what happened. Why not take a chance to recover something you lost?"

"What's there to recover?"

Calvino saw the toddler had tired of him and gone down on the floor to play with some plastic toys. "Peace of mind. Dignity. Hope. Respect. Truth. Faith in yourself and a hatred of injustice. A list of things that everyone wants and aren't for sale. The kind of things that are of the greatest value can't be bought."

"You're not a policeman, are you?"

She hadn't believed his private investigator's ID. "Like I said before, I am a private investigator."

"Why is a *farang* interested in my husband?"

The reality was Calvino was running out of leads on Valentine's estate. The only thread was the newspaper on the prayer-room floor that Prasit had placed so carefully. He must have knelt near the photograph of the remains of that dead reporter many times. The widow was a long shot, but the only one that he had.

"I know about a Thai who prayed for your husband."

"Why didn't he come with you?"

"He can't. He's dead."

The baby coughed. Nueng reached down and wiped his nose. They all looked sick and exhausted. Whatever will to resist had long since evaporated.

She opened the door.

"Maybe you should come inside," she said.

It was a simple bungalow in a small *moo baan*—a lower middle-class estate of thirty identical bungalows, tiny spirit houses, flowering bushes and stamp-sized lawns. Children's toys were scattered on the driveway. Weeds grew in the small garden. Flowers—or what had been flowers—had turned brown and were drooping from neglect. Weeds grew everywhere. Calvino removed his shoes and stepped inside. On a cabinet were framed photographs of the funeral. Mingled with the funeral photos were older photos of Pramote in a graduation gown, standing by the sea, with his children and wife, in a white shirt and tie behind a desk stacked with papers. The toddler Daeng was an infant in his father's arms; Jep, the daughter, a toddler looking very much like her brother. The man in the pictures smiled easily; confident, determined, and proud. The large dark eyes stared back. A picture of Pramote's life emerged—a graduate, a husband and father, a professional—giving flesh to the bag of bones pulled out from a well on the edge of a rice field. The widow had a lot of time to look at the photographs and go through all the things she should have told her husband but didn't get around to. The children drained her attention. There was always some button to sew, food to buy and cook, errands to run, doctors' appointments, bills to pay—and then Pramote got himself killed before she had a chance to wash her face, comb her hair and say those things people wait for another day to tell the person they love.

Calvino leaned forward on the long wooden bench that served as a sofa. Nueng brought him a glass of water and sat in the chair opposite. She gave the toddler half a banana, handing the other half to the four-year-old. On the coffee table, he saw a name card. The white card had Colonel Pratt's name, rank, and phone number. He was trying to make sense of Pratt's motive for having gone around to the house. A murdered reporter in Chon Buri was hardly within his jurisdiction. Calvino had already crawled through that hole in the wall. He had come out the other end knowing there was another reason for the colonel be poking around, probably half a dozen reasons for the colonel's presence in Chon Buri. The dead reporter was just one of the graves that the colonel was exhuming for a larger purpose yet to be revealed.

The widow saw him looking at the card. He silently drank from the glass of water. For all of the words he'd used to get him in the door, the card had made him mute. It threw him off balance. Murders happened in villages and upcountry settlements along borders and the seaport. Business rivals, upstarts, troublemakers, activists, and inevitably meddlesome Burmese and Khmer migrant workers—especially the ones who demanded things such as their pay at the end of the month—might be killed. Perhaps Pramote's widow was right—Pramote had been a fool to make a stand against such overwhelmingly powerful forces. His death had hardly made the news. Calvino was still trying to figure out Colonel Pratt's interest in such a murder.

The obvious answer was that someone in authority wanted answers.

The local authorities would likely have shared the same view of Pramote's actions as his widow's. Upcountry, a killing didn't need a green light if powerful interests were threatened, especially if warnings had been issued. After the warning, the light would stay green. There was an implicit understanding: whatever you do in your backyard is your business. Just keep out of my backyard and I will keep out of yours. Pramote had gone into someone else's backyard, stayed there, wouldn't leave, and predictably got himself whacked. There had been little outrage at his disappearance.

Less after his body had been found. Pramote had become another murder victim statistic.

Tolerance, like cholesterol, wasn't universally unhealthy. There was the good stuff and the stuff that killed you. The tolerance that allowed locals to kill outsiders with impunity was a bad tolerance. The tolerance that acknowledged that everyone was protected equally, including those with different skin, religions, and opinions, and that no one had a right to slaughter the "other," was a good tolerance. A country has grown up when its people have the ability to distinguish between the two.

The two kids played on the floor.

"You want a cigarette?" the widow asked.

He looked up from Colonel Pratt's name card. "I'll pass."

"The colonel didn't smoke, either," she said, smiling.

"We can come back to that. First, I'd like to know why your husband didn't drop his investigation into the deaths of the two Khmer fishermen?"

She angrily exhaled a blue cloud of smoke.

"He'd gone to *farang* land for three months to work as an intern on a newspaper. When he came home, he'd changed."

"How did he change?"

"His head was full of *farang*-land ideas."

"*Farang*-land?"

"America."

In the widow's mind, the *farangs* were directly responsible for her husband's murder. Without Pramote's exposure to their ideas, he would still be alive, outside weeding in the garden and playing with the children. She had a point. Abstract ideas like truth, justice, equality, rule of law, and fairness were alien weeds. And when someone tried to plant them, he found out the seedlings were uprooted before their roots could take hold. She sat face-to-face with a member of the *farang* race, a representative of those who had taken her husband's mind and turned it away from the basic instinct for survival. Calvino had talked himself into the house with the same ideas that had talked themselves into her husband's head. Calvino wondered to himself, how he could tell the widow of a man who had died for an abstraction that his death was an act of valor. The answer was he couldn't. Death was many things but one thing it wasn't was an abstraction. He watched Daeng playing with a plastic flower with an eighteen-month-old's delight.

"Did he talk to you about his work?"

"Sometimes he would tell me about a story he was working on."

"Did he talk about some foreign fishermen who had disappeared? Maybe murdered?"

"He heard some bad thing had happened to them."

"Anything specific?"

"No."

"Are you sure?"

"Sure."

Nueng wasn't making it easy. Why should she? Here was a stranger—and not just any stranger, but a *farang*—showing up without an invitation, asking questions about her husband. Pramote had been too curious and he had been taught by the Americans to hold onto a story until that curiosity was satisfied.

"Did he keep any notes on his stories?"

"I gave everything to the police in June. I told the colonel that the police already had everything."

"Did you give him anything?"

"A glass of water," she said.

"I meant about your husband."

"I know what you meant. I am not stupid."

"The colonel's my friend," said Calvino.

She stared at him as if she didn't understand.

"I've known Colonel Prachai for more than twenty years," he said. Calvino left out that he had called him Pratt for many years.

"If he's your close friend, why didn't he tell you that he talked to me?"

She had him nailed. Her eyes widened. It wasn't clear whether she believed him. How could a *farang* have a police colonel as a friend? He leaned forward from the hard wooden sofa, and wondered what else Pramote might have squirreled away. Something he might have learned from his brief stay in America.

"Did your husband keep an expense record? Phone bills, entertainment expenses, travel expenses. That kind of thing."

Nueng cocked her head, put the cigarette between her lips, reached down and stroked the neck of the toddler. "He might have."

"Could I see them?"

She removed the cigarette from her lips. "Why, you make more trouble? Isn't it enough that my husband is dead?"

"Isn't it worth finding out who killed him?"

She had the expression he often saw on Thais when asked what was essentially an existential question. To find out would be worth what to her? That would be a difficult concept to translate. There was likely no value in finding the killer. The damage was done. Justice, if it would ever come, would not return Pramote to his family. If the man who was behind the killing was untouchable, then what? Calvino had no answer; he wasn't certain Colonel Pratt would have one either.

"My husband was selfish," she said.

"Because he did his job?"

"He didn't do his job the Thai way. A man thinks of his family first. He thought of himself first," she said, stroking her daughter's hair. "He thinks like a *farang*."

Calvino sucked in a deep breath. He was about to throw in the towel. She was holding her ground; bitterness makes people unwilling to step back.

"The other papers are likely something a *farang* taught him to keep. Why not get rid of them to a *farang*?"

She shrugged and looked for another cigarette. The pack was emptied. She wadded it up and dropped it into the ashtray. Then she disappeared into the bedroom, leaving Calvino with the two kids. They stared at him wide-eyed and leery, the way one watches another species for signs of sudden movement. She came out of the bedroom carrying a shoebox. She sat down and put the shoebox on the coffee table.

"Open it," she said.

Meanwhile she tore open a fresh pack of cigarettes.

He raised the lid and looked inside at the tangle of receipts, invoices and clippings. If giving him the papers would rid her of the *farang*, then that would be a good bargain. Then she would have nothing left to remind her of Pramote's selfishness. Pramote had put his sense of personal honor above his duty to his family. Calvino understood her.

Where should he begin? It was no use arguing that what Pramote had done wasn't for himself, but for others. Her husband had been an idealist. Such a man accepted certain risks not because there was something in it for him but because he believed there was a greater good. In a world where most journalists mortgaged their souls for the greater story, Pramote had lost his life striving for something more important than just a story. For that reason alone, it was worth finding out who killed him. The widow didn't share Calvino's point of view; to her, Pramote's thinking had been rewired to think like a *farang*, and that was the source of her bitterness. Her man had died for someone else's ideals of how others should live.

"I will return them," he said, standing up to leave.

"That's not necessary. I have no need for them. They only make me remember what I want to forget."

TWENTY

A well-built thirty-something *farang* with short-cropped hair and a square jaw nodded at the box under Calvino's arm as he entered the Tequila Reef. "Excuse me, sir. I'd like to check what's inside the box."

Calvino shifted the box from his arm to his hands, deciding whether to hand it over to this stranger. "Private documents. And who exactly are you?"

"Security, sir. Hand me the box, sir."

"You're just doing your job, is that it?" asked Calvino. He handed him the shoebox.

"That's right, sir."

"Are you the owner? Or on the payroll?"

He opened the lid of the box, sifted through the papers and handed it back.

"Thank you, sir."

Pratt, who had been watching from the corner table, quickly left his seat and walked between the two men. He pulled the shoebox from Calvino's hands. The other *farang* working the security detail never lost eye contact with Calvino for a second.

"It's okay; he's with me," said Pratt. "I am expecting this box. I asked him to bring it."

"I've checked it, sir. There's no problem."

Calvino did a double-take, looking first at Pratt and then at the stranger. For the first time since Calvino had come through the door, the stranger's face relaxed; he unballed his fists. He had Special Forces written all over him. Every sentence he uttered ended in sir. The military salute offered to the colonel was sharply executed, and the stranger turned and walked back to the bar. "I was waiting for the metal detector," said Calvino.

"He's doing his job," said Pratt.

"In other words, cut him some slack. The entire world has become an international airport."

"You want to get into a fight over a shoebox?"

"You're right. That would have been dumb."

"More than dumb."

"Okay, stupid."

"A few hours ago, in Pattani, two bombs killed six people. One of the dead was an American security expert."

Calvino slowly closed his eyes and breathed out deeply. The news caught him off guard. He wished he'd known earlier. He felt foolish, having given the security detail at the door a hard time. Moving the terror out of the South was the next logical stage of escalation. Moving it into a bar filled with GIs had inherent logic.

Pratt looked across the floor. The place was filling up with Cobra Gold soldiers. Unlike the last time he had been in the restaurant, they weren't dancing and singing, rocking and rolling. They weren't listening to Eminem. A soulful Santana played instead. The men and women huddled close together, talking, nursing their beers. The music switched from Santana to Sheryl Crow, but no one was paying much attention except a solider feeding ten-baht coins into a jukebox.

"It's not a good time to carry a shoebox into a bar filled with US servicemen," said Pratt.

"I hadn't heard about the last report from the South."

"It only happened three hours ago. Security has been stepped up everywhere in the country."

A dead *farang* in the south would make all the wire services. The nearly daily murder of teachers, government officials, cops or soldiers had barely registered outside of the country.

"The world's on a perpetual high-security alert. Now Thailand has joined the club," said Calvino. "No one seems to have a clue what's dangerous and who's the threat. Or exactly where the next strike will happen."

"Everyone's on edge," said Colonel Pratt.

"The American who was killed. You remember the name?"

The expat world was a small place. There was a chance Calvino might have known the dead man. Pratt scratched the side of his jaw. He looked around the room at all the men and women. Any one of them could be next.

"Bob Dilley. He was an American journalist," whispered Colonel Pratt.

Calvino didn't recognize the dead man's name. A *farang* journalist killed in the south would make CNN and the BBC. He slid into the booth opposite Pratt and put the shoebox on the table between them. Pratt had a nearly full glass of orange juice that looked like it was room temperature. A waitress came to the booth and Calvino ordered a Mekhong and Coke.

"I talked with Pramote's widow today. She had one kid stuck to her hip while the other ran around the house eating a banana. I didn't march straight into her house and say, 'Give me the box.' I asked her if she would let me have a look. And you know what happened?"

"What happened?"

"She gave me the box. She said, 'Don't bother to return it.' And, by the way, I saw your name card on the table in the front room. When I left, the baby was chewing on it. Not the one with the banana. The toddler was teething on your name card. He'll get teeth coming soon because of you."

Pratt smiled. He seemed to warm to the idea of his card having some actual use.

"What's inside?" asked Pratt.

"I have gone through the stuff several times. I didn't take anything out."

"That's good."

"I thought you would have asked for Pramote's things," said Calvino.

"I did."

"She didn't offer."

Pratt nodded. "She must have liked you."

"It didn't seem that way," said Calvino, sliding the box across the table until it rested in front of Pratt. The waitress brought two large Mekhong and Coke and a second orange juice. She said the *farang* at the bar had paid for the drinks. It was the same guy that had stopped Calvino at the door.

Calvino turned in his seat and raised his glass to the military cop, who lifted his bottle of Singha beer in return.

"Make nice with the police, my mother always said."

"Your mother was a wise and good woman," said Pratt.

Twenty years before, Pratt had lived at Calvino's house in Queens while the family helped sort out a problem with the Chinese Triad. One evening, after dinner, Calvino's mother had reached over the table and patted Pratt's hand. "I am glad to have a second son."

"And I to have a second mother," said Pratt. It was the first time in weeks that anyone in the household had seen him smile.

Calvino had caught Pratt's eye across the dinner table. "That makes us brothers."

His mother pressed her son's and Pratt's hands together. "Brothers look after each other. Brothers take care of each other. Always."

The memory of that moment years before filtered back into Calvino's consciousness as Colonel Pratt removed the lid and began sifting through the documents, sorting invoices, name cards and newspaper clippings into separate piles. Some of the contents were in English but most were in Thai. Pratt studied a receipt, sipped his orange juice, put it on the table, and studied the next one.

"Find anything?" asked Calvino.

"That's a question I should be asking you."

"I can't read much Thai. So how would I know from the Thai stuff? If I were in Bangkok, Ratana would have it all translated by now."

Pratt looked up from an English language name card, turned it around and placed it square on the table, facing Calvino. "What about this one? And this card. The two addresses are close together."

Calvino read the two name cards.

Underneath the words *Athens, authentic Greek food*, was the Greek flag. The other read: *Harmony Massage*. If there had been a flag, it would have been a flag of convenience.

"I'll handle the restaurant and the massage parlor," said Calvino.

Colonel Pratt put the contents back into the shoebox and put on the lid. "Better yet, why not handle the whole lot? Ratana's back in your office tomorrow. As you said, she can translate the stuff for you."

"You're not interested?" asked Calvino.

"I didn't say I was uninterested, Vincent."

"But you just had a quick look. There could be a clue to Pramote's killer."

"We have a good idea who killed him."

"But you haven't arrested him?"

"What happened to the reporter is one factor."

Calvino took a long drink from his Mekhong and Coke. "And the other factors?"

Colonel Pratt shrugged and drank his orange juice.

"You're not telling me something," said Calvino, smiling.

"*Things done well, and with a care, exempt themselves from fear. Things done without example in their issue are to be feared.*"

"Shakespeare," said Calvino. It wasn't a question.

"*Henry the Eighth.*"

Calvino always expected the colonel to dig into his knowledge of Shakespeare and produce the precise quote to fit the situation. A Thai cop who had an encyclopedic knowledge of Shakespeare marked him. Colonel Pratt wasn't the defensive type. He endured the isolation that came from thinking in a different way from his colleagues. Something had been on his mind, a question that others had asked.

"Shakespeare was wise," said Colonel Pratt.

Calvino remained silent.

"Shakespeare understood that life was theater, and what is theater other than an illusion? He was a Buddhist in his heart. Life is a drama with three intervals. You and I, Vincent, have started the third act. It's our last chance to understand the nature of life before the curtain comes down."

The colonel was an enigma. If he hadn't been his best friend for many years, Calvino might have dismissed Pratt as another one of those guys who lives in a world of epigrams—a quick-reply artist skilled at producing obscure but meaningful- sounding quotes on demand.

"Fear's always been *the* growth industry," said Calvino. Make that a double espresso shot for capitalism and a triple espresso shot for Christianity.

"And it always will be, because the world is divided between those who fear not getting what they want and those who fear losing what they have."

Colonel Pratt understood that if you lifted up the prose in Shakespeare and looked inside at the mechanics, what you found was simple—the necessity for an outside enemy to act as a diversion; allowing those on both sides of the fear divide to unite against a common external threat. Sometimes it was called the third hand. Sometimes it was called terrorism. The force had many faces and names throughout history. An equilibrium existed when there was just enough external terror to keep the internal fear in check, but too much might cause fatal, everlasting damage. Thailand was on the edge of losing its equilibrium, and this made the colonel fearful.

TWENTY-ONE

THE shoebox contained a lot of junk, the detritus of an investigative reporter trying to put together a story while at the same time trying to keep track of his expenses. That evening, inside his guestroom, Calvino sifted through the invoices, clippings, notes, match covers, and name cards. He could have meditated over every piece of paper forever. It was mischievous to leave such a legacy. Sowing seeds of doubt, missed chances, evidence that could be misconstrued a hundred ways. Misfits, con artists, evildoers all had business cards. It was enough to make any man a bona fide misanthrope.

Name cards from a Greek restaurant, a massage parlor, a dry cleaner's, a couple of go-go bars along Walking Street, places where *farangs* hung out, nursing happy hour drinks and playing grab-ass with the dancers; a hotel along the beach, a Russian bakery, a car rental place, an export company, and a distribution business—they specialized in beer, whisky, and cigars. Pramote was about ten cards short of a full deck of playing cards and about eight months short of being a live player.

Calvino sat back and studied the hand that he'd been dealt by a dead man. Did he hold? Or did he call? What was the bluff? How much should he bet? There was no way of asking for another card. His decision to cut Colonel Pratt in on the hand had been rebuffed. The colonel had his own hand and was keeping it close to his chest.

There were too many places for one man to cover and most of the addresses were likely dead ends. Ever since he'd seen the newspapers in Prasit's prayer room, he'd had a gut feeling that the newspapers had a purpose. Prasit hadn't randomly laid out the newspapers in that room. The king of spades. The papers were telling a story that meant something personal. The ace of spades. There was only one problem: Calvino couldn't prove anything. But he could read a good card hand. He couldn't get the image of the newspaper photo out of his mind. The picture of a dead reporter's remains positioned in the place of honor before the prayer altar. He toyed with the Greek restaurant card. Then an idea came to him. A Greek salad was made with goat cheese. The gardener helped raise goats. He dropped the card on the bed. So the owner had killed the gardener and the reporter because some bad goat cheese was delivered? Maybe there wasn't a connection at all. It was tedious, frustrating work, like filling in a crossword puzzle in another language. When anyone wired events and people together over a given time period, they found what they believed were real connections. As everything on some level was connected with everything else, this wasn't a difficult task to do or a difficult premise to sell. From an investigator's point of view, it meant running leads down blind alleys, then backing out with one's tail between one's legs. Unless one was careful, a lifetime could be spent running up and down such alleyways. Calvino picked two alleys: the Greek restaurant and the massage parlor. He was following an old and tested Calvino Law: If you are going down a blind alley, pick one with leads a couple of doors apart.

Colonel Pratt had had no more of an idea of what to do with the contents than anyone else. The shoebox had driven him to quote Shakespeare. He might have assigned a couple of men to interview the people who gave their card to Pramote. But what would they find out? Pramote had been dead eight months. How many cards had they been given since that time? What would they remember? What would these people tell the police?

Yeah, this reporter came around and ordered a Greek salad, he liked it, he asked for a receipt and my card. It happens all the time. What did I make of it? To be frank, I didn't make anything of it. I asked him if he might mention the salad in his newspaper. He said he wasn't a food critic or anything. Then I said, couldn't he ask the food critic to give a plug?

With deadly viruses inside planes, trains, buildings and hospitals, martial law like closing hours, and killings increasingly more brutal in the south, ordinary life had been put on hold. People had stopped going to Pattaya, and what businessman didn't need a friendly reporter's help to stay in business? He'd gone as far as he could in thinking about the name cards in the box. But there were two ways to study the shoebox. Analyze what was inside and analyze what was not inside.

One of the cards absent from the box was the name card of Pramote's editor. Nor for that matter, was there a name card for anyone connected to Pramote's newspaper.

As Colonel Pratt had said, why would Pramote need the name card of his boss? He knew where to find him.

Calvino decided to start with one of the people whose card wasn't in the box and to meet for lunch at the Greek restaurant on the name card. A two-for-one blind alley.

TWENTY-TWO

PRAMOTE'S editor agreed on the phone to meet Calvino for lunch at Athens.

"I love Greek food," the editor said in perfect American English.

Calvino's Law: If you want to meet a reporter, offer to buy him a drink; if you want to meet an editor, offer to feed him.

He spotted the editor the moment he walked through the door. The man had confidence. His clothes were ultra-fashionable. Manicured fingernails. Expensive shoes. Not quite a swagger, but clearly a high opinion of himself, earned, in part, through hours of department-store mirror time. In one hand he carried a newspaper. Not any newspaper, but his own rag, suggesting he had an identity problem separating who he was from what he did for a living. He wore a freshly pressed shirt and trousers with knife-sharp creases. His face was open, boyish. Almost feminine. Calvino guessed him to be early thirties. He wouldn't have lasted a round with the muscled Special Forces guy at the restaurant the night before.

"You must be Vincent," he said, offering to shake hands. "You can call me Mike. All of my American friends call me Mike."

He shook Mike's hand. He had a firm clasp. As Calvino had just met the man, he wasn't certain how deep Mike's friendship ran with *farangs*. The restaurant had ten tables covered with identical checkered blue-and-white tablecloths.

Pictures of small Greek islands with white sandy beaches on clear, blue seas hung on the walls. There was a Greek calendar on another wall. And a Greek flag. But there wasn't a sign of any Greeks. Two Thai waitresses hovered in the corner breathing *yaa dom* from inhalers. They showed surprise when Mike walked in. He waved at them and called for them to bring the menu.

They both arrived with menus and bottled water. Neither of them showed the slightest interest in Calvino. He'd been sitting for five minutes without either waitress coming around. Now Mike was at the table, they poured his water and gave him a menu. They walked around without offering a menu to Calvino.

They couldn't take their eyes off Mike. He had the handsome smile of a *luuk-krueng*—half-Thai and half-*farang*—which made him an object of both envy and distrust. Idealization for good looks worked to give *luuk-krueng* a razor's edge advantage, but the under the surface, suspicion of the person's foreignness blunted that edge. Bringing up the subject of the dead reporter hadn't erased the smile. Calvino had a feeling Mike smiled when he slept.

"They make a great Greek salad," said Mike. "That's my recommendation."

Calvino folded the menu. "I'll have the Greek salad."

The waitress looked puzzled.

"He'll have the Greek salad," Mike said to her in Thai.

"Oh, the Greek salad."

"That one," said Calvino. "Not the Italian or Spanish or Irish salad. The Greek salad."

Mike broke a roll in half and buttered one half. "Khun Pramote was a good man."

"Was he a good reporter?"

Mike leaned back, chewing a piece of roll. He nodded to himself and stared into space as if to contemplate what this *farang* wanted to hear. What degrees of truth does he expect? What degrees of truth could he get away with? "He liked the way American reporters investigated and probed. He would have liked you. An American private eye looking into the heart of matters, getting to the bottom of things. That was Khun Pramote."

"What was he working on at the time of his death?"

"He was working on a story about the trafficking of Cambodian women into prostitution."

Mike saw from the private eye's reaction that his carefully selected piece of information had been absorbed without a blink. Mike disliked a *farang* who possessed an immunity to surprise; it robbed him of a sense of pride—more than pride, power, to witness the *farang* investigator's grateful request for more details. Calvino gave away nothing.

"You knew about the story, Vincent?"

Let the guy speculate, thought Calvino. *Keep him on edge.*

"You assigned him the story," said Calvino. He had turned the tables on the editor.

"Pramote had a bee in his bonnet. Personally, I thought it was a waste of time. Everyone knows the reality of how things actually work on the ground. Women want jobs. There are no jobs for them in Burma and Cambodia. How are they going to feed themselves and their families? If you're an attractive young woman with no education, what would you do?"

"I am more interested in why Pramote wanted to do that story."

Mike shrugged as if what Pramote wanted was of no particular interest. Of much greater interest to Mike was having a captive audience to express his own view on the prospects of peasant girls from neighboring countries.

"What other opportunity do these girls have? None but to sell their bodies. But in their village there are no buyers. Or Greek restaurants or massage parlors. Certainly there are lots of young unemployed men, but there are no buyers who have cash. So girls find a middleman who puts them in contact with a network of smugglers. And once they enter that system, they find their buyers, or should I say their buyers find them?"

"What was Khun Pramote's angle on the story?"

"He knew the girls couldn't come freely into the country without someone with influence willing to pull strings. He started asking questions. This is a very small community. If I ask one of the waitresses for a Greek salad, you know what happens? People assume that I love Greek salads. They start sending Greek salads to my office and my house with ribbons tied on the baskets, and soon I start getting requests for a

Greek salad plug in the newspaper. And then other requests, until I would have nothing in my newspaper but stories about the origin and health value of Greek salads."

"You said that Pramote was a good man,"

The editor studied him for a moment. "How good is your Thai?"

"I speak Thai."

"A lot of foreigners speak what they call Thai to their maids and bargirls. But they don't really speak Thai. They wouldn't understand if I said Khun Pramote was *sue goen pai*."

"Meaning, he was naïve," said Calvino.

"Very good, Vincent. Too straightforward. We sometimes use this for people from upcountry. It is one thing to be childlike when you are a child, but to be childlike as an adult. . ."

"A way of thinking that can get you killed," said Calvino.

Mike smiled. "You know, I think I like you."

"Saying someone is *sue goen pai* also means that they are too honest," said Calvino."

"Yes, yes, exactly. That captures Khun Pramote's personality. When you're a reporter in a backwater, you have some choices to make. You can report on local festivals, the charity fairs, run pictures of green rice fields, elephants, waterfalls, pictures of happy people splashing and having fun at the beach. Or you can run pictures of back-alley brothels, drug addicts, slums, pimps, and prostitutes, and crusade about the injustice of it all. Who is to say which vision is more honest? I told Khun Pramote to be careful. He was a reporter and not an NGO. Let the NGOs run seminars about trafficking and we cover the seminars and can report their findings. Let them take the heat."

"He didn't listen."

"No, he didn't."

Calvino thought about Bob Dilley, the American journalist killed in the blast in Pattani. He was another reporter who had been in the wrong place at the wrong time. Editors sat safe and secure in their offices like generals, while the frontline troops marched into battle. Pramote wasn't coming back and neither was Dilley.

Calvino noticed that Mike wore a wedding ring. "You'll understand how Pramote's widow feels."

"Because I wear a wedding ring?" He laughed. "That doesn't mean that I am married."

"What does it mean?"

"A wedding ring keeps away the amateurs. They see a ring and understand that whatever happens next, commitment isn't part of the deal."

He saw where Mike was headed. If truth were a mining operation, you wouldn't want to buy the ore from Mike. "You warn *yings* with the ring, and you warned Pramote off the story. He didn't listen," said Calvino.

"That's right. He didn't listen. Anyone with a wife, a couple of kids, and a career leading to nowhere takes a long look in the mirror one day and says, 'How am I ever going to dig myself out of this hole?' Most of the time they know the answer. They can't dig out. That hole only gets deeper every year. So what are a man's options? Accept the fate that has been handed him in this life or check out. And next life, remember to stay single."

The man had taken an oath of bachelorhood. The brotherhood of bachelors looked with profound pity on a man who had voluntarily locked himself up and thrown the key to a woman.

"You think he killed himself?" asked Calvino. "He kept looking into the smuggling of women business because he knew in the end a gunman would come after him? You really believe that?"

Mike paused and toyed with a chunk of feta cheese with his fork. "Like I said, I am not certain what to believe about Pramote. Other than, as I said before, he struck me as *sue goen pai*."

The restaurant owner came out from the kitchen. Fifty-something with a large gut hanging over his belt, he wore all black. An obese Zorro years after he had hung up his cape and sword and planted himself at the dinner table. One of the waitresses had told him the editor of the newspaper was having lunch with a *farang*. "Welcome to Athens," he said. "I hope that you like the food. And if you could say something in your paper, we would be grateful."

Calvino pulled out a photograph of Pramote and showed it to the owner. "Do you remember him? It would have been about nine, ten months ago."

The owner studied the photograph, turned it over as if there would be hint of the identity of the person on the opposite side. He scratched his head. In the photograph Pramote wore a business suit and tie; his hair was combed and his eyes were wide open. "I see so many people I can't remember them all."

Calvino glanced around the empty restaurant. Tables and chairs gathering dust. He had an idea the owner could remember everyone who ever came through the door. "He worked as a reporter," said Calvino.

"He worked for my newspaper," said Mike.

The owner slapped his forehead with the heel of his hand. "Oh, I remember, he came in months and months ago and . . ."

"And?" asked Calvino.

"He brought his wife and kids for dinner. It was his wife's birthday."

"Did you know he worked for the local newspaper?" asked Calvino.

The owner nodded. "He asked if I had ever hired any Khmer girls as waitresses. And I told him all my girls were Thai. I whispered so his wife wouldn't hear that if he wanted Khmer girls there was a massage parlor four doors up the road. He'd find plenty of them working there."

"Did he you ever see him again?"

The owner shook head. "Just that one time."

In Pattaya you only saw someone once before he disappeared. Vaporized. As far as the owner was concerned, Pramote had ceased to exist a very long time ago. This was the same turn-off switch that foreigners used with each other. It was no special offence to the Thais; it was just that the foreigners didn't know any better. And who could expect them to know? They liked to stay within a narrow circle of people they could trust. It was a place that attracted people who wanted to start a new life, people who had decided to go missing in action. No one asked too many questions, and the collective forgetting of individual past lives was a silent bond between them. It didn't matter if a man was on the run from an ex-wife, ex-employer, the police, the mob, so long as he stayed off the radar screen, laid low, and became one of those people others weren't hunting for. There were other kinds of foreigners, ex-military, retirees or people who had woken up and discovered they had grown old and heard Pattaya was a perfect place to run away. They were on the run from old age, which, like the police or mob, would one day tap them on the shoulder and put them in their grave. It turned out that Zorro had used a small grubstake to start up a small business and something like a mention in Mike's newspaper meant the difference between going under and getting through another couple of months until the tourists returned. It was a place where men came to hide; it was also a place where men came to die. Not of old age but at the hand of someone looking to settle a score.

Mike was already at the door when Calvino turned around with one more question for the owner.

"Where do you get your goat cheese?"

The owner smiled. There was a question he liked. "It is very good, yes?"

"Where did you say it came from?"

"A very tall man who is a piano player."

"Valentine?"

The owner nodded. "I can give you his number if you want."

"Do you remember a man who worked for Valentine? Prasit was his name. He was a gardener and worked with the goats, too."

He screwed up his mouth, "Prasit, Prasit?" Then a light went on. "Of course, I remember him."

"He's dead," said Calvino.

The owner's head jerked slightly. "You bring news of two dead men. I hope that you are finished."

Calvino took another name card from a stack near the front door. "I'll give you a call if I can think of anyone else."

TWENTY-THREE

AFTER lunch, Mike returned to his office and Calvino walked four doors down to the massage parlor. The Harmony Massage parlor occupied a shophouse constructed from concrete blocks with all the grace and elegance of a public pier. The tinted windows prevented perverts from leering at the girls sitting inside. The mirror opposite of a police interrogation room: those inside could look out and those outside were left to their imaginations. Calvino walked through the dimly lit main room. An old woman swept what appeared to be broken glass at the far end. The broom scratched the glass against the floor. Well-thumbed newspapers and magazines covered a table in the waiting area. Like the Greek restaurant, the massage parlor was empty. The only visible inhabitants were the old maid and a *mama san* sitting behind the front desk, her nose in a cheap paperback. She looked up as Calvino leaned on the desk. A price list was inside a plastic stand on the counter.

Baht 200 for an hour, Baht 400 for an oil massage.

Fix price. No negotiations.

Calvino looked up from the sign.

"Where are the girls?" asked Calvino.

The *mama san* looked over the top of her glasses. Creases and lines criss-crossed her face like a series of cobwebs; it was difficult to believe the face staring up had ever been young. She glanced over her shoulder. He saw a door framed with opaque glass like the kind used in public toilets.

"You have any Khmer girls?"

She removed her glasses and rubbed her eyes.

"You want dark-skinned girl?" she asked.

"You have?"

A moment later a girl with pencil-thin arms and legs walked in wearing baggy shorts, flip-flops and a tight-fitting T-shirt with the words: *Ready to Serve, Ready to Die*. She had green-blue bruises on her arms.

"Are you a Cambodian girl?"

"I Surin girl," she said, edgy, her smile peaking before being erased altogether.

"Nice. But I really am looking for a Khmer girl."

"Same, same," said the *mama san*.

"Either you have Khmer girls or you don't."

"You make trouble for me?"

"I am not making trouble for anybody. All I am asking is if you have any Khmer working here."

The *mama san* had hit a button under her desk with the dexterity of an executioner working on auto-pilot. A minute later, two men came running out from the other side of the door. The first one through, his fist balled up, caught Calvino in the stomach, doubling him over. The second one kicked him in the head as he started to go down. It was a perfect kick, landing square and hard. His ear rang and he saw a starburst inside in his head. The Surin *ying* disappeared, the *mama san* slipped her glasses on and turned the page in her paperback as the two men continued to punch and kick Calvino. Blood poured from one ear. He raised his hands to protect himself in time to catch the leg of one of the men, and he twisted it hard; hearing something crack, he let go. The man howled in pain; his eyes flashed a sickly white, the pupils having gone north. Calvino caught his breath, shook his head, and got to his feet as the second man—who was younger and fitter than the one wailing on the floor—threw a couple of kick-boxing moves. Calvino backed away, bleeding. The young man moved forward, kicking and punching, none of the blows landing.

Backpedaling, stumbling and nearly falling, Calvino steadied himself against a small palm tree, uprooting it from the planter. He figured that Valentine would forgive him for ripping out a living being with a hard-to-remember Latin name.

Calvino waited for the young man to give him an opening and, finding it, on the last series of kicks, the chance came. He thrust the dirt and roots of the palm tree into the kick-boxer's face, blinding him long enough for Calvino to land three hard punches that knocked out two teeth and flattened the man's nose. As he stood back, the *mama san* had put down her novel and replaced her reading glasses with another pair of glasses. She held a .38 on him, her finger inside the trigger case. He rubbed his knuckles. They were cut and bruised and throbbed. One of the Calvino's laws: Never argue with someone pointing a .38 at your midsection and asking you to leave by the same door you came in.

"I was just leaving. If your massages weren't so rough you might have more business. You might a try a sensitivity course for some of the staff. Something to think about when you are counting your money."

"You ask too many questions. People don't like. You go to Bangkok, then no problem. You stay in Pattaya, then maybe a big problem for you. You understand?"

She was speaking English. And she was holding a gun on him. Of course he understood. "Who told you I was asking questions?"

"You go now. Or there may be an accident."

"Like Khun Pramote had an accident."

The *mama san* said nothing only tightening her lips, her knuckles white around the large gun.

"I think you not live long in Thailand," she said.

"Long enough to have a good idea when it's time to leave. Glad to have met you and the boys. Next time I'll make an appointment."

One of the men—he had palm tree dirt on his face—had almost climbed to his feet when Calvino hit him hard in the gut, folding him down on the floor as the air went out of his lungs. The old woman had already moved in with her broom, sweeping around the bodies and collecting the dirt into a neat pile. She was in the line of fire. Still, it had been a stupid move, he thought. A nervous *mama san* with a gun would have happily shot the maid and him and had the local police call it a lover's triangle.

TWENTY-FOUR

VALENTINE dressed casually, having slipped into his favorite TV viewing clothing: a pair of baggy old shorts and a T-shirt. His hair was still wet. He was freshly showered and sat on the sofa using the remote to surf through a DVD with the best of National Geographic programs. In his lap was a plate of goat cheese and crackers. He never moved his eye from the TV screen as he attempted with one hand to spread a cracker with the smooth, soft white cheese. The knife kept slipping. Number One took the knife away the way a mother would from a child and finished buttering cheese onto the cracker. He opened his mouth without looking at her, the cracker or the cheese, and she slipped it inside much like one would feed a zoo animal. On his right-hand side, within reach, a bottle of white wine cooled in a bucket of ice. Another of the girls slowly turned the bottle in the ice. The air-con chilled the room, the ice chilled the bottle, and together they watched savages in hot, steamy climes, sweating and panting. Kem's job was to rotate the bottle in the bucket of ice and she was charged with the responsibility of keeping his glass filled to the half-way mark. Calvino slipped in and lowered himself into a chair. The light from the window slanted onto the floor. Valentine saw Calvino out of the corner of his eye.

"Welcome, Vincent. Have some wine and cheese."

Valentine was distracted as he spotted the program he'd been searching for halfway down the menu showing on the screen. "The glass isn't half full," he said, his eyes on Kem.

He cleared his throat. "Please pay attention. And get a glass for Khun Vincent. Hurry, hurry or you'll miss the opening."

"I could use a drink."

"National Geographic should be called the savages' channel. This is truly remarkable family entertainment. How else can a man forge a bond with his harem? A rhetorical question. Number One likes the pagan rituals of small Indians who lived on ants and snakes in the Amazon forest. I believe she likes their diet. And Number Two is quite keen on a rite of passage for young girls in Africa where village women cut off the clitoris. Number Three is a fan of Papua New Guinea cannibals with the shrunken heads of their enemies tied around their waist. And my personal favorite is a sad one. A saga about a goat-herding family in New Zealand where there is poison in the soil and half of the goats die off from cancer. I tear up each time I see the poor goats."

"Something for the entire family," said Calvino.

Valentine looked up, hitting the Pause button. "My God, what happened to your face?" His jaw dropped as he lowered his wine glass and plate of cheese.

"I can't recommend the Harmony massage parlor."

"Some savage beat you, my good man. Did you go to the hospital? Quickly, get Khun Vincent a towel and ice from the bucket," Valentine barked at Number Two. She had just returned with a fresh wine glass.

Calvino sat in a chair a few feet away from the sofa and Valentine's harem.

"My God, my dear fellow. You have suffered serious wounds and bruising."

Calvino shrugged as Number Two pressed a towel packed with ice against the side of his face. "I trust this altercation wasn't connected with your work on my behalf."

"Valentine, you are in the clear."

"I didn't mean that. . ."

"Forget about it. If it hadn't been for a potted palm tree, it would have been a lot worse."

"A palm tree?"

"You don't want to know."

The cold pack felt as good as anything Calvino could imagine. There was an age when you got beat up and somehow a few hours later it didn't seem so bad. He had passed that age into a time when a few hours later it throbbed and ached, pain shooting in every direction. The ice cut the pain, smoothed it out; feeling numb was about as close to a painless state as he could expect. On the TV screen, a mob of youth, naked and scared, shivered in the dirt as their elders, bare-breasted, danced around pounding drums and singing.

"I tell the girls that to observe the behavior of savages is an education in itself. They can see how lucky they are to be with me. And how far they have developed. And mostly how easy it would be, if they left, to slide back into the barbarity of tribes. We are always on the edge of violence and chaos. I am afraid it is our lot. And from the look of your face, some rather nasty savages took turns attacking you."

He cuddled with all of his *sanoms* and together they watched the TV. Or what seemed like all. Maew had slipped away, found Fon and brought her back to the television room. She came inside, ignored Valentine and the TV, and walked straight over to look at Calvino's wounds. She knelt down and pulled the towel away, making a clicking noise with her tongue.

"When she makes that noise with the goats, it is never good," said Valentine, devouring another cracker. He took a sip from his wine. "Is it serious?"

Fon looked up, "He needs stitches."

"This is much better than National Geographic. I am joking. Khun Fon, please render assistance to Mr. Calvino. On second thought, you may forget that he isn't a goat. And you aren't a doctor. I think after this program ends, we should drive him into town for a proper doctor to have a look."

There was a jagged cut running above Calvino's right ear. "The cut needs stitches," Fon said to Calvino.

"Can you do it?"

She nodded. He stood up and handed the towel to Number Two. "Valentine, I'll be back. We need to talk."

"If you want my opinion, you should see a proper doctor. He could lose his ear if you're not careful. Going from Vincent Calvino to Vincent Van Gogh isn't a particularly brilliant career move. Unless, of course, you can paint."

"If I want your opinion, Valentine, I'll ask for it."

"As you wish." He picked up the remote and a National Geographic special appeared on the screen showing natives who lived in a swampy area of Australia. A poisoned dart hit a wild pig and the natives fell on the screeching animal with spears and knives. The harem watched with large, unblinking eyes.

There were only a few places in the world where a man could become a sugar daddy on a beer budget. Pattaya was one of them. *Try making that work in Sidney or London or Toronto or New York,* thought Calvino on the way out. A man couldn't live on a park bench for the amount in Pattaya that covered a *tilac*, her family, a maid and three square meals, a daily six-pack of beer and the weekly short-time hotel bill. Medium wealth bought a harem and a huge estate and a cool room to watch half-naked savages on the National Geographic channel. Calvino had begun to understand why it had been so important for Valentine to restore the equilibrium of the estate. He wasn't getting full value for his money.

Outside, he followed Fon along the path, passing the kitchen on the way to the gardener's house. The Great Dane and the two smaller dogs followed behind. The smell of blood attracted not only dogs but also flying insects. In less than a minute, he was inside the small house and Fon had opened a small medical kit. She laid out the cotton balls, alcohol, scissors, and bandages. "This is going to hurt a little," she said. "I can give you an injection."

"Do you have a bottle of Mekhong?"

Fon walked over to a cupboard and pulled out a large bottle of Mekhong, screwed off the cap and poured one finger into a glass. He watched her slip the cap back on to the bottle. "You stitch and I'll pour," said Calvino.

He knocked back three fast shots. She threaded a silver needle and expertly made four stitches to close the cut above Calvino's right ear. She put antiseptic ointment over the stitches and a bandage to cover the wound. "There, you should be alright." Her touch had been soft but sure. The needle felt cold puncturing the skin; then it burnt and stung at the same time. He threw back two more shots and shivered.

"I talked with Pramote's widow."

Fon looked puzzled. "She did this?"

"A woman did this? No, let me explain. She's the wife of the reporter who was found in the bottom of the well. He'd been shot and the killers dumped his body in the well. It looked like a hit. I remember that your husband kept newspapers in the prayer room. One of the newspapers had a story about the dead reporter. I thought there might be a connection."

"You think the same person killed my husband?"

"I am not sure." He caught his reflection in a mirror hanging from the knob of a drawer. He looked terrible. His jaw throbbed; his knuckles were stiff and raw. His gut hurt where he'd been kicked. Everything ached. All he could think about was telling Fon about Pramote's widow. "But I was thinking you should meet her. I think you'd like her."

"Why do you think that? Because we lose our husbands?"

"She has a couple of kids."

Fon finished with the bandage. Most of his ear was covered in white gaze. "Then she has better luck than me."

"The way I see it, you are both fighters. But I get the feeling you are both holding back. That you know some things that you're not talking about. Information that could lead to the killer."

"*Farang* don't understand."

If he had five baht for every time he'd heard that expression, he could have retired a wealthy man. It was the automatic conclusion of last resort. Bred in part from desperation and frustration or fear, and in part from the reality that *farang* more than likely *couldn't* understand why things happened the way they did and the reasons for accepting what was often unacceptable.

Fon was holding back. He felt it.

"How many stitches?"

"Six," she said.

"A good lottery number," said Calvino.

She smiled.

"You look good when you smile. You should try it more often."

She repacked her medical kit. "I am sorry she lost her husband."

"The problem is everyone is sorry. But no one's talking to me. How can I fit the pieces together without someone helping me understand what exactly happened?" asked Calvino. "Part of the puzzle is your husband's guru. He seemed to have a lot of influence. Your husband looked up to him, admired him, and consulted him in times of trouble. At the time of his death, your husband was in trouble, and I think he must have talked to the guru about this. So you'll understand it's not unnatural that I would want to talk to the guru directly."

She busied herself repacking the medical kit.

Calvino poured another drink from the bottle of Mekhong.

"Not so good for you. He's very close to Sia Veera."

She looked up. Touched his bandages one more time.

"Are you afraid of him?"

She nodded. "But maybe you should be, too."

He drank the shot from the glass and put it back on the table. His body ached from the kicks and punches. The pain returned, fresh and immediate like a cool breeze coming off the sea. An omen or warning that by changing a couple of variables, a cool breeze became a gale-force wind. A force of nature that sank ships. One that blew down houses and buildings. One that swept away men.

"Did your husband fear him?"

Fon turned and stored the medical case away. He watched her take an amulet on a gold chain from the cupboard. She laid it on the table in front of him. "He believed this would protect him."

"Except from Sia Veera."

"You are starting to understand."

He picked it up and put the amulet in his hand.

"Please wear it."

Calvino put the amulet back in her hands. She reached forward and put it over his head. "You will need all the protection that you can get."

TWENTY-FIVE

COLONEL Pratt sat on a blanket spread on the sand, playing the tenor sax. The sea lapped at the shore a few feet away. A white spume bubbled in the wake. The water was close enough to smell the brine. The colonel lowered his tenor sax, drew the sea into his lungs and expelled the air all at once as he brought the sax back to his lips; he poured the sea mist into his music. He remembered this deserted beach from the old days when Pattaya was a fishing village. Pattaya was fifty kilometers away. In the sixties Pattaya didn't qualify as a city. It was another village with a thin string of fluorescent lights. By the time of the R&R decade starting in the mid-sixties, Pattaya Beach Road and Pattaya 2 Road had transformed the fishing village with strips of neon. And the fishermen were replaced by men with a past that mostly didn't include a boat. Not everything from the old days had changed. What remained constant was the presence of powerful men whose orders summoned up a mixture of envy and fear. The colonel never underestimated such dark influences standing like a cobra in the tall grass ready to strike a lethal blow.

He played the sax as if to cast away the shadow that fell across his soul. Veera's shadow which, like that of all strongmen, ensured those within his power lived in fear. There were no oaths sworn or loyalty pledged except to him. Justice and right were his to decide. Forces in Bangkok had decided Veera's time had to end. They suspected but lacked sufficient evidence to establish a clear connection with terrorists in the south. There was a wisp of smoke. That was enough to signal that the time had arrived to remove Veera. But arresting Veera would not be an easy battle. The strongman continued to have a strong political base. He was fortunate to live in a world squarely divided between those who lived by instinct and those who appealed to the instincts in others. To react was to survive; to reflect was to survive with wisdom.

Colonel Pratt sensed, though, that much of the world had entered an age of reaction and survival. When he stepped back, what Colonel Pratt had were two fragments of a large puzzle. Veera, the long-time provincial godfather, and intelligence reports suggesting that a terrorist named Hasam had slipped into the province months ago. Could this have happened without Veera's knowledge and consent? Terrorists like Hasam wanted a return to the world of the clan and tribe, and the strongman. If he succeeded, on the surface their victory was one for all the Veeras. The colonel wondered if Veera was wise enough to understand what lay beneath the surface. Men like Hasam possessed a ruthless, single-minded vision. They had shown they possessed a certainty of mission: finding and destroying soft targets. Would Veera have been so blinded by money that he'd fail to grasp that Hasam represented a direct threat to his survival? That Veera himself was living near the bull's-eye of the soft target? Or had he taken money believing he could control whatever would happen next? Veera didn't understand their world. Hasam's fundamentalist paradise of true believers didn't include a guestroom for local godfathers.

The Buddha taught that all life was a cycle of suffering. To crave, to want, was to ensure never-ending suffering. The colonel believed the day would come when men of wisdom would rise up and destroy men like Veera and Hasam. Until then, the terrorists and men like Veera would fuel the ambitions of reactionary forces. Men like David Jardine had been sent to his land to engage and eliminate these forces. Jardine (who worked under the cover of the Embassy) was part of a special unit with a mission, and Pratt had been enlisted in the same cause. Pratt had come to this beach to reflect, to remember and to forget.

Colonel Pratt hit a high note at the end of a riff, lowered his sax and watched the moonlight dance on the sea. A half-dozen fishing boats were anchored in the distance. The wake from a lone patrol boat cut through the moonlight. A searchlight circled the boats like a lighthouse moving across the sea. A naval patrol boat slowly crossed towards the horizon, looking for smugglers, bandits, or terrorists. The light was a snare set for a rabbit hunkered down out of sight, trying to survive. Rarely would the men in uniform patrolling the waters offshore have a second chance to catch a couple of men on a launch, speeding to shore. That would have taken incredible luck. The word was already out that new orders and rules were in place. Pressure had been placed on everyone by the Americans. The time-honored way was to announce a crackdown. Fishing boats had to fish. No supplemental income was permitted during the crackdown. No pay-offs, no exceptions. Everyone understood the main unspoken rule: crackdowns applied on sea and land. But they were never forever. They were for a time, a cooling-off period, and then business would resume. A number of the boats hadn't bothered to go out. Fishing nets hung on the decks of those boats nearest to shore. The men stayed back drinking and playing cards, borrowing money against the time when business would return to normal.

Before he turned and looked away from the sea, Colonel Pratt said, "I wasn't certain if you could find this place Vincent."

The man had been right, thought Calvino. The spot along the beach would have taken the latest technical equipment to locate. Calvino had circled the area for nearly an hour before pulling into the right small dirt path and finding Colonel Pratt's BMW parked at the end. Calvino had driven with the windows rolled down, listening as he drove. He had walked along the beach listening. If he hadn't heard the sound of the sax in the distance, he might not ever have found Pratt sitting in the dark along the beach. Standing ten feet behind the colonel, Calvino was thinking he didn't know how Pratt did this trick of knowing someone had come up behind him. The eyes in the back of the head had served him well in the past. Calvino had been careful to make no noise. This wasn't about noise; Pratt had sensed his presence. Calvino sat on the edge of the blanket.

"I heard the sax. I was thinking, you play Miles Davis real good."

"He was a genius. I am a cop who plays at the sax. I don't pretend to be real good. I like looking at things the way they are."

"And how are they?"

"You don't look so good. And you've been at the Mekhong."

"Bingo. You win any teddy bear on the top shelf."

Colonel Pratt cradled the tenor sax and looked at the sea. "There's some intelligence about an attack. Who, where, how. . . the details, no one is sure. Stuff is picked up on intercepts. Some of it useful, most of it not. This time the people who work this side of things say something bad may happen. And it may happen soon."

"I tracked down the owner of the Greek restaurant. Pramote had his card. All the owner was interested in was staying in business. A reporter died. He didn't care. The dead had his name card. So what?"

"Terror destroys the mood to eat out. People stay home. They don't want to die. The owner was thinking about his future," said Colonel Pratt.

"People forget soon enough. The bombs in Bali killed over two hundred, and everyone said no one would go to Bali for a decade. A year later, the tourists were back in Bali."

"What if they had killed 200,000? What, then?"

"You think something like that is in motion here?"

"The people in the South can't be bought. I admire that. But if they decide to expand their violence, that I can't admire. I must do all I can to stop this bad thing from happening."

Not being able to buy off the militants in the South was a challenge. They had to be dealt with on matters of principle and that was the biggest challenge of all. Religion was in the blood. So was murder. The average was thirty seconds for *that* blood to complete the cycle from the lungs to the heart through the body. A religious impulse or a murderous one followed the same pattern.

"You think something bad is about to happen?" asked Calvino.

"But it doesn't matter what I think," said Pratt.

"You know what I want?"

Pratt turned his head and looked at Calvino for the first time. "What?"

"To find out if Valentine's gardener killed himself or was murdered, and then I can go home. I want to go back to my office and my life."

"I remember when you were a man of ideals and principles."

"You get older and wiser, Pratt. What can you change? Look at the police force, the people on the take, hands in other people's pockets, accumulating wealth. And where does that leave you? On a beach, playing Miles Davis on your sax, on a mission to do someone else's dirty work. Collar a local gangster who is out of political favor. One gangster muscled another mobster for power and money. If it just stopped at gangsters then it could be contained, but it's more than that. The system gorges on the weak and helpless and if you get in the way, you end up stuffed down the bottom of a well. There are a few men like you who know this is a rotten deal. Some of them write letters or make speeches about brotherhood and compassion for one's fellow man. They are the freaks, Pratt. They actually believe that the engine that moves this well-oiled machine from day to day won't roll right over them, flattening them."

"What you are saying is, give up. That there's no point in trying to do right?"

Calvino kicked off his shoes and pulled off his socks, rolled his trousers up and walked into the sea. "Only with your family and friends. The rest of the world, they are on their own. There is no real hope for them. If they really looked down, you know what they would see?"

Colonel Pratt watched as his friend walked up to his knees into the sea.

"What would they see, Vincent?"

"That there is no net. They can't trust what they are told. They don't know who to believe or what to believe."

"You want to pack it in?"

Calvino turned with his back to the sea. He raised his arms.

"A long time ago, in New York, the Chinese Triad had a contract to kill you. You could have run back to Thailand. But you stayed and faced what you had to do."

"What I am trying to say, Vincent, is that I am not certain I can give you the same protection here. I made a promise to your mother when you came to my country. I told her I would look after you."

"Pratt, you didn't run away."

"I'll have one of my men drive you back tonight."

"You're not listening to me. You didn't run."

Colonel Pratt looked out at the sea. "It's not what I want. I look at your face. You've been beaten up. Next time could be much worse, Vincent. The people we are looking for have no problem with killing."

"The statute of limitation ran out on that promise to my mother some years ago. Didn't I tell you that?"

Calvino splashed with the palm of his hand. The water soaked his face and shirt. He splashed again. "I drank a little Mekhong," he said. He shook his head until the stitched part of his eye throbbed. "Okay, I am feeling better. Feeling alive. And what exactly did these spooks tell you about an attack?"

"Some bad men have been reported coming in. From Laos, Cambodia, Malaysia, Burma. It takes a handful of such men to change everyone's life."

Calvino walked back and sat on the blanket. "I know the party line. What I asked is who came to blow up somebody or something in Pattaya?"

"You could be back in your bed in Bangkok in a couple of hours. I'll see you have another case tomorrow."

"Do I look like a charity case? Is that what you're saying? *Go home, you can't cut it here. I'll throw you a bone to gnaw on. You won't go hungry, my old friend. You still have a few teeth left to chew.* Is that what you're saying to me?"

Colonel Pratt put the mouthpiece of the sax to his lips and played. When he stopped, Calvino had hunched over on the blanket, shivering in the night.

"What do you want, Vincent?"

"I want to talk to a man named Veera."

"Do you have any idea who that is?"

"He's *the* man."

"And you think Veera had Valentine's gardener killed?"

Calvino shrugged, looked away. "I don't know. But I'd like to ask him about a man named Sawai. He's a guru, a seer, and he was a frequent visitor to Prasit's house. I listened to one of Sawai's tapes. Prasit kept the tapes in his prayer room. Sawai seems to be in the spiritual guidance business."

"You are trying to square the circle."

"Circle? Square, or maybe it's a straight line with no connection. But I'd like to find out."

"Why not talk with Sawai?"

Calvino was prepared for this question. "In Thailand you taught me that it is better to start at the top and work your way down. You can never work your way up."

Pratt smiled, wishing he had left certain lessons untaught, as this ex-New Yorker sooner or later proved himself a more than capable student.

TWENTY-SIX

VEERA had built his estate one kilometer north of the fishing village. He had a stone wall carved by hand into the face of a cliff. One stone at a time had been cemented into place; hundreds of hands and machines had worked to erect a defensive wall, and from the top, looking out, one saw nothing but blue sea. He built walls within walls. To keep out barbarians, to keep out intruding eyes. When he finished with his great wall, he had a fifteen-foot whitewashed concrete structure that wrapped around five acres of land. Calvino braked at the main gate and waited as security men ran mirrors on long poles underneath his car, checked the trunk, made him pop the hood and checked the engine. The lid of the trunk slammed, then the hood, and they waved him inside and shut the gate behind. Two security guards escorted him from his car across the circular drive to the main house.

As he drove ahead, he saw Veera's four-story house with its Doric columns and arched windows. The building had morphed, for a moment, into a knock-off of the White House, with added features lifted from a high-class private members club complete with fountains and statues of goddesses and roaring bronze lions and rearing horses on hind legs. Flapping on top of a twenty-foot high white pole was the Thai flag. Veera was definitely a high wall man. Outer walls enclosed the immediate beach. The compound had been built to use the sea as a buffer, a defense position on the flank of the compound. The sea was also an escape hatch. As Calvino got out of his car, he looked below at the wharf and at several luxury boats rocking in the gentle sea. An arsenal of weapons and ammo had been stored in the compound and on the yachts.

Inside the gates and into the central courtyard, Calvino was transported light years away from the fishing village. Inside the door to the main house, two more security men ran airport-like scanners up and down his clothing and then patted him down before nodding that he was free to go. Another guard led him down a long corridor and through a set of enormous doors, which opened into a room large enough to park a plane. A plump man with thick, black hair combed straight back, wearing a blue silk shirt and dark trousers, sat behind a large teak desk piled with stacks of papers. A half-dozen *luuk-nong* in dark designer glasses, wires snaking into an ear, were positioned around the room like a human shield for their boss, keeping a respectful distance. The chatter he heard as he entered stopped the moment Calvino came into the room. The men in the room snapped into work mode. On any official event attended by major politicians or *jao poh*, these hard, no-nonsense men in their late twenties and early thirties with short-hair cuts and hidden eyes were everywhere from the parking lot to the lobby to the corridors with their cellphones and handguns. They wore traditional raw silk outfits: shirts with a high Chinese collar over matching trousers. The effect was to create the impression of a uniform worn by members of the same elite unit. The shirts, worn outside the trousers, were tailor-made to conceal a weapon.

On Veera's left was a young, slender Thai who appeared to have just broken into his twenties. He wasn't suited up in a *luuk nong's* uniform and that set him apart as someone special, above the crowd. Boyish, more relaxed in the way he stood, casually chewing gum, and in much closer contact to the man behind the desk, he had an easy smile. He wore a baseball cap turned around with the bill facing back, and a New York Mets T-shirt tucked into a pair of jeans. No belt, no socks.

"You must be Vincent," he said in a perfect American accent. "This is my dad. You want something to drink?"

"Water's okay," said Calvino.

"Sorry, but it looks like someone beat the shit out of you." The young man had an open smile.

"Water on the rocks." He liked the kid's style. "A piece of advice, kid. Avoid the Harmony massage parlor. Unless you are into tough love."

The kid laughed. "That place is crap. Low rent. I can take you to a much better place. . ."

The old man at the desk put up his hand and the kid stopped.

One of the *luuk nong* brought Calvino a tumbler filled with Johnny Walker Black. He knew that it was Black because the bottle was on the tray and the tumbler next to it. Calvino took the glass and looked around for a place to sit.

Veera had barely looked up from his paperwork—just to shut up the kid—and had looked at Calvino long enough to acknowledge that someone else had entered his presence. Cellphones on the desk constantly rang and one of the *luuk nong* answered in a whisper.

"My father's English isn't that great. He asked me to stick around and help translate. It's no problem. I do it all the time."

"Why all the heavy security?" asked Calvino.

Veera's son shrugged. "Not everyone's a happy camper. And we don't want the unhappy ones pulling their trailer loaded with trouble inside our compound. So we have to be careful who comes inside. You have no idea how lucky you are to be here. My father is a very busy man. But he can spend some time answering your questions."

Pratt had resources that never failed to impress Calvino. As they had walked along the beach, Pratt had promised that he would do what he could to arrange a meeting with Veera, but he couldn't promise anything. Calvino understood and thought it wouldn't happen. Then somehow Pratt had managed to get an appointment for him to meet the great man himself. No easy achievement, thought Calvino. Being a colonel helped. Veera distrusted foreigners ever since a foreign journalist had written an article about him in the *International Herald Tribune* describing him as an old-style godfather with blood on his hands and multiple sets of books for each of his businesses. Ever since, Veera had avoided *farangs* and kept a subscription to the *Trib* to see if there was a follow-up story. There never was.

The kid leaned over and whispered to his father, who put down his pen, folded his hands and studied Calvino. The Chinese-Thais had a technique for reading meaning into the structure of a man's face—*ngow-heng*. A large forehead meant a man could be trusted. The face was scanned to determine whether it had balance. There were three parts of the face that required harmony—the forehead, the tip of the nose to the eyebrows, and the tip of the nose of the chin. Drooping eyes were a bad sign, while a fleshy nose suggested wealth. For a couple of minutes Veera said nothing, taking in every element, including the stitches alongside Calvino's face. The bandages had been removed and the skin was blotchy, red and puffy with the seven stitches Fon had sewed visible to the old man. One of the *luuk nong* handed Veera a cellphone. His son translated as Veera spoke into the phone.

"If you can't get the 1/4" then buy the 3/8" sheet metal. It has to be put in tomorrow."

Veera handed the cellphone back as another *luuk nong* handed him another cellphone, "I don't want to hear delay. The cupboards were supposed to be installed in all forty-seven rooms two weeks ago. And now you are telling me another week. Maybe. And why can't you go ahead with the floors? We've already paid for the material."

The phone on his desk rang and he had two phones, one to each ear. "Why can't you fix the generator? Then get the part from Bangkok."

He handed the phones back to waiting hands. "Five minutes, no more calls," he ordered one of his *luuk nong*.

He folded his hands on his desk, his jeweled rings—diamonds and rubies and emeralds—glimmering. He switched to English. "I only go to school for six years. At eleven I worked on a fishing boat. I saved and saved until I could buy a boat of my own. Then I borrowed and bought a second boat, and a pickup truck to take the catch to market. I started to buy the catch from other boats. I invested in a truck company, and then in a hotel in Pattaya during the Vietnam War and you American GIs came to Thailand for R&R. I built road, schools, hospitals, and a football field. I worked to help my people and my village. Soon everyone comes running to me. *Help me do this, help me do that.* They think, *ah, Veera, you a rich man, you have an easy life. Everything you want, you have, everything comes easy to you.* That's what they think. But let me tell you, the more money you have, the more problem come to you. Every day is a headache.

"I have five *mia nois.* Number Three gets a BMW. Number Four gets a Volvo. Are they happy? Number Two says her car is a year older. It's a Benz. Her car is older sure, but it is worth more money. Doesn't matter. It's a year older. She's losing face. She cries that I don't love her. And the *mia luang*, the major wife, she wants an eight- carat diamond. Do you have any idea how much an eight-carat diamond costs? Until she gets her way, she's turned the kids against their father. You see this boy here? He thinks that I am mean to his mother. I don't show her respect. His brother and sister the same. What is my reward for years of support of the family, all the gifts, holidays, moments of joy and happiness? I get the silent treatment from my wife. She has lobbied *mia noi* number three and four to support her side. How much has she bribed or threatened them? Not even I can find that out. You see all these men in this room? They can't find out. Or if they do, they are afraid to tell me. You understand? My men are afraid to tell me. Of course, it doesn't stop there. A second faction comes along against Number One, Number Two and Number Five. They have decided I should take each of them to France this year. They can't find France on a map. They can't even tell me why they want to go to France. It doesn't matter. They've decided I must take them. Tomorrow these alliances will shift. Like all politics, there is no loyalty, only shifting interest. Thai politics is clean compared to the politics of the family.

"See the white envelopes on the table? There are dozens of them and inside is my money. Every day there will be a dozen more. For anniversaries, for funerals and weddings, for someone's birthday. This one is for a famous police officer, and this one, and this one. For the highway patrol. For the irrigation department. For the coast guard and fishery officials. For this councilman or that MP. For a customs officer. It is like living inside a nest alongside a hundred octopuses, and every day you wake up and find hundreds of tentacles swimming around your face. I have dreams about the suckers crawling on my skin. Not dreams, nightmares. Am I against corruption? Please may it end tomorrow. I want honesty. The bookkeeping of corruption is a nightmare. You don't dare write anything down. You have to remember everything and keep the accounts in your head. It is like dealing with wives. One gets this, they ask the other *how much did he give you? Oh, that much*, they come back, *you gave her more than me, what am I nang bam rer*? You know that is the ultimate insult. It means that you only want a woman for sex. When a woman accuses you of that, you have no choice.

"So you dig deep and fork over more cash and the cycle starts again. I sometimes wonder how it is that I have enough money for a bowl of noodles. One kid is at San Diego State University, another at the University of Western Australia, another at university in Newcastle. I have kids in more countries than the UN. I can't find half of these places on the map. But do I have their bank account numbers? Do I keep them? I have one son wanting to marry a local girl. I have a daughter wanting to marry a low-ranking police officer What can I do? Kill everyone that I think they shouldn't marry? Kill everyone who can't get a part for a generator or doesn't put in cupboards like he promised? Kill each person who lets me down? Kill everyone who comes in wanting a favor, a handout, or cheats me, or lies to me? I'd have blood flowing in rivers. Next life I come back as a Catholic. I want to be reborn as the pope. No women troubles and I get to be infallible."

When Valentine stared into his mirror did he see Veera staring back?

Veera gave the impression that he'd agreed to a meeting because he wanted an outside audience to get a few things off his chest. He looked exhausted, slumping back in his chair behind the mini-mountains of white envelopes. His son sat on the edge of the desk waiting for his old man to catch his breath. He'd heard the same complaints a hundred times.

"Dad's having a bad hair day," said the kid.

Calvino liked the kid even more.

This had been an easy translation duty for the kid. The old man had done most of the talking in near perfect English.

Being a translator for his father gave the kid face without having to open his mouth.

Only sheer will seemed to be keeping Veera going for another day, making another decision and resolving that somehow he was creating some greater good amongst a crowd of ungratefuls about to storm his compound.

The amulets around Veera's neck broadcast his belief in the occult. Calvino pulled an amulet from his pocket. Fon had folded it into his hand, and said, "It was around my husband's neck when he was found." For a man to hang himself with an amulet was unthinkable. She had intended to be rid of an amulet that had no power to protect her husband. It represented bad fortune. Failure and death. Calvino placed it on Veera's desk.

"Do you recognize this amulet?" asked Calvino.

Veera looked down and then up at Calvino. He picked it up and examined it closely. He turned over in the palm of his hand and closed his hand.

"It was owned by someone who once worked for you."

"That amulet protects a man from bullets."

"The owner is dead. Hanged. His brother had the identical amulet. He was shot."

Amulets didn't always work.

"I have many people working for me."

"The man I am interested in was named Prasit. He was a gardener. Before that he worked for you. Some say he killed himself. Others say he was killed."

"How can I know every person who works for me or claims he works for me?"

"Do you give an amulet to all of your employees?" Calvino looked around the room at the *luuk nong*. By the time he turned around and faced Veera again, everyone was smiling.

Veera's smile widened. This wasn't a happy or pleased smile. It was one that seethed from being made to look stupid in front of his *luuk nong*. He handed the amulet back to Calvino. "I said I don't remember Prasit. I gave this amulet out to many people." He paused as Calvino slipped the amulet around his neck.

"You don't remember Prasit," said Calvino.

The old man thought for a moment. "I sent flowers to his funeral. I was sorry he died."

"Prasit was close to Sawai," said Calvino, dropping the formal, polite "khun" from the name of both men. It was time to get down to business. "I'd like to talk with Sawai. I know he is your good friend."

"Ajarn Sawai, he's a very good man. He knows many things. You talk to him ten minutes and you feel something special comes into your life. I'll phone him and tell him that you want to talk to him," said Veera, raising his arms. "I think no problem with that. Anything else I can do to help you? You let me know."

Calvino rose from his chair, leaving his glass of Johnny Walker Black untouched. "The reporter who was killed. The one who was doing a story about the trafficking of Khmer women. I heard he came to the village asking questions."

"This was a very sad story. I talked to the police about this case several times. I tell them true. No one in my village would hurt that man. They have no reason. We have no prostitutes from Cambodia in our village. That business is no good. I am against those people. You ask anyone, they will tell you Veera has no need to do the dirty business."

The conversation was at an end. The kid took out his gum, balled it between his finger and thumb before sticking it onto a piece of tissue. Glancing at his watch, he said, "My father's pretty busy. So if you will excuse him, he needs to get back to work.

He was a better as a time-keeper than as a translator.

Veera rose from his desk. "Your friend said you are good on security. A professional security man, he said. What if I give you a contract to work as my personal security consultant? I can start you at 100,000 baht a month plus bonus. You give me advice on security matters. Tell me where I can improve. Many people try to harm me. You don't know how jealous Thai people can be of each other. *Id-cha taa-ron*. You know this expression? It is like your English expression, 'green with envy,' only it translates what we see that others have and want so much that it makes our eyes hot. A good security man can keep those hot eyes from burning me. What do you say, Khun Vincent? Can you work for me?"

Calvino's Law: If you don't go for the bait, you have a better chance to avoid getting caught in the trap.

"Let me think about it. You will make that call to Sawai?"

Veera picked up the phone and dialed. He spoke quickly and hung up.

"He meet you in one hour. You see how good you are? I hardly know you, and you have me working for you. You should say 'yes' to my offer."

The real reason for the meeting became clear. Colonel Pratt had sold Calvino as a possible security expert. An experienced guru who might be persuaded to sign on. Only it hadn't worked out that way. Calvino left the compound without saying whether he'd take the offer. The kid knew the answer to that one. The old man likely knew as well. When a man was desperate—Valentine being a case in point—then a rich man would pay anything to achieve one, modest goal: peace of mind. Leaving the compound Calvino thought about how one man like Veera could have been the poster boy for corruption, cronyism, and the absence of law or principle. Or from Veera's point of view, he would have seen himself as the poster boy for generosity, friendship and protection. Whatever label was put on the threads, they formed the fabric of society. Pull one out, then rip out a second one and the whole carpet risked disintegration into the familiar pattern of a Singapore or Finland. No one could separate the relative positions of the threads; good and bad were woven together. As were right and wrong. Ditto, fair and unfair. Everyone wanted to preserve the flexibility, default expression of smiles, *mai pen rai*, and gracious *wais*. How was that accomplished? No one had the slightest idea. Veera and those around him had a certain way of seeing the world, of being in the world, and of accepting the meaning and value of life. Prasit would have understood that as his widow understood it. What Calvino wanted was more basic; he searched for a way to account for the death of one man. And in the case where accountability rules marched to their own drummer, that was a tall order.

TWENTY-SEVEN

SAWAI lived in a rambling teak house sheltered behind a grove of coconut trees. It was impossible to see the house from the road. He had hidden himself away in a walled compound. The overgrown grounds had spawned a couple of inbred generations of feral cats and mangy dogs. During daylight hours, villagers often arrived asking the local guru to read their horoscope, palms, and cards. He predicted their future prospects, counseled them on how to best avoid bad omens, and claimed to cure their ills. Sawai was a faith healer and seer, and not above using hypnosis to seduce village girls. His house and activities would have provided hours of viewing on Valentine's Savage Channel. The three other houses in the compound were left unoccupied. The last occupants had fled, having claimed that ghosts and the howling of wolves haunted the grounds. It was more likely dogs howling, and the shadows of cats hunting lizards in the tall grass. From the upper windows, Sawai had been seen standing naked, his lips dripping with blood.

All of this information came from the kid. Veera's son.

The kid had walked alongside Calvino as they left the main house. The old man had ended the interview by answering a cellphone and sighing deeply as one of his wives berated him. Outside, standing beside Calvino's car, the son handed him a key. "You can use this key to open the gate. He's not all that friendly. So he probably won't come down and open it for you. Just let yourself into the compound. You'll find him in the second house on the left. Knock on the door. He won't necessarily answer. Feel free to let yourself in. You'll find him upstairs. Father phoned him. He's expecting you. And, hey, that story about Ajarn Sawai drinking blood and running around naked, it's probably an urban legend."

"Village legend," said Calvino. He looked at the key. "How do I get this back to you?"

"Leave it with Ajarn Sawai. One more thing," he said.

Calvino had the feeling the young man had been waiting to get him alone. The kid seemed lonely, as if he didn't have a lot of people to talk to inside the compound. And those who wanted to talk were scheming for something from the old man.

"What's that?"

"At Boston University I took a course in Russian literature," he said. "Did you ever hear the name Rasputin?"

"Wasn't he a mystic?"

"Man, he had power over the tsars. He had them in the palm of his hand. And he had hordes of women followers. Today he'd have his own TV show, limos, private jet, the works."

"Wasn't he the one who claimed to see the future?" asked Calvino.

The young man pulled around his baseball cap and drew the bill down over his forehead. "Yeah, a clairvoyant."

"Rasputin was a hard man to kill," said Calvino.

Veera's son nodded and gave Calvino the high-five. "I like your style," he said. "I can't remember anyone turning down the old man's offer of money. I've seen money buy everything. I mean everyone and everything."

"Does it buy Sawai?"

A crooked smile ran across the kid's face. "Yeah, you can bet on it."

Twenty minutes after leaving Veera's compound, Calvino stepped inside Sawai's compound.

At the main gate, he fished out the key and opened the Yale lock. The lock had been threaded through a heavy chain. A medieval-looking chain like that shouted that the person inside wanted to be left alone. He closed the gate and walked through the grounds. Several cats scattered and a dog barked and charged until Calvino leaned down and pretended to pick up a stone to throw. Calvino passed the deserted cottages and walked up the stairs to the main house. He knocked twice before opening the door and letting himself in. He removed his shoes and left them beside a row of shoes near the door. He had a look through the downstairs rooms. The sparsely furnished rooms were dark and hot. The salt from his sweat made the wound slicing up the side of his ear sting. He wiped the sweat away. Two steps later, he was dripping sweat again. He walked between two long teak beds. Bamboo mats covered the floor. The shutters on the windows opened onto the garden and the sunlight illuminated cobwebs around the hinges, suggesting the windows downstairs were permanently open. A gecko flicked its tongue and then darted across the wall. The dust and cobwebs were strong evidence that there was no maid in the guru's future. The kid had indicated Sawai had been bought. From the look of the place, he had sold out cheap. It was hard to imagine that a famous guru who lived alone didn't have servants. Combine face with an obsession for cleanliness, and bingo—maids, gardeners, drivers, and cooks materialized in the most humble of surroundings.

Calvino climbed the stairs to the second floor.

"Hello," he called out.

A film of gray smoke hung in the air as Calvino approached. The smoke came from an open door at the end of the corridor. Calvino walked down the corridor and peered inside.

Sawai sat on a bamboo mat smoking a cigarette. He flicked a long ash into a bowl filled with unfiltered butts.

"I am Vincent Calvino."

Sawai nodded. "I've been expecting you. Please, sit down." The voice was the same as on the tape Calvino had heard in Prasit's prayer room; it was more formal, less comforting, with an edge of suspicion.

This wasn't exactly Thai hospitality at its best. A visitor had been expected but the compound was bolted shut. He hadn't been invited into the guru's house. The shadow that fell between expectation and invitation covered guest relations in a fog of ambiguity. He would still have been waiting at the gate if he hadn't broken inside the compound using a spare key.

Sawai, like most chain smokers, had yellowish fingers; he also had the large, unblinking eyes of an executioner. He looked like he'd been freshly shaved. A scent of cologne rose from where he sat. His dress was simple: a collarless white cotton shirt and dark trousers. Joss sticks burnt in clay pots on either side of his prayer table. Through the haze of smoke, Sawai's face, round and fleshy, looked more Chinese than Thai. Behind the guru, on the sofa, two young girls no more than fourteen or fifteen read comic books, sneaking a look at the *farang* who'd come into the room. They wore school uniforms and lounged with a degree of comfort that led Calvino to believe they had been in the room before. It looked like an afternoon ritual. After school, go and see the guru, read comics, watch the mystic smoke, his eyes falling on their young bodies. A fan rotated, moving the air and ruffling the pages of their comic books. An advance warning from Veera was suddenly an understandable precaution, thought Calvino.

"Has anyone done your chart, Mr. Calvino?"

This was an interesting question. Thais inevitably called everyone including *farang* by their first names.

"No, but I have a secretary who keeps my bank book."

One of the students offered Calvino a glass of water. She slid along the floor like a slave servant of a hundred years ago, keeping her head lower than his chest. Having delivered the water, she pulled herself across the polished teak floor and resumed her place on the sofa. The buttons on her white blouse were undone, the outline of her breasts showing as she leaned forward. Calvino took a sip of the water. There was a tattoo of a coiled snake on her breasts. She lingered for a second too long. Her fingers brushed against his. He could smell her perfume.

"The water's ice cold. How do you do that?"

Her smile wasn't the innocent smile of a schoolgirl. "I make cold. I make hot."

"That makes you a thermos," said Calvino.

"Sia Veera said you had a sense of humor. That is good in a man. Women love a man with a good sense of humor. You make her laugh and she belongs to you forever," Sawai said.

"Do you make these girls laugh?"

He ignored the question, smiling. "What year were you born?"

The guru was very smooth and in control of his turf. "Year of the Dog."

"That makes you fiercely loyal to your friends. They are faithful and obedient."

Freud wrote that dreams were a kind of hallucination. Calvino wondered if he were dreaming inside the guru's house. Beautiful, nubile girls with long, slender legs stretching out like cats on the sofa. The guru would have felt at ease in Valentine's compound, as Valentine would in his. He started to wonder if the two men had ever met.

He had a number of questions: Was this staged for Calvino's benefit? What kind of game was Sawai playing? What game had he played with Valentine's gardener? Sitting across from the guru, the whispering, giggling schoolgirls in the background, Calvino had an idea why Veera's son had linked the guru to Rasputin, who also had a highly developed taste for women and orgies. And like Rasputin, it would be difficult to pin down Sawai's religious affiliations.

"I'd like to ask you a few questions," said Calvino.

"Anyone who comes at the invitation of Sia Veera is free to ask whatever questions he wishes." The amulets around his neck rattled as he shifted position.

From what Calvino had seen, it seemed that the guru's beliefs covered a range of themes—Buddhism, Hinduism, the Tao, Spiritualism, and early Hugh Hefner. His religion was served up like the small bowls of pepper, sugar, salt and sauces that a Thai restaurant delivered with a bowl of noodles. Sawai expertly spiced his client's spiritual food to suit their individual taste. Like all great chefs, Sawai had mastered the art of hooking repeat customers; those who took the bait became loyal, and loyal people did favors, brought gifts, gave him money. Local students stripped down and, in exchange for his gifts, lent him their bodies. If he was in direct contact with the other worlds, there was little in the house and compound to show that his supernatural buddies had given him advance tips on lottery numbers, horse race winners or stock exchange tips.

"Nice house," said Calvino.

"Sia allows me to occupy this house. Thanks to his generosity I can carry out my mission."

"What is your mission?"

"Bringing enlightenment."

The Buddha complex in spades, thought Calvino. Here was a country guru with a personal mission, bringing spiritual growth to his village while kicking back, locking the gates, and relaxing with a couple of young girls. It was the kind of work that would have attracted a lot of applicants. He must have some talent.

Discovering that Veera owned the well-preserved teak house in a largely unoccupied compound came as no surprise. Nor was it unexpected that Sawai lived in the house rent-free with his groupies bringing cold water for his guests and clients. Calvino guessed the guru had a finger in many pies. Close to the main source of power in the community, his power would only increase.

"Did you know a gardener named Prasit?"

"A sad case," said Sawai. He fingered a string of worry beads. The beads clicked, the only sound in the silence.

"You knew him well?"

"Very well."

"You went to his house?"

"Often. But his wife, Fon, she was a non-believer."

"What did Prasit believe in?"

"Spirits who could protect him. I tried to give him strength."

"Why did he need strength?"

"Because of his past. He did some terrible things, and the weight of his past was heavy for him to carry. The burden became too heavy."

"You think he killed himself?"

The guru nodded and sipped tea from a round Chinese cup.

"What if I told you he'd been murdered?"

Calvino watched the guru slowly put the Chinese cup back on the table. One of the girls quickly left the sofa and refilled it from a shiny porcelain pot. "Murdered by whom?"

"That's what I'd like to know. I thought you might have some idea."

The guru closed his eyes, breathed in deeply and slowly exhaled.

"Someone close to him," said Sawai.

Calvino raised an eyebrow, pulling the stitches over his right ear. The guru had told him nothing. If Prasit had been murdered, it was hardly likely that it would have been the random act of a stranger.

"What's that mean?"

Sawai's eyes opened. His fingers splayed out on the table. Long, manicured fingernails. "He was fearful of his past. I can tell you what I've told no other person. Prasit did some bad things. Not that he was bad. But sometimes good men bend to the will of others."

"What kind of bad things?"

"He carried out contracts."

"He killed for money."

The guru's eyelids half closed. His voice softened in the soothing, ethereal tones that had been recorded on Prasit's tape. The ligaments in Calvino's legs twitched. Sawai could transform himself in an instant the way a truly professional con man could switch roles on a dime. "He killed many men," said Sawai. "And he couldn't put this past away from his thought. I can say that he was a man consumed by his guilt and sin. No one could save him. I sent him spiritual guides and taught him how to call these guides to his service. All he had to do was allow those spirits into his heart. At first, these spirits gave Prasit comfort. But his sadness was too deep and not even my powers could save him."

"What about Khun Prasit's brother, Sombat? He was found shot. Was that someone close to the brother, too?"

"Sombat was drug dealer. They have a short life in Thailand."

"Fon said Sombat was never known to use drugs. They were planted on him after he was killed."

"One can never know the truth about another person."

Calvino nodded. An image of the editor, Mike, flashed through his mind. That was the first piece of truth to come from the guru, he thought. "Prasit told you his brother was a drug dealer?"

Sawai was silent for a moment. "They worked together. That's all I know."

"I have information there was a third man," said Calvino. He was bluffing, and waited to see if the bluff would be called. If the man could see events happening in the future, he could certainly see Calvino was holding a hand that should be called.

"Ton?"

"That's the one," said Calvino.

A long sigh followed from the guru and he drank his tea. Things were going in a direction that he obviously didn't like. "What do you want with him?"

"I want to meet him. Ton. That's his name, right? Can you arrange a meeting?"

The guru slurped his tea. The joss sticks had burned away. He removed several more from a plastic pack and carefully stuck them in the vase. He lit them and then a cigarette, inhaling the smoke deeply before letting it coil from his nose.

"I can arrange, Mr. Calvino."

Calvino wasn't certain what was more disturbing—the outright refusal to help or the too-quick willingness to assist. A more drawn-out, calculated and open-ended reply would have better fitted the character of such a man.

"One more thing—when was the last time you saw Prasit alive?"

Sawai withdrew the cigarette from his lips. "A couple of days before he died."

Calvino watched his eyes. A slight flutter crossed his face; those eyelids that didn't blink moved. His jaws flinched. He was lying through his teeth, thought Calvino. "How often do you see Sia Veera?"

The question deflected Sawai back to comfortable territory. His face relaxed. "Every day. I make a daily chart. There are auspicious times and dates for business. If you know how to predict these moments, you can provide a great service to others. But it takes great concentration. I can't be interrupted. That's why the gate is locked."

"Veera appreciates your guidance," said Calvino. He laid Prasit's amulet on the table before the guru. Sawai picked it up and examined it with an eyepiece.

"I help Sia Veera see his destiny."

"What do you make of this amulet?"

He lowered the eyepiece and laid the amulet on the table.

"Over the years, I've given many amulets to Sia Veera. He uses them for his protection and for the protection of his men. I may have given this one to him." For someone who was so certain about the future, the guru had a habit of making vague and disturbingly imprecise answers about the past.

Veera was downstream in the amulet distribution racket. Calvino figured that one or both of them was lying about the amulets. To connect Veera and Sawai to the dead gardener with an amulet was evidence of a relationship. It could mean nothing as handing out amulets was a common occurrence. Or, depending on the amulet, it could be a reward for service, or mean that special protection was conferred. Sawai handed the amulet back to Calvino.

"My duty is to guide Sia Veera so he avoids conflict and problems. A powerful amulet like this can help. Like powerful men everywhere, he has enemies. Such men wish to destroy him. He needs to know the path that leads him away from danger and pain. You are a *farang*. You don't understand how Thai people think. You believe what I do is based on superstition. But you are mistaken because you let your logic and science crowd out another world just because you can't see or prove its existence."

"It is a specially powerful amulet," said Calvino.

"Quite rare," said Sawai.

Not rare enough for the Prasit's widow to keep.

"Valuable?"

"It would bring a good sum," said Sawai.

Fon had wanted no money from the object. She wanted the amulet to find its way back through the mist of time and place and into the hands of the person who had given it her husband. She wished it to return as an omen.

"Even if it had been worn by a man who hanged himself?"

Sawai eyed the amulet and sat back, arms folded around his chest.

"What is it I can help you with?"

"I have a question. With all of your powers, why couldn't you help Prasit? Or did you see into the future and know that he would die?"

"I can lead a man by showing him the way, giving him spiritual guides he can call on, but I can't force him to choose a way he doesn't wish to go."

Calvino rose onto his knees. He remembered the tapes in Prasit's prayer room and how Fon had said Prasit had listened to them over and over again. "One more thing. As you seem to know about everything that happens in this village, did you ever meet a reporter named Pramote?"

"When I saw his face, I knew he was a dead man," said the guru.

"How could you know this?"

"I have a link to the future. I see things that will happen. There is no changing what will be. Nothing anyone does can alter the outcome."

"And when you saw me come through the door, what future did you see?"

"That you are doomed to love a woman you can never have."

Sawai opened a wooden box and removed an amulet. He looked at it closely and then held it out to Calvino. "Take this with you. It is very powerful. Wear it and you will have luck and happiness."

Calvino took the amulet. "So far I've managed to live alright without either."

Sawai nodded at the two teenage girls. "Would you like to take the girls with you?"

"Take them where?" asked Calvino.

"To your room of course. They might change your luck."

"I thought the amulet was supposed to do that," said Calvino.

"A man with such a sense of humor is always the saddest of men."

"The saddest is *yuen pen kai ta phang*," said Calvino. The Thai proverb for the blurry gray-eyed chicken that isn't disturbed by the heavy rain, or the idiot who refuses to see the danger of destruction about to fall on his head.

The guru sucked his teeth. "There's another Thai saying about chickens you should learn: *kai long*."

This phrase described the chicken that pecked the ground for seeds without knowing it had pecked itself into the center of a pack of wolves. It was a threat and a warning.

"If you can arrange the meeting with Ton, I'll make an effort to live with my sadness and watch out for the wolves."

On the way out, Calvino had a funny feeling that it was Veera's kid who had made him understand that he was walking into a setup. Calvino's Law: Just because you are at the top of the food chain doesn't mean you can't get eaten.

TWENTY-EIGHT

FON saw him in the distance as she groomed Wagner's brown-and-white dappled neck. Calvino passed alongside the row of rooms, stopped and talked briefly with Som, then continued with a measured, steady walk as if he knew where he was going and what he wanted when he got there. She had a feeling as he reached the gate that he'd discovered something; a piece of information that she had withheld. Now he'd returned to confront her, asking more painful questions, twisting her words, bending her memory and warping, devitalizing her spirit. She ran the brush along Wagner's spine. It was just a matter of time before he found certain things out about her husband. She had wanted to tell him—she was so close to the zone of disclosure—but couldn't bring herself to confide in a *farang* she hardly knew. A man hired by the very man who held her in contempt.

Calvino waved at her as he closed the gate and walked into the enclosure. Her hair was braided and the braids were pulled back with clips, showing face and throat. The hairstyle made her look younger.

"Som said I'd find you here," said Calvino.

She looked at the stitches she had sewn around his ear. There was still a red puffy, ragged line. "Your cut looks better."

"Someone asked if I'd had a face lift."

She smiled. "What did you tell them?"

"Only on one side," he said. "But I didn't come around to talk about my scars."

"Then why did you come?"

He leaned over the wooden railing and watched her slowly pull the brush along the side of Wagner's neck. "Why is it that I keep getting surprised? Every time I come to Pattaya I am surprised."

"Avoiding surprise is an art. Maybe they don't teach that art in Bangkok."

Calvino rubbed his eyes, grinned and took a deep breath. There was still blood in one eye from the assault. Out of the blue Fon's priceless observation confirmed what he had suspected—she'd spent her life as a gardener's wife concealing her intelligence. That was an impossible task. Intelligence insisted on asserting itself.

"We are lacking in our basic education," said Calvino.

"Not *everyone* can be taught."

He turned towards her, standing a couple of inches away.

"I can be a good student. Lesson one. Paint me a portrait of Ton."

It was her turn to look surprised.

"He's the guy who worked with your husband on special jobs. I have a good idea that you already know about that and didn't want to tell me. I understand. No one wants to talk ill of the dead."

She stopped brushing for a moment.

"My husband worked with a lot of people."

"It's my turn to paint a portrait. Killing people is *work*. Let me make it clear. Ton, his brother, Sombat and your husband worked as a murder-for-hire team. They were in the killing business. Do you understand the picture I've painted?"

She dropped the feed bucket into a trough. A couple of the goats jumped and scattered. Wagner ran off. She watched as Elgar and Bach munched the spilled feed from the ground. Calvino reached down and picked up the bucket and held it out.

Her face flushed. "I know what he did in the past. But that was many years ago."

"How would you know?"

"I would have known."

"There's something I don't understand. With your university degree, your qualification to work as a vet, you must have had a lot of men wanting to marry you. You married an uneducated gardener. It doesn't fit."

"The first time he showed up in my clinic with a sick animal I saw something in him. He had a deep compassion for every living thing. Money can't buy that. Education can't teach that. His love of nature was beyond anything I had ever known in another human being."

She started sweeping up the feed and shooing away the goats. She was thinking about the tightrope she'd been walking. She had a burning desire to establish that her husband hadn't committed suicide. To clear her husband's memory risked opening his past connections. She tossed and turned at night, seeking a way to walk that tightrope. Calvino had caused her to lose her balance. She tried to read from his expression, his voice, his words, how much he knew and how much he was guessing at, using her to fill in blanks. It had been only a matter of time before he walked to the pasture and confronted her about the bad days when her husband and Ton and Sombat had killed people. She had dreaded that moment. Now it had arrived.

"My husband's dead. What do you want me to say? That he was perfect? That he never did anything bad? You have no idea how he regretted what he'd done."

Calvino watched the goat munching. "What I want is for you to say, 'I will help you.'"

"I've already tried to do that."

"Maybe, maybe not. I can't say. But if you really want to help me, then tell me how I can find Ton. Tell me where I can find him."

"I don't know where he lives."

"Did you ever meet him?"

"I don't remember."

"I take that to be a yes."

"Really, I don't see the point of all this." Anger flashed across her face.

"Your husband, his brother and Ton took assignments from Veera."

"I told you already he worked for Sia."

"I have a theory. Good hired guns are never allowed to retire. They may stop for a short time or a long time, but they are always pulled back for another job. Your husband had a new job offer. He brought in Sombat and Ton to work with him. The same team, just like old times. Now two of the men in the team are dead, and that leaves only Ton. He probably knows who killed your husband and his brother."

"It doesn't make sense."

"Why not?"

"Ton would be dead, too."

"Did you ever hear about the walking dead man? That could be Ton. Before he finally stops walking and becomes just dead, I'd like to ask him about their last job." He walked around to where she stood. "You told Valentine that your husband hadn't killed himself. You organized the other women to back you. You knew that Valentine would be forced to do something. If it hadn't been for you, he never would have hired me. Your husband's death would have stayed a suicide. You want to know the truth. Or you wouldn't have done any of this. Now I'm asking you for some help, and by helping me, you get what you've been after. Does that make sense? You still want the world to know your husband didn't take his own life? Or have you changed your mind?"

She sighed, playing with the brush, pulling out strands of hair.

"It's true, my husband did do the bad thing. But he stopped and he was sorry for that life. He promised never to do that again. Every day he prayed to Buddha for forgiveness."

"He took one more job. I figure someone important asked him for a favor. Your husband couldn't say no."

Fon pressed the brush against Bach, who was penned between her and the railing. "He never saw that man again."

"He didn't have to. Sawai was your husband's guru. He is also close to Veera. What I am saying is, Veera had a messenger."

She threw down the brush and started to walk away. Calvino grabbed her wrist. "That's how it worked, isn't it? Sawai brought a job for your husband. Veera asked for him to do something. Just one last time."

"My husband wanted his own farm and herd. Is that so bad? Valentine has all of this. And we are Thai, and what do we have to show for our lives? He wanted more than being Valentine's pet. He wanted more for me."

"He figured Veera was good for one last big pay day. Whack someone Veera wanted out of the way. Then he'd have enough cash for the land and herd."

"You're hurting my arm," said Fon.

He released her wrist. She made no attempt to move away or break eye contact. There was something different in the way she stared at him. Not hurt or contempt or hatred. More like a woman who had decided to stop running.

"You can't run away from this. Even if you want to," he said.

He regretted grabbing her wrist. He mostly regretted judging her husband. In the real world of looters, thieves, and the rare golden opportunity, there was never sufficient moral cargo to stop the rush to claim a windfall. Prasit had simply done what most people around him were programmed to do: seize the advantage; never let the opportunity slip away. He never looked back. He only saw from the enclosure of his own hunger a shortcut to another life.

"We never talked about it," she said. "Thai men aren't like *farangs*. They keep their plans secret. They don't talk about it to their wives. You live here a long time. You have a wife?"

"No wife."

"Girlfriend?"

The conversation was getting personal.

"Believe me, a man needs to make his woman proud of him."

"He had a wife with a university education."

"You think that was easy for him?"

"I think you tried to make it easy for him. You settled for a life as a gardener's wife working for Valentine. You were so far off the frame it's hard to believe you were ever in the picture. I don't care how much his compassion touched you. It had to be hard for you and for him. Valentine was after all, as you say, an outsider. A *farang*."

"My husband understood very well that I loved him. . . that I never questioned him," she broke off and turned back to pouring feed into a trough for one of the goats.

"Question him about going back to work for Veera? You didn't need to. You were smart enough to figure it out. He suddenly had a pile of cash. He told you he was now going to buy land. Somehow it went sideways. Those who did the killing got killed. Except for Ton. And he might be able to tell me what happened to the money."

"Do you know who killed my husband?"

He had her full attention. Somewhere in her mind, she had to know he would ask about the money. No one clatters down the rungs of ladders examining potential motives for murder without asking what happened to the money.

"The question depends on who hired him to make the hit on the reporter. You *saw* the newspapers on the prayer room floor. He made a point of keeping newspapers with photographs of the reporter. Or what was left of him after they pulled the body out of the well. And the other old newspapers. All from hits going back for years. The prayer room was covered with the reports of the people he'd killed."

"That was Sawai's idea."

"Being a smart woman, you understood what was going on."

Her eyes gave her away.

"What I don't understand is why someone would want to kill your husband and his brother and leave Ton still alive. Just call me curious."

"I can't have my life back until I know who killed him."

"One more thing I've been meaning to ask. Call it another lesson in art. Did your husband show you the money?"

She shook her head. Something was spinning around in her mind. "He hadn't been paid. That is why he was killed."

"He asked for the money?"

"It was owed to him."

"He knew getting what was owed might be a problem. *Kai hen tin ngu, ngu hen nom kai.*" The chicken sees the snake's feet and the snake sees the chicken's breast. This translated as a stand-off.

A bubble of laughter rose from her throat. The *farang* had summarized her husband's situation with accuracy. "At first, I think Valentine hire someone who knows nothing. I am glad to be wrong about you."

He walked back to the guestroom, turned on the air-conditioner and poured himself a whisky neat in a glass. He sat on the edge of the bed and took a drink. She was holding back. As he was getting closer to the answer, she retreated further into silence. What was her angle? Was she after money? Claiming her husband had been killed might bring her some cash from someone like Veera. Or a bullet. Yet there was no sign that Veera was taking any interest in her or her demand to find the person who had killed her husband—she wasn't on his radar screen, another one of those little people who lined up by the hundreds every day with a problem, complaint or desire. This explained why the widow, the wave maker, was still alive. The waves still had not hit Veera's beach. Calvino started to feel that with Valentine as her cover, here was a woman who could avoid the best surveillance systems. She was very good.

At the same time, all roads and all fingers pointed to Veera, and that made it a little too easy. Veera had talked up a great story about his humble beginnings and his dedication to the village and how he was responsible for all of these people who depended on him. Calvino had heard this kind of rags-to-riches story before. In New York, he was Italian on his father's side, and he had listened as a boy when an old man who was said to be a Mafia godfather had told similar story to his uncle and father. The don said that his job was to look after his own. Blood was thicker than water. Once that premise was agreed on, then suddenly a lot of things were much easier to understand. Take an outsider: such a person could be tolerated, accommodated, but if he decided to make trouble, the outsider had better watch his back. And if any outsider came into the territory looking to make trouble for someone important and powerful on the inside, then whatever was needed to be done to remove that problem was done.

The problem had started with a couple of Khmer fisherman and escalated into a different, more complex problem. The first theory was that the two Khmer had been talking too much about sideline assignments on a trawler. The villagers said they saw nothing, heard nothing and said nothing to the police. The Khmer had vanished to the moon as far as they were concerned. Whatever the villagers had witnessed, no one could get them to talk. Not that anyone was trying very hard. The second theory was pure hatred for the Khmer. In the village, no one liked the Khmer, who were outsiders, dirty, dark-skinned people who stole their jobs; ignorant, and foreign, inferior people. Taking the next step was easier once the Khmer were no longer considered in the same category as other human beings. It made the killing easier to understand but it could have been for a hundred different reasons. A slight, a robbery, or some local drunks who got carried away when their extortion racket turned ugly.

Whatever the reason, the Khmer got themselves killed in or near the village. But the story hadn't stopped with their two murders, a second outsider, and this time a Thai reporter asking a lot of questions about the Khmer prostitutes. He got wind of the murders. He had been a journalist, and murder was always a good story. He didn't take the hint that his presence wasn't wanted. He didn't take the warning that followed the hint. What happened? He's been warned, he wouldn't listen, then he was warned again. This was the tradition. Thais normally gave a warning. When he didn't listen, he was no longer entitled to a further warning. The reporter went ahead sticking his nose into the business of the village even though his activities might lead to damaging evidence and to some important person. They got rid of him. Had him killed and dumped his body in a well. Finished. Problem solved. Peace and tranquility returned to the village. It's the way things work in New York and in Chon Buri and a thousand other places. It came from a universal instinct to protect your own kind even if that means killing strangers who stick their noses in your private affairs. That's the way it is. It is a law of nature. It is hardwired.

Whatever could be said for human nature, it couldn't stop Calvino from blaming Veera for cold-blooded murder. It was something no one could ever forgive in another. The moral cargo may have left this world, but it didn't stop Calvino from clutching onto a view about the difference between right and wrong. Killing was always the wrong thing. Whether out of revenge or personal or business conflict. It had no justification. Killing the Khmer was possible because men like Veera knew how to channel the most primitive instincts towards their own personal interest. Such ability was the true face of evil.

When he called in Prasit, the *jao poh* would have known what buttons to push. Prasit would have thought of himself as a soldier in Veera's command. If the old commander called him up, Prasit was unlikely to have said, "I can't. I am retired."

An hour later, Fon came into the guestroom without knocking. She closed the door and leaned against it as she unbuttoned her shirt. She slipped out of her jeans, and wearing only her bra and underwear, moved to the bed. Calvino finished the whisky in the glass and set it on the table. "It's been a long time since I have a man," she said.

She held his face in her hands and kissed his mouth, then his cheeks, and worked her way to the stitched wound along his ear. "It does look like a face lift scar," she said.

He pulled her on top of him, unhooking her bra. The schoolgirls at Sawai's compound flashed through his mind. Had he walked into another honey-trap? It was highly possible that she was using him to follow her husband's money. He dropped her bra onto the floor.

It had been a long time since he'd had a woman come to his room and strip down and climb into his bed. She was freshly showered and had put on make-up and perfume. She had taken the braids out of her hair and combed it out until it fell in long black waves down to the center of her back. Her tongue darted in his mouth and she let out a long sigh as he entered her. Her arms around his neck, she shuddered, eyes wide open, watching his face, watching his eyes half close, riding him slowly until the motion turned automatic.

Her nails ran down his shoulders as she arched her back and finally her eyes closed, and when she slumped back onto his body, her breath was hot on his chest. He stroked her face, pulling back the tangle of hair. Neither of them said anything for a long while afterwards.

When she finally rolled to the side, he cradled her head in his arm. He hadn't expected it to happen. He had had no warning that it would happen. And moments before he had convinced himself that Thais always signaled in advance of an attack. She had simply launched the attack.

"I want to have you the first you came to my house," she said. "Thai girls aren't supposed to think that. They aren't supposed to say this to a man."

"You're not what I'd call a typical Thai woman," he said.

She looked up and smiled at him, kissing his chest. She shook her head.

"I am a failure of the Thai educational system. Do you know why?"

"I thought you were a success," said Calvino.

"No, a failure. I learned to think. And learned to question and not accept what someone said just because he was a *poo yai*. Like many *farangs,* you meet the successes of the educational system and you think we are all like that. It's because you don't think. I am glad to be a failure. In my country, it is the failures who will one day make things change."

"Sawai tried to set me up with a tag-team today," said Calvino.

"I don't understand."

"Two teenaged girls in a honey-trap. My guess is, Veera tipped him I was coming and they were trying to compromise me. *Farang* caught with two fifteen-year-olds would have got me out of their lives for about ten years."

"Why are you telling me this?"

"So that you know what I am up against. And you and everyone else in this compound, if I keep digging into what happened to your husband. It's time to be real careful. You let me know where I can find Ton, and we can have one more chance."

"Asking questions is dangerous," she said.

"That's why most people don't bother," he replied.

"Why do you have only one more chance?"

"These guys don't give anyone a second chance."

The question in his mind was whether he had put his faith in the right woman. There were no second chances. Period.

TWENTY-NINE

DAVID Jardine had left a message for Calvino to meet him at eight o'clock inside TQ2. Calvino threaded his way along Walking Street in South Pattaya, turned into a small lane, and found TQ2 with a flashing neon sign. He was a couple of minutes early. Colonel Pratt had said on the beach that David Jardine was the terrorist specialist attached to the American Embassy, and Calvino tried to figure out Pratt's relationship with Jardine. What was the chain of command?

Jardine's voice message had been short and sweet: "I'd like to talk to you about Veera."

Jardine had caught Calvino's attention. It left Calvino with hours to sort through a deck of doubts. Had Pratt volunteered the information about the meeting with Veera? Why hadn't his friend told him? Jardine might have found out from an independent source. American agents with diplomatic credentials traditionally worked out of the embassy. With fresh bomb attacks planned in Narathiwat and links between the bombers and the terrorist group, Jemaah Islamiah, it didn't take much of a leap to believe the Americans had beefed up their local manpower. Each of them with laptops and high-tech hook-ups to secure transmissions, sorting through profiles, photographs and intelligence reports, looking to prevent the next terrorist attack.

Inside TQ2, four or five dancers in bikinis and high-heels were on a stage, moving to the tune of "Rocket Man." *Moved, moving* were active verbs; most of the dancers were closer to a state of suspended animation than movement. Angels frozen in a solid block of amber light. Young and expectant, they wondered as Calvino walked in if he were *the* customer—the one who walked through the door with a wad of cash and a desire for a good time. The *farang* who would buy them a cola, who would pay their bar fine, and the next morning buy them a gold chain, helping them execute their private business plan for a stream of cash. Mobile teenaged CEO's with one product to sell. A product that wasn't until that moment moving. That was their business: the moving of cash from a rich pocket into a not-so-rich china doll satin gown. Calvino retained all of that magic possibility and wishful thinking for about twenty seconds. All eyes on stage tracked him as he walked one level up and sat down, looking down at the stage. He avoided eye contact with the dancers. He didn't flash a smile. He didn't look happy. Most of all, he didn't look like a buyer. The angels returned to their state as angels frozen in the amber light. He'd signaled that he was an old hand, and had come for some other business. That killed the magic; they would need to wait for a new opportunity to move and cash in.

One of Calvino's laws for holding a meeting in a bar was straightforward: If you made an appointment with a stranger while investigating a murder case, ignore the bar hostess, whose job is to steer the mark to a front row stool eighteen inches from the stage, prime angel-picking terrain, and demand an isolated seat on an empty bench two levels up from the stage. Always occupy the high ground, don't make eye contact with a *ying*, and never take your eye off the door to the street even if five goddesses on the stage seek your attention. The promise of xenophilia by a bar *ying* is a con; the only *xen* that's real in a bar is xenophobia.

Calvino had originally thought that Pratt had drawn the short straw and was sent on the thankless, dangerous and difficult job of finding enough evidence to collar Veera. He figured that Veera had become too powerful and this was causing someone a major headache. Whatever the reason, the crackdown had less to do with Veera's crimes than Veera's influence. The time had run out for the old days when local godfathers were all-powerful entities inside their small feudal turfs; a new way had emerged, and in time, their influence and power was being consolidated, absorbed into a larger organization. Those who refused to go along with the times were a problem. Like dinosaurs once the climate had changed, they had trouble breathing in the new atmosphere. Veera had continued to live in a different era and, like in the Road Runner cartoon where the bird overshoots the cliff, he simply hadn't looked down. He didn't know there was nothing under his feet but a very long fall.

It didn't take rocket science to figure out that Jardine was either Special Forces or CIA, an undercover agent on assignment in Thailand. Bangkok had become spook central. They had fanned over the region. Spooks spilling into Pattaya—that was natural. After all, Chon Buri was packed with Cobra Gold troops. Not that one would have called them a soft target, but they would make a tempting target for the kind of people who liked blowing up Americans. Guys like David Jardine would be sniffing around looking to shut down trouble before it happened. Hardly an arrest of a suspected terrorist in Asia had happened without an American security detail being involved. They had their own internal system of operation. Meaning they were a law unto themselves. Calvino waited and nursed his drink. Jardine wanted something he had. What did Jardine want from him?

After receiving the voicemail from David Jardine, Calvino phoned Pratt.

"David Jardine, does the name ring a bell?" asked Calvino. "You mentioned him on the beach. Wasn't he the reason I should get out of Pattaya?"

There had been a moment of silence. "He's the reason. Why?"

One of those spooks with a name card with no title written under the name.

"I have an appointment to meet him."

"It's still not too late. Go home, Vincent."

It was Calvino's turn to pause. "You're working with him?"

"I've met him."

"I'm about to meet him."

"David's a pro," said Colonel Pratt. "He's worked in East Timor, Somalia, Kosovo."

"That almost prepares him for Pattaya."

"He's the best at what he does."

David Jardine worked in a shadow world wedged between the rotating blades of the political mandates of Washington and the practical realities of what could be accomplished on the ground, and to survive, he had to be good. Pratt's assessment wasn't something that he said about just anyone.

"Exactly what does he do?"

"I am certain he'll explain that to you."

When a tall, middle-aged lanky *farang* stood framed in the door, letting his eyes adjust to the darkness before entering, the first thing that struck Calvino was how well lived-in the face looked, crossed with lines spreading from the eyes, and how quickly he scanned the room. The *yings* on stage looked him up and down for a few seconds, locking their radar onto the target and then logging off, knowing they could never bring this one down.

Jardine scanned the upper rows and locked eyes with Calvino. He nodded and walked up the two steps and sat down, taking a cold towel from the waitress and wiping his face and the back of his neck. He folded the towel and laid it on the counter.

"Vincent Calvino?"

"David Jardine?"

Jardine didn't smile. He didn't look like he knew how to smile. He held out his hand and Calvino shook it. He was the kind of man that put a lot of stock in a firm handshake, as if firmness were a litmus test of character. Jardine's orange juice arrived in a tall glass with a straw.

"Colonel Pratt said you work at the Embassy," said Calvino.

He thought it was a good idea to immediately raise Pratt's name. Drop the dime and see where it bounced.

"Colonel Pratt is one of the few cops we trust. I understand you've known him for many years."

"Since he was a student in New York."

"He says your family saved his life."

It had been an eternity, thought Calvino. David Jardine could have opened an entire line of questions about how Calvino and New York and the colonel had come together.

The fact that he didn't meant that he already had that intelligence, or it simply didn't matter to the business he had in mind. Jardine struck him as a cautious and careful man who didn't leave things to chance. He figured Jardine had the intel on him and Pratt.

"The people I work with feel that Colonel Pratt is the right person on the ground. They trust him. And I agree with them. You save a man's life in this culture and he owes you his life."

"Colonel Pratt owes me nothing."

"It doesn't work that way. I think you know that."

Jardine sipped his orange juice, barely looking at the stage. He turned back to Calvino and he said, "I learnt two lessons. First, that the most important asset is the one honest, connected and brave man on the ground. Someone who can't be turned. You know the percentage of men who can't be turned by money, sex, blackmail?" He held up one hand and started to fold down his fingers until two were left showing in the semi-darkness of the bar. Pratt was one of two fingers. "Pratt is one of two out of a million." Calvino didn't bother to ask who the other person was.

"You said there were two lessons."

Jardine nodded. "Good, that means you're listening. Lesson number two I learned from an old hand who lived in Thailand many years. Jack Shirley. Jack said never go into a place until you first figured out how the hell you can escape. You plan your exit before you go in. Once you're inside, it's too late. When the shit starts happening and you have to run, you can't make it up as you scram. You have to mark the way out."

"If you knew Jack Shirley, you knew one of the best."

Calvino had underestimated David Jardine, who had some history with Pattaya and with Jack Shirley, one of the legendary agents of the secret war in Laos.

"That's something we can agree on. I understand that you saved the colonel from some hard times at the hands of a Chinese drug gang in New York, and that you ended up paying a high price for helping a friend. The colonel tells me that you never once complained about paying the price for that friendship."

"Did the colonel tell you what I am doing in Pattaya?"

"Investigating a murder."

"The widow thinks it was murder, the lord of the manor and the police think it was suicide. I was hired by the lord of the manor."

"Valentine, the concert pianist. I once heard him perform in Paris. Mozart Concerto in F Minor," said Jardine. "If you know anything about music, you would know that Valentine is one of the best pianists alive. And he walked away from it."

The man had done his homework.

"Why today at this bar? I thought secret agents used safe houses or limos with tinted windows."

"To see how you balance a chip on each shoulder. A couple of Mekhongs in a Pattaya bar and, who knows, one of the chips might fall off," said Jardine.

The waitress asked Calvino if he wanted another drink. He ordered a Mekhong and Coke. "Make that two," he said, and then, turning to Jardine, "One for each chip."

Jardine had shown a few of his cards. He had let Calvino know about his connection with Jack Shirley, Colonel Pratt and his murder case. There was an art in revealing just enough information to gain the confidence of another person. To create a sense of ease so they'd relax, let their guard down. Then punch hard about their attitude, call it a double-chipped shoulder complex. It had to work most of the time. As Colonel Pratt had said, Jardine was the best at what he did, and that was getting information. They were seated together because there was something that David Jardine needed to know from Calvino. He didn't have to wait until the Mekhong and Cokes arrived before Jardine turned over the next card. It was a joker with Veera's face on it.

"You think that Veera is connected to your murder case?"

Jardine wanted a debriefing on the Veera meeting and had been waiting for the right moment to bring up the subject. Calvino shrugged. "I don't know it's murder. Veera says every time someone gets whacked in Chon Buri, everyone points a finger at him. He's says he's an ordinary businessman."

"There are some bigger issues at play."

In David Jardine's world the boundaries were defined by big issues, and well-financed men met at the frontline to test each other and decide which of those big issues would prevail. Winning had nothing to do with merit or morality; like on the African savannah, survival had to do with being the fastest and strongest and most disciplined and determined.

"I leave the big issues for the big people," said Calvino. "If I can find who killed Valentine's gardener, that's good enough. You don't need my help to make the world a safer and more secure place. I wouldn't know where to start."

For the first time, David Jardine smiled. "I am not so certain I know where to start either."

After the Mekhong and Cokes arrived, Jardine seemed to relax. "The bad guys have no trouble blowing up schools, bars, discos, office buildings. That's the problem. They chose to play hardball on 9/11. Anyone who doesn't understand that the terrorists have the rules of engagement has been living in a fucking cave."

Calvino had heard this party line and understood the drill. There had been a catastrophic inflation of fear. Fear exploded at the speed of light. The masters of the new universe seized the chance to play God. Ice to water; water to steam. Such fear justified an inflated counter-reaction. Legal formalities had to be abolished. The Patriot Act was seen as necessary to rework the Constitution. Men like Jardine had been sent across the globe like post-modern missionaries to preach the gospel and make converts. Call it intelligence, call it religion—it didn't matter. Either one was a true believer or one was on the other side of the line. Hunter and hunted. Redemption came from following the sinner, pursuing him to the ends of the earth. Find him and either kill him or bundle him away to Cuba or to a base in Afghanistan. Use whatever techniques were required to make him talk—until all of his bank accounts, friends, relatives, car rentals, houses and contacts were disclosed. That wasn't salvation. That was survival. Apply to a court for extradition? No one even raised the question anymore. The courts were secular. They didn't understand the new religion. Court procedure was a relic from an old, dead world, from the age before the government became god and the new class of priest chased after the devil.

"It's a different game," said David Jardine. "You grab him, you fly him out on the next military transport and do what is needed to get the information. The information gets old quickly. The word gets out and the bad guys shift to a new set of caves. If you want to catch the ringleaders, you move fast. Vincent, we are at war, and the people on the other side are full of rage and murder and we have to stop them. If we don't act, then we will have 9/11 over and over until everything and everyone you love is destroyed."

"The government said that about the Mafia. They said that about drugs. You know what—both are still with us. No amount of weed killer gets them all," said Calvino.

"No one ever thinks we can get them all. But we can contain them."

"How do you do that unless you can contain the panic and fear that makes people feel the other side can't ever be contained? And if that's the conclusion, everyone lives under permanent siege," said Calvino.

Everyone on the covert side had joined the race to unplug the murdering machine; fueled with hatred and rage and pain, they functioned on automatic pilot, their mission to destroy the West one bomb at a time until finally nothing and no one was left standing.

"We hold a *halal* ritual for all human beings," said Jardine.

"Hit 'em or buy 'em," said Calvino.

Jardine nodded. "The world has lost nuance."

"You're either with us or against us."

Jardine flinched. "I didn't make this new world. Like you, I try to do the best I can and remember that at the end of the day, I have to live with what I do. The same goes for you. You can think what you want about me. The government. Policy debates. None of that matters right now. I want you to think about your case. The death of a gardener wasn't necessarily just another domestic murder."

It was more than normal volatility in the system. That's what Jardine meant.

Fear had the capacity of turning every death into part of the larger fight. That's what Calvino thought.

Calvino finished his Mekhong and Coke. "One piece of intelligence I can pass along: if you want a good massage, you won't find it at the Harmony massage parlor."

"I don't think you are with the program," said Jardine.

"I don't have cable. Tell me exactly—what program am I missing?"

"That we are at war with an enemy who believes God has stocked heaven with virgins for murderers."

"And what's their side? Your people, who want to kill them, believe in the virgin birth," said Calvino. "Tell me, which myth is crazier?"

"The Jemaah Islamiah operatives in Thailand aren't cartoon characters. The press refer to them as JI. What the newspaper don't report is how tough, committed, ruthless the JI are. Well trained, cunning, and well financed. I don't underestimate them. My problem is with someone who's lived too long outside of their own country. They no longer understand what others in their country value or feel."

"Colonel Pratt said I should go home."

"Do you have a home to go back to?"

"Like my mother said, you can always go home."

Calvino had lived in Thailand half a lifetime. His reaction to Jardine's world was one of anger. But he recognized that Jardine had made a point and that he'd just made a fool of himself. Expats ran the risk of falling between worlds, leaving them in the void with other expats like themselves. Invisible—and not so invisible—barriers made it impossible for a *farang* to assimilate into Thai culture. At the same time, places like America retreated into the fog of the past. The place remembered was not the same place anymore. Jardine had gone silent. He'd pushed the right button. Calvino had been about to call for the check. If Jardine wanted to bring him into the game, why not find out what the game was.

"Maybe we can help each other," said Calvino.

"That's what I've been waiting to hear for the past thirty minutes."

"What can I do for you?" Calvino asked.

Jardine looked at the stage and pointed at one of *yings* on stage. She had a plastic oval with the raised number 18 pinned to her bikini bottom. She wouldn't have stood out in a crowd; no one in the bar would be able to identify her from the other four dancers in the line-up. She had no special features. Nothing about her body was memorable. She was another ordinary *ying*; like elevator music or wallpaper, she was there and not there at the same time.

Except for one non-physical item: her friendship with an ex-dancer named Noi. Calvino misunderstood at first.

"Her friend unhooked herself from the chrome-pole-and-bikini gig and became a dive master."

"That *ying*?" asked Calvino. "A diver?"

"Not the dancer on the stage. The one dancing, her name's Dew," said Jardine. "Her friend Noi went into diving."

Calvino watched Jardine carefully to see if his face betrayed some kind of a joke. But he wasn't joking.

"Dive master?"

Jardine turned, looked at Calvino and nodded. This was the kind of turn in the road of life for a bar *ying* that sounded like pure fantasy, but stranger things had happened. Not often, but there were a few expert divers in Pattaya who had started their careers working in bars before deciding their future lay working underwater. According to Jardine, Noi had witnessed a small boat coming ashore last New Year's Eve. A pickup truck was waiting with several men. One of the men from the boat stayed on shore with a large locker. Two men helped load the locker onto the pickup. She recognized one of the men in the boat from the village where she grew up. There wasn't a lot of light, but she thought he was the captain of the trawler. She couldn't make a positive identification of the other man from a photograph. He had a beard. It was dark. He wore a mask. Months had passed. All she remembered was a small half-moon scar above his right eye.

Jardine said, "That fit one man, an Indonesian high up in our private deck of cards for JI operatives. His name is Hasam. You know what his name means?"

"I have no idea."

"Sword. Vincent, it means sword. A sword used to cut down the infidels. Wipe out the barbarians. We have reason to believe Hasam was smuggled into Thailand carrying a device that, if detonated, will kill many thousands of people. You know about a reporter named Pramote. He got himself killed investigating a story in the same village. Veera's village. Funny about all these connections in one small fishing village in the boondocks. Pramote interviewed Noi. We believe he was following up a lead and stumbled upon something about the trawler and the men and the device. Naturally, we are interested in Veera and his connection. You talked to him. He's not an easy man to get access to, even with our resources."

Calvino had been listening and watching the stage. He was prepared to agree that a lot of murders were dumped on Veera's doorstep. But that didn't mean Veera didn't kill people when a problem couldn't otherwise be managed.

"I'd like to talk to Noi," said Calvino.

"Join the list. She disappeared one night."

Calvino cocked his head. "Can't find her?"

People in Pattaya went missing in action all the time.

"That is a problem. The last person she was seen with was Valentine."

Gone missing in sex. Calvino wondered if there was a word to describe such a fetish.

THIRTY

FON sat in bed, her knees raised touching, reading a book. She had slipped into Calvino's bed. Waiting for him to return, she became bored and pulled a book off the small library shelf in the guestroom. The title had caught her eye—*Unsubmissive Women*. She read the part about how Chinese women had been bought and sold as prostitutes in America 130 years ago. An unmarried Chinese woman with a son had been sold for $105. It was a low price because of her age. The prostitute was in her thirties. Past her prime and her market value had dropped. Fon had cocked her arm to throw the book against the wall when Calvino opened the door.

"Are you going to throw the book at me?" he asked.

She lowered her arm. "Do you think I am past my prime?"

Calvino closed the door. There was only one answer when a woman in her thirties asked that question.

"You are in your prime."

The smile returned and she uncurled her legs, swung them over the side of the bed, swinging her feet, waiting and grinning. He recognized his white shirt; she had rolled up the sleeves to the elbow. Under the shirt she wore panties. He sat on the bed next to her, holding the book in his hands.

"Sometimes when you read the truth, it makes you more mad than when you read lies."

Fon's smile faded. "Nai knows I am here."

Her face looked like she was about to cry, but her eyes were flirtatious.

"He knows you were here the other night."

She floated on a cloud of sadness. "Why is it when a man sleeps with a woman, that is a natural desire and he gets a medal. But when a woman wants to sleep with a man, she's a slut."

She waited for a reply but Calvino didn't have an answer. For someone who was a self-described "failure" of the system, she had more awkward questions than any Thai woman he'd met.

"Did he fire you?" she asked.

"He thought your sleeping with me was a good interrogation technique."

"Was it?"

The jury was still out, he thought. She might have been using him as an avenue to recover the money owed to her husband. There was no way of knowing. When it came to large sums of money only a few people could be trusted not to lie, cheat or steal to keep it. Those who had more than they could spend or who valued honesty above opportunity had the best chance to rise above temptation. He wasn't certain which category Fon fit into.

"I know how to find Ton," she said. "I thought you'd be happy."

He got up and poured himself a whisky. "Thanks." He drank the whisky straight from the glass and poured another before walking back to the foot of the bed.

"You don't look happy."

She was right. He didn't feel happy, either.

"Do you remember one of Valentine's *yings* named Noi? She worked in TQ2, then qualified as dive master."

He said nothing about Jardine, or that Jardine had gathered information from a bar *ying* turned dive master who had witnessed a terrorist drop along the coast.

"She worked here a long time ago," said Fon.

"Do you know why she left?"

Fon lay down the book.

"She went back to her Thai boyfriend."

A lapidary phrase suitable for a *farang* tombstone.

Then there was Ratana. She never had a Thai boyfriend. There was always the exception that proved the rule. One exception was enough to make fools out of most men, thinking they had won. Jardine had it right. There were two out of a million you could trust. And everyone assumed the one they had chosen was one of two. Look for their tombstones.

Calvino threw back the second whisky and shivered. "I guess that kind of thing is bound to happen. She saw a life flash before her eyes. Feeding goats named Bach, Mozart and Elgar and listening to Valentine play the piano. And everything suddenly became clear. An unemployed boyfriend wasn't such a bad thing after all."

"Why do you ask about Noi?"

"Her name came up tonight."

"You go to her bar?"

"Yes, I went to her *old* bar. But she wasn't there."

"It's because I am not in my prime," she said.

"I don't understand."

"Noi is a young girl. Men like the young girl."

"I am trying to find who killed Prasit." After sleeping with Fon, Calvino found himself unable to use the phrase, "your husband." Half-dressed in his shirt, he didn't want to think of her as someone's wife. Or as someone's widow. He fell silent. It was his call. The first time a woman slept with a man, she couldn't be sure he had any desire other than sexual. If he slept with her a second time, the illusion existed that his desire for her was something more than sex. In her mind she had acquired a right of possession.

"Thanks for finding Ton's address. I appreciate it."

"You want me to go?"

He didn't know the answer himself. The meeting with Jardine had rattled him, made him confused and uncertain about what he wanted. He had a gut feeling Pratt had arranged for Calvino to meet Veera so Jardine could record the conversation using sophisticated listening devices. In other words, he had been setup. He should have seen it coming. Getting a meeting with Veera should have been impossible. He'd like to learn how Jardine had managed to get to Colonel Pratt.

Or had he? He thought about Colonel Pratt and suddenly became depressed.

He had tried to phone Pratt all evening, but the colonel's cellphone was turned off. By turning it off, Pratt was sending a message.

"Did you hear what I asked you? Do you want to me to leave?"

He stared at the bottom of his glass.

"Up to you," he said.

On the beach, Pratt had pleaded with him to go back to Bangkok. He started to understand why Pratt had pressed him to return. Calvino couldn't shake off the horrible feeling that his friend had known *that night on the beach* what was going down. Pratt had told him about David Jardine. But Calvino hadn't been careful; he wasn't listening. Colonel Pratt never tossed out a name without having a reason. *He should have told me,* thought Calvino. *He should've fucking told me.*

Fon stepped down from the bed, walked around and threaded her arm through Calvino's and led him to the bed. "Noi's boyfriend came to pick her up the day she left. Valentine refused to see her. He stayed behind his walls playing the piano. That's how he fights pain. Better than this," she said, removing the glass from his hand.

Deep in his gut, he knew that Pratt, in his own way, had told him. A couple of Americans—including David Jardine—had likely visited the village, asking questions. Veera's kid had said something he hadn't thought too much about at the time: "We get lots of *farangs* wanting to talk to my dad. But they don't get in." He could see in his mind's eye the *farangs* in suits, with short cropped hair, one of them speaking fluent Thai, asking for an appointment with Veera. The Americans followed the trail and sometimes told the Thais what they were doing. Other times they kept to themselves, searching and asking questions. They had gone to Colonel Pratt after they decided they couldn't go any further on their own. They had gone to the village to fish, throwing a line out for information. *Had anyone seen a foreigner?* Flashing photographs of possible JI agents who were known to be somewhere in the region. *Had anyone seen this girl?* Flashing another photograph, this time of Noi. No one had seen anything. No one knew anything. Veera was unavailable. No one knew when he would have time.

Calvino sat back in bed and Fon started to kiss him lightly on the forehead, working her way down to his nose and lips. Closing his eyes, he thought about Ratana. With Ratana, he felt desire, but the unspoken pact had excluded sex. It wasn't one of those permanent decisions. One day it might happen.

Fon's kiss lingered, trying to void the distraction that made him distant. It wasn't working. He told himself that a man might want a woman without wanting to sleep with her just like he might want a woman only to sleep with her. Most of the time, given the opportunity, a man would sleep with just about any woman. If men were as discriminating as women in their choice of sex partners, the world's population would have leveled off at around a million. As her lips reached his chest, he made a decision. Gently he pulled her to eye level.

"Yes, of course. It makes sense."

"What makes sense?"

"How they knew."

Colonel Pratt had left Bangkok a couple of days after the Americans and Thais caught a JI terrorist named Hambali. That gap in time had been long enough for them to get information. It was coming together inside Calvino's mind.

"I don't understand," Fon said. "Who knew what?"

He was already off the bed, buttoning his shirt. It was better that she didn't understand. What good could come from Fon knowing that a big-time terrorist had been on the run? Or that his name was Hambali who'd been caught, waiting for his passport and visa stamp? She waited for Calvino to say something. Instead, he turned around, thinking about how the cops had broken into Hambali's apartment in Ayudhaya and arrested him. How he'd gone for his handgun but had no time to use it.

She pulled one of the pillows onto her lap, nestling her arms around it.

"I've got to go."

She looked hurt. "You're not going to tell me," she said. "You found something to do with my husband's death. But it's a secret."

"How much money was Prasit owed?"

She lowered her head, pushing her face into the pillow. He waited a moment. She came up for air. Still clinging to the pillow, she said. "One hundred thousand baht."

"And you want it."

Anger flashed across her face, evaporated, and the tears fell.

"Blood money? Never. Is that what you think of me?"

He left the room without replying. His mind was elsewhere. The papers had been filled with wire-service stories and photos of a terrorist from Indonesia who had been arrested in Thailand, flown to Afghanistan and from there to Cuba. His wife had flown in from Malaysia to stay with him. The Indonesian had been tracked down on a visa run. Even terrorists made visa runs in Thailand. Suddenly Thailand had become a terrorist hot zone. The interrogators had turned up the heat on their boy. Someone finally broke him. Calvino guessed that had to be David Jardine. Jardine had said someone had been smuggled into Thailand with a dirty bomb. He also had said Pratt was one out of two men in Thailand he would trust.

Hasam, the sword, had arrived in Thailand on New Year's Day. What if he'd been ordered to keep a low profile and wait? What if he were a sleeper? A man with a destiny ordered to wait for a signal to set off a bomb. Not a Bali bomb killing a couple of hundred, but a bomb, as Colonel Pratt had hinted, that would kill hundreds of thousands. No one was certain if Hasam was his real name. They had a photograph but no positive identification.

It was time to have a heart-to-heart talk with two men.

Valentine.

And.

Pratt.

Sometimes fear hypnotized people. Sometimes fear caused hysteria. If a bomb were to be detonated in Pattaya, nothing would survive in the city, and in the world all reason and reflection would dissolve into violent impulse.

THIRTY-ONE

CALVINO side-stepped the Great Dane with a gravity-defying waterfall of slobber suspended in one corner of its mouth, and set out searching for Valentine. He checked the goat pens. No Valentine. He headed to the main house. Som, who was pottering around the kitchen area, the shelves of bottled snakes behind her, was startled as he slipped in without a sound. Her hands at her throat, she pointed towards the piano room on the far side of the swimming pool.

"No one can disturb him," she said.

Idiosyncrasy had its limits.

"Watch me," said Calvino.

The dining table was being set for the evening meal. A plate for Prasit's ghost was at the same place as before. Beyond the kitchen area, Gop, Valentine's number three *ying*, sat in shorts and tank top beneath an umbrella beside the pool reading a comic book. Her lips moved as she read. On the side table was a plate with the remains of an apple turning brown; lines of ants ferried the bounty down the leg of the table. She looked up and smiled at Calvino.

"*Sabaidee, mai?*" Are you fine?

"*Rohn,*" said Calvino, looking at the slices of apple. The ants were relentless, tireless in their work. Nothing stopped the marching columns.

Gop fanned herself. "It's too hot." But there wasn't a drop of sweat on her body.

As he approached the piano room, he heard Bach in a way he'd never heard it before. Maybe no one, not even Bach, thought it was possible. For an instant the music froze him at the door. Each note was precise, clear, hit square, with passion and speed. No one had ever played Bach like Valentine. He played for himself. He knew no bounds or limits when he was alone at the piano.

Calvino opened the set of chambered airlock doors and entered Valentine's room in the middle of his sacred practice period. The music stopped. Valentine remained hunched over the keyboard, his hands suspended above the keys. For a few seconds, he refused to acknowledge Calvino's existence. It was his way of denying that anyone could possibly have violated the cardinal rule of leaving him unmolested as he played. Calvino pulled a chair next to the grand piano and ran a hand across one end of the keyboard, the knuckles still rough and raw from the Harmony massage parlor attack.

"My God, you must never do that. Do you know how much this piano cost?"

"Tell me about Noi."

"You've destroyed my concentration."

"The Bach. I heard you playing."

"You have no idea."

"About Noi," said Calvino. "And I want to hear the story. Now."

Valentine stared at the keyboard, watching Calvino's hands, fearing a repeat of some movement that would annoy him. When it seemed the immediate danger had passed, he slowly lowered the lid over the keyboard and turned in his seat.

"Noi? My dear fellow, that is a little bit like asking an American to tell him all about someone named Jones. You must be more specific."

"This Noi worked at TQ2. She quit the bar and trained as a dive instructor. You hired her as a *sanom*. That Noi. Does her name ring a diver's bell?"

"Of course, I remember *that* Noi. What a sweet creature she was. Very affectionate and adored the goats. Two of the most important criteria in a woman, don't you think?"

"How did you meet her?"

"A friend of a friend told her that I was on the outlook for a new addition to my harem and she was frankly more than a little interested. She literally jumped in my arms."

"You offered her a place?"

"That was the idea. I made her a quite generous offer. But she stayed only a week." Valentine threw up his hands. "Then vanished without a word. Don't you think that was odd? Though, the longer I live here the less anything concerning women seems remotely odd."

"When was the last time you saw her?" Calvino figured either Valentine was lying to save face, or he really didn't know about Noi's boyfriend.

"She's not in trouble, is she?"

Calvino paused. "She might be. It would help if you would answer my question. When did she leave?"

"Let me see. . ." Valentine's attention drifted off as if he were listening to faraway music that only he could hear. He sighed, turned his head away, his eyes half closed.

He drifted back into his state of rapture. Some bubble of memory from a concert, a reception or feeding one of his goats. Glenn Gould and Bobby Fisher came to mind as Calvino watched Valentine off in an alternative universe, alone with his music, alone in time occupying a zone empty of everything but the sound of Bach.

"Was Prasit still alive?" asked Calvino. "When Noi was living here?"

The question snapped Valentine back from his fugue.

"Indeed he was. Noi arrived before he hanged himself. Unfortunately her period in my employ was brief. And bittersweet." Valentine looked wistful and sighed. "I haven't thought about Noi for a long time. Not until now. I must confess that I had completely forgotten about her. She was such a pleasant creature, and the time when she was in residence, the estate was a very different place. We knew harmony and peace. Each chord and note played the most wonderful music."

Calvino smiled at the mention of the word "harmony" as in Harmony massage parlor. "That place. It merely shows that harmony isn't always what it appears to be," he said.

"Well, maybe for you, my dear fellow. All I can tell you is that none of the current turmoil was present. That came after she left. If you find her, would you ask her to phone me?"

Valentine had little sense of irony. He spoke out of the utter, complete conviction that Calvino not only would find Noi, but that she might actually change her mind and phone him. Her return might restore the equilibrium Prasit's death had robbed from his life. He was already plotting how he would persuade Noi to rejoin the band of *sanoms*.

"Did you ever see Noi together with Prasit?"

"Vincent, you barge into my most private of places during a three-hour session and then ask me if I can possibly know whether one member of my staff might possibly wish to converse with another member of my staff. Doesn't that seem to you a slightly preposterous question? Unless you have some strange theory that Noi had something to do with Prasit's death. Which is highly doubtful. Or that she had some kind of relationship with Prasit, which is impossible. She told me that she detested Thai men."

She had left out the love in the love-hate relationship, thought Calvino.

"Do you remember how much time there was between when she disappeared and when Prasit was found dead?"

Valentine wrinkled his nose, scratched his chin, and drummed his fingers on the closed lid over the keyboard. "Let me see. It would have been. Been a few. . . You should ask my secretary, but I recall that about a week or so after her departure poor Prasit hanged himself."

"Did Noi ever have any visitors?"

He frowned. "Of course not. My creatures aren't allowed visitors. They can become a security problem. But I can tell you that Noi was unusually fearful. Som said that Noi always slept with the lights on. I say slept, but she hardly closed her eyes. Som said it was the isolation of the estate and the usual childish fear of ghosts. She had black bags under her eyes."

Noi had been haunted not by ghosts but by the fact people knew she had talked to David Jardine and the were closing in on her.

"Did you ask her if she had a problem?"

Valentine laughed, his longer, slender fingers slapping against his legs. "Thais don't have problems. *Mai mee pan ha*. Of course, I said, 'Why can't you sleep?' And do you know what she said? 'I dream I am in the bottom of the sea and my tank runs out and I know that I can't get to the top before I drown.' The poor girl had a fear of drowning. Quite extraordinary. She was a qualified dive master."

Calvino had reached the door when Valentine called to him. He was a master of timing. What he shouted was a foreign word.

"*Xenophilia*."

Calvino turned and tilted his head. "I remember this is one of your sexual fetishes."

"Not just mine. It appears to be one of yours as well. If what the staff tells me about Fon is true. It is a very small community inside the compound."

"Perhaps too small."

"Beware of wily widows. That's my advice."

"Thanks for your concern."

"I wouldn't want my private-eye distracted from his work."

"You can fire me any time."

"That won't be necessary, Vincent. But try and wrap things up in the next couple of days."

As Calvino turned again, Valentine threw out one more question. "You never asked about Noi's fetish."

"It had to do with water," said Calvino.

Valentine's eyes brightened. "You, my dear fellow, have a dirty mind."

THIRTY-TWO

CALVINO phoned his office and Ratana answered on the second ring.

"Vincent Calvino's office, how may I help you?"

She was back; perfect, she had weathered the storm.

"Any messages?" he asked.

"I've been trying to phone you. There is a new client. But you have to return to Bangkok today if you want the case."

Colonel Pratt's investigation, which was intended to take him out of the danger zone and return him to Bangkok.

"No can do. I am not finished in Pattaya."

Ratana hadn't been expecting him to reject the work. She had no idea that Colonel Pratt had been the one to find work for Vincent Calvino. It hadn't been the first time nor would it be the last.

"You know that little guy with thick glasses from New York?"

"There are a million little guys with thick glasses in New York. Which one?"

"He has a Korean wife named Soon Yi. You know him. I know that you know him."

"Soon what?"

"Soon Yi. Everyone knows her. She's young and Korean. Mia Farrow's adopted daughter."

Suddenly the name came to him. "Woody Allen."

"Yes, yes. My mother thinks that you are like Woody Allen but without the money or the fame."

Ratana had a system of remembering actors by their spouse's names. Jessica Lange translated as Sam Shepard. And Calista Flockhart as Harrison Ford. Once she had asked him, "What's his name? I can see the face but I can't remember the name. He's Annette Bening's husband. He's a really old guy. He looks like what an American President should look like but doesn't. He's really famous. What's his name? I know he's more famous than Annette but I can't think of his name."

Try Warren Beatty.

As she spoke on the phone, he thought about the widow, Fon, who translated as Prasit's wife, the obscure, nobody, ex-hitman, back-to-the-old-life-ways, hanged to death husband.

"Why does she say I'm like Woody Allen?" Calvino asked.

"Woody Allen makes her laugh."

He thought about telling her Fon had come to his bed.

What would Woody or Harrison or Warren do to make a woman laugh?

THIRTY-THREE

THE classic definition of terror is intense fear. You know the Latin word for this fear? Terror. Like a runaway freight train, it crashes straight into modern time with the same force, meaning, spelling and sound that is thousands of years old. The word should be feared. It has always been feared, and those with the power to cause fear have the ultimate power. Our enemies and our loved ones. We live in a state of perpetual terror.

David Jardine fell into silence. After a long pause, he looked up at the Buddha and a smile crossed his face. Calvino and Colonel Pratt waited for him to continue. "I wrote these words the second time I'd been shot in Vietnam," Jardine said. Confined to his hospital bed in Da Nang, he'd overheard a doctor tell a nurse that Jardine had no more than a fifty-fifty chance of making it. It had inspired anxiety and caused fear to hear what amounted to a death sentence. In the field, when he'd been shot, he'd felt pain and fear. The second time it was the same; inside the hospital, he learned that terror had many different meanings.

Ten days later David Jardine had asked the nurse to bring him paper and pen, and he wrote the words down and asked the nurse to deliver it to the doctor. The doctor had scribbled a note back, attaching the letter.

"One more day of life is worth the whole world. If you could bargain an extra week of life and the price was having your body thrown in the street to be torn apart by wild dogs, it would be a good bargain."

"Those were the words I received from my doctor. I never forgot them," Jardine said.

Jardine's job, he decided, lying in the hospital bed recovering from his wounds, was to do just what the doctor had prescribed: find one more day of life for himself and for those he loved and valued. And to do that, the mission was always the same: chase down and destroy those who live to take away that one more day.

Along the way he learned that terror had more than a feel: it had a color code. Not even the Romans with their invention of the word terror had thought of coloring the stages of terror alerts. Jardine had lived most of his life at the boundary of color code orange. Sometimes the threat of terror was downgraded from orange to yellow or upgraded from orange to red. Like waiting for traffic lights to change. Somewhere in the world an operations room was charged with choosing the color of the day for terror. Like a weather report. The chance of real, intense fear falling is ten percent. Or fifty percent. Or dig in, you have five minutes, and the color flashes across the sky and that is the last color you ever see. At that moment you are beyond terror. You are dead.

Jardine sat on the floor next to Colonel Pratt. In front of them was an enormous Buddha with thin wafers of gold fluttering as the two large floor fans in either side of the altar completed a 180° rotation. Even with the fans it was hot and sweat rolled down Jardine's face and neck. His shirt was damp and stuck to his shoulders and back.

Colonel Pratt nodded at the end of Jardine's terror story.

Jardine had been saved by a wise man, he thought.

Calvino found the two men sitting in silence inside the *wat*. A novice monk guided him to the side of the large Buddha where Colonel Pratt and David Jardine waited. Calvino sat near Colonel Pratt and leaned forward on his knees, bowing three times, *waiing* the Buddha between each bow, then sat back erect. There was a hint of a smile on Jardine's face as Calvino took his place.

"Respect is what hasn't been forgotten," said Jardine. "We are lost without it."

"We suffer because of our wants and desires. And the desire for respect is another form of clinging," said Colonel Pratt.

A silence again fell between the two men, both thinking about the nature of respect. Such a thing had once existed in America before the top one percent rented the country from the evangelicals. What was left of respect for everyone else in that kind of system? Waving of flags. It was why Calvino could never go home; the place called home had ceased to exist. Going home to a memory wasn't going home.

Calvino watched them for a moment. The colonel looked calm, almost serene.

"Valentine remembered Noi," said Calvino. "He said she had been living in the compound for a week before she disappeared. Why she left or where she's gone, he doesn't have any idea."

"Do you believe him?" asked Jardine.

Calvino looked up at the large statue of Buddha. "Valentine is incapable of lying."

"You just haven't found the things he lies about," said Jardine.

"I bow to your expertise in lying," said Calvino.

"What did he say about Noi?" asked Colonel Pratt.

"He opened a two hundred dollar bottle of French wine on their first night together. And what does she do?"

Jardine's focus was like that of a predator ready to make his move. He didn't take his eyes off Calvino; he didn't blink.

"What did she do?" asked Jardine.

"She poured Sprite into her glass of wine and then added two ice cubes."

A smile lit Jardine's face. "I like that."

"She also had nightmares about drowning and slept with the lights on. In the morning she came to the table with bags under her eyes."

"I talked with her trainer. The *farang* who taught her how to dive. You know what he said about her?" asked Jardine.

Calvino and Pratt shared a glance.

"I am certain you are going to tell us," said Calvino.

"She had laughter in her soul. The body, heart and head were all in working order, but beyond that, something in her had been touched by an artist who knew how to turn the right corner. She had something rare. He said that Noi would always belong to him and he would be comforted by the memory of her laughter."

There were women like that. But it didn't sound like the same woman Valentine had described, thought Calvino. The *farang* trainer was a very good lead.

"She left Valentine's compound a week or so before Prasit died," said Calvino. He was careful not to judge whether the death had been murder or suicide. The presence of the large Buddha statue brought a solemn, sober state, one of caution about how people died, the nature of their nightmares and the reasons for their disappearance.

"She saw something she shouldn't have seen," said Jardine. "It was her karma to be there."

"I came here to tell you what I found."

"You didn't find much, except the way that she drinks French wine," said Jardine. "Like everything French, you need to cut it by half and add ice."

"What did you expect? A map showing the location of the man we're looking for?"

Colonel Pratt bowed to the Buddha statue and rose to his feet.

"Within the good is the bad, and the bad is within the good. It isn't always a question of resources. The history of this *wat* is a good example." He walked across the open area to a pillar where a large plaque had been placed. The writing was in Thai. Colonel Pratt translated: "The building of this *sala* was funded by Veera."

He saw Jardine and Calvino looking at, what to the *farang* was, an unreadable scrawl on the plague. "Where did the money come from?" asked Colonel Pratt. "We don't really know. Does coming here knowing who built a *wat* make our respect to Buddha less? Do the resources matter? We find what we are meant to find."

"The problem with selling yourself is you no longer care about the motives of those who buy you. All you are about is the money." Jardine looked away from the sign and up at the sky. What color was terror at that moment?

"And we help those we believe deserve our help," said Calvino, looking straight at Jardine.

Jardine nodded and rose to his feet. "What we deserve is a world where people can go about their lives without worrying about the color of terror. A world where such fear goes back into the box and the lid is put on and if you don't think that is worth committing to, then we find ourselves on different sides of the fence."

"Which is another way of saying that you're either with us or against us," said Calvino.

"The Buddha teaches the middle path," said Colonel Pratt.

"And I respect his teachings. But we are at war. There is no middle path. The sooner people realize this, the sooner they can understand why everyone has to take a stand. You are on one side of the line or the other."

Men like David Jardine were true believers; they couldn't find meaning without finding their counterpart on the other side of a battle. The color codes were in their blood. "If I find out anything more, I'll pass it along," said Calvino.

In the parking lot, Calvino opened his car door while Jardine stood back a couple of feet with the colonel. "It wouldn't be a good thing if you got yourself in over your head."

"That sounds like a threat," said Calvino. "Intended to cause anxiety."

Jardine shook head. "Not a threat. Just on-the-ground realities. Civilians in war zones sometimes forget where they are. It's not a holiday."

"I'll remember that," said Calvino.

"See you around."

"I doubt it," said Calvino.

Jardine showed no emotion, turned and walked away. His car and driver were waiting. His driver stood alongside the passenger side, holding the door open. Jardine climbed inside and the driver closed the door, walked around and climbed inside. The engine was running, the air conditioner pumping chilled air. Calvino and Colonel Pratt watched as the black BMW reversed out of the parking spot and disappeared out of the entrance.

"Why is it that I don't like that guy?" asked Calvino.

"Like is less important than trust," said Colonel Pratt.

"And you don't trust him, do you?"

"He's done nothing to suggest I should distrust him. On the middle path, one stays watchful. That's not mistrust. It's prudence."

Friendships needed nourishment. Every so often Colonel Pratt would say something so simple and elegant that it provided fuel for months and months.

It was only later that Calvino found out that the abbot of the *wat* was a friend of Colonel Pratt's commander and it was the abbot who had arranged his interview with Veera. It was a world of interconnecting relationships, favors, and duties like capillaries that allowed the blood to flow throughout the civil body. Pratt's world of the middle path allowed everyone to walk that same path without knocking the other guy into the gutter.

THIRTY-FOUR

AFTER Jardine left, Colonel Pratt said, "I have something I want to show you."

"Why do you want to stick around? I've got a lead to follow up."

"This won't be a waste of time," said the colonel.

Calvino followed Colonel Pratt across the parking lot and down a passage between two *sala*s. A few country people sat on folding chairs inside the first *sala*. A young *ying* arrived a few seconds ahead of the colonel. She wore a white robe, her head was shaved, and she stepped out of her sandals before entering the *sala* barefoot. She knelt in front of a coffin and lit a stick of incense, holding the smoking stick in her cupped palms. Thumbs touching her forehead, she leaned forward. She executed the ritual like a pro, thought Calvino. In the Land of Smiles, it was always one incense stick for the dead. The ritual was a sign of respect, a prayer that the dead person would be reborn to a better life. Even for a nun, the rule was one stick of incense.

For the living wanting a better life, the idea was to make a merit ritual, or *tam boon*. The sticks increased to three: one lit for the *dharma*, another for the *sangha* and, lastly, a third set afire for the Buddha. Merit-making was a three-stick deal; for death, one stick was enough.

"Does she live in the *wat*?" asked Calvino. Not all *wats* had facilities for nuns. He was thinking that Veera had paid for much of the *wat* and wondering if it been Veera's idea to have Buddhist nuns.

Colonel Pratt nodded. "Over there." He pointed across the parking lot at a row of buildings. "They are in separate quarters."

"Also paid for by Sia Veera."

Colonel Pratt nodded. "He's making merit for the next life."

Jardine had one thing right—the threat of death was the ultimate form of terror. As everyone sooner or later croaked, the nervous types started preparing early for the eventuality that their deeds in this life were being written down in a book and the book decided what would come in the next life. Veera must have had some anxiety about the bookkeeping on the other side, because he had spent a lot of money in the *wat*. One day he'd be laid out in one of the *salas*, and the villagers and *luuk nongs* would line up, one incense stick each, kneeling in front of his coffin and praying the books were balanced and that he'd be reborn a more powerful man. Some powerful people in Bangkok were seeking to accelerate Veera's celestial bookkeeping.

In front of where the nun knelt, a wooden stand held the framed photograph of a youthful, grinning Thai who looked in his early twenties. The photo looked like it had been enlarged from a small snapshot; the deceased's grainy smile and smudged eyes peered out from a pixilated, grainy haze.

Colonel Pratt said, "He was shot a couple of nights ago. The police said he was a drug dealer. He shot at them first."

"They found drugs on him," said Calvino. There was no point in making it a question. The whole time he watched the Thai nun in front of the coffin.

"A dozen pills," said Colonel Pratt. His voice was clear and confident. Not that he believed the dead man was a drug dealer, but that he believed the evidence of drug dealing had been found.

Such a death was a set piece. If the man had been shot dead and the cops said he was a drug dealer, then it followed that drugs would be found on the body. That was a one-way package deal to the nearest *sala*. The same thing had happened to Prasit's brother. Shot to death. Fon said the brother had no previous record of drugs; pills had been sprinkled around his body. Who was to know? Pills were all the evidence required. Sombat's death was another open-and-shut case of a drug dealer killed by unknown forces.

"The rule of law is always the first casualty of any war," said Colonel Pratt, who had read Calvino's mind. The colonel was mostly right about how Calvino's mind functioned on matters in Thailand. This time it wasn't hard to hit the target. A lot of people had the same thoughts. Once the troops were sent in, that was the end of due process, prosecutors, judges, evidence, and the burden of proof. The war on drugs had been fought no differently from any other war. "In Vietnam the Americans ran a program code-named Phoenix," said Colonel Pratt. "Members of the program slipped into a village under the cover of night and slit the throat of suspected Vietcong. How could they ever be certain the throats belonged to Vietcong? They killed based on intelligence gathered by men who collected information from the field. That is always a weakness."

"You can never know."

"No one can ever fully know. Mistakes were made in the Phoenix operation."

"It's the price that gets paid," said Calvino. "Paid by those at the sharp end of the sword."

Colonel Pratt understood how a seasoned cop saw the world: people in the field sometimes had their own agenda and settling scores was a temptation. You don't like someone: he's a threat or he's shown you some disrespect or he's running some competition with your business or your wife or girlfriend. Put him on the list. Light that single stick of incense. But the flaws and shortcomings in intelligence never stopped people in the field from acting on the intelligence or investing resources in the Phoenix program. Or shooting men said to be drug dealers. The lesson was never learnt: it was impossible to rely on the honor of others to pass up the truth because either malice or ignorance always stained truth and honor. The only way to know the truth was to do your own fieldwork. So someone like David Jardine appears without any real connections. What does he do? What kind of assumptions would he make? Had there been another Phoenix-like program for international terrorists? It was the default plan of occupiers. It was the natural choice one expected them to make, and one was almost never disappointed.

The nun finished her prayer and planted the solitary incense stick in the bronze pot near the coffin. She rose and walked outside the *sala*, stepping into her sandals. She came straight over to Colonel Pratt. She wore no make-up. With her bald head and large white robes, it was difficult to tell her age. Other than to say, despite the self-inflicted demolition to her beauty, she still remained too young and beautiful to be a nun.

"Mae chee Noi, this is Khun Vincent," said Colonel Pratt.

Jardine had left empty-handed. Somewhere along the line, Colonel Pratt had made a judgment call. A command decision in the field, under fire, knowing what he decided would shape the fate of things that followed. He had chosen friendship.

Calvino *waied* her. She returned his *wai* with a slight nod. Nuns and monks don't return a *wai*. It's a rule.

He tried to imagine Noi living inside Valentine's estate with the other women, the goats, the swimming pool, the lounge chairs, the TV room with everyone huddled around watching the Savage Channel. She had been part of Valentine's self-invented world and now she was part of one a couple of universes away.

"I'd like to ask you some questions about Prasit."

"If you wish," she said.

"You knew him?"

She nodded. "Yes, I knew Pee Prasit."

The three of them walked across the grounds and found a bench.

"Would he have killed himself?" asked Calvino.

Asking a nun who had sworn a vow of truth a question was about as close as any private eye could hope to come to finding an answer connected with the truth.

"He loved life. But he was scared. Very afraid because of the bad things he had done, and the people he had worked for."

He had been living in a code red state of terror.

Why had it gone to flashing red?

Calvino smiled; he had a short list of who made the color red of terror. "Let's talk about the people he worked for. Before Valentine, he did some work for Veera? Am I right about that?"

Some say fear is your friend and there is no denying that was true. But in Thailand, ambiguity is your best friend. He waited as she looked away, picking at the hem of her robe. "Maybe. Maybe not. If you do the bad thing, you see the bad thing returning to you from every corner."

"Meaning you aren't going to tell me," said Calvino.

She neither answered nor ignored him; her stare was blank.

"Do you know who Veera is?" asked Colonel Pratt.

"Yes."

"Did Prasit know who he was?"

She nodded. "He knew."

The colonel knew the Thai way to get an answer. Calvino shrugged his shoulders like a boxer coming out of his corner for round five. A little beaten but still steady on his feet.

"Did you ever meet Ajarn Sawai at Valentine's compound?" asked Calvino.

"I saw him twice at Valentine's." Her voice broke as she spoke.

"Other than Jardine, who else knew that you were a *witness?*"

The word got her by surprise as if she had lowered her gloves and taken a slamming right hand to the jaw. Her head dropped. She stared at the ground. When she looked up, that controlled, placid face had a slight twitch above the right eye. The word *witness* had pushed the color red button. Terror alert, alarm bells ringing in her head.

"I don't know. He didn't understand me. Or why I went to Valentine's. He believed I'd gone to warn Pee Prasit."

"Warn him of what?"

"That he was in danger."

"What kind of danger?"

She shrugged and clammed up, folding her arms tightly around her body. She rocked back and forth, quietly, the way a grieving child moves, to shake out the feeling of doom and sadness.

Calvino leaned forward, his arms resting on his legs, running his fingers through his hair, exchanging a glance with Colonel Pratt. "Valentine said you were afraid of ghosts and couldn't sleep."

She nodded, tears springing into her eyes. With the edge of her robe she wiped them. "I was afraid."

"Did you warn Prasit that Veera had paid someone to kill him?"

The tears flowed. "I came to this *wat* because I no longer want to know of this world. It has only suffering for me. I did some terrible thing last life and now I am paying my debt."

"Listen to me, Noi. Did Prasit know someone was coming after him?"

"He knew. And he was so, so afraid. He knew he was going to die."

"If you have other duties, it's okay for you to go," said Colonel Pratt.

They watch her rise and slowly cross the grounds.

She had taken sanctuary in a *wat*. It was her way of saying that she had left the world, and as long as she stayed in the *wat*, she'd be safe. What was her salvation was also her prison. As long as Veera was alive, she could never leave. One could struggle a lifetime and never quite understand the struggle going on inside her head. Colonel Pratt could have easily given her up to Jardine, but he didn't do so. Jardine would have taken her out of the *wat* and put her in one of the interrogation houses, and she risked disappearing into a shadowy world, one from which many had never re-emerged. The colonel had withheld intelligence. Calvino didn't care about that. He didn't like what he saw when he looked in Jardine's mirror. Life was about deciding what you could live with looking back in the mirror.

Only death was absolute—except to a Buddhist for whom death was a transformation. And death had been all around Noi, circling above her head, plucking out of the earth and sky the people she knew, the people she loved, the people she hardly knew existed. She was someone you wanted to light a candle for, a single candle of hope that the light might shelter her from the void of darkness.

THIRTY-FIVE

THE address Fon had for Ton was two months old and as useful as a bar *ying's* promise. No one at the fleabag room had known Ton. No one in the neighborhood had any idea what had happened to him. He probably had gone home. One thing for certain: guys like Ton never went back home except to hide, and if he'd gone into hiding, he'd have left months ago.

Calvino had pretty good idea that Sawai would know how to find Ton. Calvino had phoned the guru and asked for a recent address. Instead, Sawai made an appointment to meet. For a man who never seemed to leave his compound except to visit the *jao poh* or the house of someone like Prasit, the immediate consent to a meeting came as a surprise. What wasn't a surprise was that the guru was late for the appointment. He might have had a plug-in to cosmic laws but his co-ordination with local time was flawed. Calvino paced back and forth waiting in front of the Royal Garden Plaza shopping mall, glancing now and then at his watch. He had started to sweat in the heat, so he stepped inside the Plaza.

It was no surprise when Sawai phoned and said that he had been delayed but the meeting was still on.

"Don't worry. Ton wants to meet you," said Sawai.

"That seems unlikely."

"Sure. See you below the red plane."

Calvino was worried; would the guru show? That was the question. He reminded himself that it had been the guru's idea to meet at the Plaza. The irony wasn't lost on Calvino that this was the same mall which housed the Believe It or Not museum. Sawai's instructions had been to meet below the red plane. Everyone in Pattaya knew the red plane was the fuselage of a fake plane that was suspended over one entrance to the plaza. The front half of the plane didn't exist. It hadn't been built. The size of the fuselage indicated a single-engine plane. The illusion was that the plane had plowed into the plaza and was stuck half in and half out. As landmark, it couldn't be missed. As an advertisement for the Believe It or Not museum, it already was out of date, one of those clever advertising ideas floating up from the pre-9/11 world. It screamed out World Trade Towers in New York City. *Believe It or Not.*

Sawai arrived twenty minutes late on a Harley Davidson motorcycle. He wheeled to a stop in front of the Plaza. He leaned back on the saddle, slipped the large shiny black helmet from his head and looked around. He'd parked directly below the simulated plane crash. He looked around for Calvino.

The automatic sliding doors opened and a blast of hot air from the outside shot into Calvino's face. He stepped back. One last dance with the air-con before meeting the overheated guru. Inside the mall, it had been cold enough to wear a jacket and sweater. Calvino stayed with the jacket, a .38 police special riding in the leather shoulder holster under his left arm. He waited and watched as the guru, holding his crash helmet as he spun around on the saddle of his Harley, scanned for some sign of the *farang* private eye. Sawai, with his shaved head, aviator sunglasses, and a dozen amulets hanging from gold chains around his thick neck, fingered his cellphone. The guru had come alone. Calvino didn't like the look of the setup and left the guru to roast under the sun. Toast him a medium brown, wear him down a little, make him tired and disoriented. Sweat glistening on his bald head, pellets of sweat splashed onto his crash helmet, straddling a Harley, the guru was the one who suddenly looked worried. He rang Calvino's cellphone. Calvino let it ring. Let him cook a little longer. No one paid Sawai any notice. If he had the two teenagers riding on the back, he still would have blended into the general freak show. Calvino wondered if the guru had ditched the jailbait tag-team or if they were back at his house, peeling oranges and waiting for his return.

Pattaya was a tourist attraction, part of a 24/7 non-stop freak show. Sawai was a candidate for ringmaster of the moment. The exhibits inside the museum had a hard time competing with the action on the street, which offered an unlimited possibility of staring and pointing at the dwarfs, the giants, and the bald-headed guru in designer shades.

On the phone Sawai had promised that he would arrive with Ton. That had been the purpose of the meeting: to meet Ton and talk to him about Prasit and Sombat.

But the guru had arrived alone. Beads of sweat ran down his shaved head. As the sliding door opened again, Calvino stepped out into the oven-like sun. He answered the phone. Sawai spotted him immediately, greeting him with a smile.

"Where's Ton?"

"Waiting." The guru looked him up and down. "You are going to be hot wearing jacket," he said.

"I can take a lot of heat before I melt," said Calvino.

The guru eyed him. "Up to you."

"Yeah, up to me," said Calvino. "So where is Ton?"

"At work."

Calvino smiled. "Shooting anyone I might know?"

"He works in a gym. He's a trainer. The other trainer didn't come back from lunch so he couldn't leave. He said we should go and meet him at the gym." Sawai put his helmet on, pulled up the tinted perplex faceguard and patted the seat behind him. "Let's go."

It was one of those Daniel Pearl moments. What goes through the head and what goes through the heart are distinctly conflicting messages. Ninety percent of human history screams out with one overriding lesson—don't trust a stranger. In the past, there were only two choices with a stranger, kill or be killed. The choices were written deep within the genetic code. The invention of the gun had come as a convenient way of dealing with strangers. Sawai was a stranger, and Ton he'd never met. Calvino had only a moment to consider the alternatives. He could terminate the meeting with Ton, break off with Sawai, and return to Valentine's. Or he could climb onto the back of the Harley and take a chance. The guru had, as far as he could tell, tried to set him up for a fall, using a couple of underaged girls to bait the trap. Calvino locked eyes with the guru. Sawai made a living looking into the eyes of others and convincing them he had the truth. He'd made Prasit a true believer, lending him spiritual bodyguards to protect him in the time of need. Prasit had ended up dead. Calvino felt the weight of his .38 riding against his chest. A choice equalizer in case things started to go sideways.

Calvino climbed onto the back of the Harley. "Let's go find your boy," he said.

Sawai gunned the Harley out of the mall and onto Soi 2. He drove towards Walking Street. Most things in Pattaya were 24/7 but Walking Street was also a driving street until early evening. The Harley roared down the road lined on both sides with shops, restaurants, tattoo parlors, tailor shops and jewelry shops. After dark, once all the neon lights came on, Beach Road and Walking Street and the side sois looked like a version of Las Vegas after it had been thrown into a garbage compacter and compressed down to four or five stories high. Merchants sweeping the pavement in front of their shops didn't bother to stop and watch the guru and *farang* on the Harley speeding past. The mannequins in the Believe It or Not Museum could have come to life and run down the road and they wouldn't have looked up.

Sawai parked in front of a hotel near the end of the road. The sign said "Julie Complex" sounding more like a medical condition than a hotel. "You said he worked in a gym," said Calvino.

"He does. The gym is inside," said Sawai.

Calvino and the guru walked down a long, narrow corridor. On one side was a mini-mart with bottles of Mekhong and Singha beer displayed in the window, and opposite was a massage parlor with foam mats lined side-by-side with a thin curtain separating each. Several middle-aged massage girls sat on the floor reading comic books. No customers were in his line of vision. Calvino touched his ear. Massage parlors made his ears ring and gave him a headache. At the end of the corridor, Sawai turned and started up a couple of stairs. Straight ahead were an office and the check-in counter and lobby of the hotel, and beyond was the entrance to a restaurant. But Sawai wasn't heading to the office and check-in counter of the hotel. Halfway up the stairs, he stopped and looked back. Calvino stood at the bottom of the stairs. He stared at the wall to the left of the stairs, where an Asian body builder with the body of Mr. Universe had been painted. Underneath the figure with the flexed bicep written in large bold script were the words: Golden Gym. Calvino continued up the stairs, keeping a step behind and to the left of Sawai. He didn't have a good feeling about what might be waiting at the top. In an investigation, the art was in having a sense of the percentages, working them out in his head. Did they favor the punter or the house? With all gambles, the house had an edge. Otherwise casinos would be bamboo huts rather than palaces.

He took the next step and placed his bet. His left arm flexed against the .38 police special under his armpit. Sweat soaked the collar of his shirt. He wanted to take off the jacket covering his concealed weapon.

When they reached the top, there was nothing but another corridor. Sawai pulled open a door to the lobby of the gym and walked through and into the gym area where there were rows of benches and free weights on metal racks. As they came into the gym, a couple of Thai men were working out on the benches. In the far corner, a well-built Thai dressed in dark shorts and shirt spotted for one of the weight lifters. He stood behind the bench where the customer was lifting barbells with about a hundred kilos loaded onto the bar. His arms were pumped up and his head rolled back, looking at Sawai and Calvino upside down as the trainer turned away from the bench.

"Ton," said Sawai. "The *farang* wants to talk to you."

The trainer looked away from the bench and looked Calvino over as if this wasn't what he had expected.

Calvino stared back at him, wondering how it was that this man had managed to stay alive.

Ton's hand reached into his shorts and pulled out a key, tossing it to Sawai who caught it one-handed. It was a hotel room key. *Room 402* was printed on the heavy wooden key handle.

"I'll meet you in my room. Give me five minutes to finish with my customer."

So far Sawai had told the truth. But the truth for a guru like Sawai was good for a sprint; over the long distance, lies were what let guys like Sawai pull ahead of the pack.

The request seemed reasonable.

"Okay, five minutes. Is that okay with you?" Sawai asked.

Calvino looked around the gym. Ton was the only trainer in sight and the gym had people working out. It was reasonable to let him finish. In Thailand, the appearance of things was everything. People rarely asked whether what *appeared* to be real corresponded with the underlying reality. Calvino had a habit of asking. Appearances didn't keep anyone alive. It was just the opposite. They were the best way to get oneself killed. As the hotel room key chain sailed through the air, he thought of the plane sticking out of the Royal Garden Plaza as if it had crashed. It hadn't crashed. It had been built to look like something it wasn't. As he saw the guru snatch the keys, he asked himself, *Why not step out into the lobby so that Ton could finish up the set?*

There was always a risk of the wings falling off the plane. Sometimes an investigation, no matter how much legwork he'd done, hit a dead end. More than once he had admitted to the client that he couldn't help them. Valentine would have accepted that answer and moved on to find another way to return peace to his fiefdom of harem and goats. Ton was like the plane in flight. He was real. He was on his way down. It was all working smoothly. Nothing out of place.

The windows in the room where they waited for Ton looked out over the bay. Boats anchored all along the shore and below waiters were setting tables at an outdoor seafood restaurant. The hotel had been built over the beach. From the bank of windows a tourist could watch the boats for miles, or a local could use the room as a sentry tower, watching for particular boats coming in and out of the harbor. Calvino looked at his watch, marking the passage of fifteen minutes. The Thai sense of five minutes was somewhere between five minutes and one hour. He couldn't really say that Ton was late. He was running on Thai time.

The guru switched on the television and opened the mini-fridge. He took out a can of Diet Coke, popped it open and drank from the can. He sat on the edge of the bed, he switched on the TV and surfed the channels, stopping at a game show. The guru immediately became absorbed in the game show. Watching him, it was hard to imagine that this was a man who held influence and power over Veera. Calvino stayed near the door. He thought about the probabilities of what had happened. He'd been hired to look into what appeared to be either suicide or domestic murder and had found himself on the edge of an international manhunt for a terrorist. A young woman had seen a boat come ashore with Hasam and a footlocker. Noi had recognized one of the men in the boat as the captain of a trawler. Jardine and Pratt said he was a JI operative. Jardine had talked to her and she'd gotten scared. She ran away, thinking life inside the compound of a rich *farang* would insulate her from the investigation.

Noi's presence in the compound didn't look good for Prasit. He had confessed to his personal guru about his sins, including some murders. And the guru was an advisor to some important people who might be embarrassed if this trawler captain were discovered. The safe play was to take down Prasit and his brother. The problem would be solved. Right? Well, not solved but contained. Ton was alive; one man left out of the team of three. That was strange, unless it was Ton who had been hired to kill Prasit and his brother. That way he could have proved himself a loyal soldier. The question that had been bothering Calvino was, who had hired Ton? The man sitting on the bed watching the game show snorted as he laughed.

"I have this theory that Ton was hired to kill Prasit and his brother," said Calvino.

Sawai sipped the Diet Coke.

"Prasit hanged himself. Drug dealers shot his brother. Or the police."

"That's the party line."

Calvino glanced at his watch. "I don't think Ton's going to show."

"Wait a little longer. You have a theory. I have one, too."

Sawai stared out the window at the sea. "A *ying* named Noi fall in love with Prasit. These things happen. His wife was very angry. You not know Thai lady when she's angry."

"How do you know this?"

"Prasit tell me. He said he was scared for his life. He had been fighting with Fon. She say, 'Why you have to do this? Why you break my heart this way? Why you make me lose face?'"

"Why wasn't Fon happy with a suicide verdict?" said Calvino.

Sawai shook his head and sighed. "*Farang* not understand how Thai lady think. She's a very clever woman. She knows drugs. Easy for her to give her husband an injection, put him on a chair, tie a rope around his neck and let him die. She wants more than her husband to die. She wants Noi to suffer. Dying is not so hard. We all get the chance. But suffering? That's different. No one wants to suffer. Release from suffering is what the Buddha teaches. Fon says, 'No, my husband not kill himself. Someone kill him.' At first, you think I did this. We were close. I tried to help him find the path. Or you think that Sia Veera had him killed. None of that is true. Fon is too clever. She wants you to say it was Noi who killed her husband. Women are dangerous like a cobra."

"How do you know that Noi was in the compound when Prasit died?"

The guru flexed his jaws. "Ton saw Noi in the compound that day. She had an appointment to meet Prasit. But she's too late. He's already dead. Fon says Noi drugged her husband and made his death look like suicide. Why does Noi do this? Because Prasit wouldn't leave his wife for her. You ever watch Thai TV?"

This explanation registered as a lie. Calvino had a good idea Fon would have mentioned Noi, but she hadn't.

"*Nam nao*. It means dirty water," said Sawai. "These stories every day about love triangles. It gives women many ideas. Thai women can't watch enough of *nam nao*."

"If Ton were in the compound that day, wouldn't someone have seen him?" asked Calvino. "Unless he had a secret way in. Ton seems like a well trained, resourceful man. Cunning. I can see him getting in and out without anyone noticing him."

Sawai shrugged his shoulders. "You can ask him. I don't think he had any secret. He went to see Prasit. He went to borrow money. Ton had a habit of borrowing from his friends. He saw Fon injecting Prasit with a needle. He saw Prasit sleeping in a chair by the door. He's very frightened and runs away."

There was a knock on the door. Calvino's right hand moved inside his jacket, touching the .38 police special. He moved back from the door.

"Why don't you answer that, Ajarn Sawai?"

The guru finished the can of Diet Coke, rose from the bed and opened the door. Two uniformed cops stood in the door. Walkie-talkies on their belts squawked. Handguns riding high inside leather belts, they looked all business. One cop pushed into the room and did a quick look around.

"There's been an accident," said the other cop. "You come with us now."

THIRTY-SIX

AT the bottom of the stairs leading to the gym, a small crowd had gathered. Women from the massage parlor, office workers, a security guard and some of the motorcycle taxi guys pooled at the bottom of the stairs like tadpoles on the muddy bottom of a rice paddy under the light of a full moon. They stared as two cops escorted the *farang*, and a man with a shaved head up the stairs and into the gym. Other cops kept the onlookers from following up the stairs. In the gym, a medical team was examining a body that was stretched out on the bench in the far corner. The same bench where Calvino had last seen Ton working with his customer. Ton had been spotting the customer and promising to join them in five minutes. Not far from the bench Colonel Pratt conferred with David Jardine and two other *farangs* in suits and surgical masks. One of them was dusting the bench and barbell for fingerprints. The other searched for hairs, fabric, and saliva, anything that might provide a clue as to the identity of the killer.

"You keep turning up in awkward situations. That tells me something," said Jardine.

"What does it tell you?"

"That your dead gardener is getting you into something way over where you want to be."

"You got something you want to ask me, then ask. This is Thailand. Don't tell me when I'm in over my head."

Jardine stared hard at him. "You can start by telling me what you were doing in this man's room."

"The way I see it, this is Colonel Prachai's investigation. Why don't I tell him the story and you can read his report?"

Calvino looked at the body. Ton's brown eyes stared lifeless at the ceiling. His tongue was swollen and red, extending from his mouth. It would have been a terrible way to die. Calvino remembered watching him spot the man on the bench. Ton's body lay stretched out on the same bench and the barbell with a hundred kilos of weights lay lopsided with the bar over his throat. His larynx had been crushed.

Also crushed was Calvino's theory that Ton had stayed alive by proving himself a loyal soldier. It had only been a matter of time. Calvino had been so close to questioning him. Calvino balled his hands into fists. He looked at the lifeless body and shook his head.

"I was waiting to ask him questions."

"About Prasit's death?"

"Yes."

"Interesting that you are found in Ton's room but he's dead in the gym."

"He wasn't dead when the meeting was arranged."

"Who is your friend?"

Jardine nodded at Sawai who stood a few feet back.

"A local holy man," said Calvino. "You might have seen his Harley parked out front."

"When did you see Ton?"

"Half an hour ago."

"Who was he with?"

"He was spotting for a guy on the bench."

Colonel Pratt stood silently off to the side, waiting for an opening in the barrage of Jardine's questions. He finally saw his chance.

"Vincent, did you get a good look at the men in the gym?" asked Colonel Pratt. The first sensible question that had been asked, thought Calvino.

"There were a couple of body builders over there." He pointed to the other side of the gym. "I didn't really get a good look. As I said, Ton was spotting a guy who was pumping iron on the bench. I saw his face upside down for five seconds."

"Can you identify the man on the bench?" asked David Jardine. "Was he having a conversation with Ton?"

"I saw them for a couple of seconds. The guy on the bench was lifting weights. He wasn't talking."

"Great," said Jardine. "Helpful. You saw a guy on a bench."

"I had no reason to look at him."

"You're investigating a murder. You look at everyone. That's basic training."

Calvino pursed his lips, rocking back on his heels. "You're right. I should have asked for his business card. Asked him where he was when a gardener was murdered."

"You can play wise or you can play smart. Your choice," said Jardine.

"Why don't we get our business over," said Calvino. "Then we can all go home."

"That's smart."

Colonel Pratt scratched the back of his neck and looked out the window at the street below. The guru sat on a bench opposite the body. He looked as if he were miles and miles away, another place, another universe. He'd been left out of the confrontation between Calvino and Jardine. The guru did what Thais do when *farangs* turn up the heat on each other; he turned inward. There was no percentage in getting involved in their conflicts. Let the *farangs* do what *farangs* have to do. Snarl and curse and threaten and get red in the face. Then let the winner report back when they're done with each other.

Working over the bench, the suits continued to collect evidence from the body. Ton's body looked smaller in death, broken in the way flesh and bone were pressed and smashed until the plasticity snapped and a spattering of blood and gore shot across the room, smelling vile. Finding someone killed in a gym with the murder weapon a heavy set of barbells made someone who didn't work out feel good about themselves. A couple of the *farang* suits worked over the body, brushing and touching and probing, gathering and labeling as they went.

Colonel Pratt touched Calvino's shoulder. "*Jai yen,*" he said. Keeping a cool heart with David Jardine was becoming a major effort. His style was to provoke and intimidate. It must have worked well in interrogation rooms with no windows and a single bulb hanging down from the ceiling. Getting information was one thing, but following up on that information and closing in on the man was another. All David Jardine had to show for his efforts was a woman who'd become a nun and couldn't picked out Hasam from a photo. On the staircase curious onlookers wondered why so many *farangs* had been allowed inside the crime scene and why the Thai police had excluded Thai people.

One of the *farang* suits scraped underneath the fingernails of the corpse. Another suit handed Jardine a Ziploc bag, and inside was the body of a coiled and dead snake. The dead reptile would have looked good stuffed into one of the jars in Valentine's collection.

"Have you ever seen a snake like this?" asked Jardine

"Prasit saw one before he died. His brother's body was found with one," said Calvino.

Jardine moved in closer and talked just above a whisper.

"That points to the same killer. Find the person who had access to all three men and you have your man—or woman," said Jardine. "Okay, you've given me something. And now I'll give you something. We've had been interrogating Hambali and he's given us some useful information about money transfer sources, dates, and names."

"I read that in the newspapers," said Calvino.

"He told us about Hasam."

"The man named 'Sword'."

"I'd thought you'd remember," said Jardine.

Calvino moved to the side as two medics walked past. David Jardine's attention was focused elsewhere. Beyond the medics, he stared at Sawai who, subdued and strangely quiet, stood near a couple of suits in the corner. His mystical presence was vastly reduced. Calvino made him out as another freak working a con. "Let's have a little talk with Sawai," said Jardine.

Sawai smiled as Jardine produced a photograph from an envelope and handed it to Calvino, who looked at the photograph and then passed it to Sawai. The man in the picture wore glasses and had a full black beard without a hint of gray. A puffy pudding of a face. Not a body-builder type. None of the men in the gym had a beard.

"Recognize him?" Jardine asked.

Calvino shook his head. Jardine waited until Sawai finished looking at the picture. The guru handed the picture back. "I never see this man."

The *farang* suits had finished with the body. Colonel Pratt ordered the body snatcher to lift the body onto the gurney. It took two of them grunting and sweating to lift the barbells off the body and set them on the floor.

"What do you know about snakes? Let's start with cobras," said Calvino.

Sawai pulled a face, half-disgust, half-contempt. "Ask your good friend, Valentine. He keeps snakes."

Colonel Pratt told Sawai that before he left, the colonel wanted to talk with him in the lobby. He ordered one of his men to tail the guru. Sawai stopped at the top of the stairs and punched a number into his cellphone. That was good. That was what they wanted him to do. Was he calling to let his next appointment know that he would be late? Or was he checking in with Veera? His cellphone was on their radar. After Sawai disappeared down the stairs, Jardine waited until Colonel Pratt had returned.

"Hambali also told us something else," said Jardine.

Calvino felt whatever Jardine was telling him, he wasn't giving away very much. A crumb, hoping the bird would follow the trail. "He told us that Hasam was carrying big money when he was smuggled into Thailand nine months ago. Say, fifty grand."

Colonel Pratt followed the gurney down the stairs. Sawai was one step behind him. "I'll see you downstairs," said Colonel Pratt.

That left Calvino, the *farang* suits and Jardine alone in the gym. "Hasam was carrying something else. An evil and nasty weapon intended to cause maximum harm. The man named Sword came here with a dirty bomb. He was told to wait until he received a signal. Even Hambali wasn't sure what the signal was. It had been coded, and once he was captured all of the codes were changed. Your man Prasit was somehow tied into all of this. When I said you were in over your head, it wasn't to bust your balls, it was to state a fact. There's a terrorist cell in Pattaya and it's working 24/7 to find a way to accomplish its mission. This isn't me talking. It's Hambali. He's blown up enough people to know how things work, and he's told us about all he can."

"What do you want me to do?" asked Calvino.

David Jardine smiled. "Stay out of the way. But in case you don't stay out of the way, and you happen to come across our man, let us know. It's important, Vincent. For a lot of people you used to know in New York City."

Downstairs in the lobby of the hotel, Colonel Pratt sat across from Sawai who said he had a theory about Prasit's death that he wanted to tell it to the colonel in private. The thing about gurus and fortune-tellers is they are supposed to see the future and when they don't, they inevitably come up with an explanation. "Men with bad karma can go at any time," said Sawai. "No one knows. I had a feeling this morning that Ton's time was near, and that's why I arranged for Vincent to meet him."

You can buy that and the Brooklyn Bridge for ten dollars, thought Calvino as he sat next to Colonel Pratt. Ton was about to confirm the guru's theory of the murder of the gardener. With all the deadly snakes showing up, one didn't have to look very far to find a snake-oil salesman.

"What's your theory?" asked Colonel Pratt.

Sawai explained how Prasit's jealous wife had arranged the murder of her husband and left evidence to suggest that it had been the work of her husband's lover. About the time Sawai had finished, Jardine showed up and handed Calvino a set of photographs of Indonesian terrorist suspects, including Hasam.

"Hold on to these," said Jardine. "If you run up against any of these men, give me a call." Along with the pictures was Jardine's name card with his cellphone number handwritten along the bottom. Calvino had given Sawai a perfect alibi. Jardine ignored the guru, leaving the interrogation to Colonel Pratt. The American security officer stared at Sawai and shook his head, then turned and walked out with the *farang* suits. Whatever Ton's bad karma had been, Calvino had a hunch it was interlinked with Sawai's connection to Veera.

Most decisions in life depend on whether you're looking for speed or distance. Choosing a woman, for instance. Doing a job. There had been a look in Ton's eyes in the gym; Calvino had seen something. Living long enough in Thailand, he could see those who had been defeated; it was in the eyes of certain men. Ton was one of those men. Life had worn him down. Such men are in their dreams rowing in a small boat towards a mist rolling in from the far horizon. The current is carrying their boat to the edge of a drop-off. There are those who pull against the current in fear; there are those who welcome and embrace the mist as nothing in their life will ever compare to their disappearing in it.

THIRTY-SEVEN

CALVINO nursed a Singha beer while reading through his notebook. He could see a pattern developing in his shuttle back and forth between Fon and Noi; he covered a lot of territory but never got close enough to form a picture of what had happened during Noi's brief tenure as a member of Valentine's harem. With Ton dead, the hit team that had likely whacked the local reporter had been eliminated. The links to Veera were all in the grave. Who had ordered the hit on the reporter was an academic question rather than a legal one. Sawai was in the clear and for the same reason. Had Veera and Sawai acted together? Calvino would have put money on it. Whoever made the contract had managed to deal effectively with the loose ends. With no gunmen alive, the general rule in Thailand is that the evidence of murder is insufficient to convict. That was the reason the masterminds eliminated the chain of evidence.

After he finished the beer, Calvino walked across the street and into the dive shop. He asked for the boss. He handed his name card to the Thai behind the counter, who looked at it without any reaction. "Tell the boss it's important."

A couple of minutes later, a young stocky, tanned *farang* in shorts, tank top and sandals strolled into the shop, clutching Calvino's card, sweat pouring down the side of his face.

"Are you the boss?" asked Calvino.

The young man extended his hand, "Paul Yasbeck's the name. You want to rent equipment?" He had a middle-American accent. And the look of a wholesome, all-American college fullback ten years after scoring his last touchdown, packing a bag and flying to Thailand.

Calvino shook his head. Going for a dive wasn't exactly what he had in mind. "I want to ask you a few questions about one of your former employees. Noi."

"Is she in some kind of trouble?"

"Is there some place where we can talk?

Yasbeck led Calvino to his a backroom office. Scuba tanks stood against the wall. A shelf held a row of diving masks. On his desk was a photograph of a Thai woman and three children.

"That's my wife. She's from Pattaya and that's our three kids," said Yasbeck.

"Nice family," said Calvino. He sat in a chair in front of Yasbeck's desk and took out his notebook, flipped it open, studying it for a moment. "Noi worked in a bar. After that she worked for you."

"I trained her to dive. She passed the examination for her master's certificate. You know how difficult that is?"

"That's something," said Calvino.

Yasbeck nodded his head. "Better believe it."

Believe It or Not. Divephilia: the sexual excitement of having sex underwater. Noi had been collected as another specimen for Valentine's living garden of sexual fetishes.

"Before that she worked in a South Pattaya bar as a dancer. Now she's a nun in a local *wat*. I'd say that is some career for someone who's only twenty-two years old."

"I was sorry to lose her. The customers loved learning to dive from Noi. They'd sign up for a two-day course, then sign up for two more courses. Not that she ever did anything with them. I mean, outside her job as a diving instructor. Once she left the bar, she cleaned up her act. I told her that my wife wouldn't allow any diver turning underwater tricks. Or dry-land ones either. The wife's strict about that. She kept her side of the deal, as far as I know. I was real sorry when she left."

"Was her leaving sudden?"

"Out of the blue."

"Did she say why she was leaving?"

"Her boyfriend was in some kind of trouble." Yasbeck rolled his eyes. "You take a beautiful girl like Noi. She could have any guy and what kind of guy does she pick? A loser. He'd borrow money from her and of course never pay her back. That's par for the course. Right?"

"Did you ever meet the boyfriend?"

Yasbeck fiddled with a dive meter. He looked up. "He'd pick her up after work sometimes. He never missed picking her up on payday. He never came into the shop. He sat in his pickup and waited for her to come out."

"You know his name?"

"Rangsan. I used to tease Noi about her boyfriend. I'd call him Ring-Rang- Rung."

"What kind of pickup did he drive?"

"A two-year-old red Toyota. She said he was still making payments on it and he was always short of cash."

"Do you know what kind of work he did?"

"Noi said that he worked on the coast. He'd get hired to take fish to the market. Sometimes he'd haul goats or sheep. Only most of the people around here have their own pickup trucks. His work wasn't steady. He'd go a week without a job."

Calvino made notes. "Do you know where Rangsan was from?"

"He was a local boy."

"A boy?"

"He was about the same age as Noi. Twenty-two, twenty-three. Skinny and moody and she'd paid for him to have a nose job. He said his flat nose was hurting his business. If he had a *farang* nose, then the work would flow in. She paid the six thousand baht and he got a *farang* nose but he had no more business after the nose job than before. My feeling was, the guy was a loser. She stuck up for him. But she had to know the guy was a lost cause. That's a woman for you. They don't know how to cut their losses."

"A nose job to haul goats and fish?"

Yasbeck shrugged. "She said he lacked confidence."

Calvino shook his head. "I want to go back to one thing you said earlier. You said Noi left because her boyfriend was in some kind of trouble. Do you know what the trouble was?"

"A business conflict I guess. The second she said Ring-Rang-Rung had troubles, that was enough for me. I didn't wanna know. I still don't wanna know what kind of troubles he had. I've lived in Thailand since I was twenty-one years old, and that's been for thirteen years, and I can tell you, Mr. Calvino, whenever one of the girls tells you that her Thai boyfriend has trouble, you don't ever want to go there. She wants to leave because of the boyfriend, then no matter how great she's been for the business, you have to let her go. Because she's gonna go anyway. She going into some firestorm and you can't stop that from happening." He paused, got up, and pulled a brochure from a stack on his filing cabinet. "You said Noi's in a *wat*."

"She's a nun."

"That must have been some trouble," said Yasbeck. He handed Calvino the brochure. "If you ever want to take up diving, you let me know, okay?"

"I'll let you know."

Calvino looked at the brochure. On the front was a picture of Noi with scuba tanks on her back and diver's mask pushed back over her head. She wore a bikini and looked like the kind of fantasy woman that would have any man digging into his wallet for a few days of diving lessons. He could see the attraction for Valentine.

"You can never figure out these women," said Yasbeck. "One thing I can say about Noi, the woman had laughter in her soul."

Calvino had heard the line before. Talking with the Thai boyfriend would be top of the agenda for Colonel Pratt—if they could find the boyfriend.

"Sometimes a woman doesn't understand that what she wants isn't what she really wants," said Calvino.

THIRTY-EIGHT

LATER in the afternoon Calvino returned to the *wat*. A funeral party squatting under the shade of a large tree watched him stroll along the grounds. Men and women playing cards and gambling, gossiping, others nearby milling around and watching the *farang* dressed in the jacket walking among them as they ate chicken and rice with their fingers. As Calvino stopped, an old woman dipped a cup into a plastic bucket, navigating large pieces of ice, and scooped up a glass of water. She held it out for Calvino, her toothless grin spreading across her lips.

"Hot, isn't it?" she said.

He drank the water and handed back the glass.

From the kitchen behind one of the buildings came the clattering of pots and pans from women cooking. Calvino walked away from the funeral party and found a space to sit on a concrete bench underneath a giant bodhi tree. Red and green and yellow strips of cloth had been tied around its enormous trunk. Dozens of Buddha statues and a spirit house lined with tiny doll-like figures had been stacked beneath the tree. The dolls would have been at home on the table inside Prasit's prayer room. Some ancient urge drove adults to bring dolls and place them around a tree or inside a room and to light candles and incense and pray. Fear of the unknown, the uncertainty of life. The same fear a child feels but can't express; a fear which is deep and unknowable. Sending in the dolls as proxy eased the anxiety.

Calvino saw Noi slowly cross the large dirt parking lot. He rose from the bench and waved to catch her attention. He was half way across the parking lot when she finally reached him.

"Thank you for making time," he said.

"I have a lot of that," she said.

"There's a bench where we can sit and talk."

She followed him to the bodhi tree. From this vantage point it was possible to observe anyone arriving or leaving the *wat* and the *sala*. The tree and bench occupied the high ground inside the *wat* grounds and, like the crow's nest of a ship, gave a commanding view of the sea from one side. Calvino could imagine the abbot would have positioned his spies there to watch suspect monks or nuns. A circular concrete bench had been built around the perimeter of the bodhi tree. In places the bench surface was broken and had fallen into decay and ruin, marble as impermanent as a human life. Calvino dusted off a spot and motioned for Noi to sit down. He sat next to her, facing towards the sea beyond. She stared at the sea.

"I'd like to ask you a few more questions," said Calvino.

Whatever the reason, it was clear something had made her change her mind. She hardly acknowledged him, folding back into herself in a remote silence. "It is late. You must come back tomorrow if you have more questions. I will be in trouble."

"You're already in trouble."

She had begun to rise. Calvino rose and moved in front of her, blocking her path. She tried to go around to the left; he moved left. She tried the right side and he moved at the same pace. "Why won't you leave me alone?" she asked.

"You saw something on the beach."

She turned to walk back and then stopped, half turned. "I told you what I saw."

"You told me what you wanted me to believe. But you saw a lot more. You saw something that made you afraid. It made your boyfriend Rangsan run. That's why you came to this place. And staying inside here is why you are alive."

Calvino pulled out the brochure from the dive shop with her picture on the front and showed it to her. "Rangsan drove to the diving shop in his red Toyota pickup. He borrowed money from you. When you quit your diving instructor job, you told your boss that your boyfriend was in some kind of trouble. We need to talk about your boyfriend's problem."

Noi, the master diver, still bore memories of her time working in a bar; she couldn't escape the provocative force caused when a *farang* cast doubt on her word. Pride or face, it was difficult to describe the feelings that Calvino had tapped into, but he knew bar *yings'* vulnerable spots; hitting it was the key to successfully getting her to open up. He had attacked and she had reacted. Noi sat down hard on the bench, arms folded.

"I don't lie," she said. Inside she steamed.

"Why are you angry?"

The Buddha self she sought to find had gone. As much as she tried, nothing was turning out as she wished. But she was a poor, uneducated peasant girl, she told herself, and her skin was too dark and her nose too flat and her hips were too narrow to be considered beautiful.

"Because I am a stupid girl. And ugly."

Except to farangs, she conceded to herself. Valentine had thought so, too. She had had a real chance of a new life, which had vaporized in a week. Her face pointed ahead, her eyes turned to the corner, watching as Calvino sat a couple of feet away.

"You were with Rangsan that day. You know what happened. Why not tell me what you saw on the beach last New Year's Eve?"

She shuddered and leaned back on the bench. "I already tell you and Colonel Pratt. I not tell anyone anything. I go now, okay?"

There is never a right time to pull the pin from a grenade, but once it's done, there are only seconds to make the decision that affects everything else.

"The Americans, men like Jardine, are looking for you. If he knew that you were here, what do you think he'd do? Play nice? If he asked you about Rangsan, would he let you walk away before he got an answer? If you won't talk to me, then I can see he gets this brochure. David Jardine and his friends don't strike me as men who waste time getting answers."

He rose from the bench, sighed and looked at the sea. He thought how David Jardine would use Thai proxies at the interrogation. Keeping to the guidelines of plausible deniability, watchful as the interrogators asked the questions he had requested. Threats and beatings and torture couldn't be traced to him. His hands would remain clean. It was the perfect world of no accountability and no limits.

"See you around," he said.

Noi's head turned around and the fear sprang back.

"No, don't go. Please give me a chance."

"Then tell me what you saw."

"It was my fault. I accused my boyfriend of being lazy. I think he lie to me and not try to find work. He said, 'You don't believe me? Then I take you and you watch me work. You think I lie that I have a job? Come. Come.' We drive on the highway to Sattahip. He turns off on a small road and we go to a beach. It is still dark and he is driving with his lights on. I still don't believe him. I think he is wasting my time and that my boss is right, this man is no good. Why do I keep giving him one chance after another? We are fighting when he gets out of the pickup and walks to the edge of the sea. I get out the other side and still am screaming at him. He turns and raises his hand. I don't know why. But I stop yelling at him. I walk to the beach and wait until we see a small boat with men. My boyfriend has a flashlight and he points it at the sea and turns it off and on three times. I see a light on the boat return the signal. A couple of minutes later, the boat reaches the beach and three men climbs out. They drag the boat onto the sand. My boyfriend *waied* one man. He was the captain of a trawler. My boyfriend worked for him before and the captain liked my boyfriend and wanted to help him. One of the other men was Thai. He was a relative of the captain. And the other man, I don't know who he was. He wasn't Thai."

Calvino pulled out Hasam's photograph, the one that Jardine had given him, and showed it to Noi. "Was that the man?"

She studied the photograph. "The man I saw wore a mask and had a beard."

"Could it be the same man?"

She nodded. "Maybe. I don't know."

"Do you have any idea who this man is?" Calvino shook his head.

"Rangsan said he cigarette smuggler."

"Cigarettes?"

Obviously she had no idea and it was likely that her boyfriend Rangsan knew nothing about what he was getting himself into. He had simply taken on a job from a trawler captain he had worked for in the past and that was all he needed to know. What was important at this point was to get her through the rest of the story without rattling her, making her more scared than she already was. Telling her that the man was named Hasam and he had come into Thailand for the purpose of committing an act of terrorism wasn't the path to take. One leak, and in a place where the bamboo telegraph operated at near the speed of light, the entire operation to catch him would be compromised.

"What happened after Rangsan *waied* the captain?"

"They talked a little. About how his catch was and whether he might need my boyfriend to help take the catch to market later in the day. The captain said that wouldn't be necessary. But next week he would have work for him. But now he needed a hand with something in the boat. All the men stood next to the boat. They leaned over and lifted out a big box. It looked like a coffin. I am scared, and think about *pee*—ghosts. I thought someone had died and they had put the body in the box. And we would take it to the *wat*. The four men carried the case and slid it into the back of the pickup. My boyfriend covered it with a tarp and tied it down so you couldn't see what was underneath. The captain said to my boyfriend, 'Take him where he wants to go and help him with the case.' And my boyfriend he says, 'Okay.' The foreigner stayed behind with us as the captain and his relative got into the boat and rowed out to the open sea. The three of us got into the pickup and my boyfriend drove back to Pattaya in silence. I sat in the middle, staying close to my boyfriend. The stranger stared straight ahead at the road. He had that expression of a *farang* who sits in the bar and orders one drink all night, his mind all full of things he doesn't want to talk about and you can't get near him. He won't buy you a drink. He won't do anything but hurt you. But I think maybe he's not a *farang*. I think an Arab. I stay away from that kind of man."

"Where did you drop him?" asked Calvino.

"In Pattaya."

"Where in Pattaya?"

"A construction site in South Pattaya. On Beach Road. We drove down Soi 7. It was quiet. No traffic. The foreigner told my boyfriend to park and wait. Ten minutes later he came back with three other men. My boyfriend got out and untied the tarp and helped them unload the case. When he got back into the pickup, he was smiling. I asked, 'Why are you smiling like that?' He laid out five one-hundred-dollar bills on the dashboard. I couldn't believe it. So much money paid for doing such a little thing. I was so happy and then I was scared. I asked him, 'Why do they pay you so much money? Is this drug business? Is it another bad thing?' My boyfriend said, 'Cigarette business.'"

"What did the men do with the case?" asked Calvino.

"They carried it into the construction site. Okay, smuggled goods. Not so bad. Let it be. My boyfriend is feeling good that he's got some money. And I am feeling good because he actually did have a job and he wasn't telling me a lie."

"What kind of trouble happened to Rangsan after that?"

She sighed and looked out at the sea. "He telephoned me and said he had a problem and had to go away. I asked him, 'What kind of problem?' And he said, 'You remember the night we drove to the beach and brought that man back to Pattaya.' He didn't have to say anything more. I somehow knew this would be a problem. He said that I was in the pickup and they knew my name and maybe I had a problem, too. I said we should go away together. He said, 'No. Cannot. I must go now.' I started to cry and said I didn't believe that he ever loved me. He said that wasn't true. And if he didn't love me that he wouldn't be making a phone call. He would just go. And I think, what he says is true. I know there is this rich *farang* who came to the bar sometimes. He was interested in me. He gave me his card. I go to Valentine and think, okay, it's not so bad to live in such a beautiful place and to be one of his wives. I can do this. Why not? I can live and one day my boyfriend comes back and we can start our lives over. I have my dive master license. I can always work. No problem. But it wasn't so simple. Pee Prasit knew lots of people. One day I told Pee Prasit about my boyfriend and that we had this problem. A few days later, he said it might be dangerous for me to stay at the compound. He was a good man. I am very sorry he died."

"You think that he killed himself?"

She brushed away a tear. "I don't think so."

"Would his wife have killed him?"

Noi smiled. "Pee Fon loved him very much. Impossible."

"Did you ever see a man named Ton while you lived at Valentine's?"

"He came to see Pee Prasit with Ajarn Sawai."

She was playing three poker hands at the same time. One should have been a full house. The smart money would have been to play five hands. Noi believed in her man until the end. She never thought that she should have called for a different card or that she should have played multiple hands. In her new life inside the *wat*, she had time to think about the odds of winning when the game is stacked against you. Paying for a nose job and believing that the good times were around the corner showed that she wanted a version of life that wasn't on the DVD she had drawn. Play it forward, play it back, and every time the story ends the same way. Rangsan disappeared upcountry and people all around her want her dead.

THIRTY-NINE

AT the far end of the ballroom, Colonel Pratt huddled with some top brass down from Bangkok. Tables were being setup for a thousand invited guests. A security detail was working to assemble a metal detector in front of the entrance. Security was already tight and it was about to get a whole lot tighter. The American ambassador was the scheduled speaker. Someone from the hotel security staff watched as a *farang* in a suit did a microphone sound check from the podium. "One, two, three." In less than forty-eight hours, the room would be packed with bigwigs and big faces, American and Thai ranking military officers seated at the VIP tables. American security officers were everywhere in the ballroom. A dozen men in dark suits with wires running up the back of their collars, were barking orders, checking equipment, scanning chairs and tables. Heads in sunglasses connected to earpieces. David Jardine and a couple of other suits huddled with a Thai general and two of the general's subordinates near the podium.

"One, two, testing. Testing. Can you hear me in the back of the room? Charlie, what sound level are you picking up?"

An American flag standard was positioned on one side and the Thai flag standard on the other side of the podium. Protocol on flag placement had taken the morning to hammer out. Calvino walked through the entrance to find a Thai uniformed cop blocking him

"You can't go inside," the cop said. "Unless you have ID."

The cop waited for Calvino to turn around. When Calvino stood his ground, the cop leaned forward, the thumb of his right hand riding the 9mm sidearm in a leather holster on his right hip. "You have ID?"

"I have an appointment with Colonel Prachai."

The cop shook his head. "No ID. *Mai dai.*" Cannot. Impossible. Never. Get lost. That was the general translation. No reason, no explanation given.

Mai dai is a not a simple brick wall; it is a fortress of reinforced concrete three feet thick. "Mr. Jardine is my boss. I left my ID upstairs in my room. He will be upset if I am late. You know how *farangs* get upset and they get red in the face and shout and shake their fists? Mr. Jardine has an evil temper. What did you say your name was? Just in case I have to tell Mr. Jardine why I couldn't report to him. He would want to know."

Slowly Calvino drilled through the three-foot-thick wall of impossibility.

"You said you have an appointment with Colonel Prachai." The cop was clutching at straws. That was a good sign.

"And with my boss, Mr. Jardine, too. He's going to be fucking pissed off." Calvino rolled his eyes and sighed. "I don't think I got your name."

The cop nodded, eyes narrowed, and stepped aside. "Next time state your business clearly."

Uniforms always had to win in a head-to-head confrontation—it was their training, they always had to be right. Power made them right. Only a much larger power could make them yield their ground.

"I'll remember, sergeant," said Calvino. He walked into the ballroom without ever getting the cop's name. Colonel Pratt's head was turned, talking to some other cops, as Calvino approached him from the right.

He circled around, passing Jardine, "You seem to be everywhere," said Calvino.

"I was about to say the same thing about you. How did you get a pass to get in here?"

"I said I worked for you. Seems that your name has influence with the Thai cop at the door."

"You got something for me?"

Calvino wrinkled his nose, shrugged his shoulders. "Not much. My client thinks I am taking too much time on the case."

"He might have a point," said Jardine.

"I like being thorough."

"There's something to be said for that. Remind me again why you're here."

Calvino nodded at Colonel Pratt. Jardine looked at the colonel and then back at Calvino. "I worry about Americans who get too chummy with the local police."

"Not as much as I worry about Americans who run covert operations using the local police as cover."

Jardine turned away. There was nothing more to say. The conversation had attracted the attention of the group including Colonel Pratt. Calvino walked a few steps ahead and *waied* the colonel. The superiors saw the *farang* making a *wai*. They liked what they saw—a *farang* paying respect to authority, showing submission to power and rank. A *farang* whose gesture showed that he knew the meaning of a uniform. That kind of *farang* they liked. He wasn't going to make anyone uncomfortable; no one would lose face. But it still didn't answer the question—was this *farang* part of the American contingent setting up the room? He looked different. He didn't look like government.

Colonel Pratt introduced Calvino to his colleagues and he *waied* each of them. "Khun Vincent is my old friend from America," said Colonel Pratt.

Calvino played the role. He knew what was expected. The script was one he had memorized. Dance the dance. Sing the song. Wrap his fingers into a prayer wheel and *wai* and bow. "If the Colonel has a moment, I need his advice."

They walked out of the ballroom past the cop who had refused to acknowledge Calvino's existence. "I hope that this is important, Vincent."

"I have a possible location for your man. Is that important enough?"

Colonel Pratt stopped walking.

"How did you get that information?"

"It doesn't matter how. What matters is who has this information."

"Did you tell Jardine?"

Calvino smiled. "What do you think?"

"You got this from Noi."

"She remembers where they dropped Hasam."

Colonel Pratt studied Calvino's expression. Did Noi really know this? Or had she made something up just to get rid of the *farang*? The American intelligence community with all of their resources hadn't been able to find Hasam. What if it were true? The next question the colonel had was what should he do with the information. Who should he inform? The Americans had placed a five million dollar reward for information leading to Hasam's arrest. With that kind of money, there would be jockeying to claim the reward. It had happened over the Hambali arrest. Everyone had scrambled to stake a claim to the reward, like a hungry mob hitting a buffet table. If he told Jardine at this stage, there was the risk of another headache. Fighting over money was bad enough, but the Americans would claim sole credit for the bust. They'd leave the Thais out in the cold.

"You haven't said anything," said Calvino.

"I am thinking."

"What I am thinking is that we should check out the information ourselves. It might be nothing. But then again it could be what everyone's looking for."

"You know there's a reward for Hasam's capture," said Colonel Pratt.

"Yeah, how much?"

"Five million dollars."

"What's that in baht?" asked Calvino, grinning.

"Two hundred million baht."

"Fuck-you money for this life and the next five lives."

They walked into the parking lot until they came to Calvino's car. He pulled his keys from his jacket. Colonel Pratt stared at him over the roof the Honda.

"What Noi saw happened nine months ago," said Colonel Pratt.

"It's a start. It's all we have."

"It doesn't mean that he's still there."

"He's likely long gone and holed up elsewhere."

"It's better not to tell Jardine," said Colonel Pratt.

"We should have a look around the construction site."

"How do you know it's a construction site?"

"I drove past before coming here. I wanted a look. It's one of those monster condo complexes left over from the 1997 crash. It's a shell. The usual pancake stack of unfinished concrete floors and walls. Someone must have taken a big hit. All those years and all they have to show is rusty rebar sticking like wild hairs out of eighteen floors of concrete. There's a security guard out front. It would be a miracle if it's the same guard who was on duty the first of January. Miracles like mercy are in short supply these days. We might get lucky."

The quality of mercy is not strained. It droppeth as the gentle rain from heaven upon the place beneath. It is twice blest: It blesseth him that gives and him that takes. Colonel Pratt quoted from *The Merchant of Venice*.

"I wouldn't use that one on Jardine. He'd think you've gone soft."

FORTY

IN Pattaya and Bangkok, many uncompleted projects dotted the lanes and roads like ruins from an ancient civilization which had invented concrete before it had invented money. Half-finished buildings survived as ghostly reminders of the days when everyone in Thailand believed that real estate prices could never go down. People believed all kinds of things then, and they had started to believe the same kind of things again. They had new things to fear and had forgotten about what had made them afraid before. Noi and her boyfriend had driven Hasam to a place that spoke of greed and failure. What better place to hide a terrorist than a place already defeated and humbled? The JI wouldn't have known all those months in advance that the American ambassador and ranking officers of the American Pacific Command would be in the same ballroom not more than five minutes away. They had just got lucky. Hasam had been sent to go to sleep until the time was right to wake him. Jardine had all but told them he had intercepts and information from Hambali himself that the time to awaken had been transmitted to the field. This was likely a lie. As soon as Hambali was captured, the first operational reaction of those in the field would have been to change all the codes and timetables, as they would have been compromised. Hambali would have no idea about the new schedule.

He was bluffing and Jardine knew it.

As they drove to the construction site, Calvino glanced over at the colonel. "Two men have a better chance. A Thai and a *farang* aren't going to make anyone nervous. Jardine would show up with half the Thai army and Hasam, who knows that *soi* better than anyone alive, would know, when he sees what's coming. And he slips away."

"I am in uniform."

"I brought a change of clothes. Shirt, trousers and jacket."

Colonel Pratt looked into the back seat. "Your spare set of clothes?"

"Don't worry, I haven't worn them."

"I am not worried about that. Working undercover with a civilian could get me fired," said Colonel Pratt.

"When they find out the civilian you teamed with was a *farang*, they might make you do visa runs every ninety days for the next thirty years. But on the up-side, with half of five million dollars, you could fly first class."

With the big decision already made—they would go in lone-wolf style and leave open the possibility of calling in the colonel's superiors and then the Americans if it looked like this was Hasam's roosting place—the next set of decisions could only seem easier. The decision to go undercover was beginning to look like the best of the bad alternatives.

"You could pretend to be an immigration officer hunting down illegal migrants."

"Who are you in this setup?"

An American immigration officer working on technical assistance under one of those government-to-government programs. An anti-foreign sweep wouldn't raise an eyebrow. Anyone on the site would accept the inspection as a necessary precaution. Got to protect all that brass, including politicians and foreign bigwigs, from the foreigners."

"It won't work." Colonel Pratt had taken off his policeman's shirt and slipped on the white shirt from the back seat.

"Hasam is an illegal. The last thing he wants to attract is the immigration police. That's how Hambali was arrested."

"Okay, we're not immigration police. Hey, that shirt looks good on you. You could be a businessman."

"Not a bad idea. Not a good one, either."

"We need a way in that is unofficial. No uniform, no affiliation," said Calvino.

Only a *farang* could hold such a radical thought.

"A couple of lost tourists?" asked Colonel Pratt.

"No. We're investors from Hong Kong."

The colonel warmed to the idea. "We are looking to buy the building."

"One more thing," said Calvino. "I checked around and found out the name of the civil engineer who ran the project. It turns out the engineer is working on a new condo development three *sois* away."

"Have you talked with him?"

"It's her. And I talked to her."

Colonel Pratt looked surprised. He'd never encountered a woman civil engineer in Thailand. "And you told her that your partner in the investment also wanted to meet her."

"You read my mind."

"Why the part about being immigration officers?"

"I knew you'd hate that. It made being a Hong Kong investor a much better idea."

"You thought this through, Vincent."

"I know how your mind works."

"You think you know."

He zipped up the black trousers from the back seat. Finally he put on the sports jacket over his .38 snug in its holster. "You could pass for Chinese," said Calvino.

"My grandmother on my mother's side was Chinese."

"Yeah? You know the Chinese script for housewife?"

The colonel shook his head.

"The symbol for a woman and a broom stick. This is the stuff Ratana's mother's been teaching her. What do you get when you combine the symbol for blurry vision with the one for woman? You get the Chinese word marriage."

Colonel Pratt smiled, having figured out Calvino's newfound interest in the Chinese language. "Ratana's mother is Chinese."

"What are you saying, it dissipates if it's your grandmother and not your mother?"

"Most things get watered down over time. Blood, money, desire and love."

"The jacket looks like it was made for you."

"I'll keep that in mind."

The civil engineer sat behind a desk inside her office. She worked on the third floor of a condominium site. The ground floors were full of workers carrying tools, hammering, lifting cement blocks, painting, and sweeping up. She looked up from a set of blueprints as Calvino opened the door. "Mr. Calvino, back so soon?"

"I want you to meet my partner from Hong Kong, Mr. Jerry Lee Wong," said Calvino.

"Mr. Wong, you can call me Nui." She spoke perfect American English.

"You can call him Jerry," said Calvino.

Colonel Pratt flinched. He hated the name Jerry, which had been the first name of his landlord in New York City many years ago when he was a student. Calvino had threatened to have his uncles and cousins design a new set of legs for Jerry should Jerry ever give the key to Pratt's apartment to the Chinese gangsters who had been threatening to return.

They sat down and Nui briefed them on the history of the abandoned condo project. Since Calvino's visit, she had pulled out the old set of blueprints and brochures advertising the development. A hundred and twenty-four people had paid deposits. Later when the project folded, they lost their money. The land titles office showed the developer as a company; the list of shareholders showed a lot of Isan names, people who were likely employed as maids and drivers. Calvino wondered if some of them had been on Veera's payroll. The developer had gone into bankruptcy in 1997 and all construction had stopped. The site had been abandoned. Pattaya had dozens of half-completed projects. As investors, she would show them other sites with much better prospects.

"We are interested in this one," said Colonel Pratt.

"For someone from Hong Kong, you speak English with a Thai accent," she said.

"Everyone says that," said the Colonel.

"Last life he was Thai," said Calvino.

"And who were you last life?"

Calvino started to reply but the colonel was one step ahead. "Woody Allen," said Colonel Pratt.

He'd been talking to Ratana, thought Calvino.

"For my sins, I was reborn to live in Thailand."

"Woody Allen's not dead," she said.

"It's one of those premature rebirths," said Calvino.

"And I am Vanessa May."

She is good, thought Calvino. An intelligent and fast-on-the-draw *ying*. Calvino saw her mentally running a victory lap for her Vanessa May line.

Colonel Pratt glanced up at the framed diplomas from Harvard and MIT on the wall. On Khao San Road, anyone could buy a Harvard or MIT degree. The ones in her office looked genuine. She was getting along with Calvino a little too well. It was time to shift the focus, to put her to the test, and to get on with the job.

"What kind of security is there on the building?" asked Colonel Pratt.

"It's been years. It would likely have been the standard setup. A security guard sleeping in front of the site."

She turned to her laptop computer on her desk. "Let me do a search. I probably have some information here. Give me a second to find it."

Nui wore a denim shirt with the top two buttons undone and tight jeans. A yellow hardhat with a decal reading *Safety First* sat next to her laptop. She wore an amulet; she didn't wear a wedding ring. Both were out of fashion with modern, educated Thai women. Calvino remembered Fon's description of herself as a failure of the system. The system had half succeeded with Nui. She appeared over-educated, slightly superstitious and unmarried. Calvino watched her fingers glide over the keyboard. She'd stop to look at the screen, bite her lower lip, and then type again without looking up. Nui was the kind of woman who'd been loved but not enough to have made a difference. There was nothing about her make-up or clothing other than the tight-fitting jeans and unbuttoned blouse—minor details that could be read as neglect—that suggested she was available. Call it chemistry. She had Calvino bobbing and weaving as she worked at the computer, straining to look over her shoulder. When the chemistry with a woman was right, electricity shot through the air. In the absence of chemistry, sustaining interest was like trying to strike a wet match. You got a wisp of smoke if you were lucky, but no fire. Calvino felt the flames.

Colonel Pratt couldn't help but notice that Calvino stood more erect, shoulders back, even when he hunched over the screen. He smiled, wondering if her attitude was as hard and concentrated as it appeared. She worked and didn't seem to notice that she'd attracted more than a little attention from the private eye. If anything, the young civil engineer had gone out of her way to make herself fit into the hardhat crowd of the construction site, and the result had only heightened her appeal. Thailand had not quite caught up to the new class of educated Thai women. Especially one working in an almost exclusively male field.

"Found it," Nui said, turning the screen around for Colonel Pratt to read. "The security firm's name, address and phone number."

Calvino wrote the information down in his notebook. He sat back down.

"Anything else I can help you with?"

Nui had the look of a small, sensitive woman who'd learned to survive in a tough, demanding, dangerous job, neither asking for nor giving any quarter. She looked from Calvino to the colonel waiting for one of the men to respond.

"You wouldn't happen to have the blueprints of the building?"

"I am afraid the plans are confidential."

"Meaning?" asked Calvino.

"You would need the permission of the developer to release them." She opened another file and scrolled down the page. "It's in our contract."

She turned the screen around for them to read.

"We don't have the time to do that," said Colonel Pratt.

"That's not really my problem," she said.

"In that case, can I let you in on something confidential?" asked Calvino.

Suspicion clouded her face as she looked from Calvino to Colonel Pratt.

Colonel Pratt flashed his police ID. "We have reason to believe that the building is being used for criminal activity. And I would ask that you let us have a look at the blueprints and any other information about the building."

The disclosure didn't rattle Nui. She stretched, hunching her shoulders, her small jaw clenched. "And you're. . . what?" she asked Calvino.

"His private secretary."

"That's why you were taking notes," she said.

She picked up Colonel Pratt's police ID and read it carefully before handing it back. "We are under considerable time pressure," said Colonel Pratt.

"I am Thai, and that's the first time I've had anyone in uniform ever admit that time mattered."

"Then you'll help," he said. It wasn't a question.

"Why didn't you tell me the truth from the beginning?"

Calvino raised his hand like a schoolboy. "I can answer that. It was my idea."

"Your idea? I'd say lying is never a very good idea."

"You're right. I should have told you straight up front."

Some part of the chemistry was kicking in for her as well. Only she resisted and threw up a wall of attitude. Just as she was about to close the door, Colonel Pratt cleared his throat. "We don't have time. I need this information, Khun Nui. It is important. Very important that you help," said Colonel Pratt.

It was starting to sink in that there was a police investigation and that she was about to become part of the machinery moving the police investigation forward. Her face flushed and she went back to working on her laptop. She had always played an important part in whatever she had decided to take on. She knew the plans by heart. She had only a couple of moments to decide how far to get involved in the matter. A professional's last line of defense was to bury the person demanding documents into a sea of technical documents that required an advanced degree to decipher. She began printing out documents and handing them to Calvino. Project reports. Supplier invoices. Material inventories. Cash-flow reports. Balance sheets and drawings, floor plans and model rooms. Subcontractors. The paper piled up in a stack on her desk in front of Calvino.

The construction had slowed down and finally stopped because the developer ran out of money, she explained.

Many projects had crashed around the same time. Some had been revived. Others had stayed a sprawling complex of green-netted concrete. "What you are looking at is the list of subcontractors. They can provide you with details about the construction crews who worked on the site." Nui printed out a blueprint of the building, and put it on the stack. "Finished," she said. "Anything else I can help you with?"

She knew from the look on Colonel Pratt and Calvino's faces that she had won a victory. It would take them weeks if not months to go through all the documentation and check out all the possibilities. Building an eighteen-story project produced a mountain of paper and employed hundreds of companies and workers. At the end, there was to be a condominium with three hundred units. It was, upon completion, to be home for three hundred happy middle-class families. The dream hadn't come true. The question was whether the nightmare vision of Jardine and the Americans was about to be fulfilled.

"I want to be more specific with you," said Colonel Pratt.

"That would be helpful."

"We have information that a foreigner might have setup a base of operation inside that building."

"What kind of an operation? Drugs?"

"That doesn't matter right now," said Colonel Pratt.

"Think explosive device," said Calvino.

Colonel Pratt shot Calvino a look. "I'm trying to be truthful," said Calvino.

"We cannot discuss the details," said the colonel.

Nui's mouth formed a perfect "O" and she nodded. That kind of a criminal enterprise was obviously not one that she had thought about. "This is way outside of my territory."

"Go over the blueprints with me, if that's okay?" asked Colonel Pratt.

She spread the printouts over her desk.

"Would any workers be on that site?" asked Calvino.

"No way. The building's gone nowhere for years."

"Someone could slip in unnoticed and setup living there," said Colonel Pratt.

Nui shrugged. "It's possible. But the security guard would notice if anyone lived there. Their job is to check the floors, and most of the building is exposed. No walls or windows or door. It's a concrete shell. Even if he were sleeping most of the shift, he'd notice someone coming and going. Someone living in the building would stand out."

"Okay, it's open. But if you were going to live on this site, where would you hide?" asked Calvino.

Colonel Pratt liked the way Calvino's question had made her smile. It was the kind of challenge a woman like Nui enjoyed, a puzzle, a test of her ability to fast-track an answer that only she could come up with.

She flipped through the blueprint printouts, stopping, tapping a pen, before moving onto another page. "And if you wanted to hide an explosive device where would you hide it?" asked Colonel Pratt. "In the same place or a different place?"

"You are asking a lot of questions," she said.

"We are asking the right person, aren't we?" Calvino looked up at the framed diplomas on the wall. "A Harvard-educated civil engineer would know where the best hiding spot was on any site."

"It depends on the size of the device."

"The size of a sailor's footlocker," said Calvino.

"Here," she said, turning the blueprint around so that Colonel Pratt and Calvino could both see it. They weren't certain what they were looking at; she had to explain they were staring at the central elevator shaft. "No elevators were installed. They come last because elevators are expensive. You install them after the building has been closed in. You see this space at the top? That is a small room where the relay and switching equipment are housed and spare parts for the elevator stored. It's enclosed. There are two windows that look over the shaft. You could hide a bomb in a footlocker there and it would be difficult to detect. I doubt the security guards would ever go up to that level. It's too much trouble."

Colonel Pratt rose from his chair. "You've been very helpful. Please do not mention this conversation to anyone."

Calvino folded his notebook and asked for Nui's name card.

"I could take you to the site, if that would help," she said.

She looked back and forth between Calvino and Colonel Pratt.

"It's. . ." Calvino started to say.

"Not a good idea," said Colonel Pratt finishing his thought.

"Looking at the blueprints, I might know a way someone could get in and out of that elevator shaft without anyone knowing."

Colonel Pratt stared hard at the blueprints. If what she said were true, her presence might make a difference. The downside risk was all his. No one was going to point the finger at Calvino and say, "Why did you allow this to happen on your watch?" She could get hurt, and her injury would fall on his shoulders; he'd have to take full responsibility. His superiors wouldn't stand by him. He had already gone outside the chain of command. He was free-floating, entering into that void where his actions could no longer be explained or justified. He told himself this was exactly why men stayed strictly in the chain of command and did things according to the book. He also told himself this was why they hadn't caught Hasam.

"Okay, you can come along," said Colonel Pratt. "For now, that is."

She looked at Calvino.

"If who we think is in that building is inside, he's very dangerous."

"Do I look afraid?" asked Nui.

"You should be," said Colonel Pratt.

FORTY-ONE

ON the drive to the construction site, Calvino thought how easy it would have been for Hasam to slip into Thailand on New Year's Day. It would have been easy for his JI contacts to slip cash to the security guard and ask him to leave his post early. It would have been lonely for the security guard seated on a plastic stool in front of a concrete block with piles of dirt and bricks everywhere around him. Since everyone else was on holiday having a good time with family and friends, the temptation would have been great to take the money and go. Five hundred or a thousand baht would have done the trick.

Calvino parked outside the security guardhouse. The guard came outside just as Nui was slipping on her hardhat. He was wide-eyed watching the colonel and Calvino stepping out of the car behind her. She explained that she was taking these two investors for a site tour. She pointed back at Calvino and Colonel Pratt.

"Ask him if he knows who was on duty the first of January," said Calvino.

"He wants to know what day of the week that was."

"Wednesday," said Colonel Pratt. "New Year's fell on Wednesday."

"How did you know that?" asked Calvino.

"This year is a Wednesday child. I am a Wednesday child."

"I never knew that."

Colonel Pratt looked over at his friend. "There are many things you don't know."

The security guard didn't know who had been on duty; but he wrote down the name and phone number of his supervisor. He never asked why a couple of investors would want that information. They walked into the first floor area, stepping over pieces of rebar, scattered rusty nails and weathered pieces of scrap wood. Anything of value was long gone. Nui squatted down on the floor and spread out the blueprints. "We are here," she said, pointing at the blueprint. "If we go through that area, on the other side is the elevator shaft."

A small voice in the back of Colonel Pratt's head told him that he should stop and return for backup. Another voice said there wasn't enough time. It could be a wild goose chase, but he had no choice but to follow up the lead. The information was dated; if it led anywhere, it would be a miracle. He decided it would be enough to check out the elevator shaft and drive back to the hotel before others started asking why he'd been away so long. The clock was ticking and the special Cobra Gold opening ceremony was twenty-four hours away. The Ambassador would be coming from a reception in U-Tapao. The US navy had maintained a presence at U-Tapao since the Vietnam war. No one would admit to active operations. Or to interrogation centers. *Presence* was the new codeword. It was like dark energy, which was everywhere in the universe.

In the center of the lobby was the elevator shaft. Nui knocked away a thin wall of cobwebs, walked inside the shaft and looked up at the sky eighteen stories overhead. She reappeared a moment later. "If you wanted to do some serious damage, that's where you'd hide a bomb," she said, picking the cobwebs off her fingers.

"It would be like shooting debris out of an eighteen-story gun barrel," said Calvino.

"I never thought of it that way. It would make quite a bang," said Nui. "We can take the stairs to the top."

Calvino looked at the first step and thought, *Eighteen floors of concrete stairs*. That was just what the doctor had ordered. On the twelfth floor, they stopped to rest on a landing. Calvino was out of breath, doubled over, arms resting on his legs, taking deep breaths. Twelve floors taken fast gave an indication of what kind of shape a man was in. He was in lousy shape. They looked out on the *soi* below and beyond to the sea obscured by a light rain.

"What if he's up there?" asked Nui.

"That's why you are stopping here," said Colonel Pratt.

"Because I am a woman?"

"Because you're a civilian."

"Your 'secretary' doesn't look like a Thai cop."

Calvino was trying to catch his breath, wishing his face didn't look so busted up. He had caught her staring at the stitch line over his ear. "I am not his secretary. I am a private investigator. And the colonel is right. There's nothing more you can do." He breathed in slowly, letting the air out.

"Did you have an operation or something?" she asked.

"I had a new ear sewn on. I change every couple of years. It improves my hearing."

She turned back to Colonel Pratt.

"I won't get in the way. Besides, I can show you the emergency access door. Or secret trap door, if you like Nancy Drew mysteries. This door, you'd never find it in a million years."

"Go on," said Colonel Pratt.

"The emergency access door is on the blueprint. It leads to a small room overlooking the elevator shaft."

Having caught his breath, on the floor Calvino saw a piece of paper with foreign writing. He picked it up, looked at it, and sighed. The printed letters on the paper were in Arabic. He showed it to Colonel Pratt. Nui looked at the paper, too. Neither of them could read the writing. It might have been a page from a book of poems, or scriptures, or a prayer bulletin or an operational manual. In other words, it might have been anything.

"There's a good chance our man was here," said Calvino.

"He might have found the access door," Colonel Pratt said to Nui.

Nothing was ever that easy. Jardine had said that Hasam was a fundamentalist who had been waiting for months, if not his entire life, for a special day. Curled up in the heart of a barbarous, poisonous city, waiting for his order, waiting to purify the impure. And tomorrow was the day he'd been waiting for. *Jahiliyya* was the word for this state of barbarism. True believers spent their entire lives waiting for tomorrow and that day never came. In Hasam's case, it was coming. It was less than twenty-four hours away. A Thai police colonel, a *farang* in a sports coat, and a slim, beautiful Thai woman wearing a hardhat and jeans stood between him and his virgins. The moment he saw them he would realize that his world was coming to an end. He would only need his thumb to press a button to set off the bomb. Better blow it up a day early than never have the chance at all. He would still die a martyr. He would cleanse the world.

"He occupies the high ground," said Colonel Pratt. He stood in front of the open elevator shaft on the twelfth floor. "That gives him the advantage." He looked at the paper with the Arabic writing on it. They had gone as far as they could go. "Khun Nui, it's time to turn around and go back to the car."

"I know and, 'Thank you for your help. And it would be better if you didn't say anything.' That's what you were going to say, right?"

"What I was going to say is that, given these circumstances, you had better stay with us. We can't risk anything at this point."

She smirked. "Meaning, I might be helping the man you're looking for."

Colonel Pratt folded the paper, slipped it into his pocket. His cellphone rang.

"Jardine, we might need some advice. Do you read Arabic?" Colonel Pratt nodded. "I'll meet you in ten minutes in the parking lot of Big C."

As the colonel spoke, Calvino leaned against the edge of the elevator shaft, arms folded. But he felt on edge. He had no idea what was at the upper end of that shaft. It was like waiting for a taxi in the old days when muggers lurked in the shadows with cheap handguns on the lower East Side of Manhattan. It was ever so easy to get killed and ever so easy to make the mistake that you weren't being clocked.

After the call ended, Colonel Pratt nodded to Calvino, "Time to go." He turned and started down the concrete staircase. Nui, agitated and disturbed, had turned a ghostly pale color. She was holding back the stress but it was written in white all over her body. She wrung her hands. Calvino remained the target of her anger.

"Am I under arrest?" she asked Colonel Pratt.

Calvino put a finger to his lips. "Please whisper. Your voice will carry."

She walked to the top step and waited for him to respond. He said nothing.

"Not arrest. Protective custody," whispered Calvino. He stood beside her and then started down the stairs after Colonel Pratt.

"You have lived in Asia too long." Her voice quavered as if she'd lost the ability to keep the frequency steady.

"Do you know the Chinese word for confusion? You put together the symbol for woman and the symbol for dealing with a Harvard engineer who can read blueprints."

She had been one step behind him; she pulled ahead, blocking the staircase.

"The translation is *corruption*," she whispered. Her tone lingered over the word "corruption" as if some distasteful thing had to be identified before being spit out.

Calvino should have figured her mother was Chinese. "Just testing."

"How do I know either of you are telling me the truth?"

"You don't," said Colonel Pratt.

"Have some faith, Vanessa May," said Calvino.

"This is not happening," she said.

"For everyone's sake, let's hope that it doesn't happen," said Calvino.

FORTY-TWO

JARDINE had already arrived and stood, arms folded, leaning against his car. He had shed his jacket and tie. He held an umbrella in his right hand against the light drizzle. His white shirt looked slept in and his dark trouser cuffs were damp from the rain. He was impossible to miss. Calvino pulled in the parking space beside Jardine's Volvo. He opened the door and Colonel Pratt stepped out under the umbrella. Jardine looked in the back and saw the engineer.

"You two stay put," he said, looking at Nui and Calvino.

He returned to his Volvo with heavily tinted windows. Colonel Pratt got in on the passenger side.

"What's going on here, Colonel?"

"We have a possible location for Hasam."

"Who is the 'we'?"

Colonel Pratt said nothing.

"This is a highly sensitive operation, Colonel Pratt. We can't afford having civilians fucking it up. If Hasam gets away. . ."

"You'll have my balls," said Colonel Pratt. "One thing, Jardine. Don't threaten me in my own country. Or I'll have your balls."

Jardine leaned against the steering wheel, both hands palm down on the rim.

"Okay, let's start over. What have you got?"

Colonel Pratt handed him the paper that Calvino had found in the condo. Jardine read it a couple of times.

"Can you take me where you found this?" asked Jardine.

Without a word, Colonel Pratt opened the Volvo door, climbed out and walked back to Calvino's car. A moment later, Jardine slammed his car door shut and slid into the back seat next to Nui. She slid close to the opposite door, wondering why this tall, rangy *farang* had suddenly joined them.

"What's the paper say, Jardine?" asked Calvino.

Jardine looked at the woman in the back seat and at Calvino and shook his head. He hated operations with civilians. They asked too many questions and got in the way.

"Vincent found it," said Colonel Pratt.

"Nui's the one who found it," said Calvino.

She nodded at Jardine. "Hi, I am Nui."

"Who is she?" he asked the colonel.

"A Harvard-educated civil engineer," said Colonel Pratt. There was a slight hint of pride in his voice. She was after all Thai, and pride was to be taken in any Thai who had shone on the international stage.

Jardine raised an eyebrow. "And I presume there is a reason you are here."

"I wouldn't presume anything if I were you. I thought they were Hong Kong investors. Then it turns out they're not from Hong Kong. I should ask where you're from. Assuming I can get a straight answer out of you," said Nui.

Jardine had a snapshot and in the frame of that shot was a Thai police colonel and an American national private eye on a back channel operation likely in way over their heads. "Hong Kong investors. What the fuck were you thinking?"

"It worked," said Calvino. "We got into the building."

"For the record, I never bought their story about being investors from Hong Kong," she said, looking at Colonel Pratt and catching Calvino's eye as he watched her in his rearview mirror.

"For the record, I didn't think you were a secretary," said Calvino.

"What was written on the paper?" Colonel Pratt asked.

Jardine closed his eyes and slowly shook his head. "The paper is a message. It is from the Koran and in the middle of the passage is a date and time." He glanced at his watch. "We have about an hour and a half to find him."

"We'll drive you to the probable location," said Colonel Pratt. "But we still don't have a positive confirmation that Hasam's inside. The only evidence is the paper we found."

"Nui was the engineer on the building site," said Calvino.

She explained the history of the building to Jardine, stopping to answer his questions. "From the room, he can see anyone approaching the building," she said.

"We studied the blueprints," said Colonel Pratt. "If he's inside, Nui was able to pinpoint his probable location."

It fit a pattern that Jardine knew from Bosnia to Somalia. The chances were that Hasam was holed up in the elevator tower. Jardine knew their training. Hasam would be heavily armed. He would be prepared. Men like him were pretty much meat-and-potatoes or rice-and-fish-sauce. No-frill killing machines. He also immediately understood Nui; she was one of those bicultural marvels who fell between two worlds. It was okay and not okay at the same time. The colonel would have understood the two spheres operating in tandem.

Jardine went back to his Volvo and opened the trunk removing a long leather case. Calvino popped the lid of his trunk and Jardine loaded his weapon, then closed the lid. He looked at his watch. He wiped away the beads of rain and sweat mixed together on his upper lip. With Jardine in the back seat, Calvino drove back to the condo site. The same security guard came out under an umbrella and looked inside. Seeing Calvino on the driver's side, he motioned for him to roll down the window. When he did, Colonel Pratt leaned over and showed his police ID. "Please go back to the guard house and stay there until I tell you to leave. That is an order," said Colonel Pratt.

The security guard swallowed hard, snapped off a smart salute and retreated to the guardhouse, shutting the door behind.

From the car, Jardine thought that Hasam had chosen a good operational location. It was the place he would have chosen himself. At the top, he would have an unobstructed view of the road. The colonel had been right. Putting a team of sharpshooters in place wouldn't work. Cars, helicopters and armored vehicles would tell Hasam to move up his appointment with paradise. Once that happened, he would trigger the device, and the dust from a dirty bomb would blast radiation a kilometer out in every direction. The wind would carry it for hundreds of miles, and once afloat, catching the right winds, the cloud of radioactive material would rain down over Pattaya and carry on into Cambodia and Vietnam before breaking up over the coast of China. Hasam knew precisely what he was doing choosing that spot and no doubt the site had been picked because of this advantage and location.

Calvino drove his Honda through the entrance of the building site. When they got out of the car, it would have been impossible to see how many people were in the car, or that Jardine had unpacked his sniper's rifle and mounted a night vision scope for use inside the elevator shaft. Then he removed an Uzi, slapped in a clip and handed it to the colonel. Next from the case Jardine removed a twelve-gauge sawed-off shotgun, felt inside the case for a box of shells and loaded the magazine. He leaned the shotgun against the side of the car. The last weapon was a Glock. He checked the clip; it was loaded and a round was in the chamber.

"Finished unpacking your home arsenal?" asked Calvino.

"I never leave home without it. Otherwise I might not be going back."

Nui felt cold; a shiver bolted up her spine. She looked smaller, more vulnerable and much younger standing in the open as Jardine checked all of the guns.

"You have the blueprints?" asked Jardine. "Let's have a look."

Nui fumbled with the blueprints on the concrete floor inside the parking area. Jardine could read blueprints. He didn't need an explanation of what he was looking at. It turned out Jardine had trained as a civil engineer at the Ohio State. He had been unable to get into Harvard. Nui gathered up the blueprints and they walked from the parking area into the main lobby.

Calvino checked his .38 caliber police special. Jardine watched him, leaned down, picked up the shotgun and held it out to Calvino. "Your .38 isn't going to be of much use."

Jardine immediately walked to within inches of the large empty voids that were to be used as the elevator shaft. He put a finger to his lips.

He mouthed the words, "Move back to the parking area."

Once they were outside in the parking lot, Jardine said, "I have two objectives. Kill Hasam before he detonates the bomb. And then I have," he looked at his watch, "about thirty-eight minutes to defuse the bomb."

"Looks like you found the right place for a clean shot," said Calvino.

No one needed to tell Jardine that he had only one shot.

Nui told Jardine about the emergency access door. "It could be booby trapped," said Jardine. "I have to take him from the elevator shaft."

She shrugged off his instant dismissal of the secret door. Maybe he was right, the man inside the room—if there was a man after all—might have found the door. She let it go. Her entire career had been one long head-butt against male ego. Let it go, she told herself.

"The shaft was designed for three side-by-side elevators," said Nui."

"What about the interior shaft walls on each floor? There should be a short ridge around the perimeter. A place where a maintenance man can crawl around and check the cables."

She nodded. "They should be there."

"I'll crawl inside the shaft on the sixteenth floor and balance against the ridge. I'll need someone to go on the roof and caused a diversion. If it works, we can get whoever is left inside to go to the window and look down the shaft." He didn't need to explain what would happen next.

"In New York I grew up on rooftops. I'll get his attention," said Calvino. He slung the barrel of the sawed-off shotgun over his shoulder. It smelled freshly oiled. Remington was the make of an excellent shotgun and also of an excellent typewriter. In the scheme of weapons and word-processing, both had seen better days, but for the right moment the shotgun was indispensable. No one was saying anything about the five million dollar reward; but it was working somewhere in the back of their minds.

"As this isn't New York, why don't I go as well?" asked Colonel Pratt.

"Good idea," said Jardine.

A cop was better than a civilian any day. The colonel would have some basic training and this colonel had come with about the best recommendation Jardine had ever seen in an American embassy file.

"What about me?" asked Nui. She nodded at the Glock in Jardine's belt. "Don't I get a weapon?"

"These are not free samples. They are guns to kill people. I suggest you go outside and drive the car out. That would be highly useful. If he was watching us drive in, seeing the car leave the site will make him relax. He'll think whoever came in has gone out. It is important that we catch him off guard. And your leaving is essential to this plan."

She cocked her head to the side. "This is like the Hong Kong bullshit. Why do you think I can't handle myself?"

"Can you drive?" asked Colonel Pratt.

"I can drive."

"Vincent, go with her," said Jardine. "It's a recommendation. Not an order."

Calvino walked her out to the parking area. She walked ahead, her hands shaking—from fear or anger, it wasn't clear. She didn't talk to him or look at him. She got to the car first. As he opened the car door, she took the key from his hand. "He wouldn't listen to me. I know they won't find the access door. No way."

"Let Jardine do it his way," said Calvino. "There's one chance to get it right. He knows exactly what he's doing."

"Do you mind if I take this?" she said, her hand moving towards his jacket. He caught her wrist as she went for his .38 police special.

"Not a smart move," he said.

"I have a right to be here, too."

She had started to cry. "There's no time to argue, Nui. You are letting us take him out by leaving now. Don't you get it?"

She frowned and stepped back. "How?"

"What Jardine said is right. If Hasam's watching, and he sees the car leave, it makes it easier to do the job." There had to be a term for sexual lust caused by a woman trying to snatch away your .38 police service revolver.

"Or is he proving something about doing a man's job is more important? Even if it means hundreds of thousands of people are killed so you can make your point. You understand what I am saying, Harvard?" asked Calvino.

She lowered herself into the driver's seat. Calvino leaned over the door for a last look. In another time and place, the chemistry between them would have kept them going some distance. There was nothing like a gun to destroy chemistry. He dropped the car keys in her hand.

"Go to Big C and wait for me in the parking lot. In about an hour, I'll buy you dinner."

She smiled. "Okay. Hey, good luck," she said.

"Got to go," he said.

He watched her back the Honda out, turn it around and drive towards the entrance. Suddenly she was gone. He walked back inside the building. Jardine worked over the sniper's rifle, making adjustments to the night-vision scope, glancing at his watch, getting ready to position himself inside the elevator shaft.

"She's gone," said Calvino.

"Time to move out."

FORTY-THREE

ON the sixteenth floor, Jardine stuck his head inside the interior shaft, looking for the best position to give him a clear shot of anyone above. He needed to climb in quietly and he needed an angle that would make it difficult for someone directly above to detect him. After he crawled inside, Calvino and Colonel Pratt left him in position and climbed up the last two flights.

As they walked up the staircase, Calvino thought about the security alert the American Embassy had emailed him. Phrases from that email flashed through his mind.

You may be a target of terrorists' action.

He was one step behind the colonel. The stairs looked like the back entrance to a sleazy brothel with a one-eyed monster of a *mama san* whose thighs were buttered thick by too much time and rice. Love handles that jiggled as she walked.

Maintain a high level of vigilance.

Not only was there no door handle at the top, there was no door. Any cat or bird could walk or fly inside and no one would know any different. Colonel Pratt sat low in the frame and raised his hand. He squatted down on his knees, his body stretched forward. Calvino hunched down, looking over the colonel's shoulder.

New attacks are planned that will be more devastating than September 11.

There was a man on the roof with a weapon. He was about ten feet away, looking out at the street. He had a cellphone to his ear.

Terrorists do not distinguish between official and civilian targets.

The colonel raised the Uzi with the specially built silencer fixed on the barrel; he tugged on Calvino's jacket sleeve and motioned for him to remove the jacket. Calvino slipped out of his jacket and Colonel Pratt draped it over his wrists and forearms, covering the Uzi. Firearms 101 taught that a silencer didn't eliminate all sound. Not all of the sound of Uzi came out of a barrel. The jacket would muffle most of the rest of the noise. For close work, the colonel would have preferred a Sten gun. Americans like the Uzi. Whatever the gun, for close-in work an important object was not to disturb the neighbors and, even more importantly, other friends of the man targeted, who might be heavily armed. They waited until the male, medium in height, thirty-something with a beard, put his cellphone in his pocket. Then Colonel Pratt shot him in the back of the head. Blood and brains sprayed across the rooftop and the body fell forward in the rain. No matter how you looked at it, when the clean-up squad came to the rooftop and looked at the body, one thing was for sure: suicide wasn't the immediate cause of death. Except in Thailand, where at a crime scene suicide and murder was often blurred. The man Colonel Pratt had shot had wanted to die. He got his wish. Was his death an assisted suicide?

Facilities maybe temporarily closed or suspended.

It was strange how the bulletins played like long-play albums in the head. Songs to warn of what was coming, songs for the dead and dying. Calvino stared out at the body.

Other geographic locations could be venues for the next round of attacks.

Sometimes despite themselves, the government managed to get things right. They got lucky like anyone else. Pick a lotto number and spin the wheel and wait and see if your song comes, if there is room on your dance card.

Colonel Pratt slowly moved out of the doorway and onto the roof, looking for any movement, but the roof was empty. Calvino knelt down beside the dead man, rolled him over. The dead man's forehead had been blown away. Hair matted in blood and bone. Even with half of his head gone, Calvino could see the dead man wasn't Hasam. Their first assumption had been wrong. A bamboo ladder leaned against a bunker-like structure. At the top was a door. Neither Calvino nor Colonel Pratt exchanged a word. Pratt pointed to the ladder. One of them had to climb up to the top and go through the door.

One man dead on the roof indicated he was on guard duty for someone inside. The $64,000 question was whether the five million dollar man was alone with explosives tied around his waist. Or did he have a couple of men inside to make certain that at the last moment Hasam had no doubts that paradise was exactly what it had been cracked up to be.

The colonel and Calvino walked to the outer perimeter of the bunker. The concrete structure had no windows. It had been built alongside a penthouse. While the rest of the condo building was a skeleton, the storage room had been nearly finished. They circled back to the ladder. Someone was inside the storage room. The problem was how to create a diversion, one that would cause that person to go to the internal window overlooking the elevator shaft and look down? It was impossible. *No way was the plan going to work*, thought Calvino. And there was no way to warn Jardine.

Calvino knelt beside the dead man and searched through his pockets as Colonel Pratt squatted down, holding the Uzi barrel pointing down on the roof. The barrel of an Uzi cooled down slowly. Touch the barrel after an Uzi's been fired and you end up in hospital with third-degree burns. That's Firearms 102. Calvino held up a knife, a handgun, a Golden gym membership card and a cellphone that rang as he held it in his hand. He didn't answer and instead hit the "no" button for a busy signal. Signals were funny things in Thailand. Sometimes cellphone signals dropped out; other times the network was jammed and nothing went through. Whoever was ringing had to make a judgment call about why the phone hadn't been answered. A technical problem with the equipment or network, or technical problem with the man on the other end—technical problem as in heart had stopped. As soon as the business was finished, Colonel Pratt understood the urgent need to get the phone to Jardine so his people could immediately track the incoming traffic and hunt down the callers.

These were times when fanatics used modern technology in order to return the world to the dark ages. Such men were willing to die for what they believed. They were willing to send others to die. Their goal was simple: kill as many non-believers as possible and destroy their way of life. Pattaya was the perfect symbol for what they hated. Blowing it up with the American ambassador and military in town completed the symbolism. Killing was what they had been trained to do. But it was more than training; it was their choice to kill and die. They wanted the steaming human meat of the infidels hanging from trees, blown onto the windshields of trucks and buses. They wanted to join them, to be with them.

US embassies and consulates will make every effort to provide emergency services to US citizens.

What would Ben Affleck do? What would Woody do? What would Warren or Harrison do? What would their women have them do? Whatever it was they would do, it would have been scripted, rehearsed, the dailies reviewed and the scene re-shot if needed. They made hard decisions look smooth and easy. They went home at night. A lot of people weren't ever going home if the bomb was detonated. That was what Calvino thought, squatting on the rooftop of the unfinished condo with Colonel Pratt. He felt that this might be the day to die. Hasam hits a button and there's a blank screen of nothingness. Calvino looked at the sky. He felt the rain on his face.

He had no idea what they would do. When he had pulled the cellphone out of the dead man's pocket, he'd looked at the call list. The number for the last call was listed. The dead man would have been watching the street, reporting activity to Hasam and the possibly other accomplices inside the windowless room. Their eyes and ears had been eliminated. Calvino looked around; there were no other buildings that were taller. There was nothing happening in the street below. He couldn't see the security guard.

"We have to get inside that room," whispered Colonel Pratt.

How did they separate the terrorists from the dirty bomb? It wasn't a trick question. There was no Firearms 202 manual to flip through to figure how to get the men inside to come out. Calvino stared at the dead man's cellphone. He pulled down the missed call menu and found the last phone number on the list. Then he dialed that number on his own phone. It rang twice before a voice came on with a Thai "hello."

"I want to order the double deluxe pizza with double cheese," said Calvino. He sat back facing the door at the top of the ladder and waited.

Colonel Pratt said to himself, *never again. Jardine was right. Civilians have no idea about operational procedures in the field.*

"Isn't there someone there who can speak English? I want a fucking pizza. Got that clear, shit-for-brains?"

The dead man's cellphone rang again. Calvino hit the "no" button, sending back a busy signal. He counted to five, and the door above opened and a man appeared. The shotgun blast made his ears ring as the second dead man fell onto the roof, leaving the door wide open.

"I guess it was a wrong number," said Calvino.

Colonel Pratt didn't have time to hear him as he ran across the roof, climbed the ladder two steps at a time, and slammed his back against the wall next to the open door.

"Hasam, give it up."

What did Afghan terrorism school teach them do at that moment?

Automatic gunfire shot raked overhead through the open door. Whoever was inside was firing blind.

If that's what terrorism school taught them, then the world had a chance.

They had forced Hasam to play his hand. He had nowhere to run. He could come out the door guns blazing, or he could do what he had been waiting for months to do: set off the dirty bomb. He fired again from inside. Calvino had crawled underneath the ladder. The rounds flew overhead. As long as he was shooting, that was a good thing. He needed two hands to keep the automatic weapon in operation. The moment he stopped, Colonel Pratt would swing around the door. Only the door slammed from the inside. A bolt locked into place. The man was smart, thought Colonel Pratt. The moment he heard them trying break down the door, he would shoot through it. One could be certain Hasam or whoever was alive inside wasn't in the line of fire of the door.

When a rat was cornered, it went into rat-emergency mode. The rat inside the room crawled out of the window overlooking the shaft. Above the opening for the cables was one hundred kilos of dirty bomb. He edged along the supporting beam. Colonel Pratt had kicked down the door and rolled forward into the small room. He rose up, seeing the room was empty. Calvino, two steps behind him, entered aiming the sawed-off shotgun, swinging around, pointing at shadows. At anything that moved or breathed or sighed. At the far end was a window overlooking the elevator shaft. Where was the ten mile convoy of uniforms from every branch of every service, the police, tourist police, army, marines, navy, special forces, followed by another convoy of local people wanting a cut of the reward money?

They were alone. Hasam was on the otherside of the window inside the shaft. Dark and alone and ready to die.

Jardine squeezed off a clear shot. It tagged Hasam in the shoulder. From the side of the window, Calvino peered down the shaft. Hasam was fiddling with some mechanism. It might have been a detonator. It didn't matter what it was. Calvino slowly slipped the barrel of the sawed-off shotgun along the windowsill, rose up and fired twice down the shaft. The smell of cordite mixed with dust and blood.

"Don't fucking shoot, Jardine; I am climbing inside."

"You got him," said Jardine as Hasam's blood dripped eighteen floors down the shaft.

Calvino looked around the inside.

"There's nothing here," said Calvino.

"That's because the bomb is over here," said Colonel Pratt. "We have five minutes on the digital readout."

Jardine was out of the shaft and up to the roof in less than two minutes. He hunched down on his knees in front of the device. The bomb was set to go off in less than three minutes when he set to work.

Calvino had not seen the bomb above the shaft. There were two bombs. Jardine had instinctively figured this one out. It took one crafty, ruthless, calculating devil to catch another. One bomb had been anchored with a pulley and duct-tape above the elevator shaft. That bomb had been placed so it could be lowered down the shaft and timed to explode at the same time as the second bomb, which was setup where the elevator switching equipment was supposed to be installed in the storage room. Only there would be no future or switching equipment. Hasam was on his way to paradise. Unless Jardine got it right, in a couple of minutes there would be a billowing of debris and dust; clouds would form over-head and float around the heavens poisoning the infidels, making them suffer for their pleasures and privileges and wrong-headed ideas about God and his plans to take mankind back to the hunter-gatherer level of development.

Terrorists learn to build in redundancy. They weren't rocket scientists but their instincts told them that not everything always goes as planned. They needed a backup system of destruction. Infidels might have found one bomb, but would they find two bombs in time? That was the question.

Terrorist actions may include suicide operations, hijackings, bombings or kidnappings. Remember this is a warning.

What does that piece of information tell you? Nothing.

It leaves out the redundancy possibility. They might try all four things at the same time, or one after another, leaving you to catch your breath.

"It's a standard detonator stuck into four kilos of C-4," said Jardine, working on the canister housing. "A dirty bomb throws off radiation for hundreds of miles and the half-life lasts a very long time." After he defused the bomb designed to drop down the elevator shaft, he performed the same operation in the switching room. He wiped the sweat from his brow and lay back on the floor, eyeball-to-eyeball with his handiwork. "They used the same mechanism on both bombs. Figure out one and you've nailed the other bomb."

A Thai police colonel and an American private eye had broken into the room. They were still alive. The private dick had lucked out and killed Hasam. That was a miracle in Jardine's book. Disabling the bombs was a piece of cake. Except for one problem. The bomb casing on the second device in the switching room had been booby-trapped. Jardine had nearly been fooled. It was setup just like the bomb in the shaft. These men were well trained. They had wanted a backup. And that would lull a man in a hurry into making a mistake. They had planned on one bomb being taken out and the next one doing the job because the enemy would make the wrong assumption. Two bombs. Each having the same mechanism. That would have been the kind of carelessness they had prayed for. Assumptions based on sameness—whether a bomb or a woman—were the most deadly ones anyone could make.

They had all been less than a minute away from paradise. Once it was over, Jardine and the colonel spent thirty tense minutes getting into the room, rolling over bodies, checking Hasam's body in the elevator shaft. An hour later bomb squad experts and dozens of other uniforms were all over the roof, the storage room, bagging bodies, gathering evidence and taking statements. The cellphones taken from the dead men were already being analyzed for the record of calls. If they had been smart, they would have used prepaid cards for each call. Throw the card away. Make another call. Throw the card away. Never use the same card twice. Were they that smart? Probably not, since one of the men who was shot had answered the phone. No one should have been phoning inward.

American and Thai uniforms carted the defused bombs one at a time onto the roof for inspection. Calvino heard one of the American uniforms say the two bombs would be flown out of Thailand, taken apart piece by piece, inspected and labeled to unravel where the parts came from, finding the bastards who sold the parts and putting them on a list of cards for more reward money. As for the dead men on the roof and the bomb, which were being taken down eighteen flights of stairs, the Americans wondered as they finished the interrogation how to play back the operation.

"You think we'll ever see any part of the five million?" asked Calvino.

Colonel Pratt shrugged. "Is that why you were here? For the money?"

Calvino looked ashamed. "It's a lot of money."

"And you were the one who killed Hasam," said Colonel Pratt. "Is that what you want me to write in my report?"

"It's probably in violation of my work permit."

"Most likely."

"Nui should get part of it. Without her, we'd never have found him."

Colonel Pratt nodded. "I'll see what I can do."

Washington would settle the reward issue later. Handing out rewards kept people onside. Kept them loyal and expectant, hoping to be of service the next time. For a larger amount of the pie—and everyone loved big fat pies—revisions were necessary, if not mandatory. As he watched Calvino walk away, the colonel remembered the lesson from Sun Tzu's *Art of War* ". . . yet [generals] begrudge bestowing ranks and emoluments of one hundred pieces of gold [to spies] and therefore do not know the enemy's situation. This is the ultimate inhumanity. Such a person is not a general for the people, an assistant for a rule, or the arbiter of victory."

He thought of calling Calvino back and quoting from Sun Tzu.

He decided it was better to leave that battle for another day.

FORTY-FOUR

VALENTINE sat at the end of the dining table reading the *Bangkok Post* and sipping a large glass of fresh orange juice. Som stood ten feet away at the counter preparing his coffee. Calvino walked past the swimming pool. The rain slanted against the aqua blue water. The overhanging palm leaves and plants were a brilliant liquid green. Flowers along the back of the pool drooped with rain pouring off the petals. The baby goats pranced around the table and chairs. Chopin, who was pure black, jumped onto a chair and onto the table. Som ran over and pulled her down to the floor where she scampered off to the corner, knocking over a plastic water bottle. The brown-spotted, four-day-younger Haydn chewed the corner of a white cloth laid over the top of a ten-liter water bottle next to the fridge. They jumped, ran, pranced, and pissed on the floor. Valentine looked up from his newspaper. Calvino had a look of disgust as a 12-day-old goat named Chopin squatted and pissed on the tiled floor.

"It's only water," said Valentine. "Bring Mr. Calvino a cup of coffee."

Som mopped up the urine with a small throw rug. Making Valentine's coffee, keeping the baby goats off the furniture and cleaning up after them had Som looking more ragged than usual. Things were so bad in Burma that life in Valentine's compound and her chores were as close to paradise as she was likely to come. Calvino stepped over a puddle left by Chopin, pulled back a chair and sat down at the table.

"Prasit was murdered," said Calvino.

"Yes, perhaps he was. What a pity. Did you find his murderer?" asked Valentine.

"It's one of two men."

Valentine stroked Chopin. "Who are they?"

"You and Sawai. You both had access to the compound and you both had a thing about snakes."

"And what is my motive to kill my own gardener?"

"He was squeezing you for money."

"Blackmail?"

"Was he?"

"Good God, no. My life is an open book. Do you see me hiding anything?"

The answer was that everyone had something to hide. The question was what Valentine had buried and what Prasit had dug up. Sawai's motives were not in doubt. His connection was with Veera; he was working to keep his *jao poh* out of harm's way by dispatching a hit team and leaving snakes on the bodies to confuse the authorities.

"Sawai is the other possibility."

"The guru? What evidence do you have for this conclusion?"

"Insufficient evidence for a Thai court." Calvino had no illusions that Sawai could be arrested based on mere assumptions, no matter how plausible. The *luuk nong* of a *jao poh* would go down only if there had been a video camera on the scene showing him killing someone. Even then the tape would likely go missing and the witnesses' minds would go blank.

"That's rather complicated. You've solved the crime but can prove nothing. We must be in Thailand." Valentine let out a hooting laugh that scared the baby goat.

After he recovered, Valentine sighed. "I suspect that's the end of it. It doesn't matter."

Calvino disagreed; it mattered to him. "Did you ever meet Sawai?"

"He once brought me a lovely cobra for my collection." Valentine pointed to the shelf; inside one of the bottles was a curled-up baby cobra.

"That was thoughtful of him," said Calvino. "You might have told me that before."

"You're the private investigator. You didn't ask me."

Valentine grinned. "Did you?"

Calvino lowered his head.

It s not satisfactory. But what can you do? What can anyone do? asked Valentine.

Calvino wished sometimes he had a perfect record of asking the right person the right question at the right time. Most of the time it was hard enough finding any reasonable conclusion. People got themselves killed for all manner of reasons. But it was always in the fine print or through the small detail that a truly motivated murderer could be discovered. Sawai had used the police crackdown on drug dealers as a cover to kill Prasit s brother. He had made Prasit s death appear to be a suicide with a backup scenario that pointed either to Valentine or Fon. He d hired someone to hit Ton using Calvino as his alibi. That was hubris. It was outright in-your-face bravado. Catch me if you can. He knew he wouldn t be caught. He was a master of opportunity and sheltered under the cover of a powerful man. The snake was his signature.

"It doesn't matter. Don't take all of this so personally. It's time to move on. I've moved on."

"Moved on to what?" asked Calvino.

"I am expanding the herd. I want a hundred more goats. And I am hiring new staff and building new facilities and buying more land. In six months I will produce one hundred kilos of cheese a week. Our cheese will be sold in the best shops in Bangkok. I plan to sell to Harrods."

"I've told the police that Prasit was killed in this compound," said Calvino. "They may come around and ask you some questions."

"That's hardly my affair. People are killed all the time in Thailand. They have to be killed somewhere. It's only the law of averages that sooner or later one of them is done in on your property."

Valentine was hard work. His precise opinions on everything were as fixed and rigid as the musical scales. He reached over and patted Chopin on the head.

"Can you imagine, this beauty is a twelve days old goat? Look at her size. The way she runs and jumps. Think if a human baby could do that. Think if Frédéric Chopin could have done that. He would have been composing for the piano at six months old."

The world of goats was a far more appealing one to Valentine. Measured food, set feeding times, and a sure-fire source of milk within months of birth. "I stopped in to let you know that I am going back to Bangkok tonight. I wanted to let Fon know what I've found out. Whether you care or not, she deserves to know."

"Fon's given me her notice. Can you imagine that? She's resigned. She leaves tomorrow. The others can go with her. I hope that they do. They've been nothing but a misery. The goats need happy and contented workers. I need happy people working for me. I want smiling faces. Busy bees that love these babies as much as I love them."

There was nothing more to say to Valentine. He leaned over and cuffed Haydn around its long Nubian ears and made smacking noises with his tongue. Calvino slipped out without saying goodbye and walked across the grounds to the gardener's house. Fon was inside packing a suitcase. She didn't seem surprised to see him standing in the doorway.

"I quit." She was smoking a cigarette.

"I heard," he said, slipping off his shoes and stepping into the room.

She had packed a case small enough for an airplane carry-on. Her life's possessions fit into a case small enough to fit in the overhead compartment of a 747. She folded a blouse and laid it on top. She walked across to the fridge and poured Calvino a glass of water. All that remained in the fridge was a bottle of water. "It's for the best," she said. "I am not angry with him. If he doesn't want me here, I should go."

"I can't prove it, but I would says the odds are that Sawai killed your husband."

She stopped pouring the water. "Sawai?"

"He had access. Khun Prasit trusted him. He knew that your husband had worked on hit for Veera. And they got scared when Noi moved into the compound. My guess is that Sawai did it himself, or he might have sent Ton to do the job. I can't prove any of this. Plcase understand. Ton's dead. And there's nothing but circumstantial evidence to show the connection between Sawai and Ton, or that either of them actually murdered your husband. But I wanted to let you know that you were right. Your husband didn't kill himself."

Fon finished pouring the water and handed him the glass. "My husband shouldn't have gone back to that old life. In Thailand we have something called *kreng jai*. You know this?"

Calvino nodded. "It means you can't tell your boss 'no' even though in your heart you know that what he is asking you to do is wrong and you don't want to do it."

"He didn't want to kill that reporter. I know it in my heart. But he couldn't follow his heart."

"Where will you go?"

She wiped a tear that spilled down her cheek. "There's an animal clinic in Bangkok run by one of my old classmates. She said I could have a job anytime. The time has finally come around to see if that job is still open."

"And if it's not?"

"Nothing is certain in the world. But I know that I will survive."

"About the other night," Calvino said, putting down the water glass.

"I know that you have someone in Bangkok, if that's what you want to tell me."

"What I wanted to say is that you're no failure. You taught me a lesson. Not to make assumptions. Failure is sometimes the best card to draw for success. If you ever need anything, let me know," he said.

As she inhaled deep on her cigarette, a wisp of a smile crossed her lips, "Sure. Once two paths cross, they are crossed forever."

Neither of them wished for a long goodbye. Nor did they need any further explanations. He had the feeling, though, that sometime, somewhere, they would meet again. He leaned forward to kiss her and she offered her cheek.

Calvino left the gardener's house and Valentine's compound. On the way out, the dogs ran after him; the giant slobbered on his jacket sleeve. He stood in the driveway, his car door open, taking one more look at the gardens in the rain. A thick film of white clouds rolled across the black clouds leaching thunderheads, boiling and spilling out to the far horizon. The world did go on. Nothing ever stopped for long. Now and again, there was a pause, and people pondered why someone died and how, and not long afterwards, those clouds passed and the rain stopped and the gardens bloomed and the new goats ran across vast lawns.

FORTY-FIVE

"YOU noticed the lines on my face? They're from the mask." It was a statement. She'd worn the mask for two weeks. Her mother had let her lower it to have breakfast, lunch and dinner. Otherwise she checked the stretchy straps that cut into her daughter's cheeks. In her mother's house Ratana had become a child again. Unable to speak her own thoughts clearly. Unable to be heard by the adults. Lost in those close quarters, she felt her freedom had slipped away, replaced by a system of rules to obey. She could have been eleven again.

He had noticed them straight away. Deep cuts running from the hairline away from the ear and down the cheekbone. A deformity had set in, marking her. Cosmetics were invented to give a woman's cheeks a red glow and her lips a fuller, puffy-from-the-after-sex glow. The lines left on Ratana's face by the mask were about death. Not life. Not sex. The affirmation was another world beyond sexual coupling.

"What lines? I don't see anything." There were lies to tell a woman, lies you would go to the grave before admitting.

"Everyone else said they saw lines. You didn't see anything? You're a trained observer. This is what you do best. And you see nothing?"

Ratana wasn't any woman. She was a clever woman. She'd known exactly how to challenge Calvino, hitting him in the center of his private-investigating heart. He had been through Valentine's harem, Fon and Nui and all of them had called upon every single moment of concentration, to see what really was and not to let feelings interfere. With Ratana, though, it was different. He didn't know which way to jump.

"Maybe I noticed a little."

"But you said you didn't notice."

There were the dreadful words "you said." They had a special meaning and the way of reading them was to understand a cardinal Calvino's Law: Never contradict yourself or give a hint of light under an otherwise solid black door of deniability. With a woman, that is.

"What I meant to say..." He knew that he was drowning. "Yeah, there was something, but not enough to say I noticed."

She smiled. "Did you learn that in law school? To talk that way? To be so quick?"

"*You* graduated from law school," he said. "So you know that lines are never fixed."

"You're doing it again."

He leaned against the wall. "I learned that from Colonel Pratt." He turned and started to walk back to his office. He turned around, the puzzled look on his face evaporating. "I am glad you're back," he said. He opened his mouth, paused, examining the way she brushed her hair back. It was longer than he remembered. For a long moment he said nothing, as if she would somehow rescue him from the moment, "You bring out the best in me, and I'd like to think I bring out the best in you."

She thought for a moment. "The best," she said.

He disappeared behind the partition and sat behind his office desk. Ratana had laid out the morning newspapers. Once again she had broken the siege of her mother. That meant she had another year of work before a new attempt would be made to separate her from the private investigations office of Vincent Calvino. He wondered as he sat down behind his desk if the mother's resolve would gradually wind down into an uneasy acceptance. He didn't have an answer and he knew better than to ask Ratana. Any hint of a suggestion that her mother might be a problem was unacceptable. The most liberated Thai women shared the same faith: Mothers were gods. And like all god mothers they could sometimes act in an arbitrary fashion. But they deserved to be worshipped.

At the bottom of page three was a photograph of Veera with a couple of politicians and a couple of businessmen. They were all smiling. They were at a construction site. He read the story. The businessmen worked for the expressway contractor. The contractor wasn't one of Veera's companies. He had moved aside and let someone on his turf and he was smiling about this.

Around the corner, at Starbucks, he found Colonel Pratt reading the newspaper with a double espresso. Calvino sat down at the table.

"Have a look at page three," said Calvino.

Colonel Pratt cleared his throat. "I saw *the* story."

"The story within the story—meaning there's insufficient evidence against Veera," said Calvino. "He cut a deal."

"Without the white there can't be black."

"You had him."

"He was never mine to have."

"You got used. They used you to pressure him."

"You see only part of the story."

"Meaning?"

"If Veera concedes the ground one time, the next time will be easier, and the time after that easier still until everyone knows he's no longer the invincible kingpin. His time is limited, Vincent. You mustn't see total defeat as the only way to victory. Sometimes it is wise to learn that if you win a little bit everyday and over time, what you wish to see happen, happens. The old era is fading. It won't be gone tomorrow. But if I can help break the power of someone like Veera even in small measure, I have served my country."

As Colonel Pratt finished his espresso, Calvino wondered whether Veera would be replaced by another gangster. And the cycle of *jao poh* would once again take root. Rather than a new era, was this a continuation of the old way with new faces? He didn't have an answer because there wasn't one. Some would say evil changes its clothes and face but the old body marches ahead to the same tune. The optimist believes that eventually good wins over evil. Colonel Pratt was on neither side of the dual equation. He was a Buddhist. In his world evil stayed and faded away at the same time, things became worse than before and better than before in the same space and time. There was no contradiction in such forces existing side by side. Calvino tried to see the world through Colonel Pratt's eyes. Sometimes he caught a glimpse of that world. Mostly he suffered from double vision.

"About the reward money," said Colonel Pratt, putting the cup back on the saucer.

"A decision has been made?" Calvino held his breath. "Anyone we know on the list?"

"Nui."

"The engineer with the Harvard degree?"

"Washington loves the fact she's an American-educated young woman. Bright, articulate and ready to go on camera. She's in New York being interviewed on network TV."

"They'll get two hundred million bucks' worth of publicity."

"Five million isn't enough." Colonel Pratt reached across the table and grabbed Calvino's shoulder. "There will be a price on her head."

Did I ever tell you she tried to take my gun?

"You were the one who said she should get the reward money."

"But not the whole fucking five mil."

"Let me buy you another coffee," said Colonel Pratt.

"Yeah, thanks, that will make my day."

Later, after returning to his office, as hard as he tried, Calvino couldn't concentrate on his work. It was an insurance fraud case. The insurer thought the deceased hadn't really died but had faked his death with the help of his wife. He shook his head. Inside the rim of real unresolved deaths was a parallel universe of fake deaths for insurance money. He walked along Sukhumvit Road and heard someone calling his name.

It was Ed McPhail, "Hey, buddy, I saw that Thai engineer friend of yours scored the big five million. I thought you had something to do with that case. Wasn't this supposed to be your big year for dough?"

"The government didn't see it that way."

"I saw her picture. She looks like that singer Vanessa May. And you let her get away? Are you crazy?"

Calvino sighed, dropped his chin.

"Barking-dog crazy," he said.

"It gets better. CNN said she was getting her own reality TV show. *Finding Them*. Contestants are ordinary people who get a set of blueprints and have twenty-four hours to locate the terrorists' cell. They're armed with paint guns. Meanwhile, terrorists setup ambushes and try to whack the contestants. It sounds like the kind of crazy concept that appeals to most married couch potatoes."

"Think how making her a hero plays in the Middle East. Like Colonel Pratt said, she's a natural. A tiny Thai woman takes out a group of JI professionals planning to blow up an entire city."

McPhail leaned back, letting the smoke curl out of his nose. His eyes were half closed, and slowly he opened them wide and stared at Calvino.

"Fuck it. When does the ordinary guy ever get a chance? There's always some guy at the top of the heap. He's got the most brains, is hung like a stallion, and he's totally fit, handsome, young, together, passionate and loveable. There's got to be one guy like that. Who is he? Where does he live?"

"He never goes out. He doesn't have to leave his apartment," said Calvino.

"What does he do about lining up women? Nothing. He's got a system of perpetual home delivery. Tag-teams line up outside his door like pizza delivery workers, waiting for their turn to jump into his bed. He's God. He doesn't have to pay. *Yings* are free for him. They never think he's wrong or stupid or fat or old. He's God, and God is always right, clever, slender and young. He's the man."

"Or the woman."

"Hey, she stole that reward money; that's a pissing shame."

"She deserved it."

McPhail shook his head. "There's got to be one guy who has it all."

"Valentine comes close."

"I know about that guy. He's a nut. Forget him. He's not even on the long list."

"See you around, McPhail."

"Take care of yourself, Bud."

Calvino stopped outside of Villa market, looking at the stalls selling fresh-cut flowers. The flowers reminded him of Valentine's gardens. Only these were no longer alive. Cut from the earth, they would be in vases for a few days before being thrown out. He thought about what Colonel Pratt had said and what it meant. Life was a transitory, temporary journey. And on a rainy day in the city the mist seemed closer, and beyond was the roar of the falls.